LT FIC GRIFFIN W
Griffin, W.E.B.
The double agents  /

# THE DOUBLE AGENTS

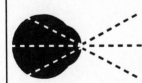

This Large Print Book carries the
Seal of Approval of N.A.V.H.

# THE DOUBLE AGENTS

## W.E.B. GRIFFIN

## AND WILLIAM E. BUTTERWORTH IV

**THORNDIKE PRESS**

*An imprint of Thomson Gale, a part of The Thomson Corporation*

**THOMSON**

™

**GALE**

Detroit • New York • San Francisco • New Haven, Conn. • Waterville, Maine • London

Thorndike Press® Large Print Core.

The text of this Large Print edition is unabridged.

Other aspects of the book may vary from the original edition.

Set in 16 pt. Plantin.

LIBRARY OF CONGRESS CATALOGING-IN-PUBLICATION DATA

Griffin, W. E. B.
    The double agents / by W.E.B. Griffin and William E. Butterworth IV.
    p. cm. — (The men at war series) (Thorndike press large print core)
    ISBN-13: 978-0-7862-9489-3 (hardcover : alk. paper)
    ISBN-10: 0-7862-9489-2 (hardcover : alk. paper) 1. United States. Office of
Strategic Services — Fiction. 2. World War, 1939-1945 — Secret service —
Fiction. 3. Large type books. I. Butterworth, William E. (William Edmund)
II. Title.
PS3557.R489137D68 2007b
813'.54—dc22

2007015299

Published in 2007 by arrangement with G. P. Putnam's Sons,
a member of Penguin Group (USA) Inc.

Printed in the United States of America on permanent paper
10 9 8 7 6 5 4 3 2 1

**THE MEN AT WAR SERIES
IS RESPECTFULLY DEDICATED
IN HONOR OF**

*Lieutenant Aaron Bank, Infantry, AUS,
detailed OSS
(Later Colonel, Special Forces)
November 23, 1902–April 1, 2004*

*Lieutenant William E. Colby, Infantry, AUS,
detailed OSS
(Later Ambassador and Director, CIA)
January 4, 1920–April 28, 1996*

★

It is no use saying,
"We are doing our best."
You have got to succeed in doing
what is necessary.

— *Prime Minister Winston S. Churchill*

When you get to the end
of your rope,
tie a knot, and hang on.

— *President Franklin D. Roosevelt*

# I

## [ONE]
## SCHUTZSTAFFEL PROVISIONAL
## HEADQUARTERS
## MESSINA, SICILY
## 0810 26 MARCH 1943

"You'd very likely be shot for saying such a thing," SS Standartenführer Julius Schrader said.

SS Obersturmbannführer Oskar Kappler — an athletic thirty-two-year-old, tall and trim, with a strong chin, intelligent blue eyes, and a full head of closely cropped light brown hair — did not trust his voice to reply. The lieutenant colonel stood stiffly and simply stared at the colonel, a pale-skinned portly thirty-five-year-old of medium height who kept his balding head cleanly shaven.

"Of all people, my friend, this you should understand," Schrader added.

Taking care not to spill coffee from the fine porcelain china cup that he carried on its saucer, the Standartenführer rose slowly from his high-backed leather chair, then moved out from behind the polished marble-topped wooden desk that dominated the large office.

Kappler's eyes followed Schrader as he walked across the floor, also highly polished stone, past oversize portraits of Adolf Hitler and Joseph Goebbels — the images of the Nazi Germany leader and his propaganda minister struck Kappler as more oafish than inspiring — and over to one of the half-dozen floor-to-ceiling windows with heavy burgundy-colored drapes pulled back to either side.

Sipping from his cup, Schrader looked out at the busy Port of Messina and, five kilometers distant across the Strait of Messina, to the toe of the boot that was mainland Italy. The morning sun painted the coast and rising hills in golden hues and turned the surface of the emerald green sea to shimmering silver.

Schrader sighed, then added pointedly but softly: "Or, perhaps worse, you would be sent to suffer a slow death in a concentration camp."

Both men — Nazi officers in the Sicherheitsdienst, known as the SD, the intelligence arm of the Schutzstaffel, also called

10

the SS — knew far more about that than they wished. Punishment for anything less than total commitment to *der Führer* and the success of his Third Reich was swift and brutal. And they both personally had witnessed incidents in which those merely suspected of being suspicious — civilians and soldiers alike — had been summarily shot or shipped off to spend their final days toiling in the death camps.

For those so sentenced, a bullet served as the far better option, even if self-administered . . . as it sometimes was.

Obersturmbannführer Kappler wanted to speak but found it hard to control his voice so that it did not waver.

Schrader surveyed the port. Cargo vessels flying the flags of Germany and Italy were moored at the long docks, loading and unloading, the cranes and ships creating long, defined shadows in the low angle of the sun.

At anchor inside the sickle-shaped harbor were warships — two aging destroyers and a heavy cruiser of the *Regina Marina,* the latter easily twenty years old — from the Third Division of the Italian navy.

Schrader thought, *The ships look beautiful in the morning light, but the fact is, the merchant vessels have been weeks late getting here. Supply to all of our ports in Sicily — es-*

*pecially those in the south and far west — has been getting slower. Food, munitions, everything.*

*And the* Regina Marina *treats us like some kind of stepchild, providing only weak, aging vessels for our protection.*

*It is hard not to agree with my old friend . . . though I dare not say it.*

Schrader, still looking out the window, stated in a matter-of-fact tone: "We go back very far, Oskar. I have always supported you. Yet I must strongly counsel you not to continue with such talk and will, even at great risk to myself for not reporting it, ignore that you ever said anything of the kind."

He turned to glance at Kappler. He saw him looking off into the distance, slowly shaking his head in frustration if not defiance.

Kappler cleared his throat, swallowed — and found his voice.

"Juli," he began softly but with determination, "I, of course, have always appreciated everything that you have done for me. And I certainly value your counsel. But . . ."

Schrader held up his hand, palm outward, in a gesture that said *Stop.*

"But nothing," he said. "You will serve here as ordered, as will I, and we will honor the Führer and the Fatherland. Period."

Kappler looked at his friend, who for the last year also had been his superior in the SS office in Messina. Their friendship dated back a dozen years, to when they had been teammates on the university polo team in Berlin. Schrader, then in far better shape, had held the key position of number four player while Kappler had been number three.

Then as now, Kappler knew Schrader expected him to follow his lead.

"But, Juli, I have heard from sources in Berlin that Hitler will not be able to defend Sicily adequately. With his focus on fronts of higher strategic value — France, Russia, others — he cannot afford to send the forces necessary to do so. And when that is realized by the Italian military — who some say would just as well fight against us, which is to say not fight any invasion — we'll be left to defend this pathetic island alone. We'll be overrun."

He walked over to the window and stood beside Schrader.

"Take a closer look out there, Juli," Kappler said, making a dramatic sweep with his arm. "What do you see? A tired old city — no, not even that — a tired old town that has been neglected by its own people. And what has Mussolini done for Messina? Same that

13

he's done for all of Sicily: nothing but promise after promise, all of them empty. Yet here the Sicilians sit, so close that they can almost reach out and touch the shore of Italy — and its riches."

He paused, then pointed to the northwest, where the low masonry buildings at the edge of the city gave way to much-lesser structures — fashioned of really no more than rusted corrugated tin and other salvaged metal and wood scraps — near the foothills.

"And there," Kappler went on, his tone of voice becoming stronger. "Those shanties. Do you think that any one of the tens of thousands in those miserable conditions have any reason to fight for Mussolini? No. Of course not. Nor does the average Sicilian feel loyalty to him. And certainly not the real leaders, the members of the Mafia — many of whom, you will recall, you and I helped *Il Duce* imprison. They feel exactly the opposite. They despise Mussolini." He paused. "They despise *us*."

Schrader made a *humph* sound and shrugged.

"What do you expect?" he said. "This is war —"

"But," Kappler interrupted, "you would think that we're an occupying force. We're not. These people do not know — or choose not to acknowledge — that we're fighting on the same side, Juli."

He let that statement set in, then added: "If you do not agree, then answer this: How do we go about ensuring their allegiance?"

He looked at his friend. When finally there was no answer, only silence, he answered the question himself: "We do it with threats, Juli, with coercion and fear. Just as you and I fear being found not to be in complete and total lockstep with" — he made a wave of disgust with his hand toward the portraits on the wall — "the high party and its ideals."

Schrader looked at Kappler, then at his coffee cup, and drained it.

"This is complete nonsense," Schrader said. "I have been given no intelligence that says —"

"Do you really believe that they would *tell* you that? From what I hear, no one tells the Führer anything that the Führer does not want to hear. His temper is legendary."

Schrader snorted. "So it is said. I would not wish to have been the unfortunate one who had to report the news last month of von Paulus's defeat."

Kappler nodded solemnly.

The Wehrmacht had been dealt a devastating blow by the Russian Red Army. Field Marshal Friedrich von Paulus and his Sixth

15

German Army — strung out too far while battling a wicked Stalingrad winter — had been damn near obliterated.

It was a loss that even now Hitler had not come completely to comprehend — quite possibly could not, considering that people were prone to report that which would keep them alive . . . not necessarily that which the Führer needed to hear.

"Precisely," Kappler said. "And apparently that temper is worsening with his misfortunes of war. First, he basically loses North Africa and — worse — refuses to concede it. Now, mere months later, this travesty in Stalingrad. What makes you think he is even thinking of Sicily? Maybe he's more concerned about Corsica and Sardinia. They're closer to the mainland. If I were him, I would pull back and protect against mainland invasions closer to home — particularly ones from the east and west — battles that I can win." He exhaled audibly. "Not save some island."

He looked at Schrader, who returned the look but said nothing.

Kappler then quietly offered: "You know there have been attempts on Hitler's life."

"Rumors," Schrader snapped.

Kappler nodded and said, "Possibly. But credible ones. He's weakening."

Schrader stared at Kappler, looking in his eyes for something that he feared Kappler might be holding back from saying.

Schrader knew the Kapplers were an old family well connected in Dortmund — and thus well connected at high levels in Berlin thanks to Oskar's industrialist grandfather's steel mill in Ruhrpott, the Ruhr Valley, supplying critical materials to the war effort — and Kappler could very well have access to quiet information that Schrader never would.

"Only a fool would try to assassinate him," Schrader finally said, reasonably.

"Only a fool would try *and fail.*"

Schrader stiffened and with a raised voice said, "You're not suggesting —?"

"I'm not suggesting anything, Juli," he said evenly. "I am saying, however, that there appear to be real cracks in Hitler's grand plan. And that wise men make their own plans for different courses of action."

Schrader walked wordlessly over to the desk, took a deep breath and exhaled, then picked up the carafe from the sterling silver coffee service at the front edge of the desk. He gestured with it, offering Kappler a cup.

"Sure you won't have some?" he asked, his voice now casual, and after Kappler shook his head Schrader shrugged and poured

17

himself a fresh cup.

"Different courses of action," Schrader said conversationally. "What does this mean?"

"Just look at what Hitler has sent us to prepare for a possible invasion. Not men, not matériel. No, he has left us *Il Duce*'s tired army to fight with our own thin forces."

As Schrader absently stirred three spoonfuls of sugar in his coffee, he said, "There is no reason we could not get additional reinforcements."

Kappler made a sour face.

"Come now, Juli. The German forces have only so many men and we're losing what we have at a growing rate. If Hitler were planning to reinforce Sicily, why would he have us overseeing Sturmbannführer Müller's work? And let me remind you what that professor from the university in Palermo said: that such weapons do not discriminate. That they are as likely to kill us as they are any enemy."

Schrader made eye contact, pursed his lips, and nodded. He returned to his leather chair, sat, and sipped at his coffee slowly and thoughtfully.

He knew that Kappler was of course privy to all of the secret SS operations on Sicily and that these included Müller and the plans for chemical and biological weapons.

For one, Kappler was the supervising officer of the SS major — Hans Müller, a high-strung twenty-eight-year-old with a violent temper matching, if not surpassing, that of Hitler — who was in charge of the Palermo SS field office and its operations.

Near Palermo, in an ancient seaside villa, the SS was advancing the Nazi experimentation — begun in the Dachau concentration camp — of injecting Sicilian prisoners with extract from mosquito mucous glands to keep alive a strain of yellow fever. That was to say, until the sickened hosts died of malaria. Then new hosts — often members of the Mafia brought in from the penal colonies that had been established on tiny outer islands just north of Sicily — were infected with the disease that the SS had imported.

For another, Kappler was aware — although Müller as yet was not — that shipments had begun of crates labeled SONDERKART.6LE.F.H.18 T83 that contained 10.5cm howitzer shells. These were not the usual *ack-ack* antiaircraft munitions for firing from the Nazi's light field howitzers. These rounds contained the chemical agent code-named T83 that attacked the human central nervous system.

Commonly called Tabun, the German-developed chemical was one of the easiest to produce on a massive scale and was efficient to a horrific level. Mostly odorless and colorless, it quickly caused its victims to have convulsions, restricted breathing, triggered loss of bowel control — and, ultimately, loss of heartbeat.

Death by Tabun was relatively swift . . . but intensely painful and gruesome.

Kappler knew that Müller was not aware of the Tabun munitions, nor that a first shipment was already in the Port of Palermo, aboard a cargo ship, mixed in with other military goods and listed on the manifest, more or less innocuously, by its code name.

Müller did not know because Kappler had decided not to tell him until he thought it was necessary to do so.

In short, Kappler had told Schrader, he did not trust the hothead with knowledge — let alone control — of such a powerful weapon and Schrader quietly had concurred.

After a moment, Kappler asked, "What do you have to say about that, Juli?"

Schrader leaned back in the leather chair, staring at the coffee cup, and with an index finger slowly rotated the cup on the saucer as he considered it all.

*How do I agree,* Schrader thought, *without encouraging Oskar to take one step too far, to act on a "different course" perhaps too soon?*

He sighed.

"I will allow that what you say is conceivable —" he began.

*"Ach du leiber Gott!"* Kappler flared. Dramatically, he raised his hands heavenward, palms up, and looked upward, as if seeking divine input. "Of course it is, Juli! And that is why I speak of this with you, my friend, so that wise men can make plans, not just be left twisting in the wind . . . a deadly, contaminated wind."

Standartenführer Julius Schrader looked exasperated.

"Yes, yes, Oskar. So you have said. Yet you have not shared with me what these different courses of action might be."

Kappler approached the desk, then went to the coffee service and poured himself a cup. He started to pick up the cup, then, for some reason, decided otherwise.

He buried his face in the palms of his hands, his fingertips massaging his temples. After a moment, he removed his hands, looked at Schrader, and quietly said, "I have also heard — from trusted sources other than those I have mentioned — that there are certain members of the SS who are setting up routes to safety should we not win this war. Routes for them, for their loved ones. And then there are other routes, ones that set aside their funds."

Schrader stared into Kappler's eyes. After a long moment, his eyebrows went up.

"Yes," Schrader said. "I have heard of that, too."

Schrader leaned forward and placed his cup and saucer on the desktop. The fine *clink* that the porcelain made as it touched the polished marble seemed to echo in the silence of the large room.

"I have also heard," Schrader said, his tone quiet, his words measured, "that those caught making such plans — or even suspected of such — are being charged with treason . . . and so are being dealt with in a vicious fashion. And if you and I have heard of this 'planning,' then no doubt it is known to —"

There was a faint rap at the door and both men turned quickly — and more than a little nervously — toward it.

The massive, dark wooden door slowly swung open just enough for a boyish-looking young man — easily a teenager — in the uniform of an Italian naval ensign to step through. He stood at an awkward attention and saluted stiffly.

Kappler noticed that the ensign's uniform was mussed, that he had a crudely shorn haircut, and that his eyes appeared to be without thought.

*He doesn't look old enough to shave,* Kappler thought as he and Schrader absently returned the salute. *He looks, in fact, like a very simple boy, one plunked off a farm . . . or maybe out of the shanties . . . and stuck in the first sailor suit they could find, never mind the fit or lack thereof.*

*"Herr Standartenführer?"* the young ensign said tentatively.

"I am Standartenführer Schrader," Schrader said with what Kappler thought was a touch too much authority. "Where is Tentente de Benedetto?"

Italian navy Lieutenant Antonio de Benedetto — a fifty-five-year-old Sicilian, five foot two and one-eighty, with a sun-baked complexion as coarse as that of the volcanic rock of nearby Mount Etna — had two months earlier been recalled to the *Regina Marina* and there assigned to serve as the chief naval aide and liaison — and, it was strongly suspected, chief spy — to the Messina SS provisional headquarters.

He of course had been neither requested nor needed, but the Italians insisted that they be allowed to properly serve their SS guests and comrades-in-arms. And so the squat Sicilian had become a fixture around the office.

The young ensign looked uneasy and avoided eye contact with Standartenführer Julius Schrader by looking five feet over his head, to a point on the high wall near the portrait of Hitler. He still held his salute, though now it was not quite so stiff.

"He is ill, *Herr Standartenführer.* I am Guardiamarina Mentesana. I was asked to take his desk today, as no one else was available."

*Christ!* Kappler thought. *They send us children and old men to fight a war!*

"Guardiamarina Mentesana," Standartenführer Julius Schrader said stiffly. "Did anyone, perhaps even Tentente de Benedetto, inform you that you are to wait to be admitted after you knock at the door? That you do not simply knock and then enter?"

Guardiamarina Mentesana's eyes, still fixed on a point on the wall five feet above Standartenführer Schrader's head, suddenly grew wider.

"No, *Herr Standartenführer.* I was not so informed."

As if suddenly remembering he was still saluting, he quickly brought down his hand, then held out a folded sheet of paper as he walked to the desk.

"This message just came in, *Herr Standartenführer*. It is marked 'Urgent' for you. I thought I should deliver it immediately, and that is why —"

"*Danke,*" Standartenführer Schrader said, taking the paper. "That will be all."

"Yes, *Herr Standartenführer.*"

Guardiamarina Mentesana saluted, turned on his heels, and marched back to the door, then went through it.

When the door was pulled closed, Kappler said what he was thinking: "That's what we can expect to repel the enemy? Children? It is bad enough that the Italian men are ill equipped and poorly trained. What can we possibly expect of their children?"

Schrader was unfolding the sheet of paper as he replied, "Never underestimate the effectiveness of youth, my friend. I seem to recall a young man at university who, time and again, rode polo ponies into battles."

Kappler snorted.

"Battle?" he began. "I seem to recall that the teams were reasonably evenly matched, and that we shot wooden balls, not bullets." When he saw Schrader's expression change dramatically, he said, "What? What is that about?"

"It's from Müller."

"*Müller?* Why is he not messaging me?"

"He reports explosions from unknown causes," Schrader said as he calmly refolded the sheet and held it out to Kappler, "and felt that I should be directly made aware of them. According to this, protocol would appear to be the least of our worries. . . ."

As Kappler took the sheet, he muttered, "The bastard."

He scanned the message.

*"Schiest!"*

He looked at Schrader, then said more softly, "The Tabun?"

Schrader nodded just perceptibly.

"Berlin won't be pleased that we allowed this to happen," Schrader said.

Kappler didn't reply for a moment. Then he said: "Worse. If word gets out that we have a nerve agent, and thus there are plans to use it, Churchill may make good on his threat to retaliate in kind. . . ."

"I believe it was the American President Roosevelt who said that," Schrader offered.

"Churchill, Roosevelt — does it matter?"

Kappler saw in Schrader's eyes that he clearly understood the ramifications of that.

"No," Schrader said. "Of course not. You

should leave for Palermo at once, Oskar. Take whatever and whomever you think necessary. Report back as soon as you can."

## [TWO]
## 37 DEGREES 51 MINUTES 01 SECONDS NORTH LATITUDE 11 DEGREES 13 MINUTES 05 SECONDS EAST LONGITUDE STRAIT OF SICILY ABOARD THE *CASABIANCA* 1025 26 MARCH 1943

"Commander, there is absolutely no question in my mind that that cargo ship had to be a total loss," United States Army Air Forces Major Richard M. Canidy said, his dark eyes intense. "I used enough Composition C-2 to blow up a vessel damn near twice its size. What's not clear is what kind of" — he paused, glancing at the ceiling as he mentally searched for an appropriate description — "secondary destruction was caused by the cloud created from the Tabun burning in the hold."

Commander Jean L'Herminier, chief officer of the Free French Forces submarine

*Casabianca,* nodded. There was no mistaking the human horror that was meant by the nerve agent's "secondary destruction."

The two were meeting in private in the commander's small office, just two hatches down from the control room. The ninety-two-meter-long Agosta-class sub, submerged to a depth of ninety meters and cruising under battery power at a speed of eight nautical miles an hour, was en route to Algiers, Algeria, from the northwestern tip of Sicily. The executive officer had the helm for this leg, the last on what for the *Casabianca* promised to become a regular route for covert missions in the Mediterranean Sea.

The commander's dimly lit, drab-gray office held little more than bare essentials — a metal desktop, three metal chairs, and a framework on one wall with navigation charts of the Mediterranean. The desktop, which doubled as a plotting table, had two collapsible legs on one end and, on the other, was attached to the wall by a long hinge so that the top could be folded up flat and out of the way.

Canidy sat on one side of the desktop, in one of two armless metal chairs; across from him, in the single metal chair that had arms, was L'Herminier, now leaning back with his hands behind his head, fingers interlaced.

28

At five foot seven and maybe one-forty, the thirty-five-year-old L'Herminier — who carried himself with a soft-spoken confidence — comfortably fit the room's tight surroundings, as would be expected of such a seasoned submariner.

Not nearly at ease in the tight confines, however, was Canidy, whose big bones and wide shoulders on a six-foot frame made the twenty-six-year-old seem somewhat like the proverbial bull in the china shop. And Canidy's energy right now — intense, smoldering just under the surface — did little to diffuse that impression.

L'Herminier knew that while Canidy carried authentic papers stating he was a major in the USAAF, Canidy was in fact with the Office of Strategic Services. Since mid-December, L'Herminier had also been working for the organization; the *Casabianca* was serving as a spy delivery vehicle.

*I know little about Canidy,* the commander thought, *but I like him. And my gut tells me that, until he proves himself otherwise, he is a man of his word.*

The admiration was mutual.

For one, Major Canidy knew what Commander L'Herminier had done just four months earlier. Many people knew — including the Nazis, if not Hitler himself — as it had become damn near legendary.

On November 27, 1942, as Nazi Germany carried out the personal orders of its furious leader to retaliate against Vichy France for its cooperation with the Allies in the taking of North Africa — Operation Torch — the German SS raided the southern France port of Toulon in an attempt to capture the French fleet there.

The French had ordered those vessels to be scuttled.

Dozens of ships were burned and sunk at their moorings. But — against odds, not to mention against orders of the admiralty of Vichy France — L'Herminier commanded his crew to dive. As the *Casabianca* came under enemy cannon fire, she made way for Algiers.

There, in newly liberated North Africa, the captain and crew of the somewhat-new submarine (it had been launched not quite seven years earlier, in February 1935) joined the Free French Forces.

L'Herminier's brave act had been a remarkable one in that it at once saved the warship from either destruction or falling into the hands of the Nazis and preserved it and her skilled crew for use against the Axis powers.

Canidy's admiration of L'Herminier also

came from personal experience with the commander, whom he found to be a real professional.

When Canidy had first approached the submariner with the vague outline of his proposed mission in Sicily and his request to be inserted by sub, L'Herminier quickly had said, "Consider it done."

It had been no problem in large part because, shortly after joining the Allies, Commander L'Herminier had begun doing something very similar to what Canidy requested.

On December 14, 1942 — only weeks after fleeing Toulon — Commander L'Herminier had maneuvered the *Casabianca* just off shore of Corsica, the Axis-occupied French island in the upper Mediterranean Sea.

The sub carried her complement of four officers and fifty-plus men. Also on board: two teams of OSS agents.

Using the method that L'Herminier himself had developed for the secret landing of spies, he carefully surveyed the coast by periscope, found an area suitable for putting ashore a small boat, then slipped the sub back out to sea, flooded its ballast, and sat on the bottom of the Mediterranean till dark.

Under cover of night, L'Herminier then returned the submarine to within a mile of the position he had found on the shoreline, and, with the sub's deck just barely awash so as to keep a low profile from enemy patrols, ordered the launching of a dinghy.

A pair of *Casabianca* crewmen, armed with Sten 9mm submachine guns, then rowed ashore the first team of three OSS men. They carried with them equipment (machine guns, pistols, ammunition, wireless radios) and money (several thousand Italian lire, a million French francs).

After the OSS team began to make its way inland, the crewmen rowed back to the sub, and then the sub returned to her spot on the sea bottom to await a second insertion.

Thirty hours later, the last of the OSS spies and supplies were ashore.

And nine days after that, PEARL HARBOR, the code name for the clandestine wireless radio station, sent a message in Morse code to OSS Algiers Station — and became the first OSS team to successfully transmit intel from inside enemy-controlled Europe.

Henceforth, on a daily basis, the W/T (wireless telegraphy) link relayed order of battle information on the Italians and Germans to an OSS control in Algiers. This intel was then decrypted and forwarded across town to Allied Forces Headquarters, where it came to be enthusiastically embraced — and helped to establish the fledgling OSS as a bona fide supplier of enemy intel in the Mediterranean Theater of Operations (MTO).

As historic and reaching as the mission had been, however, it had not been without error. During the second insertion of OSS agents, the dinghy had capsized and its two sailors had become stranded on the island with the agents.

It wasn't exactly a disastrous turn of events — the crewmen were, after all, French and thus could assimilate, and, it was expected, aid the agents — but it certainly had not been planned.

The *Casabianca* found that it had no option but to return to Algiers, where plans were drawn up for another mission to Corsica that would serve to rescue the two crewmen and resupply the OSS teams.

In the course of such planning, Dick Canidy's request came up, and Commander L'Herminier had voiced his opinion of the mission.

"It would only be a bit of a detour to and from Corsica," L'Herminier had said. "Consider it done."

The new plan thus called for Commander

L'Herminier to put Canidy ashore on Sicily, exactly as L'Herminier had put the OSS teams on Corisca — with the hopeful exception of dunking him in the drink — and then continue on to Corsica, where the sub would resupply the teams there and collect the pair of stranded sailors.

Canidy, meanwhile, was to locate a professor from the University of Palermo who had great expertise in metallurgy — and whose skills were a critical asset to any country with an interest in the development of advanced weaponry — and convince him that it was in his best interests to leave Sicily with Canidy.

If, however, the professor would not allow himself to be so persuaded, Canidy's orders were to take him out — in the absolute worst possible sense of the phrase — thus depriving the Germans and Italians of his expertise in their advancement of such new weaponry.

Canidy was also to reconnoiter the area, keeping an eye out for locations and, if possible, personnel to set up OSS stations on Sicily like that of Pearl Harbor on Corsica, as well as collect anything else that would be of military intelligence value.

In a short time, Canidy got more than anyone had bargained for.

For starters, the professor shared evidence that the enemy had biological weapons in its possession, then, at the eleventh hour, pointed out the existence of chemical weapons as well.

Canidy had carefully put to use his Composition C-2 plastic explosives to get rid of both.

And when the submarine returned exactly on schedule six days later for the extraction, both he and the professor were more than ready to get the hell out of there.

That extraction had happened the previous night.

Now, this morning, with the professor sound and secure in a bunk room of the submarine, the suitcase at his feet packed with all the scholarly writings that he could carry out, Canidy had borrowed a ship's typewriter and written the mission's after-action report.

Canidy then had confirmed the critical points of his report with the professor, then composed a brief top secret message that would need to be sent by the sub's commo room as soon as possible, and then finally requested the private meeting with the commander of the *Casabianca*.

In L'Herminier's office, Canidy handed over the typewritten message.

"We need to encrypt this at the earliest opportunity," Canidy said, "then radio it."

On the five-hundred-nautical-mile leg

35

from Algiers to Sicily's Mondello, the sub had run as hard and fast as conditions allowed — sometimes ten knots, sometimes dead in the water at depth to avoid detection by German and Italian ships on patrol.

Heading back would take her at least as long, and Canidy knew his report could not wait for that time frame.

News of the nerve gas would be enough to get attention right away. He decided there was no reason to muddy the message with the discovery of the yellow fever — which was detailed in his after action-report — and would save it for a subsequent message, or till they reached OSS Algiers Station.

*There shouldn't be anything left of the villa and its lab, anyway,* Canidy thought.

L'Herminier took the sheet and his eyes fell on it:

---

TOP SECRET

OPERATIONAL IMMEDIATE

26MAR43 0900

FOR OSS WASHINGTON EYES ONLY COL DONOVAN; OSS ALGIERS EYES ONLY CAPT FINE

---

```
BEGIN QUOTE

PACKAGE COLLECTED AND FLOATING HOME.

URGENT: NOTE THAT PACKAGE CONFIRMS
REPEAT PACKAGE CONFIRMS BEYOND ANY
QUESTION THAT ANTACID EXISTS AT COLLEC-
TION POINT PLUS OTHERS.

DETAILS TO FOLLOW ON ARRIVAL..

CANIDY

END QUOTE

TOP SECRET
```

L'Herminier folded it and put it in his tunic pocket.

"Consider it done," Commander L'Herminier said agreeably. "Soon as it is safe to surface."

"Thank you," Canidy said.

L'Herminier looked like he had a question.

"Something on your mind, Commander?" Canidy said.

"Antacid?" he said simply.

Canidy raised an eyebrow.

"My code words aren't always appreciated," he said.

"But *antacid* for a nerve agent?" L'Herminier said, not making a connection and thinking something must be lost in the translation.

"I think it's fair to say that if you had a bout of stomach acid," Canidy said, somewhat darkly, "a dose of Tabun would cure you of it for good."

The commander's eyebrows went up in recognition.

*"Oui,"* he said softly. "That and everything else."

# [THREE]
## THE OVAL OFFICE
## THE WHITE HOUSE
## 1600 PENNSYLVANIA AVENUE, NW
## WASHINGTON, D.C.
## 1125 27 MARCH 1943

"Bill!" Franklin Delano Roosevelt called fondly. The President of the United States of America propelled himself across the room in the wooden chair that he had had specially fitted with wheels. "Such a pleasure to see you again so soon."

William J. Donovan, a stocky, silver-haired, ruddy-faced Irishman, stood in the doorway to the right, which led to the office of the President's personal secretary.

"Come in, *General,*" Roosevelt continued as he rolled closer, smiling, with his ivory cigarette holder clenched between his teeth.

Roosevelt took great delight in the use of the rank. When Donovan had returned to the employ of the United States government in 1941 at the request of FDR, he had been a civilian using the honorific title of "Colonel," which he had in fact been in the First World War.

On Tuesday, March 23, when he had been given his new commission, he became Brigadier General William Joseph Donovan, USA.

It was a title more appropriate for the man whom FDR had made America's spymaster.

Donovan forced a smile. He was pleased to find Roosevelt in a pleasant frame of mind. The President had been under a lot of stress of late, plus clearly in some pain from the cruel effects of the polio that had nearly killed him in 1921. Donovan was sorry that the news he bore would no doubt squash those good spirits.

Still, he knew that Roosevelt was the kind of man who knew he should hear bad news when that's what it was. He demanded to hear it — undiluted and never, ever withheld.

Donovan put out his right hand to meet Roosevelt's.

"Mr. President," he said, "you're looking especially well."

"I'm feeling especially well," Roosevelt replied, shaking Donovan's hand while warmly gripping his forearm with his left hand. "I wish I could tell you what it is — because I'd damn well bottle it for use on my darker days — but, with the exception of the glorious weather on this spring day, I don't have an inkling . . ."

His voice trailed off.

Roosevelt sensed in Donovan's eyes that, despite the smile, there was something troubling his old friend terribly. And FDR knew that that took something very serious indeed.

It was a matter of official record that "Wild Bill" Donovan had been one hell of a soldier in his day. In World War One, on the battlefields of France, he had earned his silver eagle and the Medal of Honor — his country's highest honor for valor — while with the "Fighting 69th," the National Guard regiment from New York City.

Roosevelt remembered the wording of the MOH citation being along the lines of: *After then Lieutenant Colonel Donovan personally led an assault against a strongly organized enemy position, and his troops suffered heavy casualties, he moved among his men in exposed positions, reorganized the decimated platoons, then accompanied them forward in attacks. When badly wounded in the leg by machine-gun fire, he refused to be evacuated and instead continued fighting the enemy until his unit withdrew to a less-exposed position.*

A determined man of great integrity — who inspired loyalty, led by example, didn't back down — Franklin Roosevelt had known Bill Donovan since their days as classmates at Columbia Law School more than thirty years earlier.

Roosevelt recognized that Donovan shared more than a few of his own qualities. Topping the list: being one tough and shrewd sonofabitch. And an extremely smart one, of course.

An ambitious Irishman, Donovan was self-made. Between wars he had become a very successful — and very wealthy — attorney in New York City, and, with that, a power behind the political scenes, not only in New York but in Washington.

Roosevelt was neither professionally nor personally bothered by the fact that Donovan was a solid Republican who had opposed FDR's New Deal, which conservatives termed "socialist" when they were being nice, something far less polite when they weren't.

What mattered to FDR was the man's character, not his politics, and he was glad that they were pals.

He was even more grateful that whatever Donovan told FDR as being factual, FDR could take it as that.

Roosevelt, ever the savvy politician, long had used his friends with great wealth or high connections — and especially those with both, because he knew that heads of state never put themselves far from deep pockets — to serve as his eyes and ears around the world.

Donovan was no exception.

When FDR had served as assistant secretary of the Navy, he'd attached Donovan to the Office of Naval Intelligence, and, in 1920, secretly sent him to Siberia to collect intelligence. When, in 1935, the belligerent dictator of Italy, Benito Mussolini, invaded Ethiopia — dirt poor and essentially unarmed — Roosevelt, in his first term as President, had dispatched Donovan to supply him trusted information on that one-sided "war." And, in 1940, as another Fascist — the charismatic German chancellor, Adolf Hitler — waged an unchecked war of evil across Europe, FDR twice sent Donovan across the pond.

Donovan's first trip that year, in July, was a relatively quick one to England.

"Find out if our cousins can beat back that bastard Hitler," Roosevelt had told Donovan.

Donovan had done so, and, in August, reported back that the Brits were not likely to be pushing the German forces anywhere anytime soon but, at least for the time being, they could protect their country — especially with the help of neutral America.

The second 1940 trip began in the middle of December and lasted for nearly three months, covering the Baltics and the Mediterranean.

Donovan reported his newest findings to the President in March 1941. Roosevelt's fears of the spreading of Fascism and Communism — and the free world's ability to contain them — grew faster than ever before. These threats were real, and he felt that they could not be underestimated — abroad, clearly, but also in the United States.

Thus FDR, being a shrewd, smart sonofabitch now in his third term as President, knew that despite the cries of the isolationists who wanted America to have nothing to do with another world war it was only a matter of time before the country would be forced to shed its neutral status.

And the best way to be prepared for that moment was to have the finest intelligence he could.

And the best way to get that information, to get the facts that he trusted because he trusted the messenger, was to put another shrewd, smart sonofabitch in charge — his pal Wild Bill Donovan.

The problem was not that intelligence wasn't being collected. The United States of America had vast organizations actively engaged in it — the Federal Bureau of Investigation, the Office of Naval Intelligence, and the Military Intelligence Division chief among them.

The problem was that the intelligence these organizations collected was, in the word of the old-school British spymasters, "coloured." That was to say, the intel tended first to serve to promote the respective branches.

If, for example, ONI overstated the number of, say, German submarines, then the Navy brass could use that intelligence to justify its demands for more funds for sailors and ships to hunt down those U-boats. (Which, of course, played to everyone's natural fears as the U-boats were damn effective killing machines.)

Likewise, if MID stated that it had found significantly more Axis troops amassing toward an Allied border than was previously thought, Army brass could argue that ground and/or air forces needed the money more than did the swabbies.

Then there was the turf-fighting FBI. J. Edgar Hoover and Company didn't want any Allied spies snooping around in their backyard.

It followed then that if the agencies had their own agendas, they were not prone to share with others the information that they collected. The argument, as might be expected, was that intelligence shared was intelligence compromised.

There was also the interagency fear, unspoken but there, as sure as God made little green apples, that some shared intel would be found to be wanting. If that should happen, it would make the particular agency that had developed it look bad. And *that,* fear of all fears, would result in the reduction of funds, of men, of weapons, et cetera, et cetera. In short, the loss of importance of the agency in the eyes of the grand political scheme.

Thus among the various agencies there continued the endless turf battles, the duplications of effort — even the instances, say, of undercover FBI agents arresting undercover ONI agents snooping around Washington, D.C., and New York City.

Roosevelt had had enough. A master of political maneuvering, he had an answer.

On July 11, 1941, the President created a new department. He said it would collect all information critical to national security — from the FBI, ONI, MID, from anyone and everyone — analyze it, and act on such information as necessary.

This new office, logically, was named Coordinator of Information.

And he appointed William J. Donovan as its director.

Donovan would report directly to the President. His pay: one dollar per annum.

Roosevelt was quite pleased with himself. This was a natural extension of what Donovan had very much been doing for FDR for years, dating back to when FDR first had attached Donovan to ONI.

But not everyone could be described as being overjoyed.

If the existing intelligence organizations

did not play happily together before, there was certainly no reason to expect them to embrace the new kid on the playground. Particularly with the new kid answering only to the President and having access to the vast secret funds of the Office of the President.

There were howls of protest, which Roosevelt more or less managed. But the top brass that made up the Joint Chiefs of Staff eventually prevailed upon the President that an organization evaluating intelligence of the military and for the military should not be outside the military. And certainly not answerable to a civilian. (Donovan's unquestionable credentials be damned, this was bureaucratic battling at its best.)

And so on June 13, 1942, the COI evolved into the OSS — the Office of Strategic Services — and was duly placed under the Joint Chiefs of Staff.

On paper, Donovan now answered to General George Catlett Marshall, the Chief of Staff, who in turn answered to the President.

In reality, however, the door to the Oval Office — and any other place the President of the United States might be — was always open to FDR's old friend and confidante.

The President released Donovan's forearm,

47

then his hand, and then rolled the chair back two feet, the high spirits seeming to drain from him as he did so.

Roosevelt quietly spun his chair, and began wheeling it toward the ornate, wooden presidential desk — what was known as the *Resolute* desk, as on the orders of the Queen of England it had been finely crafted from timbers taken from the retired HMS *Resolute* and then in 1880 given by Her Majesty Queen Victoria to Rutherford Hayes, who was then the President of the United States.

Donovan saw that spread across this magnificent desk, next to the wire baskets holding decrypted secret messages and a half-full water glass, were the tools of FDR's lifelong hobby of stamp collecting. There were scissors, a magnifying glass, a thick album, and, next to a well-worn guidebook with dog-eared pages, an eight-by-ten-inch manila envelope torn open to give ready access to its mass of stamps from around the world, newly collected and packaged for him by an admirer in the State Department.

Bright sunlight filtered into the Oval Office through the tall windows and doors, gloriously lighting the great two-story interior of the thirty-five-by-twenty-nine-foot room. The glossy white walls shined. The intricately patterned woodwork of the floor glowed. The details practically popped in each of the representations of the Presidential Seal on the room's ceiling and in its floor.

Roosevelt stopped at the windows. He thoughtfully looked out at the Rose Garden and its fanciful foliage beginning to bloom, then across the well-manicured grounds of the South Lawn. He grunted and nodded appreciatively, puffed his cigarette, then finally maneuvered his chair around the big, royal blue banner that was the President's Flag. It hung from an eight-foot-tall staff standing near the wall behind the desk, opposite the flag of the United States of America, also on a tall staff.

Donovan followed the President across the Oval Office. He stopped at the three finely patterned silk-upholstered armchairs arranged in an arc in front of the desk and sat down in the center one.

After a moment, the President looked across the desk and straight into Donovan's concerned eyes.

"What is it, Bill?" Roosevelt asked. "May I ask about the family?"

Roosevelt knew that he could of course ask about Donovan's family; as friends for decades, and as both husbands and fathers, they felt a genuine fondness for one another's family.

Still painfully fresh in their minds was the memory, not quite three years earlier, of Donovan's beloved daughter Patricia having died when her car overturned near Fredericksburg, Virginia. Roosevelt had made sure then that every arrangement for her final resting went without difficulty for Donovan, including Patricia's place of burial in Arlington National Cemetery.

"The family is fine," Donovan said, "as I hope is yours."

"Yes, yes. Quite," the President said. He coughed twice, puffed his cigarette, then pursued, "And Dave?"

Lieutenant David Rumsey Donovan, United States Navy, was twenty-eight; he had been born two years before Patricia. Roosevelt was particularly fond of him — he was close in age to FDR's son James, and the three of them were products of Harvard.

Donovan smiled warmly.

"Dave's fine, too, thank you. What do you hear from Jimmy?"

Donovan knew Jimmy Roosevelt well and liked him very much. As his father's confidante, in 1941 Jimmy had been, in addition to other presidential assignments, temporarily attached to the COI to minimize the bureaucratic attacks on Donovan's — and, really, FDR's — fledgling organization.

More recently, Major James Roosevelt, United States Marine Corps, had been a Marine Raider on the Makin Island raid in the Pacific and awarded the Navy Cross for his heroism in that battle.

"Still successfully dodging enemy bullets," Roosevelt said proudly.

"We're very lucky," Donovan said softly.

"Yes, we are, Bill."

After a moment, Donovan went on: "Dave is helping plan for Operation Husky."

Roosevelt saw that after the mention of the code name for the Allied invasion of Sicily, Donovan had paused and his face had changed expression.

"And I'm afraid," the director of the OSS finally said, "that that's what I'm here for."

"Sicily?" the President said. He took a long puff from his cigarette in its holder, exhaled, then added, "I know you're not asking to keep David from the fight for Sicily — I'm sure he's hoping to get in the thick of it. So what about it?"

"Mr. President," Donovan said, his deep voice formal and somewhat stiff, "I'm here to report that there is nerve gas on Sicily."

The President, his face stoic, took two puffs on his cigarette, turned his chair to look out at the South Lawn, then exhaled

51

the smoke toward the glass.

After a moment, Roosevelt said unemotionally, "Tell that to me again."

"Frank, it's true," Donovan said reasonably.

FDR, still looking out the window, ignored the informality.

"General Donovan," the President said, his patrician voice an even tone, "indulge me."

"The Germans have nerve gas on Sicily, Mr. President," the director of the Office of Strategic Services repeated formally.

FDR turned in his chair and snubbed out the cigarette in a round crystal ashtray with far more force than was necessary.

Donovan now saw anger in FDR's face.

Roosevelt quietly reached across his desk, opened a silver box that held a dozen or more loose Camel cigarettes, took out one and worked it into his holder, lit it, then inhaled deeply before slowly exhaling a significant cloud of gray-blue smoke.

He remained silent, lost in his thoughts as he absently fingered the stamps in the open envelope on the desk.

Then Roosevelt suddenly banged on the desk with his fist. Stamps went flying. The scissors hit the floor.

"Goddamn it all to hell!" the President exploded.

It was an uncharacteristic act. In all their years, Donovan had known Roosevelt to project calm, particularly at moments of bad news.

*The tension or pain — or both — is worse than I feared,* Donovan thought.

"Yes, Mr. President," Donovan, whose temper bordered on the legendary, responded. "My thoughts exactly."

After a moment, when the President seemed somewhat sure of his anger not getting away from him, he said, "How did we come about this information? And why is this the first I have heard of it?"

"Candy," Donovan said. "And I just had it confirmed through radio traffic with the OSS station in Algiers."

"Candy?"

Donovan nodded.

"Dick Canidy," he explained, "two days ago blew up a cargo ship that had the nerve gas onboard. I personally sent him on a mission in Sicily to bring out a professor, a metallurgist, we wanted for the Manhattan Project."

Roosevelt nodded.

The Manhattan Project — TOP SECRET PRESIDENTIAL — was FDR's race to build the atomic bomb before Nazi Germany built its own. Albert Einstein and a number of other distinguished scientists who had fled Europe for the freedom of America had convinced Roosevelt that it was only a matter of time before scientists learned how to harness the power of a nuclear reaction and create the world's most powerful weapon — one producing the explosive equivalent of twenty thousand tons of TNT. FDR understood that whoever won the race for such a weapon also won the war.

Quietly supplying the Manhattan Project with whatever it needed — men, matériel, smuggled scientists, whatever — had become the OSS's number one priority. Number two concerned the enemy's development of jet aircraft, and the OSS hotly sought in any way it could to steal, delay, and destroy the Germans' plans for superiority in the air war. Thus, this wasn't the first scientist whom Canidy had helped nab, and so neither was this the first time he had come to the attention of the President.

"The evidence of nerve gas, is it conclusive?" the President asked, measuring his words.

"As yet, there is no hard evidence. But there appears to be no reason to doubt the professor. He said that there was nerve gas. Canidy believes him."

"That's really not enough to go on, Bill,

now is it?" the President said reasonably.

Donovan exhaled audibly.

"Canidy is no dummy," the director of the OSS replied somewhat defensively. "He's one of my best men. That's why he's basically working directly for me."

"Is that wise? Is it a good idea to send one who's a bit of — what did I hear was the phrase? — 'a loose cannon'?"

Donovan frowned as his face flushed.

"Franklin," he said, his voice beginning to rise, "I've heard that crack about Canidy, too. I will tell you that he gets done what has to be done in whatever way necessary, even if — no, *especially* if — that gets ugly and complicated. Unfortunately, his methods often offend those stiff-shirt types who have been afraid to color outside of the lines ever since they were in diapers."

Donovan heard what he just said, and how loud he'd said it, and paused.

He threw his hands up, and exhaled audibly.

"Excuse me for that little outburst, Mr. President."

The President of the United States leaned his head back and laughed out loud.

"That's the Wild Bill Donovan I know," the President said fondly. "And you're absolutely right, Bill. No apology necessary. I should apologize to you. I've heard that same loose-cannon phrase attached to you, and felt it was as unfair to you as I believe you feel it is to Canidy."

He took the two last puffs of his cigarette, then looked intently across the desk. "You're not done yet, are you?"

After they silently looked at one another a moment, and after Roosevelt snuffed out his cigarette and reached for another, Donovan spoke up.

"I'm afraid Canidy came across more than that," Donovan said.

"More?"

Donovan explained: "The professor — Rossi — showed Canidy a lab that the SS had set up. They were injecting prisoners with yellow fever."

The President took the cigarette holder from his mouth.

"My God!" FDR said. "Germ warfare, too? That's as bad as the damn nerve gas!"

Donovan nodded. "The lab — a makeshift lab, actually, in a villa — was supposed to have blown up, too."

"Supposed to?"

"They had to leave before they actually saw it go up," Donovan explained. "But they did see the explosions of the ship that had the gas on board."

The President looked at Donovan a long moment, mentally measuring it all, before replying.

"Let me see if I have this straight," Roosevelt said finally. "We know that a ship was destroyed but don't know conclusively that it had nerve gas. And we know conclusively that a yellow-fever lab existed but don't know that it was in fact destroyed."

"That, I'm afraid, is correct. But as far as I'm concerned —"

"Bill," the President interrupted, "I need irrefutable evidence. Can we get that?"

Donovan considered the question a moment before replying.

"If the villa did explode," the OSS director said, "then all we're going to find there, basically, is a mass of rubble."

"And if the ship did have the nerve gas?"

Donovan looked down, his memory flashing images of the bloody battlefields of France in the First War — and of the unspeakable horror that was mass death. It was a mental image that had faded with time but would never completely go away.

He gathered his thoughts for a moment, then looked back at FDR.

"If the nerve gas was on there," Donovan said slowly, "then the evidence of it is right now all over Palermo."

The President frowned. He understood that meant that the Germans had in a roundabout fashion — with the help of one OSS agent — caused a heinous death on the very citizens of Sicily they were there, in part, to help protect.

"The Germans will be quick to cover their tracks," Roosevelt said.

"You can't just go in and clean up something like that. Lingering signs — the irrefutable evidence — will be around a long time. Weeks, maybe months. Longer, if they use mass graves instead of burials at sea."

Roosevelt nodded thoughtfully. Then he said, "I've long feared that that damn Hitler would eventually use chemicals. Not so much germs, but certainly gas, never mind the Geneva Protocol."

Formally, the "Protocol for the Prohibition of the Use in War of Asphyxiating, Poisonous or Other Gases, and of Bacteriological Methods of Warfare," the Geneva Protocol, signed in 1925 and put in play in 1928, outlawed the use of chemical and biological weapons. It read, in part: "Whereas the use in war of asphyxiating, poisonous or other gases, and of all analogous liquids, materials, or devices, has been justly condemned by the general opinion of the civilized world. . ."

Donovan knew that in war any number of

ruthless dictators — those clearly *not* civilized — might regard it as nothing more than a piece of paper.

Which was to say, patently ignore it.

"Technically, the Germans did not set off those munitions," Donovan offered. "And the Geneva Protocol forbids the use of such weapons. It doesn't address storage or shipment —"

"Which," Roosevelt interrupted, "you well know is why we have Arkansas and Colorado working day and night."

By "Colorado," the OSS director knew that the President was referring to the Rocky Mountain Arsenal there. And that "Arkansas" was the Pine Bluff Arsenal. The U.S. Army secretly manufactured chemical warfare (CW) munitions at the huge facilities. Testing of the nerve gas had taken place in mock CW exercises in Utah. Tons of the munitions had been and were being stockpiled in top secret locations . . . including overseas.

Roosevelt motioned with his cigarette holder as he added pointedly, "I meant it when I said that we would retaliate in kind."

Donovan nodded solemnly.

The President paused in thought, then went on:

"Let's suppose that the ship did in fact

contain nerve gas. Hitler doesn't know that we know who set off the munitions. He's likely going to think that we think the Germans or Italians did it knowingly, either intentionally or accidentally. He cannot take the chance that somehow we do not know about the incident, because that would mean not being prepared for any possible retaliation on our part. Regardless that it would be retaliation for something he didn't do." He looked at Donovan. "You with me?"

"Yeah."

"So he's going to spend a lot of effort making sure we don't find out about the use —"

Roosevelt suddenly had an extended coughing fit. After it ended, he took a sip of water, cleared his throat, then added: "Yes?"

"Yeah," Donovan repeated. "You'd certainly expect that."

Roosevelt snorted.

"He's just damn lucky Churchill doesn't know about it," FDR said. "With the slightest excuse such as this, Winston would in a moment float Berlin away on a cloud of mustard gas."

Donovan nodded solemnly again.

Roosevelt shuffled in his seat, sat up a bit, and cleared his throat.

"Here's what's going to happen," FDR said earnestly. "I will keep an eye on the

Ultra messages" — he gestured at the wire baskets of decrypted enemy message traffic; Ultra was the code name for the Allies' supersecret breaking of the German cipher machine, Enigma — "for any mention of this. And I will make it known to George Marshall, without mentioning my source, to quietly keep an eye out."

FDR would not reveal where he got the information because both men knew that Marshall would not be happy with this meeting between them. The way it was supposed to work was that Donovan reported to Marshall and Marshall reported to the President. That was chain of command and how such intel was supposed to reach Roosevelt.

But Donovan knew — and he figured that FDR suspected — that General Marshall, USA, likely would kick it down to General Eisenhower, USA, and get his brethren's take on it before carrying it to FDR.

General Dwight D. Eisenhower was commander in chief, Allied Forces Headquarters. AFHQ (pronounced "aff-kew") was in Algiers. Ike's command included British General Bernard Montgomery and his British Eighth Army.

"With all due respect, you do realize that all answers cannot be found in Ultra," the director of the Office of Strategic Services said carefully. "Clearly, it's invaluable. But Ike's people — both the Americans and the Brits — are putting their blind faith in it. If Ultra says something and they can corroborate it by other means, then they act on it. But if it's not in Ultra, then it doesn't exist — which is why, apparently, they're underwhelmed by Canidy's discoveries."

Roosevelt nodded.

"I do realize that," he said. "So then it's up to you."

"You want us to get the evidence?" Donovan said. It was a statement more than a question.

"I damn sure need it before I can" — Roosevelt struggled for the right words — "go forward."

His face then grew hard.

"You know, I expected this out of those damn ruthless Japs — which was why I reluctantly allowed our nerve gas production to move with such speed and size — but not from that crazed goddamn Austrian corporal. I thought he'd had more than his share of gas when he fought in the First War and that he'd sworn it off."

Roosevelt looked deeply into Donovan's eyes.

"Get me that evidence, Bill."

"Yes, Mr. President. But despite the horror

I expect we'll find, it won't be easy."

"Why?"

"Ike has made it clear that he's controlling all the strings in the MTO. It's hard to blow your nose anywhere near AFHQ without his explicit permission."

Sensitive to the accusations that the American troops were unbloodied and undertrained and thus not meshing well with their more-battle-hardened British counterparts, Eisenhower was taking great pains — some said being a great pain — about the British and Americans coming together seamlessly to work under one leader.

And that leader was Ike. And Ike was being all-controlling.

"What exactly was the reaction at AFHQ to Canidy's findings? You said underwhelmed?"

"More like denial. 'We'll take it under advisement,' they said, not believing our fledgling OSS could possibly know something they don't. And they're hiding behind Husky — they're (a) not going to spend resources checking out what they declare not to be and (b) not going to risk having such an investigation possibly tip off the Germans and Italians that we're about to invade the islands."

Roosevelt looked at Donovan and nodded.

"I see," the President said. "Well, we have

to find out the real facts about what is on the island, and quickly. If they have those evil weapons, they must have the plans to them. And, if so, we have to decide if we're going to respond in kind or not — and, if not, then . . ."

He let that thought go unspoken.

The OSS director, after a moment, said, "What we can do, Mr. President —"

"You and your loose cannon Canidy do what you have to, Bill," FDR interrupted. He paused, waiting for the provoked response that didn't come. Then he went on: "I don't want to know details, because, if I do, I'm afraid that I won't be able to deny to Marshall, or whomever, that I do."

The President puffed thoughtfully on his cigarette holder, bluish gray clouds filling the air immediately over his head. He appeared pleased with himself.

"And that, General Donovan, my old friend, is why I put you in business."

# II

## [ONE]
## PORT OF ALGIERS
## ALGIERS, ALGERIA
## 1125 30 MARCH 1943

Ensign Zack Lee, U.S. Navy — a wiry, five-foot-seven twenty-one-year-old, fair-skinned, with buzzed white-blond hair and a pair of disproportionately large ears that stuck straight out from his very round head — was not sure exactly what to expect when he had been sent to meet the Free French Forces submarine *Casabianca*. He'd simply been ordered by the motor pool lieutenant (junior grade) to go down the hill to the docks and bring Commander L'Herminier directly back to AFHQ.

What Ensign Lee *was* sure of, however, was that he planned to carry out the order without mishap.

The motor pool lieutenant (j.g.) had told him, "Some light bird named Owen on Eisenhower's staff has a bug up his ass that the sub driver is not to go anywhere but from the boat right to Owen's office." Without looking up from the crossword puzzle he'd been working, he added, "Screw it up and you'll wind up getting reassigned to a DLM in, oh, say, el Golia."

When Lee had replied, "A DLM in el Golia, sir?" the reply had been, "Ensign, that would be Desk, Large Metal, in the Algerian hellhole called a desert. Now, get the hell down there!"

Ensign Lee, wearing summer whites, his newly issued butter bars shining brightly in the Mediterranean sun, hoped that he was not going to have to wait too long, as he now was beginning to drip with sweat.

Lee had already managed an impressive string of screwups during his short hitch — the biggest being picking the Navy in the first place. He'd joined in large part, he had hoped, to get away from the dreadful dry heat of the sunbaked Texas Panhandle. He'd been born in Amarillo, raised an hour's drive north in a desolate dirt patch called, appropriately enough, Cactus, Texas. And he'd just graduated from Texas Technological College, there on the high plains in Lubbock.

Now, not at all overjoyed about being assigned as a motor pool driver to ferry AFHQ flag officers and the like, he stood leaning against the front right fender of a 1941 Plymouth P11.

The four-door staff car he drove was another that the Navy had decided for whatever reason to leave in its civilian configuration — this particular one with the body and wheels painted in a baby blue color, and its bumpers, grille, window trim, and hubcaps still in shining chrome. There was one obvious modification that may have met some military standard: US NAVY had been stenciled in black, four-inch-high block letters across each of the back doors.

He mopped the sweat from his forehead, very much aware that hoping for an assignment at sea had been a colossal screwup on his part. He realized that he had, very simply, traded a dreadful, dry Texas heat for a dreadful, humid subtropical heat.

Not to mention a dreadfully boring job, one he was determined to rise above.

And not screwing up certainly was one way to accomplish that.

Lee watched the *Casabianca* being nudged to her berth by small tugs. Her deck was busy with what clearly were Free French sailors. They steadily and calmly readied lines fore and aft, while watchful gunners stood by the antiaircraft weaponry. A small group of five or six men crowded

67

the conning tower.

*Wonder if one of them is the captain?* Lee thought. *And which one?*

When the boat was stopped dead in the water alongside the dock, the sailor activity increased dramatically. The speed and agility impressed Lee, who wondered what life on a sub would be like.

*Can't be worse than a motor pool driver. It sure looks more exciting.*

Once the submarine was secure, a nonregulation gangplank was produced — *Looks like something they could've made in junior high woodshop* — and run from the sub's deck down to the smooth stone edge of the dockage.

Ensign Lee watched in amazement as two male figures — *What? Passengers? They sure don't look like Free French sailors* — made their way toward coming ashore.

The first figure walking toward the gangplank was a big man with dark hair, imposing — probably six feet tall, with wide shoulders — and a confident stride. He wore nice, casual tan slacks, a lightweight, dark brown shirt that was buttoned down the front, and a navy blue Greek fisherman's cap. Slung over his shoulder was a black duffel made of what looked like a rubberized fabric.

*Must be waterproofing, or something that*

*sailors use. But is that a pistol butt sticking out above his belt buckle? I'll be damned! He's got himself a .45 tucked in his waistband!*

Trailing the tall man by some ten feet was another tall figure, this one almost completely concealed in a traditional Arab outfit — a white gandoura cloak, a burnous cape, and on his head a fez wrapped in white cloth. He carried — very carefully, very slowly, as he apparently was having more than a little difficulty with his footing on the deck — what looked very much like a large leather suitcase.

"What's with the Arab and the suitcase?" Ensign Lee muttered aloud.

His Texas tongue made "Arab" come out *"A-rhab."*

He thought, *Must be a heavy one, too. He's using both hands on that handle.*

Lee watched with rapt fascination as the big, imposing man moved quickly to the foot of the gangplank and then stopped to look back at the Arab. He clearly looked to be in a rush . . . and not necessarily pleased with the Arab's slow pace.

The big, imposing man waited till the Arab had reached him, then held out his hand for the suitcase.

The Arab did not seem sure that he wanted the big, imposing man to take the suitcase. There then ensued what Ensign Lee thought to be a somewhat comic tug-of-war.

*This is getting to be a pretty good l'il show,* he thought, grinning.

The big, imposing man then let go of the handle, said something to the Arab, and gestured toward the narrow gangplank.

The Arab looked at what he was gesturing toward, tentatively placed a foot on the gangplank, and then apparently understood what the big imposing man was trying to tell him. Which appeared to be that the gangplank was (1) not only narrow but (2) also not exactly the most stable of conveyances to carry a heavy suitcase across for a man who was experiencing an obvious loss of footing.

The Arab let loose the suitcase handle.

The big, imposing man then made a dramatic sweep of his arm and slight bow, to say, à la Alphonse and Gaston, *Please, after you, sir.*

As the Arab began his slow trek across the gangplank, the big, imposing man turned back to the conning tower, where three men in naval officer uniforms still stood, watching.

The big man then raised his right arm high above his head, made a slow, exaggerated wave of good-bye to the officers, and then saluted them. When the officers had returned his salute, the big man picked up the suitcase, turned toward the foot of the gangplank, and with no apparent effort followed the Arab ashore.

*I'd better go down and find L'Herminier before I foul my prop,* Ensign Lee thought, pleased with himself for picking up seaman lingo from his lieutenant even though he was stuck ashore. He started walking — almost marching — the thirty-yard distance to where the gangplank met the dockage.

About midway, he intercepted the Arab and, coming up quickly behind him, the big man.

Beneath the white cloth that wrapped the fez and most of the face, Ensign Lee saw two chestnut brown eyes staring down at him. Then he saw the eyes dart toward the second man and then the fez nod in that direction.

At exactly the same time, there came a shrill whistle from the big, imposing man. Ensign Lee looked and saw that the man was waving for him to come to him.

Ensign Lee started in that direction, walking calmly and purposefully.

"On the double!" the big man added. "We're in a hurry!"

*What the hell?* Lee thought, but picked up his speed till they met.

"My orders are to pick up Commander L'Herminier and ferry him to AFHQ," Lee said with what he hoped was more than a little confidence.

The big man stared at Lee a long moment, clearly thinking.

He turned, pointed at the sub, and said, "I just left the commander in the . . ."

He looked at the conn tower, which was now empty.

"Dammit!" the big man said, then turned back to Lee. "Look, I just talked with him. I know he'll be at least an hour before he disembarks — he told me as much because we're going to the same place. So if you're here for that, then I'm sure he won't mind you running us up first. It's near AFHQ."

"Sir," Lee said, mustering more confidence, "my orders are to pick up Commander L'Herminier and ferry him to AFHQ."

The big man made a face, then said, "So you've told me. And I'm telling you that he won't mind you giving us a lift, then coming back for him."

Ensign Lee looked more than a little dubious.

"Take this," the big man went on, ignoring Lee's look and dropping the heavy suitcase on the ground at the ensign's feet.

"We're in a hurry."

*Don't screw this up!* Lee thought.

Ensign Zack Lee, in his best formal tone, said, "Sir, those are not my orders."

The big man looked pissed as he adjusted the duffel strap over his shoulder.

"Who did you say you were?" he said.

"Ensign Lee, sir. I was sent —"

"And you will, Ensign Lee. Right after you run us up the hill. Aye, aye, Ensign?"

The big man raised his eyebrows as if to say *What're you waiting for?*

Ensign Lee, clearly thinking, stared down at his feet. He noticed again the Colt semi-automatic .45 ACP pistol tucked behind the big man's belt buckle.

As Lee considered his options, he glanced past the big man toward the sub. There, naval support vehicles, including four GMC 6 x 6 trucks and a couple of Plymouth P11 sedans, were pulling up near the gangplank.

*If Commander L'Herminier gets in one of those instead of mine, who knows where he'll go? With my luck, nowhere near AFHQ.*

*And, oh, boy, would my ass be in a crack then. . . .*

Lee's eyes nervously darted to the big man, then to the sub, then back again.

"If you don't mind, sir," Lee said, "I'll just

check at the boat. It'll take only a second."

"Christ!" the big man fumed, then looked toward the Arab, who stood waiting almost at Lee's car. The big man then put his hands up, chest high, palms out. "Okay, Lee. Do what you must."

"Yes, sir," Lee said, his voice relieved. "Thank you for understanding, sir."

Ensign Lee marched purposefully toward the gangplank.

When Lee was more or less halfway there, he heard behind him the sound of a door shut. It sounded like the Plymouth's.

He turned and saw that the big man had closed the left rear passenger door after the Arab had gotten in, and now was himself in the process of getting in behind the wheel.

In the time it took Ensign Lee to utter "What the hell?," the big man had fired up the Plymouth's engine and begun driving out of the busy dock area.

"Hey!" Lee shouted as he took off toward it at a trot.

The car disappeared into the web of city streets. Lee stopped in his tracks.

"Aw, dadgumit!" he said and looked around to see if anyone had seen what had just happened.

He sighed.

*There can't really be any Navy guys in the desert.*

*Can there . . . ?*

# [TWO]

Canidy, his foot heavy on the accelerator pedal, briskly wound the Plymouth through Algiers, the car's eighty-seven-horsepower six-cylinder straining on the inclines. He aggressively tapped the horn when the mass of pedestrians — and the occasional donkey-drawn carts — clogged the narrow cobblestone-paved streets, taking care to play the clutch just right because the low-geared, three-speed transmission had a nasty habit of bucking on the hills.

Canidy had instructed Professor Rossi to stay down on the backseat out of sight. And every now and then, particularly at the sudden moments requiring heavy braking and during the rounding of blind corners, Canidy could hear from the backseat Rossi's groans or gasps or murmurings, these last sounds he decided being directed to a higher power.

Moving ever farther up the hillside of white buildings with red tile roofs, the view of the harbor and sea growing greater and wider below, Canidy sped along, scanning the city streets for familiar landmarks.

After a few more minutes, and more than a few turns, he said somewhat excitedly, "Aha, there's the Hotel Saint George!" He then upshifted, accelerated past that grand old building that served as the base for the brass of AFHQ, slowed only slightly as he hung a left at the next intersection, then accelerated again up the hill.

"You're one lucky man, Professor," Canidy called back in a cheery tone as he made a right turn onto rue Michaud and backed off the gas. "You're in the hands of a natural navigator, a human compass, a — oh, shit!"

Canidy braked heavily and quickly nosed the car to a stop at the curb. He tried unsuccessfully to hide behind the delivery truck that was parked across the street from a large villa painted a faint shade of pink.

When he had set the brake and killed the engine, he heard Rossi murmur a final prayer, then a sigh.

"Sit tight, Professor," Canidy called back quietly. "We need to wait here a moment."

"*Buon,*" Rossi whispered in reply, his tone suggesting that he was not at all disappointed.

Canidy stared across the street. Parked at

the curb in front of a large villa was what had first caught his attention: a great big Army staff car.

Unlike the Plymouth, this 1942 Cadillac had been completely made over with military markings, including the painting of its body in olive drab and its bumpers and other chromed parts blacked out. At the front and back were places designed for the holding of small flags and of small signage — ones that Canidy knew very probably displayed the stars of a general officer of the United States Army. Specifically, Dwight D. Eisenhower, Supreme Commander Allied (Expeditionary) Forces.

There were four people on the sidewalk near the car. One was a mean-looking civilian male who was absently sweeping the walkway with a makeshift broom fashioned of palm fronds while keeping an eye on the other three. Canidy recognized him. He was the villa owner's vassal, Monsieur Khatim, a tough, old Algerian who Canidy knew carried a curved *khanjar* dagger — its double edges razor-sharp — in a sculpted scabbard on his hip just inside the overfold of his off-white robe.

Two wore the uniforms of senior officers in the United States Army. One was a captain, whose face Canidy could see and whom

Canidy knew well, the other a lieutenant colonel, whose back was to him. The third was a good-looking Irish woman in her midthirties who wore the uniform of the British Motor Transport Corps; she stood stiffly, holding open the right rear passenger door.

*That's Ike's Caddy, all right,* Canidy thought.

*And that has got to be his driver — the one who they say he's slipping it to on the side. Hell of a fine-looking woman.*

*But I don't think that's Ike talking with Stan Fine.*

*Must be his light bird fluky, Ol' Colonel Whatshisname.*

Captain Stanley S. Fine, U.S. Army Air Forces, the acting chief of station of OSS Algiers, was thirty-five years old, a tall, ascetic Jew who had left his position as a high-level Hollywood studio lawyer. He joined the Army hoping to be a fighter pilot but wound up with command of a B-17 squadron, then found himself recruited for the OSS.

Fine, nodding in a slow, measured manner, looked somewhat annoyed by the conversation with the lieutenant colonel, a tall, athletic-looking man who — at least from the rear — bore a striking resemblance to Eisenhower.

*Maybe that's why Ike keeps this guy around,* Canidy mused. *Body doubles make great bullet magnets. Or maybe Ike just uses him as a diversion.*

Fine appeared to have just about had his fill of whatever Colonel Whatshisname had to say and his eyes started to roam. Canidy saw Fine glance his way, and Canidy began smiling and waving broadly like a long-lost friend.

Fine seemed first to notice the baby blue Plymouth not quite hidden behind the truck, then did see the excited motion from behind its steering wheel, and then figured out what — or, more precisely, *who* — he was looking at.

A practiced lawyer of considerable skill, Fine kept his poker face, but still quickly returned his attention to the lieutenant colonel.

At that point, the lieutenant colonel apparently had at last reached the end of his speech. Fine nodded one last time, and they exchanged salutes.

The lieutenant colonel turned and moved toward the car door, which still was being held open for him. He looked up and down the street as he did so. Just as he started to climb in the backseat, he noticed the baby blue Navy staff car parked behind a big truck across the street.

He studied it for a moment, wondering if he actually was seeing a man slumped behind the wheel and napping under a Greek fisherman cap that was pulled down over his face. Then he decided that if that was indeed what it was — he'd seen his share of some strange things happening here in Algiers — it was a matter not worthy of his time. And he slid onto the Cadillac's backseat, allowing the door to be closed behind him.

The good-looking Motor Transport Corps driver ran around the front of the car and got in behind the wheel.

Fine stood by and watched as the Cadillac pulled away from the curb. When it had driven out of sight, he walked quickly across the street toward the Plymouth.

Canidy was already standing out on the sidewalk and in the process of opening the rear passenger door.

"Once again," Stanley Fine said by way of greeting, "your timing is impeccable and your luck apparently without limit."

"Was that who I think it was?" Canidy said, shouldering his rubberized duffel bag.

The bag was all that Canidy had carried into Sicily. It had held a change of clothes, a Johnson light machine gun, six magazines of .30-06 ammunition for the LMG, four mags of .45 ACP for his Colt pistol, ten pounds of Composition C-2 explosive, two packages of cheese crackers, a one-pound salami, and a canteen of water. With the exception of the C-2 and food gone, it still held the same items.

He offered his hand to Fine. "Good to see you, Stan."

"You, too," Fine answered fondly as he shook Canidy's hand, then gave a friendly pat to his shoulder. "Welcome back. And if you thought it was Ike's right hand, then your skills of deduction remain in top form, too."

"No," Canidy said with a straight face, "what I meant was, Ike's secret piece of ass?"

Fine laughed. "That was his driver, yes. Kay Summersby. Beautiful woman. Beautiful *newly divorced* woman. But that's all I know. Rumors of Ike's activities are legion. . . . So who knows?"

"Divorced?" Canidy said with a smile. "That's interesting."

"Don't even think about it, Dick."

"Oh, even I don't live that dangerously."

He turned to the car.

Professor Rossi was expending some effort to sit upright, then slide himself and his suitcase out. Once finally on the sidewalk, Rossi awkwardly adjusted his burnous cape and rewrapped the cloth around his fez and head.

"Professor," Canidy said, "say hello to your new best friend, Captain Stanley Fine."

"My pleasure, Professor," Fine said, looking up and down the street suspiciously. Then he nodded toward the villa. "If you don't mind, let's get you out of sight."

The professor made a grunt and nodded, then started to grab the suitcase. He found Canidy's hand already lifting it. This time, there was no tug-of-war over who would carry it.

As Canidy started to lug the case across the street, he saw that Fine still was scanning the immediate area.

"Where's your driver?" Fine said.

"Oh, I expect he'll be along eventually," Canidy called over his shoulder and continued toward the villa without further explanation.

Fine just shook his head, then looked at the professor and motioned for him to precede him to the villa, where Monsieur Khatim waited at the door.


# [THREE]

Drinking coffee from a heavy white china mug, Canidy stood looking out wooden slatted French doors that opened onto a balcony. A warm breeze blew in, lightly scented with sea salt and lilacs. The room before the war had served as the primary of two main dining areas of the Villa de Vue de Mer.

The grand, four-story Sea View Villa — a French Colonial–style mansion solidly built of masonry in the 1880s high on the lush hillside overlooking the harbor — had been let to the Office of Strategic Services for the sum of ten dollars per annum and the promise that it would be preserved and protected. Its owner was the widow of one of Wild Bill Donovan's law school pals. Pamela Dutton — formerly of New York City, Capri, and Algiers, and now simply of Manhattan due to the war — had a line of designer women's shoes, once manufactured in Italy, that carried her name.

Canidy was convinced that the very nice clothes he'd borrowed two weeks earlier from the vast closet off of the villa's master bedroom — and that he now wore — had belonged to Mr. Dutton . . . or perhaps one of Madame Dutton's recent suitors.

*Hell if I care who they belonged to. They're comfortable, and they help me blend in damn better than any Army uniform. And I intend to help myself to more while I'm here.*

The villa's eight bedrooms were on the two

upper floors. The master had its own bath. There were shared baths for the others, one on each floor at the end of the main hall. The second floor, which actually was at street level, had the two dining areas, a kitchen, a pair of lavatories, and a large living area. The bottom floor, tucked into the hill yet with its own view of the sea, had been for entertainment, complete with a formal ballroom.

Now an OSS station, the Villa de Vue de Mer had a permanent staff of about twenty, most wearing U.S. Army tropical-worsted uniforms, some with and some without insignia. There was a transient group of another fifteen or so who wore anything but military outfits. These latter ran the training camps and came and went on irregular schedules, using the villa only as their base.

Three of the four bedrooms (including the master) on the top floor had been filled with rows of folding, wooden-framed cots. Close to the roof and the small forest of antennae newly erected there, and situated in the middle of the floor, the fourth bedroom had become the commo room. It was crammed with tables holding the wireless, two-way radios and teletypes and typewriters and chairs for the operators who encrypted and decrypted the W/T messages. Its wooden door had been reinforced with steel, a wooden beam with brackets added on the inside, and an armed guard posted outside at all times.

The third-floor bedrooms had been made into basic offices for the permanent staffers, with mismatched chairs placed in front of makeshift desks, rows of battered filing cabinets, and, on the walls, frameworks that held charts detailing the Mediterranean Theater of Operations and current and future OSS ops therein.

The first-floor ballroom had been converted into a warehouse storage area, heavy wooden shelving and stacks of crates containing everything from the necessities of an office (typewriters, typewriter papers and ribbons, safes with gold, silver, and the currencies of half a dozen countries, et cetera) to field equipment (W/T radios with their assorted parts, wooden racks holding a small armory of weapons of both American and British manufacture, crates of appropriate calibers of ammunition, Composition C-2 plastic explosive, fuses, even a large wardrobe featuring a variety of enemy uniforms taken from prisoners of war captured in North African campaigns).

With the exception of the two dining rooms doubling as conference areas, the second floor remained mostly unchanged.

Canidy looked at Fine and Rossi seated opposite each other at the room's large, round, wooden dining table. Fine also held a china mug steaming with coffee. Professor Rossi sipped tea from a glass cup. On the table in front of Fine was a short stack of papers.

Canidy gestured toward the stack with his mug. He said, "As I wrote in my after-action report, Stan, there were three distinctive explosions, each one larger than the last. Then came a fantastic plume of fire that lit the night."

He stopped, swallowed a swig of coffee, then added, "It was an impressive sight. Wouldn't you agree, Professor?"

Fine studied Rossi. With the fez and its cloth wrap now on a nearby chair, he could get a good look at the fifty-five-year-old's slender, thoughtful face.

"The explosions were as the major says," he said evenly, his English thick with a Sicilian accent. "The inferno had to have totally consumed the vessel."

"Including the Tabun?" Fine asked.

Canidy said, "I would think so, Stan —"

"Including the T83," Rossi interrupted. "However, the burning would not necessarily have rendered the agent ineffective. In fact . . ."

His voice trailed off. He took a sip of his tea.

"In fact what, Professor?" Fine pursued. "I know you've been through all this with Major Canidy, and it's in his report, but I'd like to hear it again. From you. You might think of something you forgot before."

Rossi nodded.

"My area of expertise is metallurgy, I believe you know, Captain," the professor went on conversationally. "Not chemicals, per se. But it is commonly understood that a cloud created by such a fire would serve as a method of dispersal, a rather rapid one, in effect carrying the T83 across everything in the near distance . . . and farther, depending on winds and the size of the cloud."

"Jesus," Fine said softly.

Fine exchanged glances with Canidy — who appeared somewhat saddened when he raised his eyebrows in a *Yeah, I know* look — then turned back to Rossi.

"And it would have been effective in that state?" Fine asked. It was more a statement than a question; Fine already had read in Canidy's report that that was the case.

Rossi nodded again.

"Not as much had the nerve agent been delivered undiluted from a munitions shell," he said. "But, yes, people, as well as animals,

would have suffered the severe effects —
*would be suffering* its effects."

Everyone was silent a moment.

"And if it did not burn?" Fine then said.

"I really don't think that this could be the
case," the professor replied. "There could
not have been anything left of the ship's contents."

"But, hypothetically," Fine pursued, "if the
shells maintained their integrity in the fires
and simply went down with the ship?"

Rossi shrugged.

"Very well," he replied. "*Hypothetically,* if it
went to the sea bottom the salt water would
corrode the metal of the shells. Eventually —
probably years but possibly sooner — the
shells' seal would fail. Then the T83 would
leach into the water, then to the surface, possibly in such volume as to poison the harbor
and anyone close to it."

He paused.

"Incidentally, it is a fact — not a well-kept
one and not at all hypothetical — that the
shells themselves are prone to leakage. Great
care must be taken in their transport . . . and
in their salvage, if your thinking is that they
could be retrieved intact from the harbor
bottom."

Fine and Canidy exchanged a long look.
The instability of the shells was something

that they had not known.

"And," Rossi said finally, "this was only the first shipment. I heard that more was coming from Messina, possibly already en route."

Fine glanced again at Canidy, then turned to Rossi and said, "Would you mind excusing us for a moment, Professor?"

Rossi nodded, then suddenly yawned, covering his mouth with his right hand.

"This has been quite exhausting," he said. "I'd actually like to lie down. Would that be possible?"

"Of course," Fine said, then raised his voice: "Monsieur Khatim!"

When the tough old man almost immediately appeared in the arched doorway, Canidy realized he had been standing a silent guard outside the door.

Khatim leaned slightly forward in a bow that conveyed *At your service*.

Captain Stanley Fine said, "Monsieur Khatim, please show our guest to his room." He turned to Rossi, and added, "You'll please forgive the accommodations. When we got here, the beds were all infested. Now we have no more than cots."

"That will be fine," Rossi said, standing and putting down his teacup. "My alternative right now would be to be back in Palermo."

# [FOUR]

"I know what you're going to say, Stan," Major Richard M. Canidy said after Professor Arturo Rossi had been made comfortable and Canidy had refilled their coffee mugs.

"You do?" Captain Stanley S. Fine said. "Then you're way ahead of me, Dick, because I don't know what the hell to say right now."

He sipped at his mug, watching Canidy return to the French doors, then look out in silence, his back toward Fine.

"There was no option, Stan," Canidy said finally. "I had to blow up the Tabun; I couldn't leave it for the Germans. Deadly cloud or not. It was a split-second decision, and —"

"And one that I agree with."

Canidy turned. He looked at Fine for some time, took a sip of coffee, then nodded thoughtfully. His eyes showed some relief.

"Thanks, Stan. I appreciate that. I hope we're not alone in holding that opinion."

He sighed.

"You know, all the way back on the sub, after Rossi told me about the deadly cloud, I was sickened at the thought . . ."

He stopped himself, then suddenly looked back out at the sea.

*Jesus! What the hell is the matter with me? I'm babbling.*

*Yeah, I'm sickened at the thought of all those people in Palermo in the wrong place at the wrong time.*

*But why does that bother me?*

*This is war. And I didn't put the goddamn gas there.*

*So why then am I suddenly concerned about innocent . . .*

*Oh, shit!*

*Ann!*

Canidy heard Stan Fine's comforting voice behind him.

"Dick, you didn't know," Fine said loyally.

Canidy turned, and, as he looked at Fine, he said softly, "Ann?"

The look on Fine's face was shock, then anger.

"Dammit!" he said, and thrust his right hand into his tunic. "I'm sorry, Dick. I'd forgotten —"

"It's okay. Obviously, so had I."

Ann Chambers was more than Canidy's sweetheart. She was the one woman who had made him look hard in the mirror and consider that by God there might be something to having a relationship that lasted longer than a half rotation of the earth.

But three weeks earlier, Canidy had gone to her London flat and found that, while he had been in the States, it and most of her street had been demolished by a Luftwaffe bombing — and that she had gone missing.

Fine produced a sheet of folded paper and held it out to Canidy.

"From London Station. I put it in my jacket to keep it separate of this stack." He gestured at the table. "I didn't want to forget it. Lot of good that did."

Canidy took the sheet and unfolded it.

"It's basically good news," Fine went on, "don't you think? Not everything we'd like, of course. . . ."

Canidy read it, swallowed with some effort, then said, "So they still haven't found her, or any trace."

"Dick, that strikes me as positive. Otherwise, they'd be reporting that her body was found in the rubble of her flat. And they are making every effort to locate her."

*He's right,* Canidy thought. *Ann is smart as hell, more than able to take care of herself.*

*But my memory of her bombed street — and the thought of her being an innocent casualty in this damn war — no wonder I feel bad for those sorry bastards in Sicily.*

"You're right, of course, Stan," he said, folding the paper and putting it in his pocket. "Thank you."

"I wish I could do more," Fine said.

"Me, too."

Canidy glanced out the doors at the harbor, out to the sea, and said, "You know, Donovan didn't tell me what I was looking for in Sicily besides Rossi, only to keep my eyes open, that I'd know it when I found it."

"And you did."

"But I thought that it was the villa with the yellow-fever lab. . . . And then, as we were leaving the dock, Rossi told me about the Tabun . . . and I just blew it up."

He turned and looked at Fine and said, "You know, maybe David Bruce is more right than I want to admit. I am a loose cannon, in way over my head."

Colonel David Kirkpatrick Este Bruce was the distinguished, high-level diplomat currently serving as the OSS London chief of station. At forty-five, he had more than twenty years — and a wealth of experience — over Canidy. And he was not hesitant to let him know that.

Fine made a face of frustration.

"Dammit, Dick. You know better than

that. You're not going to get any false sympathy out of me. You had your orders and you followed your orders, and you did it damn well."

Canidy didn't respond to that. Instead, after a moment, he went on, his tone matter-of-fact, "I thought and rethought it on the sub and about the only thing that I came up with that was positive about the gas was the fact that the sea was flat calm that night. Not even a bit of a breeze."

"So if the Tabun did go up," Fine finished, "the cloud didn't go far."

Canidy nodded.

"Right," Canidy said. "We were sitting there on the fishing boat — the *Stefania* — waiting for the sub, about twelve klicks northwest of the explosion. Which was why we had such a good view of the show . . ."

"And the *Casabianca* got there right after that?"

"Uh-huh. Like clockwork."

"And another — what? — half hour for you to get out of the boat and into the sub?"

"Just shy of that, maybe twenty minutes from the moment it surfaced to the order to dive. L'Herminier's a real pro. So we weren't endangered by the Tabun. Trust me, I had the sub's doc keep a close eye on Rossi and me for symptoms. But I'm not sure where

94

the *Stefania* went after dropping us. She was supposed to come here."

"After your messages en route," Fine said, "I had some discreet questions asked down at the commercial docks."

"And?"

"The *Stefania* is en route to here, fishing on the way, of course, as both a cover and a genuine source of income. She's due in tomorrow or the next day, though that does not mean anything. They said she's often late, especially if there's a mechanical problem."

"Like a bullet to the engine block?" Canidy suggested. "After the cargo is looted by a German patrol boat?"

Fine grunted.

"They didn't say that," he said, "but I could see it as being problematic."

"I understand that that's a common occurrence," Canidy went on, "particularly for captains hesitant to surrender their tuna . . . and/or whatever they might be smuggling."

"Well, so far there is no word from her — which can be read pretty much any way anyone wants to read it. Bottom line: They were not too concerned."

Canidy shook his head in resignation. "If they went back into the port for any reason . . ."

"But why would they? A ship had just blown up. Who'd go into an inferno?"

Canidy shrugged.

"Changing the subject somewhat," Fine said, "what about the villa with the yellow fever?"

Canidy raised his hands, palms upward, and shrugged again.

"Hell if I know, Stan. Rossi had two assistants who had access and who he said he trusted completely. I gave them the C-2 and then taught a very basic demolitions course — where to place it for best effect, how much to use, et cetera. But we did not stay offshore long enough to see the villa blow. Which, now that we know what we do about what happens when nerve gas burns, I can't say I'm disappointed."

"But we don't know if the villa went up."

Canidy frowned.

"No, Stan, we don't."

"And we don't know, really, if there was gas and if it burned, and if it *did* burn what damage it caused."

"No, and no, and no."

"So small wonder that my new friend Lieutenant Colonel Owen says no one on Eisenhower's staff believes any of this."

"They don't think that we found the nerve gas," Canidy asked, "or they don't believe that it exists?"

"Both, as best I can tell," Fine said. "I'm having a little trouble discerning exactly what to them is worse: one, that they don't know about it or, two, that we, *you,* do. Regardless, it's clearly caused some concern at AFHQ, enough to merit our personal visit from this pompous Owen."

"Does that mean they're actually going to act?"

Fine grunted derisively.

"Hardly. That, again as best I can tell, was the purpose of the visit. By definition, not to mention by Ike's supreme order, AFHQ speaks for *all* Allied Forces here, the Brits included. And AFHQ's position is that they have the situation under control, thank you very much for your concern. Or, as Owen put it, 'Ike asked me personally to thank you for your input.' Which, basically, was a smack at the OSS, translation being: 'How could you new kids on the block possibly have anything over the British who've been playing the spy game for centuries?' "

Canidy shook his head. He knew that the early beginnings of what would become the British Secret Intelligence Service, known as MI6, could be traced back to when Henry VIII sent agents slinking around Europe.

"Christ!" Canidy flared. "Ed Stevens

warned me about that sonofabitch. Said he was glad Owen wasn't nosing around London Station anymore. Now I know why. I despise aides who love reminding you at every opportunity who they work for — worse, who they speak for, therefore their words carry the same power as their boss's."

Lieutenant Colonel Edmund T. Stevens was David Bruce's number two at OSS London Station. A West Pointer — not a diplomat with an assimilated military rank — Stevens understood Candy as an operative and thus held a far higher opinion of him than did Bruce. Fine was acutely aware of the dynamics of all this, as he had served as Stevens's deputy prior to being sent to OSS Algiers.

Fine nodded. That certainly had been his experience with Lieutenant Colonel Warren J. Owen. He had also observed how Owen had used it as a sort of double standard.

When delivering orders from Ike that would be well received, Owen would agree with you that the man was brilliant and that he had no doubt whatsoever in his mind that you would perform admirably in the execution of the orders.

But when the orders were not what anyone wanted to hear — let alone eager to execute — Owen delivered them with the proverbial ten-foot pole while quietly agreeing with you that "the old man has lost his mind, but what can I say except that his orders are his orders and don't shoot the messenger, and all that."

*And that was definitely how he just presented himself today . . . merely a messenger.*

Fine wondered how a wet-behind-the-ears Warren J. Owen could have schlepped his books through Harvard Yard for four or more years and completely missed every damn course that could have created in him some — *any* — backbone.

Being a Harvard-trained lawyer, Fine personally knew plenty of graduates of that great institution, each of whom had come out with enough character for five men — FDR certainly chief among them. People with conviction, ones who did not use their *Hahvard* sheepskin as evidence enough of their stellar status in the rarefied air of civilized society.

Still, Fine figured that Owen had to have learned something worthwhile along the way — *Maybe from advanced courses in How to Cover Your Ass by Always Citing Regulations?* — or Eisenhower would not keep him around.

Candy looked curiously at Fine.

"What're you thinking about, Stan?"

Fine smirked.

"What a spineless bastard Owen can be," he said, then paused. "Grudgingly, however, I have to give the guy credit. His capacity for speaking at great length but actually saying nothing is remarkable."

"What do you mean?"

"He was here for almost an hour, and the only thing that I can tell you that I know he said for sure was that they had your information and that they had the situation under control. He shared no information from their intel. We could have just as easily been discussing the weather, for all I got out of it. Actually, now that I think of it, he did spend an annoyingly disproportionate amount time talking about the heat here."

Canidy laughed. Then he shook his head.

"What is it that Donovan says?" Canidy said. " 'If it wasn't for the fighting amongst our own, I'd have had this war with the real enemy won long ago.' "

"Something like that," Fine said, grinning. "I shouldn't smile. It's not funny at all."

"Speaking of our fearless leader," Canidy said, "any idea what good ol' Colonel Wild Bill thinks about all this?"

"That's good ol' *General* Wild Bill," Fine corrected.

Canidy turned, his eyebrows raised. "Really?" he said.

"Indeed. While you were gone — on the twenty-third, before you were headed back here — FDR had him placed back on active duty and made him a brigadier general."

"That's good news."

Fine smiled. "Yes, indeed it is."

Stanley Fine was quite aware that it had taken Richard Canidy quite some time to come to hold William Donovan in high regard. Fine knew that because he had known Canidy a long time. Fine's history of bailing out Canidy went back far before either of them had become part of the Office of the Coordinator of Information and the Office of Strategic Services — well before either organization even existed — back to when Fine was starting out in Hollywood and Canidy was in prep school in Iowa.

The young Stanley S. Fine, Esq., the ink still damp on the *juris doctor* diploma hanging on the wall of his movie studio office, had been the lawyer for the actress Monica Carlisle when she had sent him to the Iowa school.

Miss Carlisle was known at "America's Sweetheart," and the Hollywood studio PR flaks worked hard to maintain that image — and to keep secret from her adoring fans the fact that she had a young son, fathered before the war by a German industrialist.

And so it had been Fine's mission to smooth over the hysteria that had resulted from a practical joke performed by Eric Fulmar — who the sultry actress herself more or less refused to acknowledge existed — and his buddy, a troublemaker by the name of Dick Canidy.

The joke had backfired, causing a Studebaker President to erupt in flames and, with it, a lot of tempers. Fine had shown up with a new replacement car and a calming influence over those who could have pressed charges. And with the damage thus limited, the friendship between Canidy and Fulmar — and their relationship with Fine — had become solidified for life.

Canidy went on to pursue his dream to be a pilot, and in 1938 graduated (cum laude) from the Massachusetts Institute of Technology with a Bachelor of Science, Aeronautical Engineering. That had been on a Navy scholarship, in exchange for four years of postgraduation service. By the time he entered the Navy, he'd already accumulated a commercial pilot's license, an instrument ticket, and three hundred fifty hours of solo time.

A career in the Navy would have seemed the natural path for such a skilled aviator.

Not Canidy. He made no secret of the fact that he felt constrained by the rigid ways of the service and that he was determined to stay only so long as to make good on his agreement. He swore not to serve one damn minute more than was contractually required to repay the cost of his education — and was already entertaining an offer of employment at the Boeing Aircraft Company, Seattle, Washington.

But then, in June 1941, with barely a year left to his commitment, a grizzled, gray-haired man named Claire Chennault showed up at Naval Air Station Pensacola, where then-Lieutenant (Junior Grade) Richard M. Canidy, USN, was spending long days in the backseat of a biwing Kaydet, as a Navy instructor pilot for fledgling flyboys.

The legendary General Chennault suggested that the United States of America was soon to join the raging world war and Canidy was kidding himself if he thought his country was going to just let him walk with his skills out of the military.

"Son," the crusty WWI fighter pilot said in his coarse Southern accent, "you damn may as well go ahead and believe in the Easter Bunny, Santa Claus, *and* the fucking Tooth Fairy. There'll be no time in the ramping up for war to adequately train all the new pilots that're going to be needed. And you'll be front of the line."

Chennault said that he was pulling together a group of volunteers — with FDR's approval, if not direct order, though this was implied and not discussed in any more detail than necessary with Canidy. These top pilots would fly in support of the Chinese, specifically the protection of the two-thousand-mile-long Burma Road that was the critical route for getting Western aid to China.

On behalf of Chiang Kai-shek, Chennault could offer Canidy a one-year contract flying Curtiss P-40Bs against the Japanese. Pay was six hundred dollars a month — twice what Canidy was getting from the Navy — plus a five-hundred-buck bonus for every Jap he shot down.

Ever on the lookout for number one — himself — Canidy took it. He'd decided it was as much for the money as for the honorable discharge from the Navy that it came with.

Being a Flying Tiger in Chennault's American Volunteer Group (AVG) was not easy work — it was, in fact, damn dangerous — but Canidy quickly found his place and almost immediately had reaffirmed his belief that he'd been born to fly.

Yet it seemed that as soon as he had discovered that he not only loved being a fighter pilot but was damn good at it — five kills on one nasty sortie alone, making him a certifiable ace — a pudgy, pale, self-important-looking bureaucrat by the name of Eldon C. Baker showed up one day in December 1941 on the flight line at Kunming, China.

Baker came across as a supreme prick. But also a very highly placed prick — in his suit coat pocket he carried orders personally signed by the President of the United States — and he said that, as the U.S. had just joined the war, he was there to recruit Canidy.

Trouble was, he added, it was into an outfit described as so secretive that he (a) could not tell Canidy what he would be doing and (b) that in order for there to be no questions asked as to his disappearance — and thus no awkward answers that might reveal secrets — a cover story would have the newly minted ace whisked away under a cloud of disgrace.

That did not necessarily bother Canidy — "I really don't give a rat's ass what anything thinks of me," he'd muttered when informed of the need for the cover story — but leaving behind his buddies did.

*Still,* he'd thought, *if whatever it is that I'm*

*wanted to do is important enough for the President to send this asshole clear around the damn world to get me, then that's that. Pack the bags. . . .*

Besides, being out of the AVG would mean he no longer would be getting shot at by the Japs. He figured it was only a matter of time before their Mitsubishi A5M 7.7mm machine-gun rounds found his ass. More important, he figured that taking the offer put him one step closer to getting the hell out of his military service obligations.

Back in Washington, however, he found that it all was somewhat more complicated than that.

The supersecret outfit turned out to be the Office of the Coordinator of Information, run by Colonel William "Wild Bill" Donovan and answerable only to Roosevelt himself. And it needed Canidy for his connections to help smuggle a French mining engineer prized by the Germans — and thus the Americans — out of North Africa.

Then Canidy got really pissed.

Pissed at this supersecret outfit, pissed at having left the AVG, pissed at himself for his options.

Or lack of options.

He had a choice: either agree to this "mission of considerable risk" or, now that he was privy to top secret information, be locked down in a secure institution for "psychiatric evaluation" for an unspecified time — *habeas corpus* be damned — which was to say, a very long time, at least the duration of the war, in order to keep the information safe.

Canidy, still pissed but smart enough to keep his mouth shut, chose the mission. In due course, he was given the assimilated rank of major and presented with credentials stating that he was in the United States Army Air Corps and another (for when the first did not get him what he needed) stating that he worked for the Office of the Coordinator of Information, which carried a presidential priority.

The mission had turned out to be of considerable risk indeed, not to mention had required cold, ruthless decisions, ones he found himself not necessarily enjoying but perfectly capable of carrying out.

He realized it was a situation not unlike the one he had discovered as a Flying Tiger in China: that he more or less liked what he was doing and he did very well at it.

This was not lost on Donovan and his top spies in what the COI now was called: the Office of Strategic Services. An unusually natural operative, Canidy proved expert at espionage and sabotage and more — at the "strategic services" deemed important to winning the war.

Over time, Canidy was given — which was to say, Wild Bill Donovan had assigned him indirectly at first, then directly — more and more responsibility.

There were missions to nab more engineers and scientists (ones with expertise in nuclear fission, the development and manufacture of jet aircraft, manned and unmanned), missions to smuggle uranite for the Manhattan Project's development of the atom bomb, and missions to modify B-17s into explosive-filled drones that could be flown from England into German assets (submarine pens, plants manufacturing fighter jets, et cetera).

Most recently — within the last month, in New York City — Canidy had found himself dealing with the Mafia in the extraction of Professor Rossi prior to the Allied Forces' early planning of the invasion of Sicily.

It had been the top mafioso himself — one Charles "Lucky" Luciano, in a New York State slam on prostitution and racketeering charges but still the acting "boss of all bosses" — who had directly helped Canidy make connections on and off the island.

Canidy carried in his possession a personal

note from Charlie Lucky that asked of any-one so able to please provide Canidy what-ever aid possible. It was a carte blanche in-strument that Canidy now expected he would desperately need to use to find out about the nerve gas.

And so Fine, in short, understood that Canidy had become "almost" the perfect spy. "Almost," because he'd also become what no spy was supposed to be . . . indispensable.

"I don't think it's so much what Donovan thinks about all this," Fine began, then reached for the stack of papers before him on the table and fingered down through it until he came to what he was looking for. He pulled out a typewritten sheet, held it out, and went on, "This came back in response to your second message, the sit-rep sent from the *Casabianca.*"

Canidy walked over to the table, took the sheet, and read the decrypted message:

| | |
|---|---|
| TOP SECRET | ___ STATION CHIEF |
| OPERATIONAL IMMEDIATE | ___ FILE |

```
COPY NO. 1

                    OF 2 COPIES ONLY

27MAR43

FROM OSS WASHINGTON DC
TO OSS ALGIERS EYES ONLY CAPT FINE

BEGIN QUOTE

MAJ CANIDY IS HEREBY DIRECTED BY HIGH-
EST AUTHORITY TO USE ANY AND EVERY EX-
PEDITIOUS  METHOD   NECESSARY   TO
COVERTLY REPEAT COVERTLY SECURE AB-
SOLUTE EVIDENCE OF ANTACID AND/OR SIM-
ILAR AS REPORTED.

BRIG GEN DONOVAN

END QUOTE

TOP SECRET
```

" 'By highest authority'?" Canidy quoted.
" 'Any and every expeditious method'?"

"I'd say the President has taken a personal
interest in your discovery," Fine said. "And
clearly he's aware of possible obstacles and
wants this done quietly."

Canidy grunted.

"So I'm going to have to go back in. And, Stan, I'm going to need help. Help on the island and help in keeping clear of AFHQ."

Fine nodded.

"Both will be a challenge," Fine said. "We've already had some trouble, not counting today's visit from Owen."

"Why both? And what kind of trouble?"

"Help on the island is difficult because basically AFHQ has declared it off-limits. We've been told that we can plan for the invasion, collect intel, but we are not supposed to go there." He paused. "I understand — though not necessarily agree — as to why. Hell, anyone with a map can make a rather well-educated guess what Hitler considers possible in the way of Allied intentions."

"Sure," Canidy said. "He sees that we can go from here into Sicily, then up through Italy. And, alternatively, from here up through southern France. We know he's bracing for a cross-channel invasion of western France, as he's been using forced labor to build defensive positions all along the coast. And then there's an attack from across the Balkans. And, of course, the Red Army has Hitler looking nervously over his shoulder to the east."

Fine sipped his coffee and nodded.

"Hitler just does not know which one when," he said.

"And each one — location and D-Day — is a huge variable by itself," Canidy put in. "Torch was first expected to land in May. Six months is a long time to wait, especially if you're not sure you've got the right spot."

"Exactly," Fine said. "And Hitler cannot defend them all . . . and wait it out. So the trick is to fool him as to exactly which island and when. Done right, he sends his defenses to where we say, then we take advantage of his weak spots. But if, say, you get caught in Sicily now, Dick, and his intel is telling him that we're amassing troops and ships here and in Tunis, it would be clear we're preparing for an invasion."

Canidy's eyebrows went up. "And next is, as we know, Sicily."

"As of today, right. Never mind what you found there. OSS London is helping our cousins with one very quiet operation that's meant to fool the Germans and Italians into believing that the invasion will be on Sardinia and Greece. Meanwhile, we — OSS Algiers — are supposed to be concentrating on training teams for the French *réseau.*"

Canidy knew the *réseau* — for "resistance network" — was in large part the *maquis,* young men who refused to be slaves of the

112

German occupation. They had fled into France's woods, where the Allies planned to insert teams and supplies to help them wage guerrilla war.

"Tell me about the trouble you mentioned," Canidy said.

Fine got up from the table. He walked over to the open French doors, then went through the doorway. Canidy followed him onto the balcony.

"You'll recall Club des Pins, the resort that's down there on the beach?" Fine said, pointing to the western end of the coast that was visible.

"Yeah," Canidy said. "The one that the SOE is using for its finishing school, right?"

Special Operations Executive was the British saboteur and operative arm. The OSS was emulating it, and had named theirs, accordingly, OSS Special Operations.

"Right. The teams are modeled after the OSS teams we have in Corsica."

"We had the reinforcement teams on the sub," Canidy said.

"Of course. So you know each has an officer and three men, a liaison and two radio operators, who report to him." When Canidy nodded, Fine went on: "So the SOE is fine-tuning their people in radio operations, Morse code, encryption, map and compass,

hand-to-hand combat. There's even a jump school and a demolitions school."

"Their people? I though we had our guys there, too."

"A handful. We maintain a presence in the interest of 'Allied cooperation.' But for the bulk of our men, it just wasn't working out."

Canidy's expression showed that he was surprised.

Fine explained: "Our guys were being treated — in that fine, subtle English way, but it was there nonetheless — as sort of stepchildren. The training for the Brits' missions always seemed to take precedence and we were left on a space-available basis. 'Sorry, old chap, that was the last spot on the plane. We'll put you top of the queue to jump tomorrow.' And, of course, the next day there was another reason why we got bumped."

"So much for Ike's declaration that we're all in this together."

"I like Eisenhower," Fine said, "and respect him immensely. But you and I know that the OSS must by its very nature operate on a far smaller scale."

Canidy nodded. "We have — what — maybe ten thousand serving in the OSS?"

"I heard almost twelve thousand at last count. Total."

"Okay, call it twelve. And figure half of that number are in Washington."

"Uh-huh. And with his masses, Eisenhower, on the other hand, is too caught up in the big picture to want to worry about us. After seriously stumbling at Kasserine Pass, he wants to prove that the Americans can run the show — 'A seamless Allied force able to act as one,' I've heard him say — and in so doing he's both bending over to accommodate our cousins and being damn near deaf to anything that goes against that."

The disaster at Tunisia's Kasserine Pass in the Atlas Mountains had taken place only weeks earlier. Erwin Rommel's Afrika Korps had hammered the hell out of Allied forces made up mostly of the U.S. Army's II Corps. The Germans boldly forced them back fifty miles, while inflicting huge casualties, taking prisoners, and capturing critical matériel, everything from weapons to fuel. Eisenhower eventually struck back successfully, but there was no denying grave mistakes had been made up and down the lines of command.

"And our cousins are taking advantage of that?" Canidy said.

"You know the Brits and their snooty air of superiority. They're brash. It's creating friction for Eisenhower. And it's certainly affecting how they treat the OSS and our intel. They're making the point at AFHQ that if they don't say something exists, that if their far superior intel-gathering services don't know about it, then, *ipso facto,* it cannot possibly exist."

"So if us new kids on the block don't get our fair share of instruction," Canidy said, "what do we do?"

"We set up our own finishing school," Fine said.

"Okay. When?"

"Already done."

"Really?"

"You underestimate me, my friend."

Canidy grinned. "That I never would do."

"There's a small place we took over called Dellys, about sixty klicks east of here," Fine explained as he gestured to the right, toward the eastern point of the coast on the horizon. "It's sort of a miniature Algiers, with a port, an ancient casbah, assorted buildings like these" — he gestured at the city below — "just smaller and fewer, and not much else. We've got four or five fishing boats and a dozen or so small rubber boats. With these we practice putting the agents ashore. And we'll use the aircraft to drop agents in."

That got Canidy's attention.

"Aircraft?" he said.

Fine nodded. "We got our hands on a couple C-47s. Darmstadter did. And —"

"Darmstadter?" Canidy said, excited. "He's here? With Gooney Birds? This is getting better by the second."

"Yeah. A week ago he arrived with the aircraft. I've got him on a *very* short TDY. He's getting the aircraft squared away; they're out at the airport, someone with them at all times to keep them from disappearing. He brought pilots with him, then the plan is he'll head back to England, back to the Aphrodite Project."

*Like hell,* Canidy thought, visualizing the B-17s being turned into Torpex-filled drones. *Not if I decide I need him.*

"Hank's a good guy," Fine went on. "And a decent pilot."

"Agreed." Canidy grinned, and added, "Not as good as me, but then few are, said he with overwhelming modesty."

Fine shook his head, grinned, too, then went on, "And no one knows more than he does about dropping sticks of paratroopers than Hank."

"Agreed again," Canidy said, then thought again about the twin-engine transports. "Can we get more Gooney Birds?"

"Why?"

"Why not? We could call it Canidy Air

Corps just to piss off the Brits. And maybe Colonel Pompous."

Fine laughed. When Candidy didn't laugh, too, Fine's expression suddenly changed.

"You're not serious, Dick, are you?"

Candidy made a devious face and shrugged.

"I don't know, Dick," Fine said cautiously. "Everyone is fighting over scraps here. We're lucky to have the two we do."

Candidy put up his hands, chest high, palms outward.

"Okay," he said. "Just asking. I'm trying to get an idea of what we have immediate access to, and what assets I'll have to acquire, shall we say, by other means. If it turns out we need more, I can always play the OSS trump card as a last resort."

"Good thing you're better practiced at theft," Fine said. He was smiling again.

"Who, me?" Candidy said with mock indignation, his hands on his chest. "That's an unjust characterization, Counselor! I'll have you know that I prefer the term 'borrow,' as I always return that which I take . . . perhaps not in the condition in which it was acquired, but return it nonetheless." He paused. "Unless that proves to be impossible. Then I don't. But my intentions — like my heart, dear sir — are pure."

Fine shook his head in resignation.

Canidy grinned, then with some finality went on:

"Okay, so we have some challenges. My immediate one is finding the *Stefania* and seeing what they know about the status of Palermo. It's been four days since I blew up the ship; the cleanup has to be well under way. Then I need to find out when the *Casabianca* sets sail again and if I need to get that date moved up. And then, or maybe before, I need to set up an SO team for Sicily, so we can run a *réseau* — or whatever the hell the Sicilian word for *réseau* is."

Canidy thought: *And keep a low profile so that Ike and his flunky Owen — and anyone else who can bloody well spell AFHQ — don't know what I'm doing.*

"Get Darmstadter to run you out to Dellys," Stan Fine said. "You may find what you need at our school. Know that Corvo is out there with Scamporinio, Anfuso, and some others."

Canidy had met Max Corvo in Washington, D.C., in '42, shortly after the chief of the OSS Italian Division, Earl Brennan, had recruited the twenty-two-year-old U.S. Army private. Of Sicilian descent, Corvo had strong connections — family, friends, business associates — both in America and Sicily. He spoke Italian as well as Sicilian dialects. Despite his age and rank, he was put in charge of OSS Italy SI (Secret Intelligence) and quickly manned his section with a dozen Sicilian Americans to serve as SI field agents. Victor Anfuso and Vincent Scamporino, both young lawyers, were among his recruits.

Canidy knew that as far as AFHQ was concerned, Corvo and Captain Stanley S. Fine were the official face of the OSS here. Canidy was attached to neither OSS Italy nor OSS Algiers. On paper, he was in charge of the safe house known as OSS Whitbey House, which made him the number three man in OSS London, behind David Bruce and Ed Stevens.

But right now, Canidy worked directly for OSS Washington; he was Wild Bill Donovan's wild card.

Canidy reached into his pocket and pulled out the stamped-metal fob that held the key to the Plymouth.

"On my way," he said.

"You'd be wise to use one of our cars," Fine said reasonably. "Less conspicuous, as I suspect someone is very likely hunting that Plymouth. And Owen, I think, noticed it as he left."

Canidy considered all that a moment, then nodded.

"Dammit, Stan, I hate it that you're always right. *Almost* always. But you know how much I hate returning something that I just borrowed."

Fine snorted.

"Yeah, I do," he said, "but give me the key, anyway."

Canidy tossed the fob with its key to him.

Fine raised his voice slightly. "Monsieur Khatim!"

The leather-tough Algerian appeared almost instantly at the arched doorway.

"Please run Major Canidy out to the airport in my car, then take this Navy staff car" — he tossed the key to Khatim, who Canidy noted snatched it out of the air with catlike speed and grace — "back to AFHQ without letting them know you're doing it."

Wordlessly, Monsieur Khatim bowed slightly and turned and left.

Fine looked at Canidy. "I'll check on the *Casabianca*'s schedule with L'Herminier," he said, "and also, as an alternative, see what other sub might be available."

"Good idea," Canidy said. "Thanks, Stan."

"Anything else you can think of?"

Canidy shook his head.

"Not right now, but you know there's always something . . . and I usually discover it at the worst possible moment."

He scooped up his black rubberized duffel, went to the doorway, then stopped and looked back at Fine.

"Wait. Here's an obvious one," Canidy said. "I'm going to need the professor's help. Sit tight on him till I get back, will you?"

"Sure. Any idea when that'll be?"

"As soon as I can, Stan. As soon as I fucking can."

# III

## [ONE]
## OSS LONDON STATION
## BERKELEY SQUARE
## LONDON, ENGLAND
## 1501 30 MARCH 1943

Lieutenant Colonel Ed Stevens — who was tall and thin and, at forty-four years old, already silver-haired — stood in the doorway to the office of Colonel David Bruce. He held a message from OSS Algiers Station and waited for his boss to get off the phone.

The distinguished-looking chief of station, whose chiseled stone face, intense eyes, and starting-to-gray hair caused him to appear older than his age of forty-five, had out-stretched his left hand and signaled *Just another minute* with his index finger.

Stevens filled the time listening to the one side of the conversation, as the Metropolitan-Vickers radio in the corner of the office droned out yet another stiff bit of classical music courtesy of the British Broadcasting Corporation. He enjoyed classical music. But much of the BBC's selections were uninspired, and Stevens found himself looking forward to the breaks in the music for the BBC's regular readings of the Allied cryptic message traffic: *"And now for our friends away from home: Churchy wishes Franky a happy birthday, Churchy wishes Franky a happy birthday. Adolf needs a shave, Adolf needs a shave. . . ."*

Stevens was not learning much about Bruce's call.

The chief of station's contributions were limited to multiples of "I understand" and "Right" and a few grunts. Then, almost exactly a minute later, he finally said, "Thank you, Mr. Ambassador," and placed the handset in its cradle. He stared at the phone with disdain, then looked up at Stevens.

"That," Bruce announced, "was not good news."

He waved Stevens to take a seat on the

couch opposite the desk.

"I couldn't quite pick up on who it was let alone what it was about," Stevens said. "Winant?"

Bruce nodded. "I could almost hear him without benefit of the telephone."

The U.S. embassy at One Grosvenor Square was but blocks away from the Berkeley Square building that housed OSS London Station. The embassy stood near the house on the corner of Duke and Brook that was where America's first minister to the Court of St. James's — John Adams, later President John Adams — had lived, beginning in 1785.

Bruce was not particularly fond of John G. Winant, the ambassador extraordinary and plenipotentiary. He did not necessarily dislike the man — Winant had twice served as governor of New Hampshire and was, like Bruce, a product of Princeton — but was quite wary of him.

He could not put his finger on what exactly it was about Winant that caused the caution flags. There were his quirks, as might be expected of such a high-profile politician, but Bruce recognized something else — some disturbance, some imbalance, deep down. Something as yet not fully developed that could — and probably would — erupt at

124

some point.

And Bruce was wise enough to maintain a healthy distance so as not to get caught in any aftereffects when it did.

David Bruce was not playing pseudo shrink in his analysis of the man. The very intelligent — some said brilliant — Bruce had personal experience with the oddities of the human condition. His wife suffered from mental illness. They had thrown a lot of money at the problem — Bruce had made his own fortune before marrying Alisa Mellon, one of the wealthiest women in the world — and in the hiring of the best medical minds, and the picking of said minds, he'd in his own way come to be somewhat of an expert layman.

Yet whatever the problem there may or may not be, David Bruce knew that Winant had a direct line to the Oval Office. (Literally. Word was that AT&T billed the embassy a small fortune — more than ten dollars a minute — for his calls over the transatlantic line.) Not only was Winant, as the Ambassador to the Court of Saint James's, the personal representative of the President of the United States of America, he was also one of his buddies. He had long enjoyed FDR's generosity. Roosevelt, before appointing Winant to his current position in London, had in 1935 made him the first leader of the newly formed Social Security Board.

Colonel David Bruce looked at Lieutenant Colonel Ed Stevens.

"Ambassador Winant informs me, as a courtesy, that his legal attaché has been contacted by Brandon Chambers."

The legal attaché, Stevens knew, was the agent of the Federal Bureau of Investigation attached as a liaison between the embassy and the FBI headquarters in Washington, D.C.

"No doubt Chambers is looking for Ann," Stevens said. "Can't blame him for that."

"No, but we *can* blame Canidy."

"How so?"

"Because the father wants to know how he can find Canidy. He figures, reasonably, that if he finds Canidy, he finds Ann. It did not help — actually, it hurt, as he took offense — when the FBI agent professed ignorance of something called 'the OSS.'"

Stevens whistled softly. "Wish it were that simple. I know Dick does." He paused, then wondered aloud, "I wonder how he came to look for Dick in London?"

He was immediately sorry he had said it when he saw Bruce make a face.

"It doesn't hurt," Bruce said, "when your daughter lets you in on a secret or two along the way. Even without benefit of Canidy's indiscretions, Chambers can put two and two together. He's a man of considerable resources. And, apparently, temper. The ambassador said that Chambers demanded to be put in touch with the OSS office here — or, better, Canidy directly — or he'd take his request as high as he'd have to."

There were many secrets in the OSS stations in London and in Washington, but the relationship between the stunning Southern blonde and Dick Canidy wasn't one of them.

Ann Chambers, twenty years old, had gotten herself a job as a war correspondent for the Chambers News Service. It was obviously no coincidence that she shared her name with her employer's; her father was the chairman of the board of the Chambers Publishing Corporation and the Chambers News Service was a wholly owned subsidiary of that. The corporation also held total interest in nine newspapers and more than twice that many radio stations.

Her employment, however, had not been a blatant bout of nepotism.

In the summers of her high school years, Ann Chambers had worked part-time at *The Atlanta Courier-Journal,* making herself useful in the family business as best she could. She did anything from moving mail and fetching coffee for editors to checking page proofs in order to edit out typographic and other errors. Occasionally, she had been given short features to write from her desk.

Human interest pieces came naturally to her, and she excelled at chronicling how newlyweds had come to meet, then fall desperately in love and marry. These articles appeared in the Sunday "Weddings" section. They became very popular with women readers — married and single alike — and thus with advertisers, too.

And it was there that Ann really began to better understand two very important things. One was the family business: bring in the readers and the ad dollars follow. And the other was: that she had a very marketable skill.

So when Ann decided that marrying Dick Canidy was to take precedence over her studies at Bryn Mawr, and to do that would require following him to London, and to get to London would require a legitimate civilian occupation deemed necessary in the eyes of the War Department, she had not had to look very far.

Brandon Chambers, however, did not think women in general should be in harm's way — a veteran of War One, he embraced the idea of the fairer sex keeping the home fires burning — and he sure as hell didn't believe his daughter should.

Brandon Chambers was a big man — both in business and, at two hundred thirty pounds, in girth — and not of the sort to give in easily. He was accustomed to getting his way. But when he balked at Ann's idea, he found that he had met his match in his daughter.

She had explained to him in a logical manner that either he could hire her or his competition would.

"Mr. Cowles," she had said in her soft, sweet Southern accent, "has kindly offered me a correspondent position in the London bureau of *Look.*"

Gardner Cowles was the owner of the hugely successful magazine, as well as quite a number of other properties that competed directly with those of the Chambers Publishing Corporation.

Brandon Chambers would just as soon gouge out his eyes than see his daughter's byline in *Look,* never mind having the skills of a Chambers making money for that sonofabitch Cowles.

And so it was that Ann Chambers had come to England to work for the Chambers News Service.

While her dashing Dick Canidy disappeared now and then on some secret mission to win the war, Ann had set about the serious business of capturing the war in words for those back home. She worked writing scripts for the newsman Meachum Hope on his *Report from London* radio broadcast. And she had developed her own human interest series — "Profiles of Courage," newspaper articles about the extraordinary efforts of everyday citizens in war-torn England — and each week had sent out a new installment across the Chambers News Service wire.

Until her flat had been bombed during an attack of London by the Luftwaffe.

"You are aware," Lieutenant Colonel Ed Stevens said, "that I have been in touch with Andy Marks, the CNS bureau chief here. Canidy gave him my name as a contact if Marks heard news of Ann."

"I'm aware," Colonel David Bruce replied agreeably.

Bruce walked a somewhat fine line with Stevens. He knew that Donovan had personally recruited Stevens, a West Pointer who had resigned his commission before the war in order to work in his wife's wholesale food business, and who, because of that, had lived

130

and worked in England. Donovan had noted how Stevens handled with ease the difficult upper-crust Englishmen and had tapped him for OSS London Station as much for that valuable skill as for his military expertise.

"As far as Marks knows," Stevens said, "we're no more than another bureaucratic layer for the Army Air Forces, a logistical office."

Bruce grinned. "Which is not exactly untrue."

"We spoke daily when Ann Chambers first went missing," Stevens went on, "then went to weekly. Marks waited as long as he could — ten days — before passing the news to the home office. Read: her father. Marks had had reporters disappear for a few days for any number of reasons and had hoped that that was the case with Ann. He didn't see any sense in worrying the family and had seen to it that there had been a bureau-wide effort not to draw attention to Ann's absence. But then it was inevitable that before long someone got suspicious, and Marks said he couldn't respond with a lie, so he took the bull by the horns. . . ."

Bruce's eyebrows rose.

Stevens quickly added, "I didn't mean to suggest her father . . ."

"It's all right, Ed," Bruce said. "I know you didn't."

"Anyway, I feel responsible for where we are now."

"How is that?"

"I told Dick that I would keep on top of what was going on with Ann and let Dick know of any news. I went with Marks to inspect the bombed flat. The Civil Defence rescue crews had combed through the rubble and come up with nothing. Which we felt was better than if they had found her in there. Anyway, we gave them Ann's name and our names and numbers, and they promised to get in touch. . . ."

Bruce shook his head slowly. "I know. A long shot."

"Marks said he'd have his reporters ask around as they went about their day-to-day duties, covering the city. It seemed sufficient . . . especially as she hadn't been found in the rubble. . . . People turn up all the time."

"Assuming that she went off to wherever," Bruce put in, "it's curious that she has not sent word she's fine. That she hasn't perhaps suggests she's not. But . . . it could be anything, Ed, and you shouldn't take it personally."

Both men sat in quiet thought for a moment.

"You know," Stevens then said, "I'm surprised that her father didn't get my name from Marks and then contact me."

"I'm not. I'm more surprised that I don't have a message from Bill Donovan or FDR, instead of a courtesy call from the ambassador. People like Brandon Chambers go right to the top of the food chain."

Bruce stood, methodically brushed the creases from his trousers, then walked over to the windows and looked out at the gray day.

"Knowing that," Bruce went on, "we had better, as you put it, take the bull by the horns."

"Message General Donovan?" Stevens said.

"Certainly that," Bruce said, turning and walking back to his desk. "Having the old man talk with Canidy is impossible. So I'd say we need to find Ann, and fast. Certainly before the FBI sticks its nose in it. It seems to be that or have her old man raise enough hell — or spill enough ink — to bring the OSS out of the shadows."

"Hoover would love that," Stevens said.

John Edgar Hoover, director of the Federal Bureau of Investigation, had been silently furious when President Roosevelt shared with him his ideas of how the United States should deal with espionage and counterespionage. Hoover believed it to be the purview of his federal police force. But FDR had told him that (a) he was not only giving those duties (worldwide, with the exceptions of the Americas, which remained with the FBI) to what then was the COI (later the OSS), but (b) he was heading it with one of Hoover's longtime rivals, William Donovan.

Ever since, Hoover had made every attempt to prove that the President had made a grave error of judgment . . . and to rub it in, which invariably involved quietly feeding the information to reporters.

"It would serve as a fine example as to why this should be his territory, not Donovan's," Bruce said. "Hoover in a heartbeat would bring in his whole lot of agents — under the auspices of hunting down Nazis and Nazi sympathizers headed for the States — to make us look bad. He knows how fearful FDR is of the fifth column."

"We don't know how much Chambers really knows about the OSS," Stevens said.

"No, we don't. Probably more than we'd like and he'd admit. But I've met him. He's a good man. A veteran. A patriot. He understands the importance of keeping secrets. Yet . . . when a man is worried about his daughter, all bets are off as to what he will or won't do. Especially if a man as formidable as Brandon Chambers believes he's being lied to by the FBI."

"So we're in a race to find Ann," Stevens said.

Bruce nodded solemnly.

"Charity Hoche," Stevens added suddenly.

Bruce looked at him a moment.

"Yes. What about her?"

"It just came to me. She and Ann were at Bryn Mawr."

There was recognition in Bruce's eyes. He immediately had a mental picture of the tall, radiant, very smart — and very well-built — blonde. Charity Hoche was from the Main Line of Philadelphia, her family well-connected, which, in large part, explained why Wild Bill Donovan personally had approved her recent transfer from OSS Washington.

*And,* Bruce thought, *she's a shining example of why some derisively refer to the OSS as Donovan's Oh So Social club.*

*Which isn't entirely fair, to the OSS in general and to Charity Hoche in particular.*

*Charity, connected or not, has a master's degree in political science, earned* summa cum laude. *She's worked hard for Donovan, surprising everyone with her worth to the organization . . . to the point Donovan says she has the Need to Know here on a par with Ed Stevens's.*

*She's shown me she's certainly no wilting lily.*

*And, Jesus, those magnificent breasts. . . .*

"Good thinking," Bruce said. "Put her on it. She's still out at Whitbey House. . . ."

"Consider it done. I'll track her down. And you'll get me the message for General Donovan?"

Bruce reached across his desk for a sheet of blank paper, then pulled a pen from his shirt pocket. "Right now. Before I get one from him."

Stevens held up the sheet that was in his hand. He nodded at the paper and said, "How do you want to act on Stan Fine's request?"

Bruce looked at the paper, his eyes intense.

"You mean Dick Canidy's request?" he said pointedly.

"It's from Stan Fine."

"But it's Canidy's. I know it. You know it."

"Okay, Canidy's request," Stevens said agreeably. "How would you like to respond?"

"Any idea why he wants to delay that scientist's travel to the States?"

"None whatsoever."

Bruce looked deep in thought, then said,

"It's really not for us to decide. Professor . . .
Professor . . ."

"Rossi," Stevens furnished.

". . . Professor Rossi is an expert in metals.
Through his association with the University
of Rome, he's a contemporary of Professor
Dyer, who Canidy pulled out of Germany
last month, who now is in the States working
on the Manhattan Project."

Stevens wondered why Bruce had just
gone through the *You know it's Canidy, not
Fine* song and dance and now was telling
him what Bruce knew they both already
knew about Rossi and Dyer.

Then he decided that Bruce was subtly reminding Stevens he was still smarting over
another message from OSS Washington —
one handwritten by Donovan — that had
been personally couriered by Charity
Hoche. She'd delivered it on February four-
teenth, and ever since had left Bruce somewhat paranoid.

It had informed him, in the gentle but
commanding manner of which Donovan
was master, that a mission put on by the
President himself was taking place in Bruce's
backyard. Donovan had explained that
Bruce had not been told till now because he
hadn't had the Need to Know. Further —
and what really had poured salt on the open

137

wound that was Bruce's badly wounded ego — was that Stevens, Bruce's subordinate, *did* have the Need to Know.

Donovan had attempted to temper that by writing that Stevens had been given only limited details, just enough so that he could act if any actions by Bruce or OSS London Station threatened to blow the presidential mission.

On one hand, Bruce had more or less understood the logic of the mission taking absolute precedence. On the other hand, however, knowing that his deputy had been considered more worthy of having highly classified information than he was made him furious.

Worse, when he calmed down a little, it had caused him to wonder what other ops there might be that he'd been deemed not worthy of knowing about. And so he felt he was entitled to a little pettiness about being left out of the loop in the past . . . and now wondering what might be going on under his nose without his knowledge.

"I'll relay the request in here," Bruce said finally, tapping the sheet of paper with his pen. "Let Donovan make the final decision. We know he likes to hold all the cards. Meanwhile, message back to Fine that Rossi can stay, pending approval of OSS Washington."

Stevens stood, started for the door, and said, "I'll get right on —"

There was a knock at the door.

"Come!" Bruce called.

As the wooden door began to swing open, Stevens reached for the doorknob.

An attractive brunette in her thirties peered through the opening. She had a quizzical look on her face.

"Sir?" Captain Helene Dancy, Women's Army Corps, said tentatively.

"Yes, Helene?" Bruce replied a little impatiently to his administrative assistant.

Dancy answered: "There's an unusual call from the Admiralty —"

"I cannot take it right now, Helene," Bruce interrupted, tapping impatiently with his pen.

She looked at Bruce.

"Not for you, sir," Dancy said. "It's from naval intelligence" — she looked at Stevens — "and it's for you, sir."

Stevens heard Bruce stop the tapping . . . and thought he saw him squint his eyes.

"It's a British officer, Colonel Stevens," she explained. "A Major Niven. Quite a distinctive voice." She paused. "He sounds very much like the movie star, you know?"

"David Niven," Stevens offered.

"Yes, sir."

"What does Niven want?" Bruce put in.

Dancy looked at Bruce, then again at Stevens.

"Sir, he said that he's at Admiralty with a Commander Fleming, and that the commander, quote, needs to know straightaway where you wish the cadaver to be delivered as it appears to be thawing, unquote."

" 'Cadaver'?" Bruce parroted. "A *frozen cadaver?*"

He looked at Stevens, who looked back wordlessly with raised eyebrows.

## [TWO]
### AÉROPORTE NATIONALE ALGIERS
### ALGIERS, ALGERIA
### 1605 30 MARCH 1943

Major Richard M. Canidy, USAAF, watched "his" baby blue U.S. Navy P11 staff car leave in a cloud of reddish dust as it drove through the gap in the airport perimeter fencing, then off into the distance. Monsieur Khatim was at the wheel, en route to return the vehicle to AFHQ. They had had no choice but to take the baby blue staff car to the airport — conspicuous or not, and, as it turned out, they'd had no trouble — because when they

140

got to Fine's car, they found its left rear tire had gone flat.

Canidy wasn't sorry to see the Algerian leave. Khatim had avoided any conversation on the drive out, answering Canidy's casual queries with nods and grunts. But Canidy was sorry to see the car go. He realized that just now was likely the last time he would see it. He looked at the Hamilton Chronograph on his wrist, did the quick math, came up with six hours, and figured this was the first time he had given up a "borrowed" vehicle — car, jeep, aircraft — in so short a time.

Khatim had dropped him at the very far side of the airport grounds, barely in view of the main base operations of the airport, which itself was little more than an old one-story masonry structure pockmarked by bullets during OPERATION TORCH. On the roof of the building was the rickety control tower. The macadam of the runway and taxiway was a patchwork, the holes blown there temporarily packed with dirt and crushed stone. All of the airport appeared to be in various levels of repair by AFHQ and the local civilians they had hired to handle the manual labor.

The facility, if that was an applicable description, that served the OSS aircraft was set up behind a boneyard of WWI aircraft —

a couple of cannibalized French Spad XIIIs, a rotting German Fokker D.VII resting upside down on what was left of its bent top wing — and assorted worn-out, rusted airfield equipment.

It was really nothing more than a dusty, sunbaked spot beside a dirt strip that led to the taxiway. It had an old Nissen hut. The two Douglas C-47s were on either side of that, the main wheels of the low-wing taildragger transports chocked with what looked like parts scavenged from the Fokker.

Canidy walked toward the small hut. Designed by the British during the First World War, it was made of corrugated steel bent to form an inverted *U*. Wooden walls capped the ends, each with a single-man door, two windows, a louvered vent above the door, and three pipe vents in the roof. The cramped quarters accommodated four men.

As Canidy approached the hut, and the empty fifty-five-gallon drum by its front door, he found in the air the familiar strong smell of aircraft hydraulic fluid. He smiled; the smell triggered more than a few thoughts.

It was said that with the exception of the two-place, single-engine Piper Cub, the Gooney Bird was the Army Air Force's most forgiving aircraft. He agreed with that.

On one level — as that of an aeronautical engineer — he appreciated its fine design. It wasn't sexy, like a Lockheed P-38 fighter, but it was elegant in its utilitarian simplicity. On another, far more important level — as that of a secret agent stranded in enemy-occupied territory — he genuinely loved the Gooney Bird because it had saved his ass.

Darmstadter had put one down in an impossibly small spot in Hungary (one that Canidy had enlarged by clearing out its trees with Composition C-2 plastic explosive), then, against all odds, barely got the airplane the hell out of there.

The C-47 was the AAF's version of the Douglas DC-3 airliner. They were coming out of the Douglas plant by the thousands, and were being used as personnel transports and cargo aircraft — mostly carrying paratroopers or towing gliders in support of airborne operations. The C-47's two, twelve-hundred-horsepower Twin Wasp radial piston engines took it to an impressive twenty-three thousand feet.

Canidy also knew the fuel-efficient Twin Wasps — so named for the engine's two rows of fourteen cylinders — gave the Gooney Bird a range of more than two thousand miles. That meant without modification — the adding of auxiliary fuel cells, say, which

Canidy had done before — it could easily make the trip from Algiers to Sicily and back.

*Though,* he thought, *the Luftwaffe there on the island might have other ideas.*

Canidy looked at the closest Gooney Bird, the one on the left side of the hut, and saw that there was some motion in the cockpit. The aircraft on the right side of the hut had two men standing on wooden ladders by the starboard wing. They held wrenches and rags and were bent over the opened nacelle of the engine. A third man, stocky, with hands on his hips and his back to Canidy, stood between the fifty-five-gallon drum and wing, looking up at the engine and supervising.

As Canidy passed the drum, he raised his left hand, then swung it down hard, smacking the lid of the drum. The deep *wham!* sound that his open palm made when it hit the thin metal of the empty drum was stunning.

The supervisor came about a foot off of the ground.

The two mechanics jerked their heads up, one banging his head on the nacelle, the other trying to recover on his wobbly ladder.

"Sonofabitch!" the mechanic who hit his head exclaimed.

"Who in hell —" the supervisor began to roar as he turned toward the noise.

The mechanics watched as a big man in civilian clothing — he looked American but his clothes weren't — grinned broadly as he walked up with his arms open wide to their boss. In one smooth motion, the man placed his hands on both sides of the boss's head — and kissed him wetly and noisily on the forehead.

"It's me in hell, that's who!" he said cheerfully, his accent clearly midwestern American. "Miss me?"

Then he looked up at the mechanic who was rubbing his head.

"And a sonofabitch, if you like," he added. "Sorry about your head. That wasn't the response I'd hoped for." He hooked his thumb at the supervisor. "The lieutenant's here was."

Canidy looked at him and laughed loudly.

"You came about four feet off the ground, Hank!"

The mechanics on the ladder smiled in appreciation.

"Jeez, Dick, you sure know how to make an entrance," First Lieutenant Henry Darmstadter, USAAF, said fondly, wiping the wet kiss from his forehead with his shirtsleeve, then holding out his hand.

Darmstadter was twenty-two years old and had a friendly, round face.

"How are you?" Canidy said, shaking the hand.

"Great. What in hell are you doing here?" Darmstadter said, his tone pleasant.

"I need a favor. I need your airplane."

"You never did beat around the bush," Darmstadter said, smiling. "But you can't have this one. Not unless you want to use just the one engine." He paused. "But, then, *you* might. And you're the only pilot I'd trust to do that."

"Is it broke bad?" Canidy said.

Darmstadter stuck out his lower lip and shook his head. "Nah. They think it might just be a magneto."

"What about the other one?" Canidy said. "Is it airworthy?"

Darmstadter studied Canidy.

"You're serious about taking a plane, aren't you?"

Canidy nodded. "I'm in a helluva hurry. Stan Fine said you could run me out to Dellys, give me a tour, make introductions."

Darmstadter considered that, knew better than to ask questions — Canidy would confide if and when it was necessary — then checked his watch.

"We've got some jumpers due here for us

to run them out there in two hours," he said. "Can it wait till then?"

"I'd really like to get out there and back yesterday," Canidy said.

"Okay," Darmstadter nodded, then turned to the mechanics. "You guys'll be okay if we make a run?"

"Yes, sir," they replied almost in unison.

The mechanic who'd hit his head grinned and added, "Better than okay, if you get him and his surprises out of here."

"Surprises?" Canidy said. "I'd call them little tests. They're good for you. Didn't your mother ever tell you 'Never let your guard down' or 'Watch your back'?"

"How about 'Payback is hell'?" Darmstadter said to Canidy with a grin.

The mechanics smiled as they went back to work.

Darmstadter said, "Get that bird fixed, guys, and we'll be back in a bit."

Darmstadter turned to Canidy and looked at the duffel on his shoulder.

"You look ready to go," he said, then nodded toward the Nissen hut. "Let me go inside and get my flight bag, then we're out of here. Okay?"

He opened the door to the Nissen hut, and Canidy could see inside. There was a single lightbulb hanging above four bunks built of raw lumber. The shelving that held army field manuals and a few other books had been constructed from old ammo crates.

Canidy nodded.

"Sure," he said. "I think that while you're doing that, I'd better see to my bladder."

"Piss tube's over there in the shadow of the Fokker."

"Taking leaks on the Krauts, are we?"

"It was someone else's idea, but seemed fitting enough to me," Darmstadter said, then went inside the hut, the door slamming shut on its spring behind him.

The crew who had been in the other Gooney Bird, readying it for flight, had not been disappointed with Darmstadter's announcement that he was taking their aircraft and that they could have the other one when it was fixed in an hour or so.

As Darmstadter worked out those details, and made the preflight walk-around inspection of the aircraft, Canidy had made his way forward and strapped himself into the copilot seat.

When Darmstadter appeared in the cockpit and found him there, he said, "What? You don't want to fly left seat?"

"I thought you knew that I only fly the ones that can breathe fire," Canidy said.

Darmstadter glared at him.

Canidy went on, "You know, ones that go *rat-a-tat-tat* and *boom-boom?* I leave the operation of airborne buses to those pilots whose lips tend to move when they read the checklist."

Darmstadter shook his head as he settled into the pilot seat and retrieved the checklist.

He said, "With all due respect, *Major,* you can be such an ass sometimes."

Canidy smiled smugly.

The C-47 taxied to the threshold of runway 32, stuck its nose into the prevailing light wind coming off the sea, then, after engine run-up, roared down the strip and went wheels-up for the sixty-kilometer flight to Dellys. All the while, Canidy watched Darmstadter with the critical eye of the flight instructor he once had been at Naval Air Station Pensacola.

The C-47 copilot usually handled the business of putting the gear up and down, setting the flaps, running the radios. Darmstadter never asked Canidy to lift a finger. He effortlessly covered all the tasks.

*And he didn't even move his lips when the read the checklist.*

Despite the fact that it was safer to have the copilot read the checklist and work the panel, leaving the flying itself to the pilot, Canidy took no offense. He knew it was not a case of him not trusting Canidy, or of him showing off, or even of him being reckless.

Darmstadter simply loved to fly, to truly be pilot in command.

And as Canidy looked coolly out of the airplane, casually following Darmstadter's movements and being quietly impressed, Canidy was reminded how fine a pilot Darmstadter was, and how he almost missed the chance to become one.

Because he sure as hell had not started out as one.

The fact — not to mention the irony — was that Darmstadter, Henry, Lieutenant, United States Army Air Forces, almost wound up as a navigator, a bombardier, an aerial gunner — anything but a pilot in command of an aircraft.

Reason: The then nineteen-year-old had damn near flunked out of basic flight training. Despite his genuine enthusiasm to fly, his skills as a pilot had been rather rough, and compounding that problem were his bad bouts of airsickness.

What had saved his ass was a combination of two things. One, there had been a severe shortage of pilots. Two, there had not been a shortage of rough-around-the-edges fledgling flyboys in Darmstadter's class who also suffered from airsickness.

If the AAF elimination board had resorted to disqualifying everyone with less-than-polished skills or with airsickness — or with both — and declared them unfit to fly, then the result would have been a great number of empty cockpits . . . and thus grounded aircraft.

Resigned to the fact that they had to fill slots, the elimination board took another look — a long, hard book — at each candidate who had a problem with airsickness. (The ones left, that is. Half a dozen guys had simply gotten sick of being sick and quit to pursue other land-based assignments.) And the elimination board had then decided that Darmstadter held the dubious honor of being the least bad of a bad class.

They gave him another chance. They said that if during his probation period he could show he could perform aerobatic maneuvers without getting disoriented — or airsick — then they would see that he would earn his wings to fly, say, two-place, single-engine Piper Cubs. Fighters and bombers clearly being beyond his scope of competence.

The enthusiastic Darmstadter was determined.

Turning the phrase what goes up must come down on its head, he figured what doesn't go down can't come up and stopped eating on the days he knew he was going to fly. The result had been that he still got a little light-headed, but the throwing up was history. And with that resolved, he'd been able to successfully complete the aerobatic maneuvers.

The board made good on its condition of probation, and he soon pinned on his wings and butter bar and headed for advanced training.

It was there that he found the board also meant what it had said about what he would be flying — or not flying.

He had been sent to learn to fly the small twin-engine transport C-45.

Not a problem, he'd thought. He still would get to fly.

But then, just as he was about to graduate, he dumped one. Taking off solo in a C-45, he lost an engine. Miraculously, he'd had barely enough altitude to pull a three-sixty and, despite landing downwind, get the plane back in one piece on the runway — where he lost the other engine.

No sooner had he escaped the fuselage and made it across the tarmac than the fuel ignited and the aircraft exploded in a magnificent fireball.

And he found himself in front of the elimination board again.

The seven members debated his actions in
his presence. One declared that he should
have followed Standard Operating Proce-
dures, including adjusting the aircraft to fly
on a single engine and to circle the field until
able to land properly, into the wind. Another
member gave him the benefit of the doubt,
saying no one but Darmstadter really knew
what had happened, and how could it really
be a pilot's fault when both of his engines
crap out?

The elimination board voted in secret, and
Darmstadter (by a single yea, he later
learned) passed. He then transitioned to
learn how to fly the C-47, and, following his
successful graduation from that course, had
been sent to England to fly Gooney Birds.

But not in the left seat.

His place was in the copilot seat. And
there, he'd spent countless hours picking up
time — and skills — with superior pilots in
command, as they practiced low-level flights
for dropping parachutists, towing gliders,
and such. In the process, he'd also picked up
— on top of an automatic time-in-grade promotion to first lieutenant — enough flight
hours, plus landings and takeoffs, to qualify

as an aircraft commander.

Then one day his troop carrier wing commander had made an announcement to the pilots he'd gathered in the maintenance hangar. Eighth Air Force needed volunteer pilots, the commander said, for a "classified mission involving great personal risk."

Two of the Gooney Bird pilots there wanted nothing more than to be fighter pilots — and knew that towing gliders and dropping parachutists was not the career path for them. They jumped at the opportunity.

Hank Darmstadter admitted that he (1) would have loved being a fighter pilot but (2) knew that, with his history, did not for a minute stand a chance of becoming one. Nor did he really believe, as might the other two pilots, that this dangerous mission would put him in at the controls of a fighter plane.

*But,* he'd thought, *sounds interesting. What the hell? Why not apply? Probably won't make it, anyway. . . .*

Just when enough time had passed since he'd filled out the questionnaire that he knew he'd been passed over, though, sure as hell an order had arrived that said for him to immediately report to Eighth Air Force.

And, very shortly, he discovered that he'd very likely done a dumb goddamn thing by volunteering for this secret outfit called the Office of Strategic Services.

The mission — smuggling some important people out from under the noses of the damn Nazis — had been dangerous. But it had also been exciting, far more than tugging gliders through the sky. And in the process he'd saved the ass of one Major Richard M. Canidy.

Darmstadter got Canidy's attention when he pulled back on the throttles of the C-47's Twin Wasp engines. It was exactly half an hour after they'd gone wheels-up. He tapped Canidy on the shoulder, then pointed directly ahead of them toward the coastline, where the green hills led down and met the emerald sea.

"Dellys," Darmstadter's voice said in Canidy's headset.

Canidy looked and nodded. He saw the small city of low white buildings set into the hillside, with a small, semicircular harbor at the bottom, and thought that Dellys did indeed look as Stan Fine had said, "a miniature version of Algiers."

Canidy glanced at the altimeter and watched the needles creep counterclockwise as the aircraft settled into a slow descent.

They had been flying at a thousand feet

above ground level (AGL), which he knew was considered the standard height from which to drop paratroops — *Once again,* Canidy thought, *Hank proves old habits are hard to break* — although he was more than aware that in certain conditions AGL altitudes of five hundred and six hundred feet were quite common.

*The closer you drop men to the ground, the less time they spend in the sky floating to earth as easy targets.*

He noted, too, that the airspeed indicator showed one hundred forty miles per hour. That of course was the target speed for turning the jump light from red to green.

*Darmstadter's consistent. He still flies like they trained him, before we snagged him. Which, of course, is why we snagged him . . . to drop agents by parachute.*

*Saving our ass in Hungary was just icing on the cake.*

Canidy sat back and relaxed as Darmstadter maneuvered the aircraft to just shy of the western edge of the city, then made a gentle, flat turn out over the sea, and then turned again to roughly parallel the coast.

They were at a little more than a hundred feet off the deck and coming up on the shoreline somewhat quickly.

Canidy wasn't concerned; he knew Darmstadter could skim the bird along the tops of the waves and still land with his wheels dry. But Canidy did wonder where the hell he was going to put down. There wasn't a flat spot anywhere he could see that would be big enough to accommodate the Gooney Bird.

And, right now, with the peak elevation above Dellys looking to be at about a thousand feet above sea level, they presently were on a direct vector into the side of the land rise.

Darmstadter, showing no apparent concern, pointed toward the eastern end of Dellys.

Again his voice came through Canidy's headset: "There's the Sandbox."

Canidy followed to where he was pointing and found at the edge of town, right along the seawall, a compound that covered a whole block. It had a one-story tan-colored building that looked like a schoolhouse. The compound was ringed by a high wall built of white stone. There was a large courtyard, and in the half of the courtyard that was dirt Canidy saw lines of men going through what looked like hand-to-hand combat.

The Gooney Bird buzzed the compound. Then, with the Twin Wasps roaring from Darmstadter's big push on the throttles, the aircraft quickly gained altitude, then turned to the south and easily hopped the ridge.

Barely a moment later — just as Canidy made out a small, crude dirt strip dug out on the backside of the ridge, with a Nissen hut at one end and a jeep parked under a tarp strung alongside the hut — Darmstadter, in a flash of hands, slightly retarded the throttles, extended the full flaps for landing, and dropped and locked the landing gear.

They were on the ground in no time and taxiing toward the Nissen hut and jeep. Canidy noticed that an armed guard was standing in the shade of the tarp.

After Darmstadter had shut down the Twin Wasps, Canidy undid his seat harness.

"Hank," he said, patting him on the shoulder, "I was going to try to make up for my apparently offensive comment earlier and tell you that that just now wasn't half-bad flying."

"Thank —" Darmstadter began.

"But," Canidy continued, holding up his hands to stop him, "I'm afraid the compliment would probably go right to your head. And then you'd go do something dumb, like dump another plane, and I'd feel responsible for having let you feel overly confident."

Darmstadter looked at Canidy and

laughed appreciatively.

Then he gave him the finger.

# [THREE]
## OSS DELLYS STATION
## DELLYS, ALGERIA
## 1655 30 MARCH 1943

The drive over the hill into town took about twenty minutes. Darmstadter, having left the C-47 under the watch of the guard, steered the jeep though the narrow cobblestone streets of Dellys. When he came to the driveway of the compound, he brought the vehicle to a screeching stop in front of a massive wooden gate in the tall stone wall.

Without Darmstadter tapping on the horn or making any other effort to signal, the closed gate began slowly to swing open. Canidy wondered why, but when he looked around, and then up, he was not surprised to see a sentry in what had to be an emplacement hidden atop the compound wall.

Darmstadter stepped on the accelerator pedal, popped the clutch, and shot the jeep through the opening. The gate, moved manually by a young man in fatigues, was closed behind them.

Darmstadter looked at Canidy.

"Welcome to the Sandbox," he said over the whine of the jeep.

"What was it before?" Canidy said. "Some government facility?"

"Close. A Catholic missionary boarding school for boys. Some French folks thought they could save some local orphans while spreading the divine message. Don't know how successful they were. . . ."

Canidy grunted.

"That explains the high walls," he said. "Keeps out those prying eyes wondering what the infidels are up to."

As they rolled through the compound, toward the main building, Canidy saw in the courtyard the lines of men he'd seen from the airplane. Close up, most looked to be Frenchmen in their twenties and thirties, with a few appearing to be American or Franco-American.

*Maybe first-generation Americans?* Canidy thought.

The instructors, somewhat older, looked decidedly American.

In the courtyard, confirming what Canidy had thought when they had flown overhead, the lines of men were practicing hand-to-hand combat.

Elsewhere throughout the compound, men

were engaged in various activities. There was one group of ten agents, sweat-soaked and with bulging backpacks, that was running along the perimeter wall. Gathered in the shade at the base of a tree, six men, in three teams, were bent over open suitcases. Canidy recognized that they were working on Morse code skills, and that each two-man team had a SSTR-1 set — the "suitcase radio," an ordinary-looking green suitcase with a receiver, transmitter, and power supply hidden inside.

The jeep turned a corner, and Canidy saw that across the drive from the main entrance to the building was a telephone pole some twenty-five feet tall. It bristled with climbing spikes and was topped by a six-by-six-foot wooden platform. A parachute harness was tethered by parachute cord tied to two heavy-duty steel springs bolted to an overhead beam. The landing zone (LZ) was a pit of loose sand directly below.

Two men were at the top, standing on the platform, one helping the other adjust the parachute harness. The fit and muscular helper, by all appearances the instructor, made some hand motions, then yanked on the harness straps to test them. Then he gave the somewhat-overweight jumper — who had the soft features of perhaps a banker or other businessman more at home at a desk than a guerrilla training camp — an encouraging pat on the back.

The jeep pulled into a parking area alongside another jeep and Canidy and Darmstadter got out.

Canidy stopped at the front bumper, looked up at the platform, and watched the jumper.

The man in the harness hesitantly stepped to the edge of the platform.

He peered over it.

He looked back at the instructor, who motioned casually with his head, as if to say, *Go on, you can do it.*

The jumper peered back over the edge.

He closed his eyes . . . and stepped off.

He dropped like a rock, wailing as he went.

Then the tethered line snapped taut, and the jumper bobbed a few times under the tension of the springs before coming to a rest, gently swinging three feet above the sandpit LZ.

"Nice jump, Pierre!" the instructor called down. He had an American accent. "Next time, though, lose the scream, huh?"

Pierre, hanging his head with relief while staring at the sand LZ, didn't reply.

Canidy then heard a voice with a slight Italian accent call behind him, "We've been expecting you."

Canidy turned. He saw two men in Army fatigues without insignia coming down the stone steps at the building's main entrance. Both had dark olive skin and close-cropped black hair and bushy black mustaches; one was about six feet tall, the other a head shorter. He recognized the short one as Max Corvo.

"We got a heads-up from Algiers on the landline," Corvo said, offering his hand to Canidy. "Good to see you. Max Corvo."

"I remember," Canidy said, shaking his hand. "Nice to see you, too."

"Vincent Scamporino," the tall man said, offering his hand.

"Dick Canidy," he replied, taking the hand.

Canidy glanced at Darmstadter.

"And you've met the terror of the skies here?" he said.

Corvo turned to Darmstadter.

"I thought we'd come to some agreement about those buzzings," he said seriously.

"Major Canidy here grabbed the wheel. I was just trying to get control of the aircraft back before he killed us all."

Corvo, a stern look on his face, studied Canidy.

Canidy shrugged. "He said I should get a

close look at the Sandbox."

Corvo looked at Darmstadter's blank expression and sensed he was having his chain pulled.

"All right," Corvo said finally. He looked at Canidy. "Let's go to my office and talk in private. I've got work to do."

The building construction of the old Catholic school was not unlike that of the villa that served as OSS Algiers Station. It was of a similar sturdy masonry design but more utilitarian, and certainly not as nicely furnished. Its hard surfaces amplified the softest of sounds and caused louder ones to echo.

The room that Corvo called his office had actually been a classroom, one that the church had thoughtfully supplied with a wooden crucifix that filled the space between the top of the doorframe and the ceiling, and, on the wall near the small window, amateur artwork in charcoal of what looked to Canidy's eye to be biblical scenes.

And that was how Corvo had left the room set up: a teacher's wooden desk and chairs, at the front of the room in front of the wall that held the wide blackboard, and the remainder of the room filled with two dozen wooden student desks, with hinged wooden writing surfaces, in three rows of eight desks each.

Judging by the size of the desks, Canidy guessed the room had served to instruct boys who were ten or twelve years old.

"Help yourselves to a seat," Corvo said, leaning his buttocks against the front edge of the teacher's desk. "Captain Fine said to give you whatever you ask. Tell me what I can do for you."

Canidy noticed that Darmstadter didn't move toward a chair, just leaned against the wall. Then Canidy looked at Corvo and wondered if he was the one now doing the chain pulling. But when Scamporino squeezed himself into one of the student desks, Canidy realized that Corvo wasn't.

"I think I'll stand," Canidy said finally. "I've been sitting a lot lately."

"Something to drink?" Corvo said.

"Maybe later, thank you. I'm in a hurry, so let me get right to the point."

"Please do."

"I need intel out of Palermo and I need it right now. And I need to set up a wireless team long-term," Canidy said.

"Okay," Corvo replied more than a little dubiously.

"Stan Fine says you have people, connections?" It was more a statement than

165

a question.

Corvo looked somewhat surprised, then said, "In Sicily? Sure I do. My family is there" — he motioned at Scamporino in the chair — "Vincent's is. And Victor Anfuso's. Most of the men with me do. They're their uncles, grandparents, cousins, whatever." He shrugged. "AFHQ told us to get ready, but until they give us the go-ahead that we can get in there we're screwed. So we just train here with the French Resistance teams and wait."

Canidy snorted.

"Not good enough," he said.

Corvo stiffened.

"What is that supposed to mean?" Corvo said.

Canidy glanced at Darmstadter, who shook his head slightly.

*Yeah . . . I don't need to get off on the wrong foot here,* Canidy thought.

"I mean," Canidy went on in a calm, reasonable tone, "that I can't wait for that."

"I have to for all kinds of reasons, not just AFHQ," Corvo said, feeling the need to explain. "Look, I could bring only ten recruits from the States; that's Vincent and Victor and eight others. We're assembling teams, and training them, as best we can. We found some Sicilians among the prisoners of war that were liberated here and are trying to integrate them."

"Are they good?" Canidy said.

"They're taking a lot of work," Scamporino offered. "But I can tell you that they're motivated. And a couple are quite ruthless. I don't know who they hate more, Hitler or Mussolini."

"Have you been able to tell if any of them, maybe these ones you call ruthless, are connected with the Mafia?"

"No," Corvo immediately replied. It was as if he had been expecting the question. "I can't work with the Mafia."

Canidy looked at him. "Can't or won't?"

Corvo crossed his arms on his chest.

"I made it clear back in Washington," he said emphatically, "that anyone with connections to the Mafia cannot be trusted, and that the Sicilians we do have — our relatives, their extended family, and others — are."

Canidy nodded as he considered that.

*He profoundly believes that,* he thought. *Maybe he's right. But I can't rely on it, and it's not worth arguing now. Somehow, I don't think he'd be too impressed right now if I shared with him my letter of introduction from Luciano. . . .*

"Do you have any teams close to being

ready to go?" Canidy said.

Scamporino shook his head.

"Not even close," Corvo added. "But we have plenty of time."

Canidy grunted.

"Maybe you do," Canidy said.

"What's that mean?"

"I told you, I'm in a hurry. I don't have the luxury of time." He thought for a moment. "At the risk of this next question annoying you, too, I'll say it, anyway."

Canidy noticed that Corvo was practically glaring at him.

"What are the odds," Canidy went on, "that one of these former POWs of yours is a *V-männer?*"

"A what?" Scamporino said.

"That's what the Germans call their spies —" Canidy began to explain.

"Not a damn one!" Corvo interrupted.

"— It's short for *Vertrauensmänner,*" Canidy went on evenly, his attention still on Scamporino. "It means 'trustworthy men.' "

Canidy looked at Corvo. "Not one? That's too bad."

Corvo looked as if he could not believe his ears.

"Why in hell would you say that?" he said.

"Because he might make a good CEA."

Corvo glanced at Scamporino as he

thought about that a moment, then said, "A double agent?"

Canidy nodded.

"I believe the OSS likes to use the term Controlled Enemy Agent," Canidy said, then added, "You might take another hard look. Just to make sure."

Corvo looked like he was about to explode.

Canidy held up his hand, palm out.

"Before you fly off the handle," he said, "consider your source. That they were in the POW camps during Operation Torch could mean they were just in the wrong place at the wrong time and simply got swept up with the real bad guys. Or . . . it could mean that there's one or more who were in a Nest, that they'd been pins on the map when we came through, and now, oh so conveniently, denounce the Nazis and Italians."

"Pins on a map?" Scamporino said.

Canidy noticed that even Darmstadter now was looking curiously.

"Max," Canidy said, "does Pins on the Map Syndrome mean anything to you?"

He shook his head. "Sorry, Major."

"You can call me Dick," Canidy replied.

The look on Corvo's face showed that he appreciated the gesture.

"It's the first I've heard of it, Dick," he

said. "The syndrome, that is. Keep in mind I'm new to all this."

Canidy knew that when he had been recruited for the OSS, Corvo had worn the stripe of an Army private on his uniform.

"In many ways, me, too, Max," Canidy said, then, after a moment, added, "I gather that *Nests* and *Asts* are unfamiliar terms also?"

Corvo nodded. Scamporino shrugged slightly.

"About how many men do you have, Max?" Canidy said.

"Everyone included," Corvo said, "about thirty."

"How soon can you round them up?"

Corvo looked at Scamporino and raised an eyebrow, passing the question.

"Fifteen minutes?" Scamporino answered.

Canidy nodded as he considered that. He looked at this wristwatch.

"You mind if I speak with them as a group?" Canidy said.

"Captain Fine said to give you what you want."

"Get 'em in here," Canidy said. "I can do this quickly, especially if I only have to do it once."

Canidy looked at Darmstadter.

"This will be good for your education,

too, Hank. You might want to take advantage of picking out a good seat before the rest arrive."

# [FOUR]
## OSS WHITBEY HOUSE STATION KENT, ENGLAND 1630 2 APRIL 1943

The three-vehicle caravan wound down the rain-slick narrow country road that cut through dense forest. Lieutenant Colonel Ed Stevens's olive drab 1941 Ford staff car was in the lead. Behind it was a British Humber light ambulance — a large red cross within a white square painted on its side panels and its back doors — and trailing the ambulance was another U.S. Army '41 Ford.

As they approached the grounds of Whitbey House, Stevens noticed the faded cardboard signs nailed to trees and affixed to stakes driven in the ground. These the Brits had placed every twenty meters around the perimeter of the lands of Whitbey House. They bore the now barely legible legend GOVERNMENT ESTABLISHMENT ENTRY PROHIBITED and the seal of the Crown.

The procession came to an unmarked gap

in the trees that was an ancient lane which wound into the forest.

Stevens's driver steered the Ford through the gap and began winding up the lane, and the trailing vehicles followed.

Stevens smiled.

Before the war, when he'd been living with his family in London, he liked to take his wife and sons on Sunday drives to admire the countryside. And now, despite the war — *Or maybe in spite of the damn thing, because it's refreshing to get out of that dreary London* — he discovered that he enjoyed the trip all the more. He found Whitbey House, and its storied history, to be absolutely magnificent.

Whitbey House — the ancestral seat of the Duchy of Stanfield — consisted of some twenty-six thousand acres. This included the eighty-four-room Whitbey House itself and its various outbuildings (garages, stables, et cetera), the village of Whitbey on Naer (population: 607), the ruins of the Roman Catholic abbey of St. William the Martyr, St. Timothy's Anglican Church, a ten-year-old, forty-six-hundred-foot gravel runway with an aircraft hangar, plus various other real property that had come into the hands of the first Duke of Stanfield circa 1213.

Like most of England's "stately homes," Whitbey House had been requisitioned for the duration of the war by His Majesty's government. The government's need for space had been bad enough — damn near insatiable — but when the United States entered the war, it quickly became unbelievably worse. U.S. air, ground, and naval forces arrived in the British Isles, and all of these people — and the supply depots they brought with them — required their own places.

Once requisitioned, Whitbey House had passed from the control of His Majesty's Office of Properties to the War Office, then to the Special Operations Executive, then to the Office of Strategic Services.

Shamelessly copying the Research and Development Station IX of their counterparts in the British Special Operations Executive — "Because *they* know what they're doing," Wild Bill Donovan had said, only half in jest — the OSS set up the facility as a safe house and, as the Operational Techniques School, a training base for agents.

*What Dick Canidy more accurately called the Throat-Cutting and Bomb-Throwing Academy.*

There had been "improvements" to the property, beyond the Brits' cardboard warning signs that hung faded and limp on the perimeter.

A kilometer up the ancient lane, a shoulder had been added to either side of the road, one wide enough for vehicles to be able to turn around. A low stone wall crossed the shoulder, from the trees to a gatehouse, and served as a barrier. The Kent Constabulary supplied constables to man the gatehouse around the clock. The constable's job was to serve as the first level of security, passing those with proper clearance while turning back the casual visitors curious about the estate.

Stevens saw that after the constable — this one a rather portly fellow stretching his uniform buttons to the point of popping — had checked their identification and cleared the caravan to pass onto the estate, the constable cranked a U.S. Army EE-8 field telephone. He then reported to the sergeant of the U.S. Army Guard at the next barrier that he had just passed three authorized vehicles, the first carrying an American lieutenant colonel.

This next barrier, far out of sight of the roads bordering the estate and the first barrier, was protected by tall coils of concertina, a razor-sharp barbed wire. Plywood signs hung from the concertina at intervals of fifteen meters. These bore a representation of a skull and crossbones with the legend: PERSONS TRESPASSING BEYOND THIS LINE WILL BE SHOT ON SIGHT.

Stevens was quite aware that the skull and crossbones and rolls of concertina were American, and that the guard was U.S. Army infantry.

That was because, just outside of the barbed wire, there was an American infantry battalion housed in a tent-and-hut encampment. While the OSS station did not need the twelve hundred men of a battalion, the soldiers had been stationed there anyway, the reasoning being that the battalion had to be stationed *somewhere,* so why the hell not show the British that the Yanks were serious about keeping safe the secrets of their new OSS.

The officers of the battalion had been told that Whitbey House housed a highly classified organization and that its mission was to select bombardment targets for the Eighth Air Force. The officers had no reason to doubt that, but it wasn't uncommon for them to wonder among themselves — "My God, George, *eighteen hundred men?* What the hell else is in that old house?" — if this wasn't a bit of bureaucratic overkill to guard one lousy facility.

The battalion's four companies were on rotation. As three companies carried on routine training (keeping themselves available as needed), the fourth provided the guard force between the concertina and a third barrier.

This third barrier enclosed just over three acres around Whitbey House itself. It consisted of an eight-foot-high fence of barbed wire, with concertina laid on either side of the fence. Atop poles planted every thirty meters were floodlights, three to a pole.

Past this point, the forest became manicured, and Stevens marveled at the two-kilometer-long path they followed. He knew that it had been carved out centuries before, designed not as the quickest route from Point A to Point B but, in order to accommodate the aristocracy's heavy carriages, as a route that was as level as possible up to the house.

They emerged from the forest, and there, at the end of a wide, curving entrance drive, was Whitbey House itself. Stevens smiled. The structure was so impressively large — three stories of brick and sandstone — that he could not take it all in without moving his head.

At the final U.S. Army guard post, the officer of the guard checked ID cards against a list of authorized personnel. Beyond him, Stevens saw Canidy's Packard parked in front of the front door of Whitbey House.

It was a custom-bodied 1939 Packard. It had a right-hand drive. The driver's compartment bore a canvas roof, and the front fenders held spare tires. It was just the type of car that belonged at a mansion like Whitbey House.

After the OSS had moved in, the Packard had been discovered behind hay bales in the stables. It hadn't been there by accident. It had, in fact, been hidden, put up on blocks and otherwise preserved from the war for the duration and six months.

Canidy had appropriated it for his own use, lettering U.S. ARMY on its doors and adding numbers on its hood. For protection at night, a strip of white paint edged the lower fenders, and the headlights were blacked out except for a one-inch strip. And he'd assigned a stunning English lady sergeant as its driver.

Only Canidy would be so bold as to declare that no British bobby or American MP would have the nerve to stop such an impressive automobile and ask for its papers. And, accordingly, only Canidy could get away with that.

Stevens grinned, then, as he got out of the car and glanced at the ambulance — which, for some reason, was now blowing its horn — he thought, with some concern, *I wonder how in hell Dick is doing?*

# IV
## [ONE]
## THE SANDBOX
## OSS DELLYS STATION
## DELLYS, ALGERIA
## 1720 30 MARCH 1943

A crowd of men streamed into Max Corvo's "office," the first ones filling the wooden school desks that were empty and the rest collecting at the back of the room. Canidy saw their eyes on him, all of them studying the stranger in civilian clothing standing at the front of the room.

Canidy scanned the crowd and was impressed at the wide range of men who were willing to fight — and die — opposing the Germans and Italians. Some of them — like Pierre, the parachutist, whom he saw seated in the middle of the crowd — were well-educated men, men of some wealth. You could see it in their eyes that they were thoughtful, intelligent. Others were of more

178

modest means and schooling, many of them tradesmen, hardworking men not afraid to get their hands dirty, even if that meant slitting Nazi throats.

"Good afternoon, gentlemen," Canidy began, speaking slowly, his raised voice easily filling the room. "Thank you for interrupting your work on such short notice."

He paused as he paced before the blackboard. He glanced around the room, then went on:

"You don't know me. I don't know you. Maybe that will change in the near future. Maybe it won't. For right now, simply consider me a visiting instructor."

Canidy let that sink in a second as he looked around the room, making eye contact. He noticed that a couple of the men were made uncomfortable with that. They looked away. He made a mental note on them, particularly the one with a thick black beard who appeared somewhat nervous.

Then he went to the blackboard, located a piece of white chalk, and picked it up.

"I'm going to make this presentation short and sweet," he said, looking at the men, "as we all have important work to do. But I believe what you're about to see and hear is important background for what you're doing."

He turned to the board.

"Okay," he began, and, with the chalk, wrote ABWEHR, centered near the top of the blackboard, then drew a box around it. "I'm sure you're all familiar with this."

He turned to look at the others and then went on. "Germany's real use of the Abwehr was to get around the Treaty of Versailles. As you know, with the end of the First World War the 1919 treaty was signed in order to keep Germany contained, keep its balls in a vise. The treaty said that Germany could not engage in espionage or other covert 'offensive' intelligence gathering. But it did allow a 'defensive' counterespionage. So they had —"

He turned back to the backboard and tapped the white box.

"— the Abwehr."

To the right of the box, he wrote AMT AUSLANDSNACHRICHTEN UND ABWEHR.

"Anyone translate?" Canidy said.

"Simply," a voice with a French accent said, "the Office of Foreign and Counterintelligence."

Canidy looked to see who had answered. It was Pierre, the parachutist.

"Right, Mr. —"

"Mr. Jones," he said, his French accent somewhat mangling the pronunciation. It came out a nasally *Mee-ster Joe-nay.*

*Pierre Jones,* Canidy thought and smiled inwardly.

OSS agents did not use their real names in training camps, and usually only went by their first name. The cover helped protect them in the event that the agent sitting next to him was indeed a *V-männer* or just a low-level snitch who later could rat him out.

"Of course," Canidy said and wrote the translation underneath the German as he repeated it. "OFFICE OF FOREIGN AND COUNTERINTELLIGENCE."

He circled the last word, then tapped FOREIGN.

"The treaty allowed Germany's military attached to its embassies and such to overtly gather information — the 'foreign' — and the Germans of course did exactly that. The treaty also allowed Germany to have its own security force, and so the 'counterintelligence.' "

He tapped the circled word.

"But it was under this legitimate service that Germany conducted its illicit activities — its international secret service."

He paused to let that sink in.

"Thus," he said, then stopped, and above ABWEHR wrote HIGH COMMAND in its own box and drew a line linking the two boxes. He went on: "Thus, the Abwehr, under the High Command, really began as an illegitimate, underground organization, its secret purpose to gather covert intel . . . all against the faith of the Treaty of Versailles."

"Not that that damn Hitler abides by any agreements, anyway," Scamporino said.

"Unfortunately, very true," Canidy said, and immediately thought about the bastard violating the chemical warfare treaty by putting the Tabun in Palermo.

He cleared his throat, and went on: "By the time Admiral Wilhelm Canaris took over the Abwehr in 1935, Germany's rearming was pretty much in full swing, and the Abwehr quite powerful. Today, it's even more so, and the reason why we need to know all that we can to defeat them."

He saw that some of his students were starting to get a glazed look in their eyes.

"Okay, I'll try to make this next part fast."

He turned back toward the blackboard and, below the box with ABWEHR, he drew four more boxes on the same line. Then he drew lines from each new box to the ABWEHR box, forming what looked like a four-tine fork.

"The Abwehr has four main sections, called *Abteilungen,* or Abt for short. And each Abt has men from the German army, navy, and air services."

He wrote ABT I in the first box, ABT II in the second, ABT III in the third, and ABT Z in the last.

"Abt I is espionage," he said, and wrote ESPIONAGE in the box, "commanded as of this month by Colonel Georg Hansen."

He wrote the name in the box.

"Oberst Hansen is a bit of a roughneck, but, as one might expect of someone in such a position, he is energetic and efficient at his job."

Canidy in the next box wrote SABOTAGE, SUBVERSION, and after a dash put COL. ERWIN LAHOUSEN.

"Like a great many of Hitler's officers — like Hitler himself — Oberst Lahousen is an Austrian. He comes from a military family, and so is very much a natural at what he does" — Canidy tapped the box — "sabotage and subversion."

In the Abt III box, Canidy wrote SECURITY, COUNTERESPIONAGE, and COL. EGBERT VON BENTIVEGNI.

"This one, I'm sure you gather, is what once was the legitimate arm under which the illegitimate Abwehr once operated."

And in the last box, Abt Z, he wrote Z = "ZENTRAL" OR ADMIN. and COL. HANS OSTER.

"And this one is the administrative section. A critical component, if only for its layers of bureaucracy that with luck we could target in order to cut off, or at least cause to delay, the lifeblood of money, munitions, et cetera, destined for German agents."

He looked around the room. A few men, the more intelligent-looking ones, were writing down what he'd put on the board. The vast majority, however, simply sat and stared back blankly.

"Questions at this point?" Canidy said.

The room remained silent, the men looking either reluctant to speak or, more likely, just disengaged.

"Anyone?" Canidy pursued. "If I don't know the answer, I'll just get it pooma."

There now were flashes of curiosity in their eyes.

"Pooh — *what?*" Darmstadter suddenly said, innocently . . . then looked embarrassed at his outburst.

Canidy grinned. "You surprise me. Of all people, I'd have thought you'd be the one who knew pooma up and down."

Canidy turned to the board and wrote the word on the board.

Then, tapping the appropriate letter as he went, Canidy said, "Pulled Out of My Ass. Pooma."

The room erupted with appreciative laughter.

After the sound of that settled, a young man at the front raised his hand. He appeared to be Sicilian, or Sicilian American, about twenty years old.

Candidy pointed to him. "Yes?"

"The odds of me running into Oberst Lahousen," the young man said, motioning at the blackboard, "well, let's just say I'm not holding my breath it's going to happen. So how exactly does all this fit with what we're doing?"

*There's an American flavor to his speech,* Candy thought. *Maybe one of Corvo's ten recruits he brought over. . . .*

Candy nodded.

"Okay," he said, "I understand what you're saying. But it's important to understand the big picture — Know Thy Enemy — so that you can understand the ones that you will come in contact with."

The young man nodded, his unruly black hair bouncing.

Candy turned to the board and wrote PINS ON THE MAP SYNDROME.

He looked at the men, and said, "Anyone heard of that?"

An intelligent-looking Italian American of about thirty raised his hand.

"Is it like where you keep track of your salesmen by putting pushpins with different-colored heads on a map representing your sales territory?" he said clearly with the accent and experience of someone who had been in America for some time.

*Definitely one of Corvo's recruits from the States.*

Canidy nodded.

"Very much so," he said. "It is, in other words, the tracking of assets. But something more. The syndrome part has, as you might expect, a psychological component."

Canidy turned to the board and began writing again.

"First, let me outline this."

He turned and pointed at the young Sicilian American and said, "You mentioned Oberst Lahousen, so I'll use Abt II. But know that all the Abts are structured in this manner. Abt II is a good example, as it was the parent of the Brandenburg units, the ruthless German special ops that took out the partisans in Yugoslavia in '41. These are the type of forces you can expect to fight."

He drew another box at the top of the board, then wrote ABWEHR HQ in it. Under that, he put another box, drew a line linking the two, and in the lower box wrote AB-WEHRSTELLEN ("ASTS").

"There are some twenty-plus Asts within the Reich," Canidy said as he drew another box, this one under ASTS, "with a dozen or more in occupied territories. Each Ast has smaller *Nebenstellen*" — he wrote that in the new box and added NESTS — "and these Nests can have even smaller teams that specialize, called *Aussenstellen,* or 'Outstations.' "

Canidy noticed Corvo and Scamporino nodding, having recognized the terms ASTS and NESTS.

He finished writing all that, and went on:

"Then there is the *Kriegsorganisation,* 'KO' for short, or 'War Organization.' This operates in neutral countries — Switzerland and Sweden, of course, Spain, Turkey, et cetera — with either a diplomatic or commercial cover. It is the Abwehr's overt presence, but the Abwehr does not act against its host. KO serves as a base of operations."

When he finished, he turned to the crowd and said:

"All of these have representatives from each of the German services, and all of these, we have found, do not have any true centralized control or direction from above. Therefore, the Abwehr is not always well run. And, occasionally, not well run at all."

There were murmurings.

"Do not misunderstand me," Canidy quickly added. "It *is* often effective, and you should not underestimate it. But there are Abwehr weak links." He paused. "Here's where the syndrome kicks in. We have found, as I'm sure you have seen here among the German POWs, that Nazi officers tend to be rather proud of themselves —"

Someone in the crowd snorted loudly. That caused others to chuckle.

Canidy went on: "A genuine arrogance —"

"Like that goddamn Hitler!" the young Sicilian American interrupted.

Appreciative grunts of agreement rippled through the crowd.

*Do I need to tell them to shut the hell up until I'm finished?*

He was about to say exactly that when he realized that the outbursts proved that the men now were engaged with the subject. Snapping at them would be the equivalent of him pissing on their fire. So, instead, he embraced it.

"Yes, 'Like that goddamn Hitler,' " Canidy repeated.

Darmstadter saw the young man's face practically light up.

*Canidy's good at that,* Darmstadter thought, *making the guy low on the team feel like he's king.*

Canidy went on: "Hitler's arrogance is their example and they mimic it. Now, to feed this arrogance, these officers need power, and the more people they control, then the more power they appear to have — among their men and their superiors."

"The more pins on the map!" the young Sicilian American said suddenly.

"You got it," Canidy said. "And this, you might expect, tends to fuel itself. And competition rises between officers who oversee the spies and their controllers. They think that if, for example, ten agents are good, a hundred has to be ten or more times better. So ignoring whatever talent their recruits may or may not have — or even what loyalty — they fill their ranks with as many men, or women, as possible."

He paused, letting that set in.

"And here's where the payoff comes for us: The Asts and Nests — again, acting independently, without direction from above — recruit and train their own spies, then send them on ops. Ast Berlin could, for example, send agents to, say, Porto Empedocle not knowing that Ast Hamburg and Ast Munich already had agents there. And Hamburg and Munich may not know of the other's existence."

He paused, glanced at the board, then continued:

"These agents sent into the field may be without talent, but they are not so stupid as not to recognize this arrogance *and* the fact that they can play to it. They feed the officer information — good, bad, indifferent — and the officer adds that to the information from his other agents, then passes it all up the line to impress his superiors. Meanwhile, the agent skims money he's given to pay his sources, demands higher payment for his work, lies about his expenses. His loyalty is only to himself. And, clearly, that loyalty has a price."

He paused.

"And that, gentlemen, is one of the major weak links of the Abwehr — if not *the* weakest link."

There were nods of understanding in the crowd.

Pierre, the parachutist, then said, "You're not suggesting that only the Krauts are corrupt, are you?"

*Shit,* Canidy thought, looking at Pierre. *Good question.*

*Answer: "Not no but hell, no. We've got our own agents rotten to the core."*

Then he wondered: *And how much of what I just went over was already perfectly clear to* someone here?

"Oh, no," Canidy said. "You're going to find that on our side, too. It's, unfortunately, human nature."

"Then what's the difference?" Pierre pursued.

*Christ, another good question.*

*Am I being naïve about this? And he's seeing right through it?*

*Because the real answer is: "Not a helluva lot."*

*But . . . there is one difference, however small it might be. And sometimes it's the small thing that saves the day.*

"Very simple," Canidy said, looking around the crowd, then making a dramatic sweep of the room with his right hand. "*We* want to fight to win. When you were approached, no one in here volunteered for fear that, if they didn't, they'd be sent to a concentration camp, or shot on the spot, or that their families would be. Right?"

He saw a few heads nodding in agreement.

"Now, without a doubt, there are those with ulterior motives, perhaps even someone in this room" — he glanced at one of the men whom he'd earlier made uneasy with his eye contact; the bearded man now busied himself making notes from the blackboard — "but we have ways to weed them out. As my father, and, I'm sure, your fathers, too, said, 'Good always overcomes evil.' "

He let that sink in, then continued:

"Now, knowing all I've told you here, and knowing what you're learning here at the Sandbox, there should not be a doubt in your minds that you and I will be successful fighting for the freedom of our countries, for the freedom of our families." He paused for dramatic effect, then, raising his voice, said, "We're going to kick the living hell out of them and win this goddamn war!"

The crowd erupted with hoots and applause.

Canidy looked around the room, smiling.

*Jesus, I think that I just may have pulled that off.*

*Or, as the case would be, I did it pooma.*

*When in doubt, always wave flag and family in their face.*

Canidy glanced at his watch, then held up his hand as a wave good-bye.

"And with that, gentlemen, I have to go."

There was more polite applause as the men got up from their seats.

Canidy walked over to Corvo.

"I'm sure I'll be back sometime soon, Max," he said. "Meantime, keep an eye out for what we discussed."

*Because I'm going to take over one of your*

*teams for Sicily. And if I can turn an enemy agent here, so much the better.*

"Will do, Dick," Corvo said. He looked at the board, then added, "And thanks for this."

As Scamporino walked up, Corvo said to him, "We need to save what's on the board. Get a picture of it, huh? Or write it down . . . whatever."

Scamporino nodded. He looked at Canidy and offered his hand.

"Thanks for that lesson. And, particularly, the pep talk. The men needed it more than I realized."

"You're welcome," Canidy said, shaking his hand.

Scamporino turned to Darmstadter, patted him on the shoulder, and said, "See you soon, Hank. Take care."

Then he left the room.

As Canidy started to follow Scamporino to the door, he glanced again at the charcoal scenes from the Bible.

Two thoughts struck him, both concerning his father, the Reverend Dr. George Crater Canidy, headmaster of St. Paul's School in Cedar Rapids, Iowa.

First was that he knew that his father would know exactly what they were, right down to citing chapter and verse for each.

His father was, of course, expert in such study.

Second, that he had just served as teacher to a class of students, just as his father had done for decades.

Dick Canidy loved his father dearly. Yet he wondered how his father would feel knowing that he was part of an organization using the facility that had once been a boarding school for Catholic boys — not unlike St. Paul's and its sons of devout Episcopalians — for the training of spies and saboteurs and assassins.

*"And you shall know the truth, and the truth shall set you free,"* Canidy suddenly remembered. *From the Book of John — chapter 8, verse 32.*

*Like father, like son?*

*Don't kid yourself, Dick.*

*Dear ol' Dad, God bless him, would not like this shit one bit.*

# [TWO]

Darmstadter raised the landing gear and retracted the flaps of the Gooney Bird after their departure from the dirt strip at Dellys. He then pushed the yoke slightly forward, leveling off the plane, and adjusted the throttle back just slightly, settling in on a due easterly course right along the coastline.

The sun was to their back, a little more than an hour from setting and starting to create long shadows across the ground ahead of them. After a few minutes, Darmstadter pointed in an animated fashion at eleven o'clock out the windscreen.

"There they go," he said over the intercom. "Headed for the Sandbox."

Canidy looked out that direction, and saw another C-47. The sunlight set it off in the blue sky.

Canidy saw that it was approaching the western edge of Dellys. Then he saw, in quick succession, eight figures drop from the back of the aircraft — then their parachutes pop open one after another. They floated down, all nicely lit by the sun, and landed somewhat scattered. Then the aircraft disappeared over the ridge, headed in the direction of the dirt strip on the other side.

Canidy looked at Darmstadter and gave a thumbs-up.

Darmstadter nodded, then caused the Gooney Bird to make a slow turn, so that the needle on the compass came to rest on 200 degrees. That would result in a more or less direct vector to the airfield at Algiers.

Canidy went back to looking out the windscreen. Nothing he saw really registered, as he mentally went back over everything that had just happened at the Sandbox.

He was disappointed. He realized — again — that he'd come away from the OSS finishing school with pretty much zip. While the trip had not been a total waste of time — he, of course, had been able to share his talk with the agents there — he desperately had to make some headway of his own here soon. . . .

Suddenly, Darmstadter banked the aircraft. He was turning away from the Algiers airfield, on a course out over the sea.

Canidy looked at him for an answer.

Darmstadter's voice came over the intercom: "Algiers control is routing me out and around the long way. Not the first time it's happened. Damn sure won't be the last."

Canidy nodded, resigned to the fact that that amounted to yet another small delay for him.

He turned to watch the waves, lost in thought.

*Everyone back in that room at the Sandbox is fighting to defeat Hitler — if not exactly for the same honorable reasons.*

*Donovan told me before sending me into Sicily that to a man everyone is working some angle to come out on top after the war.*

*Just among the damn Frogs there's the Communist Francs-Tireurs et Partisans; the Organization de la Résistance dans l'Armée, followers of Giraud; De Gaulle's Forces Française de l'Intérieur; and a deadly mix of other warring subfractions.*

*Christ knows how many we will deal with in Sicily. But clearly the usual suspects. Including my new friends in the Mafia.*

*What was it Donovan told Hoover? "I know they're Communists, Edgar. That's why I hired them."*

*Communists, Fascists, mobsters — the Boss isn't afraid of working with anyone to win this damn thing.*

*But then neither are FDR and Churchill.*

*Just consider that damned Stalin. His belief that "One man's death is a tragedy, but a million deaths is merely a statistic" doesn't exactly qualify the sonofabitch for sainthood.*

*Pulling these various factions together — or at least managing them in our own way — is how Donovan expects to do that.*

*They're really on their own side. That's a given. And most likely why that bearded bastard in the classroom would not look me in the eyes.*

*But we do have the upper hand. They all need our training and weapons and money. And they all know we can go into every last*

*one of their countries, behind enemy lines,
and sabotage anything we don't want them to
have — power plants, heavy factories, railroads — just take out the equipment short-
term if they cooperate or, if they don't, call in
the bombers and blow the hell out of everything.*

*Just like a certain spook blowing up a muni-
tions supply ship full of nerve gas in Palermo.*

*Shit. . . .*

Canidy looked down. He shook his head,
hoping to clear it, then looked again out the
windscreen.

*What the hell?*

He put his fingers behind his aviator sun-
glasses and rubbed his eyes.

*Am I seeing things?*

Shielding his eyes against the glare of the
low sun, he looked down at the surface —
and the long shadow cast by a fishing boat
down there.

He tapped Darmstadter's shoulder. Holding his left index finger upright, he made a
circling motion.

Darmstader immediately understood,
scanned the sky for other aircraft, and stood
the Gooney Bird on her starboard wing, putting her belly toward the sun.

That cut the glare, and when Canidy
looked out the windscreen, his direct view

was now that of the ocean surface.

"Well, I'll be damned!" he suddenly said.

He motioned to get Darmstadter's attention, then pointed at the ocean surface, signaling for him to take a closer look.

Darmstadter banked the aircraft a little more for a clearer look, then saw the shape of the small boat and its shadow. He nodded, leveled off, then pushed the yoke forward, the nose instantly dipping.

*God does take care of fools and drunks,* Canidy thought, *and I qualify on both accounts.*

Canidy got on the intercom.

"Can you get all the way down on the deck, Hank, so I can be sure?" he said. It was a statement more than a question.

Darmstadter made turns so that the Gooney Bird would approach the fishing boat from the stern, keeping to its port side so that Canidy, in the copilot's seat, would have an unobstructed view.

As they closed on the aft of the boat, brightly lit by the sun, Canidy could see four people at the transom. They watched the aircraft, and no doubt wondered what the hell it wanted.

"Not too close," Canidy said over the intercom. "Never know who has an itchy trigger finger."

Darmstadter raised an eyebrow and nodded.

They flew closer, and Canidy was sure he could make out the tall, solidly built man whom he knew to have an olive complexion, thick black hair and mustache, and a rather large nose. He'd last seen him five days ago, when Canidy and professor Arturo Rossi stepped off that boat and into the submarine.

In a flash, the Gooney Bird caught up to the boat and blew past. Canidy had just enough time to glance at the faces aboard — *Yep, that's Frank Nola, in the flesh* — and to read what was painted on the ship's bow just below the rusty anchor: STEFANIA.

*Sweet Jesus,* he thought, smiling. *They did get out okay.*

*Or at least look like they're okay.*

Then he raised his left hand so that the palm faced down, rocked it left to right, then with his index finger poked repeatedly toward Algiers.

Darmstadter nodded in understanding.

He waved the wings of the Gooney Bird at the crew of the boat, then gained altitude before heading for the airfield.

# [THREE]
## OSS WHITBEY HOUSE STATION
## KENT, ENGLAND
## 1655 2 APRIL 1943

It had been a ghastly, mind-numbing day. The weather had turned dreadful and dreary — again — the gray-black clouds rumbling with the threat of rain. Worse, the day's paperwork had seemed endless. And as twenty-two-year-old Charity Hoche walked quickly down the wide corridor to her bedroom, heels tapping rhythmically on the parquet flooring, she knew that there was only one thing that could even begin to make up for it.

*I've been working since five o'clock,* she thought. *I deserve this. Twelve hours is enough.*

Charity Hoche was accustomed to getting what Charity Hoche wanted.

*And no damn war is going to change that.*

She unlocked the sturdy paneled door to the bedroom and entered, then locked the door behind her. After first removing her shoes, then her first lieutenant's uniform, she took care in slipping off the fine silk stockings, panties, and brassiere. Then Charity pulled on a thick cotton robe, lifted her shoulder-length hair out from under its collar and made a ponytail, then padded barefoot into the adjacent bathroom.

She went directly to the huge black marble bathtub.

She turned on the tap and water began to gurgle into the tub. Then she walked to a cabinet, opened the door, and removed a jar of Elizabeth Arden bubble bath crystals. She had brought two dozen jars with her when she had come over from the States, not quite two months ago. Her stockpile was down to eighteen, as she had judiciously given jars — and some silk stockings — to the other women at Whitbey House.

She carefully poured two scoops of crystals into the running water, adjusted the taps, then returned the jar to the cabinet. When the tub was about half full, she dipped her right big toe in the water to test the temperature. She winced — it was quite hot at first touch, but then she became accustomed to it — and slid off her robe and stepped both feet into the tub. She slowly lowered herself in the water, the layer of bubbles swallowing every part of her body but her head.

"Ahhh," she said, contentedly.

A rumble of thunder rattled the windows.

As her body warmed and her muscles began to relax, her mind became less cluttered with the day's mundane tasks that had driven her to numbness — and settled on the one thing that dogged her.

Charity desperately wanted to be of the frame of mind not to give a damn about what people thought of her.

*Like Dick Canidy does,* she thought, reaching for the oval bar of Pear's Soap and the facecloth next to it. *He couldn't care less.*

But Charity — reared on a twenty-acre estate in Wallingford, one of the plusher suburbs of Philadelphia, and educated at Bryn Mawr — couldn't bring herself to do that.

*I do care.*

And she did not think that having a socialite's image and being taken seriously had to be mutually exclusive.

*It's not either-or, dammit.*

She felt tears welling, told herself they were from exhaustion, and wiped them from her cheek. She rubbed the soap bar in the facecloth, creating a lather, then softly began soaping herself.

Initially, when talk began of her coming to England, it was thought that she would simply do for Whitbey House what she had done so well for the House on Q Street in Washington, D.C.

The House on Q Street was used as an OSS safe house, as well as a hotel of sorts for transients the OSS could not put up elsewhere in D.C. Charity had run it and its staff — while acting as a sort of superhostess — with the precision of a Swiss timepiece, and there was no reason to believe that she could not do the same at Whitbey House.

And Whitbey House — and Bob Jamison — would soon desperately need the help.

First Lieutenant Robert Jamison, a pleasant, red-haired young man, was adjutant, working directly for Dick Canidy. He handled the requisitioning of everything for the OSS station from bedsheets to plywood sheets, laxatives to explosives. And he handled all the paperwork. All Canidy had to do was scribble his name in the signature block authorizing said requisitions — hundreds of them each month. Sometimes, Canidy didn't have to do that; Jamison occasionally signed Canidy's name in his absence. Canidy encouraged him to do so, having explained that that was in keeping with the true nature of his job, relieving Canidy of all the administrative burden that he could.

Bob Jamison had performed superbly — perhaps too well. While he was grateful to work for someone as decent (if demanding) as Dick Canidy, he wasn't exactly thrilled to be stuck ordering laundry soap and such. He longed to contribute something more to the war than being what he called a chief clerk.

He wanted to go operational.

Both Dick Canidy and David Bruce thought that Jamison had the brains and talent for that. He had demonstrated it recently in the setting up of a target for a test of the B-17 drones. That mission had required working with regular military elements (army and navy) who did not have the Need to Know why they had been sent to build massive wooden frameworks on a remote English coastal cliff, nor how it was that almost to the minute the last nail had been hammered home a B-17 "accidentally" crashed into the framework, the aircraft's "pilots" having safely parachuted out before impact.

Jamison had come up with plausible cover stories — in fact, had put together the whole project for the test of flying an aircraft by remote control into the phony "sub pen." No one ever questioned the crash as anything but what Jamison had explained.

As more and more such OSS operations were mounted out of Whitbey House Station, someone had to procure — through channels or other unconventional methods — the matériel to carry them out. Jamison, of course, was the man, and, being damn bright, had over time put the details of so many missions together into a larger picture.

And *that* was what had ruined his chances of going operational.

The Rule One was that no OSS personnel with knowledge of OSS plans other than their own could go operational. And Jamison knew too much about what was going on in and out of Whitbey House Station — the very things that the damn Nazi Sicherheitsdienst gladly would carve him apart, little piece by little piece, in order to learn — and so he was left to do what he did best.

With Canidy disappearing now and again — Canidy being the exception to any rule that Canidy chose, including Rule One — Jamison had simply carried on with his own duties while filling Canidy's as he was able. What he could not handle or did not have the authority to handle, Lieutenant Colonel Stevens took care of either from his office at OSS London Station or from personal visits to the safe house.

Charity Hoche's arrival at Whitbey House, with the grand if somewhat vague title of "Deputy Director (Acting)," only served to solidify in Bob Jamison's mind the fact that he was stuck as chief clerk.

Charity had sensed some friction from the start, particularly when she came to understand that the early word had quickly circulated through Whitbey House that she would be working for Jamison "taking care of the women."

What followed was a subtle, behind-the-scenes tug-of-war between them for control.

Officially, Canidy was in charge. And, officially, Charity was his acting deputy. Not Jamison. But she made a very real effort — sometimes successful, sometimes not — not to push it. She was smart enough to know that the much-liked Jamison could just as well make her job difficult as he could make it easy.

Charity Hoche and Bob Jamison had gotten along reasonably well as he had showed her the ropes. She liked him, and not only because he hadn't made things even more awkward by making a pass at her. He was a nice guy, outgoing and agreeable.

And, over time, she came to understand his frustration, especially when he'd told her about being turned down to go operational, and why.

*How awful,* she'd thought. *I wouldn't want to be told I've done so well at my job I can't do anything else, then have someone brought in above me.*

She understood that that was the source of the friction, and so was a little afraid — if that was the right word — that it might turn to resentment for her being put in charge of Whitbey House in Canidy's absence, even though they both understood how the system worked.

Her rank of first lieutenant did not help. It was an assimilated one, and only recently made, meaning that First Lieutenant Jamison had far more time in rank and thus was technically her superior. But he had also pieced together the information that she held some super–security clearance — he had no idea it was on par with that of Lieutenant Colonel Stevens's Top Secret–Presidential, but he knew it was up there — and that the way the OSS worked was, Jamison could bloody well be a major general, but if Donovan said she was in charge, then, by God, Major General Jamison — or whoever — was going to cheerfully carry out her orders, even if Donovan had to have her made a lieutenant general for that to happen.

Jamison had been around the Office of Strategic Services long enough to know anything was possible, no matter how the real military world operated.

While Charity took care not to abuse her

power, she did understand that there was a distinct difference between being in charge and disliked and being in charge, liked . . . and ineffectual.

*You can't make everyone happy,* she thought, holding the facecloth under the running faucet and rinsing it. *You have to break eggs to make the omelet.*

From Day One at Whitbey House, she'd been determined to prove herself, just as she had accomplished proving her worth in Washington to Wild Bill Donovan. He initially had had his own doubts about her when she first arrived at the House on Q Street. And, clearly, the Philly socialite had earned the Boss's respect.

David Bruce had let Charity read the personal note that Donovan had written to him. In it, the director of the OSS explained how Charity had come to get that security clearance ("I needed a clerk-typist and file clerk with the intellectual ability to comprehend the implications of the project, and to deal with the people involved," he'd written) and how she came to be in England ("As a result of growth in the project, we cannot risk that something might slip past Ed Stevens's attention. My decision is to send you Charity, who, on my authority, has the Need to Know on anything there").

"The project," of course, was the most important one of the war — the Manhattan Project, the pursuit of the atomic bomb.

She knew that she certainly could "comprehend the implications of the project." Beyond the simple fact that whoever built the nuclear device first would win this maddening world war, many would die in the quest to achieve it — some of whom she very likely would know.

And would love.

And that brought up "the people involved."

Quite a few of these people, at one time or another, had come through Whitbey House.

*Like Jimmy Whittaker,* Charity thought, as she adjusted the faucet and added more hot water to the tub.

She knew that Captain James M. B. Whittaker, U.S. Army Air Forces, had been pulled away from Whitbey House and sent on an OSS mission to the Philippines — but not before getting romantically entwined with the Dutchess.

*And likely in this very marble tub,* Charity thought, reaching up to undo her ponytail and begin washing her hair.

Captain the Duchess Elizabeth Alexandra Mary Stanfield, WRAC, was the liaison officer of His Majesty's Imperial General Staff to OSS Whitbey House Station. The enormous property belonged to her — and to her husband, an RAF wing commander shot down and more or less presumed dead.

Whittaker — who was wealthy beyond imagination, and, in fact, owned the OSS safe house on Q Street — could, and *did,* address President Roosevelt as "Uncle Frank." Whittaker had attended St. Mark's prep school with Canidy and Eric Fulmar, and all were like brothers.

These latter two, Charity also knew, had been operational more than once in support of the Manhattan Project. Last she'd heard, they now were operational in preparation for the invasion of Sicily — oddly enough, something about running with the mob, Canidy in Algeria and Fulmar in New York City.

Then there was Canidy and Eddie Bitter. They had been in the Navy together, as instructor pilots at NAS Pensacola. Bitter was a cousin of Ann Chambers — *My God, what about Ann? Where the hell can she be?* — and it had been with Ann at her family's plantation in Alabama that Charity had met Canidy and Bitter. It was right before they had gone off to join what she later learned was the American Volunteer Group in China and Burma, the "Flying Tigers."

Now, she knew, Commander Edwin Bitter, USN, was over at Eighth United States Air Force, Fersfield Army Air Forces Station, with elements of the OSS hidden in the 402nd Composite Wing that was a cover for the explosives-packed B-17 drone project.

And Bitter and Canidy had been Flying Tigers with Doug Douglass — who now was Lieutenant Colonel Douglass, commanding officer of the 344th Fighter Group, Eighth United States Air Force, Atcham Army Air Forces Station. He had just returned from flying temporary duty on an OSS mission to Egypt.

Using a definition of "love" that was *an intense feeling of tender affection and compassion,* Charity Hoche knew that these "people involved," as General Donovan had written, did love one another.

And that she loved them.

There was, of course, another definition of love, a deeper one — *a passionate feeling of romantic desire and sexual attraction.*

This Charity saved for Doug Douglass.

Doug, twenty-five, was slight and pleasant-looking — Canidy ribbed him by calling him a West Pointer Boy Scout, each of which he'd been at different times — but Douglass's intense intelligent eyes revealed something far more.

For one, he was a natural fighter pilot. Painted on his P-38F's nose were ten small Japanese flags (each "meatball" signifying a Japanese kill), six swastikas (for the killing of six German aircraft), and the representation of a submarine (he'd bounced a five-hundred-pound bomb into one at the German pens at Saint-Lazare).

And also there on the nose of the Lockheed Lightning, in newly painted flowing script, was *Charity.*

Doug Douglass officially was not in the Office of Strategic Services. But with the mission to Egypt, that door appeared to have been just now opened to him. Charity expected it to happen any second — between Dick Canidy bending his own rules by letting Douglass hang out at Whitbey House and Doug's father being Wild Bill Donovan's number two in Washington, and now this TDY, he certainly qualified for membership, honorific or otherwise.

*And I don't know if I like that or not.*

*Because I don't know how it is going to affect us.*

At the House on Q Street, even in the presence of Donovan and Doug's father, Charity had made no effort whatsoever to conceal the fact that she had her eyes locked on Doug Douglass. She had thrown all of her energy into getting assigned to be closer to him.

Charity Hoche was determined to marry Doug Douglass and then take him home and make babies.

Not necessarily in that order.

She had hoped that that in fact had happened back in early February — "I think we made a baby," she'd told him lovingly — and had gone on to explain that a woman's desire to carry a man's child was the single most heartfelt indication of love that there possibly could be.

While a baby had not then been begun — *There'll be other opportunities for that* — she had succeeded in sowing another seed.

Doug clearly returned her love — exhaustingly, at times.

She was glad. But she wasn't surprised.

Charity Hoche was accustomed to getting what Charity Hoche wanted.

*And no damn war is going to change that,* she thought again.

Charity's thoughts were interrupted by the blaring of a truck horn from the front of the house. A *lorry* horn, she decided, as it had that peculiar British bleat to it.

She stood and looked at the large window by the tub. Moisture from the tub had formed on it, and she could not make out anything outside the window but vague shapes — what looked to be some small parade of vehicles.

She unlatched the window, then pushed it open a crack. Cool air drifted in, and she got goose bumps.

There, in the drive before the front door, she saw a British Humber light ambulance, with a red cross within a square on its sides, and two olive drab Ford staff cars. It was the ambulance that was blowing its horn. And there was an Army officer getting out of the staff car parked ahead of it.

*That's Ed Stevens!*

*And what's with the ambulance?*

Someone came out of the front door of the house and waved to Stevens.

*Shit! Jamison!*

*I've got to get down there.*

She stepped out of the tub, making a large puddle on the tile flooring. She grabbed a towel, quickly rubbed it about her hair and head, then dried her body, her arms, and finally her long legs. She dropped the towel on top of the puddle, then padded back into her bedroom, where she threw on her uniform.

Once dressed, she felt something odd. When she glanced down at her shoulder-length blond locks, she saw that they were dripping on the uniform.

"Shit, shit, shit!" she said softly.

She stormed back into the bathroom and wrapped a fresh towel around her head.

*It's either the towel or a wet uniform.*

She returned to the bedroom, slipped her shoes on, then went quickly out of the room and down the wide corridor, the fast taps of her heels echoing down the hallway.

She ran down the stairs to the first floor. Then she went down the center corridor of the left wing of the mansion, to what had once been the ballroom. Now it was the dispensary. She entered.

The former ballroom had been set up with sixteen field hospital beds. The beds were in two rows of eight each on either side of the high-ceilinged room. A small flat-roofed enclosure, fashioned from raw sheets of plywood over a framework of two-by-fours, was at the far end of the room. This "building" was remarkable in that it held an office for the two doctors assigned to OSS Whitbey House Station, two examining cubicles, a dentist chair and equipment, a pharmacy, an X-ray room, and a complete operating room.

One of the physicians and a nurse were making the late-afternoon rounds, attending to one of the ten patients, when she came running up.

"I need you both now, please!" she called. "Follow me!"

There was a small crowd gathered at the rear of the British ambulance as Charity Hoche arrived in great haste with the doctor and nurse. The large rear panel doors of the Humber light ambulance were swung open wide.

The only person she recognized was Bob Jamison. Most of the others were in British uniforms. Lieutenant Colonel Stevens was nowhere in sight.

"Who is it, Bob?" Charity said, looking inside the open doors.

"You don't —" the young driver of the ambulance, a moonfaced, somewhat-portly British private, began.

"Don't *You don't* me, Private!" First Lieutenant Charity Hoche heard herself suddenly snap. "I'm in charge here."

The driver, who looked to be barely out of his teen years, held up his hands chest high and palms out as a sign of surrender.

"Right, miss," he said agreeably.

She glared at him, and he immediately stood stiffly, stamped his foot, and saluted sharply, palm outward and fingernails flat to his forehead. "I mean, YESSIR, *Left-*

enant, SAH!"

The driver of the ambulance was looking above Charity's head. His eyes twinkled.

"And might I say quite a lovely towel, SAH!"

He snapped his saluting hand to his side.

Charity's eyes grew large. With a struggle, she ripped the dampened towel off of her head, then threw it to Jamison. It hit him in the chest with a damp *thud,* leaving a wet mark on his tunic. He caught the towel before it fell to the ground.

She turned on her heels and looked at the doctor and nurse.

"In there!" Lieutenant Hoche ordered and pointed in the back of the ambulance, rather unnecessarily.

As the doctor and nurse peered inside, Charity heard a somewhat-familiar British voice say, "I'm afraid it's a bit late for that."

Charity turned to see Lieutenant Colonel Stevens coming down the steps to the front doors with a British officer on either side of him, one in an Army uniform and one in a Navy uniform.

The Army officer looked somewhat familiar, and when he spoke it was with the familiar voice she had just heard.

"So sorry," he said with a smile. "Had to visit the loo."

Lieutenant Colonel Stevens and the Navy officer just grinned.

The doctor had stepped into the back of the ambulance. He knelt beside a closed metal container that was more than large enough for a person to fit inside. Its lid was connected to the main box by a long hinge.

Charity Hoche had never seen anything like it. But then there was a very long list of things in England that she had come to see for the first time — that horrid haggis, for instance, being at the very top. She knew that there had to be someone injured inside of it — why in the world otherwise would they bring a body in a box to Whitbey House?

"There's nothing to be done here," the doctor said, his tone matter-of-fact.

"And just why is that, Doctor?" Lieutenant Hoche demanded.

"I'm afraid he's right," the British Army officer added softly as he lit a cigarette.

Lieutenant Hoche looked at him defiantly and said, "Surely there must be something that we can do."

She looked at the doctor as he pulled up on the metal lid of the container, opening it just enough for puffs of what looked like fog to come floating out.

"Dry ice," the doctor said, and added, "The 'patient' would appear to be frozen solid."

"Wha—" Charity began.

"Quite right," the British Army officer said to Charity. He puffed his cigarette, exhaled a small cloud of smoke, then said with a smile, "As my old friend Groucho Marx says, 'And please don't call me Shirley.' "

First Lieutenant Charity Hoche, all eyes on her, did not know what to say.

After a moment, Stevens broke the awkward silence.

"Lieutenant Charity Hoche, may I present Major David Niven?"

"I'm pleased to make your acquaintance," Niven said formally, offering his hand.

Charity, still not quite sure what was going on, automatically shook it as she replied evenly, "And yours, Major."

Stevens motioned with his hand toward the Navy officer beside Niven.

"And," Stevens continued, "this is Commander Ian Fleming."

Charity thought that Niven and Fleming looked very much alike, with the exception being that Niven had a thin mustache. They were in their early thirties, tall and slender, with dark hair and deeply intelligent eyes. They carried themselves with a real confidence.

"Commander," she said with some authority, slowly recovering from the awkward moment.

"A pleasure," Commander Fleming replied, shaking Charity's hand. "And," he added, motioning toward another naval officer standing nearby, "may I present Lieutenant Commander E.E.S. Montagu of the Royal Navy?"

Montagu stepped forward. He was of medium height, with a slender face and, Charity noticed, very warm, considerate eyes.

"It is my honor to meet you, Lieutenant," he said, taking her hand in his.

"Commander," Charity repeated politely. Then, glancing at Niven and Fleming, she added, "I'm happy to address you gentlemen by your rank, but we tend to forgo the formal use of such here. Please call me Charity."

Niven immediately pointed to Montagu, then Fleming, then himself, and said, "Ewen, Ian, David."

There was a sudden deafening rattle of thunder, and from the gray-black clouds came a driving rain of fat, cold raindrops.

With a raised voice, Stevens quickly said, "I suggest we take this meeting inside."

The downpour then turned even heavier.

Niven and Fleming calmly motioned with a grand sweep of their arms for Charity to lead the way to the front door. She took off at a half trot.

As Stevens, Fleming, Montagu, and Jamison began to follow, they overheard Major Niven address the ambulance driver.

"Private, kindly bring the Genever straightaway."

"YES, SAH!" the private replied with another exaggerated sharp salute.

# [FOUR]
## THE PUB
## OSS WHITBEY HOUSE STATION
## KENT, ENGLAND
## 1850 2 APRIL 1943

The pub was a very large, dark oak–paneled room with twenty-five-foot-high ceilings from which heavy, ornate chandeliers hung at the end of long, thick chains. The pub was packed. A dull roar of lively conversation filled the room, clouds of cigarette and pipe smoke floating up and around the chandeliers.

Against one wall was the cocktail bar, also of dark oak, and it was busy, with a standing-room-only crowd of men two deep. Opposite the bar were tall French doors that led out onto a stone terrace overlooking the rolling country hills and, barely visible in the distance, perimeter fencing and concertina wire.

The pub's old, scuffed upright piano, one more or less still in tune, was angled off the wall at the far end of the bar. A tall, big-boned lieutenant — who had Hungarian features, and whose left foot was in a brand-new plaster of paris cast — sat at it, expertly banging out a lively version of "Alexander's Ragtime Band." His half-empty highball cocktail glass sat on the scarred varnish of the piano lid, vibrating with the tune.

At the far end of the room was a ten-foot-tall carved stone fireplace surrounded by a wall of bookcases. And on either side of the fireplace, appearing as if sentries on duty, stood a pair of ancient suits of armor — the one on the right with a cigar butt strategically placed (one might say crammed) in its face shield, a battered USAAC cotton-twill-and-leather-brim crush cap set atop its helmet, and a woolen scarf in the Royal Stewart tartan pattern wrapped around its neck.

Around the room were arrangements of large and small circular tables, with heavy sofas and armchairs covered in age-softened dark green English leather. Like the bar, the sofas and chairs were filled with an animated crowd of drinkers and smokers.

Right next to the fireplace — and the dashing suit of armor — was one of the larger tables. Seated at it were Lieutenant Colonel Edmund T. Stevens, First Lieutenant Charity Hoche, First Lieutenant Robert Jamison, Commander Ian Lancaster Fleming, Lieutenant Commander Ewen E. S. Montagu, and Major James David Graham Niven.

All were more or less still wet from the sudden rain shower. Beneath Charity's tunic, her blouse, while already straining at the buttons to conceal her ample bosom, was just about transparent — and quite distracting. She appeared oblivious to the situation.

"What can I offer you gentlemen to drink?" Charity said. "Some of your country's nice scotch, perhaps?"

She saw Niven glance at Montagu, who returned the look with a somewhat-serious gaze.

Niven turned back to Charity and — silently grateful that it was a pleasant experience to look her in the eyes and thus avoid gazing at her bosom — said, "That's very kind of you, Lieutenant —"

"Please, it's Charity," she interrupted and smiled warmly.

He smiled back.

"Ah, yes. Right. Thank you, *Charity*. What I was going to say was, I believe we should touch on this bit of business before getting into all that."

"No coffee? Or tea?" she suggested, then realized she was falling back to the hostess mode she had used so well in Washington.

"I'd truly like to get into the good stuff," Niven said, "and the sooner we cover the business, the sooner that can happen. It's preliminary and should not take long."

"Of course," Charity said, nodding understandingly.

She then turned to Commander Fleming.

"I seem to recall seeing you in Washington?" she said. It was more a statement than a question.

She saw Stevens nod, glanced at him, then back at Fleming.

"With General Donovan?" she added.

"That's right," Fleming replied. "But, no offense intended, I remember addressing him as 'Colonel Donovan.'"

"President Roosevelt," Ed Stevens explained, "just gave him his commission, Ian."

"Excellent," Fleming said, smiling. "Well deserved. I'll have to remember to send him a note."

Stevens was aware that Fleming knew Wild

Bill Donovan better than everyone at the table knew their OSS boss.

Ian Fleming — who came from a well-to-do family, his father a member of Parliament and his father's father a financier with very deep pockets — had been a journalist and then a stockbroker. When World War II started, Fleming was already commissioned into the Royal Navy and serving under the director of Naval Intelligence.

In London, during one of the fact-finding missions to Europe on behalf of Roosevelt, Donovan had become very friendly with Fleming. Over many drinks at Fleming's club (Boodles, founded in the eighteenth century at 24 St. James's Place, and now mere blocks from OSS London Station), Fleming had shared his views on what did — and, more important, what did not — work in covert and overt intelligence organizations.

Donovan had been fascinated, and he eventually asked Fleming to draft a plan for what in his opinion he believed would be the most effective of all secret services. With this plan, Donovan began formulating his own structure, which eventually found its way into FDR's hands — and became the working instrument for what would become the Office of the Coordinator of Information and then the Office of Strategic Services.

"I have had the genuine pleasure of visiting with Col — *General* — Donovan in Washington at his office," Fleming said. "Most of our time together, however, has been over drinks at Boodles."

Charity smiled warmly, showing a perfect row of beautiful white teeth.

"I thought I did recall you," Charity said in her finest Philadelphia socialite voice.

Lieutenant Colonel Ed Stevens noticed that and he smiled. Her tone reminded him of the code name he and Wild Bill Donovan privately had given her: Katharine Hepburn.

Charity turned to Niven.

"And forgive me for not quite remembering," she said, "but I cannot quite put my finger on why is it that I find you so very familiar."

Ed Stevens heard that, too — and laughed out loud.

Charity quickly looked at him.

"David is an old friend of Stan Fine's," Stevens said.

"Really?" she said to Stevens.

She looked at Niven. "Then you were in Washington as well?"

"An old *Hollywood* friend," Stevens clarified.

Charity's eyes grew larger as she suddenly

made the connection. She put her hand over her open mouth.

"I am *so* sorry," she said warmly.

"As am I," Niven replied with a grin. "As a rule, I tend not to collect barristers among my friends. But as a skilled barrister will tell you, there are always exceptions to the rule, and, with Stanley, I'll certainly make one."

"No," Charity said, softly putting her hand on Niven's forearm, "what I meant by that was that I am *so* sorry that I did not recognize you as David Niven the actor. I loved you in *Bachelor Mother.* Very, very funny. And that Ginger Rogers — what a delight!"

Niven looked her in the eyes — trying to keep his from drifting down to her breasts — and nodded.

"Yes," he said, his tone mock-saddened, "I am painfully aware that that was your meaning. I was trying to move past the fact that I am no longer so well known nor working with the likes of Miss Rogers. I suppose we all make sacrifices for this war, and that, alas, must be my contribution."

There was polite laughter from around the table.

"In actuality," Fleming said, "we all know that David's plight is not quite so terribly dire. One visit to the bar at the Claridge — where, I might add, Sir Down-on-His-Luck here maintains a suite — proves my point. He, in fact, still has his work, one job in particular being the reason we are here."

"Really?" Charity said.

"We need to use David's talents," Fleming went on, "as well as yours."

"Mine?" Charity said. "I understand David's, but what can I possibly do?"

"It has to do with our friend," Fleming said, "the one we brought in the ambulance."

"Oh, yes!" Charity said, suddenly remembering. "I've been meaning to get to that." She paused. "I do apologize for my behavior when you arrived. I must have looked half raving mad."

"Quite possibly completely raving mad," Niven said, smiling brightly, clearly in jest. "But how were you to know? Frozen patients are not exactly a common occurrence. I've been frozen stiff on stage, but nothing like that."

Charity smiled warmly, flashing her beautiful teeth.

"I do appreciate your saying so, David," Charity said, again using her finest Philadelphia socialite voice. "If you'll pardon the phrase, I was afraid I'd made an ass of myself, especially with your driver."

Charity thought she'd noticed Jamison react to that pronouncement, but when she glanced at him he just smiled politely back at her.

She looked at Fleming.

"You mentioned David's talents," she said. "And mine? What would that be?"

"For starters, Charity," Lieutenant Colonel Ed Stevens said, "we probably will need you to write a love letter or two."

"Excuse me?" she said.

"For the man," Niven said.

"What man?"

"Our friend in the box," Niven said.

Charity looked as if she could not believe her ears.

"You want me to write a love letter to . . . a frozen dead man," she said, clearly not believing what she was hearing.

"Actually, letters plural," Niven said. "I'd have Ian here do it — he fancies himself the writer, you know — but I suggest that he's not exactly skilled at writing from a woman's point of view. And certainly nothing remotely involved with lustful prose" — he paused and grinned at Fleming before finishing — "from the viewpoint of either the female or the male."

Commander Fleming made an obscene gesture with his hand at Major Niven.

"I do hope you'll pretend that you did not see that, Charity," Fleming said. "I like to believe I'm above such acts, but Niven here unfortunately brings out the Sandhurst lad in me."

There was more laughter around the table.

Charity said, "You two were at the Royal Military Academy?"

Fleming nodded.

"We both attended Sandhurst," he said, "but I did not fare as well there as David. We met elsewhere."

Niven laughed.

"Indeed we did," Niven put in. "Would you like to hear the story?"

Montagu was about to say something when Fleming replied, "Wild horses could not stop you from telling it again. You actors never quit. So out with it!"

Niven made a face at Fleming, then turned his attention to Charity.

"I'll make it brief. I was visiting Boodles for my first time. They gave me a tour of the place, then let me loose. I decided to sit by the windows, to watch people walk past while I enjoyed my drink. I didn't realize I was in the silence room."

*Yet another English item of note to add to my education,* Charity thought.

She said: "The silence room? It must be the opposite of this place."

"Quite. It's where one may be left to his

own thoughts," Fleming explained. "The only speaking is with the waitstaff."

"I thought this was *my* story!" Niven said, looking at Fleming.

Fleming shrugged but smiled, unapologetic.

Niven went on: "About the time I settled into a deep, soft leather chair and put my feet upon its ottoman, a large old gentleman with an impressively large walrus mustache came into the silence room. He appeared unhappy to have the company as he glared at me. He found a chair nearby and set about to stare at me —"

"Then began making a *hurrrumph* sound," Fleming interrupted.

Niven picked up the story: "And *hurrrumph* after *hurrrumph.* He then set about to reading his newspaper, making all sorts of noise while flipping the pages. Finally, he called for the waiter, and as he again stared at me he said for the waiter to bring him the list of members. When he got it, and studied it, he made one last *hurrrumph,* glared at me, and left the room. I took advantage of this opportunity to also leave the silence room — only to run right into a rather rude gentleman who I found was laughing uncontrollably at me."

He looked at Fleming, who now was laughing.

"True story," Fleming said. "I stopped laughing long enough to say that I had waited an eternity for someone to be caught using the chair that the eldest member considered his favorite and thus his own! Oh, it was a sublime scene."

"A true story indeed," Niven said, shaking his head and grinning. "And ever since, Ian and I have had a history of running into each other. Such as now."

Montagu looked a bit anxious.

"Yes," he quickly put in, his tone serious, "can we get back to the matter at hand?"

Niven and Fleming made exaggerated motions for Montagu to take over.

"Thank you," Montagu said, then looked at Charity.

"There's much more to do than simply write the love letters," he said. "We have to give our man a life."

"A life?" Charity repeated.

Niven nodded. "Quite. Before we give him a swim."

"A credible life the Germans will believe," Montagu explained.

"One everyone will believe," Niven added.

"Right," Montagu went on. "We have our man. Now we need to create a cover for who he is . . . was."

"Who . . . was . . . why . . . ?" she said, confused, then looked at Niven. "Did you say 'swim'?"

"Charity," Lieutenant Colonel Ed Stevens said, "we brought the body here because what we're going to do within a two-week time frame is absolutely critical to the success of the Allied landing in Sicily. It requires complete secrecy, and we decided that a safe house such as Whitbey House was the best place we could hide a frozen cadaver and not have questions asked or covers blown."

Stevens let that sink in, then, after a moment, decided not to go on. It was clear there was too much information being supplied at once — or, perhaps, not enough — and this really wasn't the place to get into details. He noticed that even Bob Jamison looked confused.

"I realize this is quite a lot to consider. I know it took me some time to swallow," Stevens said, finally. "Complete details to come tomorrow. In the meantime, welcome to Operation Mincemeat."

"Mincemeat?" Charity repeated, and immediately had graphic mental images of her first haggis.

"Ah!" Major Niven suddenly said, looking across the room and starting to half stand and wave. "There he is — finally!"

Charity Hoche looked over toward the

234

door. She saw the driver of the ambulance standing there. In his arms, he cradled what looked to be a very heavy brown canvas bag. He returned Niven's wave, and began to make a direct line through the crowd toward them.

At the table, the private placed the bag before Niven with a *thud*. From inside the bag came the *clank* of heavy glass hitting together.

*That,* Charity thought, *sounds like a booze bottle in that bag — booze bottles.*

"Well done, Private!" Major Niven said loudly. "Now, you may go shine my shoes, brush down my wardrobe, and the sundry other noble tasks of a good batman."

The private, who stood five foot nine, stared at Niven. Then his moon face changed to an expression of amusement. His eyes twinkled.

"With all due respect, *Major,*" the private replied, as he took an empty chair from the adjacent table and pulled it up to the table beside Niven, "you can shine your own goddamn shoes."

Everyone at the table stared at the private, who was now reaching into the bag and pulling out a bottle of clear liquor.

Looking again at Niven, the private went on:

"I just drove that ambulance all the bloody way out here, just oversaw the securing of its frozen passenger in the bloody basement, and now I believe that I have bloody well earned a taste of Genever." He paused. "SAH!"

Niven turned to everyone at the table and dramatically said, "You will please excuse him. As you must know, the war has made good help so very hard to find."

At that point, the private looked at the major — and gave him the finger.

"And I mean that in the most respectful manner, SAH!" he said with a grin.

Major Niven laughed.

When he saw the look of shock on Charity's face, Niven said, "Oh, everyone, please forgive my rudeness. Allow me to introduce my batman, Private Peter Alexander Ustinov." He looked at Charity. "He too is friendly with one Stanley Fine, Esquire."

It was a moment before Charity found her voice.

"You're also an actor?" Charity said to Ustinov.

"A lousy one," Niven answered for him, "if you consider how he plays the role of batman."

Ustinov gave him the finger again.

"And I offer that one with quite a bit more

malice than the first," Ustinov said.

Niven made a dramatic, wide-eyed face and slapped his chest with an open palm.

"Well, then," Niven said, "that must mean only one thing!"

"Precisely!" Ustinov said.

"Private, hand me the Genever," Niven said formally. "I hereby declare this the commencement of Attitude Adjustment Hour. Make that *Hours,* plural!"

Charity saw that Commander Fleming was shaking his head. But she also saw that he was grinning widely.

Lieutenant Colonel Ed Stevens was smiling, too.

And Lieutenant Commander Montagu seemed resigned at this point to the course of events becoming out of his control.

Ustinov took the bottle of liquor he had pulled from the bag, placed it in front of Niven, then glanced over his shoulder at the bar.

"Appears to be a bit crowded over there," he said to Niven.

Niven looked to see, then said, "Not a problem."

He stood, walked over to the dashing suit of armor, and pulled the sword from its baldric. He raised the weapon above his head and pointed its tip across the room.

"To the bar!" he cried out.

This, of course, caught the attention of the crowd at the bar, as did the fact that he had started in their direction. They watched in rapt fascination.

But whether from the fog of booze or from the disbelief in what was happening — or, more likely, from the fact that everyone there was either a student or graduate of Dick Canidy's Throat-Cutting and Bomb-Throwing Academy — no one moved from their place.

And this did not go unnoticed by Ustinov. He quickly got up from the table and went after Niven to intervene.

By the time Ustinov reached Niven, the would-be swashbuckler had stopped in his tracks and quickly brought down the sword.

"Damn blade is heavy!" Niven announced. "And Errol Flynn made it look so easy at the beach house. The sorry bastard must've used a prop."

Ustinov grinned. He had heard the legendary stories of the wild parties thrown for the Hollywood crowd at the bachelor pad that Niven had shared with Flynn. Their wry neighbor, one Cary Grant, had dubbed the dwelling "Cirrhosis-by-the-Sea."

"I can handle things at the bar," Ustinov said.

Niven looked at the bar crowd. Most of the men had turned their attention back to their drinks and conversation. Then he looked at Ustinov and said, "Very well, Private."

As Niven marched back and returned the sword to its baldric, Ustinov went to the bar — then behind it. Both returned to the table at the same time. Ustinov carried a tray, on which were a bucket of ice, two tall, heavy glass shakers, a strainer, and six martini glasses. He put the tray on the table.

"Very good, Private," Niven said. "Well done."

He looked at the crowd at the table and intoned formally, "On behalf of the British Empire and Winston Churchill, I bring to you the Prime Minister's personal martini cocktail recipe. Would you allow me the privilege of sharing it?"

Everyone was grinning.

Charity said formally, "As we have been instructed to interact with our British hosts in any and every positive way possible, I do believe it would be an honor."

Niven smiled.

"Delightful," he said. "Then, with the assistance of my batman, off we go."

Niven lined up the six glasses in two rows of three. Ustinov held up the bucket of ice toward him.

"First, as I'm sure you're aware, one must chill the glass," he explained.

Niven then placed ice cubes in the glasses and spun each glass by delicately turning the stem back and forth between his thumb and forefinger.

With Ustinov continuing to hold the ice bucket, Niven then filled one of the tall, heavy glass shakers with ice. He uncorked the bottle of liquor and poured the shaker just shy of full.

"We keep a healthy stock of Genever in the closet of Private Ustinov's room at the Claridge," he said with a conspiratorial wink to Charity.

"Genever?" Charity asked, prepared to learn yet another new foreign item.

"It's along the lines of gin," Niven explained. "Wheat or rye is used as the spirit base of gin. Juniper berries flavor it. *Genever* is the Dutch word for 'juniper,' and so some overachieving Brit along the way decided to shorten that to *gin*. Which is not exactly correct, as Genever is actually a mixture of rye, wheat, corn, and barley. Our British gin, however, has accents of citrus — the peels of lemon and orange — its pale color coming from aging three months in charred oak barrels."

"Fascinating," Charity said.

"Don't be too impressed. He used to be a booze salesman," Fleming said drily. "In the States, of all places. Ever hear of Jack and Charlie's?"

"In New York? Of course, the '21' Club," Charity said.

"That's the one," Fleming said.

Charity found herself going on: "Jack Kriendler and Charlie Berns are cousins. They opened a speakeasy in Greenwich Village to pay for school. After a few moves, it wound up at 21 West Fifty-second Street."

"Well done," Stevens said.

Charity blushed.

*The one damn thing I know about in all our conversation,* she thought, *and it's the history of a bar my father took me to when he was in the city on business.*

Charity looked at Niven, who now had covered the tall glass shaker that was full with the other shaker and proceeded to vigorously shake the liquor and ice inside.

"Coincidentally, the key to a perfectly chilled beverage is twenty-one shakes," Niven announced. "Not twenty, not twenty-two. Twenty-one exactly."

"So it is true you were the first bartender at '21'?" Charity said.

Niven shook his head. "Not bartender. I was a twenty-two-year-old chap fresh out of

Sandhurst when I went to work as the first salesman for Charlie's booze. He was calling it '21' Brands. It was 1934, the year after the Yanks repealed prohibition. I was an aspiring actor who was exactly that — aspiring — and I desperately needed money. Used to be a photo of me on the wall."

"Still is," Ed Stevens said.

Niven separated the shakers and put the strainer on the mouth of the one with the chilled liquor in it. Ustinov dumped the ice from the martini glasses back into the ice bucket. Then Niven began pouring each glass three-quarters full.

"Glad to hear I'm still famous somewhere," Niven said to Stevens, then looked down at the martini glasses. He turned to Ustinov. "Are we not forgetting something?"

There was a moment's hesitation, then Ustinov said, "Oh, yes."

He produced a half-liter bottle of sweet vermouth from his trouser pocket.

"So sorry," Ustinov said, a grimace on his moon face.

Niven held out his hand, waving his fingers in a mock-impatient *I'll take that* motion.

"Now, this is the very critical part," Niven said. "One Mr. Churchill was very kind as to instruct me."

With great drama, he unwrapped the foil from the top of the bottle of vermouth, then quickly worked the cork free.

"Watch carefully," he said.

He dramatically moved the bottle of vermouth far away from the glasses, then, holding the cork between forefinger and thumb, he swiftly passed the cork over the top of the glasses.

He then quickly returned the cork to the open neck of the bottle and pushed it in noisily with a smack of the palm of his hand.

Charity Hoche let loose a pleasant peal of laughter.

"Very nicely done," she said. "I believe that would be what is called a dry martini."

"Very dry," Niven said, smiling.

"And it should be noted," Fleming added, "shaken, not stirred."

Niven picked up one glass, raised it to his lips, took a sip, then sighed.

"Perfection!" he exclaimed.

He motioned to the other glasses.

"Please, enjoy."

After the first of the martinis disappeared, Major David Niven instructed Private Peter Ustinov to begin preparing a second round using the Prime Minister's personal martini recipe.

Lieutenant Ed Stevens emptied his glass, then got up from his chair. He walked around the table to where First Lieutenant Charity Hoche sat conversing with Commander Ian Fleming.

Stevens touched her lightly on the shoulder.

"Excuse me for interrupting," Stevens said. "Charity, before we get too deep into this next round, could I please have a word with you?"

She looked up at him, as if awaiting some explanation.

Stevens added, "Just a bit of housekeeping before the night gets away from us."

He nodded toward the main door.

Charity Hoche stood, and everyone else at the table still seated also stood.

"If you'll please excuse me," she said.

As Stevens and Charity left, everyone but Ustinov, counting aloud as he stood shaking the shaker, returned to their seats.

Stevens and Charity walked to the doorway, then went through it.

Outside the pub, in the main corridor of Whitbey House, the noise level dropped noticeably.

"Good," Stevens said. "Now I can at least hear myself."

"What's this all about?" Charity asked.

"This is not something that David or Ian could not hear," Stevens explained. "I just wanted to make sure that you heard it, that it didn't get lost in the noise in there, and you could have time to think about it."

"Okay."

"This situation with Operation Mincemeat. David Bruce still is smarting about having been left out of the loop for the Manhattan Project. Now that wound has been reopened because he thinks he's also been kept in the dark on Mincemeat. He thought that I knew about the op, and it took some real work from David to convince him otherwise."

Charity nodded.

"I had no idea about it before David and Ian called yesterday after they had run into John Ford."

Ford, at forty-seven, was a real heavy hitter in Hollywood. Now he was using his award-winning filmmaking skills on the front lines — and getting injured in the process. The documentary he'd made in 1942, *The Battle of Midway,* had won an Academy Award.

Stevens went on: "He's the chief of our Field Photographic Branch. He has been helping set up shop at London Station and getting ready to go back into the field. When Niven found out that he was there, he took the idea of Mincemeat to him. Next thing I know, I'm involved."

"And so you moved the op out here."

"It was the logical thing to do," Stevens said. He paused, then went on. "But there's another pressing problem that brings me out here."

Charity's face was questioning.

Stevens explained: "I need you to find Ann Chambers as soon as possible."

"I have no idea where she is," she said. "I've been thinking about her, wondering, but I don't have a clue."

"No one does. And that's the problem. Her father is demanding to know what we know, to know what Dick Canidy knows."

Charity's eyebrows went up.

"Dick," she said, "doesn't know anything. He's in Algiers."

Charity felt for Dick and Ann; she damn sure knew what it meant to be in love . . . and separated by war.

"I know," Stevens said. "And Ann Chambers's father —"

"Brandon. He's got real clout," Charity interrupted.

"Brandon Chambers does have real clout. And he's been on the phone to the FBI trying to find the OSS and Canidy."

"Oh."

"Yeah," Stevens said. "Oh."

"I wonder if he's tried to get to him through Eddie Bitter," Charity said. "And couldn't, and that's why he's gone to the FBI."

"Why Bitter?"

"He and Ann are cousins," Charity said. "Their mothers are sisters, Mrs. Chambers and Mrs. Bitter."

"That's right. I'd forgotten that."

"But I doubt that Eddie would tell his Uncle Brandon much — if anything. About the OSS, that is. Does he know where Dick is?"

"No," Stevens said. "And Canidy sure wouldn't have told him."

"Brandon Chambers won't give up until he gets what he wants."

Stevens nodded. "And that's why you're going to find Ann — and give Brandon Chambers what he needs — before we get any more attention than we already have."

Charity nodded slowly.

"Let's go back in before our drinks spoil," Stevens said with a smile. "We can pick this up in the morning."

They walked back into the pub.

As they approached the table, Major David Niven noticed with some disappointment that Charity's blouse was now dry.

He held up a full martini for her to take, brought his up in a toast, and declared: "Tonight we drink, for tomorrow we ship our man to sea."

"Next week," Montagu corrected.

Niven looked at him over the top of his martini, said, "Whenever," then swallowed half his drink.

# V

## [ONE]
## PORT OF ALGIERS
## ALGIERS, ALGERIA
## 2135 30 MARCH 1943

Dick Canidy leaned against the side of the warehouse as he watched the unloading of a pair of forty-foot-long wooden-hulled fishing boats. The vessels were moored on either side of a T-shaped dock that was at the far eastern end of the port, a ramshackle area separate from the main military dockage. The longshoremen had been steadily off-loading wooden boxes filled with iced-down fish for longer than the ninety minutes that Canidy had stood there in the dark shadows.

After Canidy had left Hank Darmstadter

with the C-47 Gooney Bird at the airfield, he had stopped in at the OSS villa to drop off his duffel, which held his change of clothing and the Johnson light machine gun and ammo, and to get exact directions to Francisco Nola's dock from Stan Fine.

Fine had warned Canidy not to expect anything like a warm reception when he arrived and he'd been right. Almost to a man, the rough-looking longshoremen had given Canidy glares that clearly related that they did not like being watched by a stranger, even one supposedly known to Francisco Nola.

Canidy caught himself yawning long and hard.

*Damn, it's been a long day!* he thought, when he'd finally finished. *And it's nowhere near being over.*

He once more checked the chronograph on his left wrist.

*Four hours! Where in hell is that boat?*

On the flight back to the airfield at Algiers, Canidy had calculated time and distance and come up with an ETA of the *Stefania* making it to the dock. According to his figuring, the boat was now was an hour and two minutes overdue.

*It was a rough figure but not* that *rough.*

*Either my math's faulty or something's gone wrong.*

*I'm guessing the latter. . . .*

Beside each fishing boat, a boom mounted on the pier was being used to lift the boxes of iced fish from the holds. It was labor-intensive, as the block and tackle and the pivoting boom were manually operated.

With two men pulling on the rope of the block and tackle, the boxes of fish were lifted out one by one. Then another man pushed on the boom to swing each box from above the boat to above the pier. Then the two men at the rope lowered the box to a wooden pallet waiting on the pier.

This was repeated until the pallet had a load of four boxes. Then two other men used a manual lift with steel wheels that fingered into the openings of the pallet, then raised the pallet and its load. With one man pulling on the lift handle and one pushing on the boxes, they maneuvered the fish along the pier and up into the warehouse.

As a load was wheeled past Canidy, he looked at the fish — *Fair-sized blackfin tuna, he thought, maybe sixty-pounders* — and studied the men, who he saw tried not to make eye contact. The one pulling on the handle stopped to open the wooden sliding door. Canidy noticed that he and the others looked less like they were Algerians and more like the Sicilians he'd seen in Palermo.

*Sicilian Mafia, like those on Nola's boat.*

*I really don't like these guys, but I have come to understand them better.*

*Ironically, the fact that they're known as such miserable shits plays in my favor. No one would believe I'm connected — especially to the* capo di tutti capi. . . .

The "boss of all bosses," Charles "Lucky" Luciano, was in the big house, New York's Great Meadow Prison in Comstock. The Guinea thug could have been serving time for any crime on his lengthy rap sheet — running booze, heroin, numbers, not to mention murder.

But, of course, it had been a woman — *women* — who'd done him in.

Luciano was doing time on a record sentence of thirty to fifty years for prostitution racketeering. His hookers had testified against him on charges that finally had stuck — ensuring that the son of a bitch was the one who ultimately got screwed.

Major Richard M. Canidy, U.S. Army Air Forces, had a connection with the ruthless Charlie Lucky because Luciano — ever the savvy operator — still was running his very big, very effective, and very illicit syndicate from his cell.

When OSS Director Wild Bill Donovan

had decided to send Candy into Sicily —
first to find, and then to extricate, Professor
Arturo Rossi before some German SS officer
put two and two together and came up with
Rossi's connection to Professor Frederick
Dyer, whom Candy had just smuggled out
through Hungary — it had been suggested
that Candy would need help from some
type of underground resistance group there.

And without question the underworld of
the Mafia was the best connected, both in
Sicily and in New York City.

As it happened, there in fact had been a recently established relationship — one kept
very quiet — between Charlie Lucky and the
Office of Naval Intelligence (ONI).

The Battle of the Atlantic was raging, and
German U-boat wolf packs were being
damn deadly in their attempt to strangle
England by shutting down the supply lines
sailing from America. Convoys of 441-foot-
long Liberty ships ferried food, fuel, munitions, men, and more to war. Each convoy
contained scores of ships, each ship the
equivalent load of some three hundred rail-
road cars. And Nazi torpedoes were blasting
more and more of them to the Atlantic
Ocean bottom.

It was thought that there existed the very
strong possibility that the so-called fifth col-

umn of German sympathizers in New York City was giving aid and comfort to the wolf packs — anything from sending the U-boats signals that contained intelligence on the convoys to providing boats with food and bladders of fuel for replenishing U-boats in the night.

ONI's Third Naval District was responsible for securing the waterfront in New York, Connecticut, and part of New Jersey. But it was no secret that the Mafia really ran the docks, just as it had its presence in the bars, the restaurants, the hotels — in damn near every business.

Nor was it any sort of secret that Charlie Lucky, despite the mob's run-ins with law enforcement, enjoyed this lucrative position. Clearly, he would not want that balance upset, that control lost. He had whacked many enemies — and more than a few former associates — to obtain it. And, if necessary, he could order hits from his jail cell.

ONI approached Murray Gurfein — the extremely bright thirty-year-old head of the Rackets Bureau of the New York County district attorney's office — with an idea: They should get the mob to root out the subversive elements.

Gurfein agreed. He personally and professionally knew Moses Polakoff, the high-powered lawyer who counted among his deep-pocketed clients one Charlie Lucky. He arranged to meet him for drinks at the Oak Bar of the Plaza.

There, looking out the hotel's enormous plateglass windows overlooking Central Park, Gurfein made his point: Luciano should cooperate, or he could wait for the Nazi Fascists to arrive.

With the glow from the flames of the torpedoed Liberty ships off Long Island clearly visible at night from New York City, the implications of this were not lost on the very intelligent Polakoff.

Before long, Luciano had agreed to help — some said for special considerations, such as a reduction in his sentence, which Gurfein vehemently denied.

The Mafia began keeping its own watch for Germany sympathizers. It also provided union cards to men from Naval Intelligence as cover, getting them jobs, for example, as dockhands (where they could monitor fuel sales), aboard fishing boats (to spy on waterway traffic), and in hotel cloakrooms (to dig through the pockets and briefcases of suspected fifth column types).

Wild Bill Donovan, who, of course, had made his fortune as a New York lawyer, and who was accustomed to acquiring the best and the brightest for the OSS, tapped Gurfein. And when Donovan prepared Canidy to go into Sicily, he had had Gurfein brief Canidy on the mob, and make arrangements for Canidy to begin his own relationship with them.

No matter how much Canidy could intellectually rationalize what Donovan had described as "dancing with the devil," he was still unsettled — *Maybe "disturbed" is a better word,* he thought — by his dealings with the Mafia.

Canidy's rationalization included the understanding that most people seemed satisfied with the simplistic mind-set of *Them vs. Us* that defined who fought on which side of the Allied–Axis struggle. He knew, however, that the reality of the situation was not that clear-cut.

You had to be able to use whatever resources you could in order to achieve the ultimate goal of winning the war.

*And that means dancing with the devil.*

*Quoting Churchill, "If Hitler invaded Hell, I would make at least a favorable reference to the Devil in the House of Commons."*

Canidy's first dance — his first meeting — had been with Joe "Socks" Lanza.

The forty-one-year-old street-tough wiseguy was the business agent of Local 124,

United Seafood Workers Union. As such, he controlled the Fulton Fish Market — in lower Manhattan, in the shadow of the Brooklyn Bridge, and across the East River from the Brooklyn Army Base and Terminal that loaded Liberty ships. This made him an important man in the mob — the enormous market moved fish from the entire eastern seaboard, Maine to Florida — and he took his orders from Luciano.

Charlie Lucky got word to Joe Socks that he considered Canidy's request for help to be in line with what they already were doing, and almost immediately Canidy found himself aboard a fishing boat talking to a Sicilian named Francisco Nola.

Nola had made profound declarations of his dedication to fight Hitler and the Berlin-Rome Axis. His reasons, he said, were many.

For one, Nola's wife was Jewish, and they had had to flee from Sicily to America for her safety. Then the Italian dictator Benito Mussolini, fearful of the power of the Mafia, ordered his vicious secret police OVRA — the Organization for Vigilance Against Anti-Fascism — to sweep through Sicily and systematically arrest suspected mafiosos. Some of Nola's relatives had wound up in the penal colonies on the small volcanic islands north of Sicily, in the Tyrrhenian Sea.

Nola offered to aid Canidy in any way he could. And he more or less had been a man of his word, ultimately helping Canidy find Professor Rossi in Palermo, then shuttling them by fishing boat to the submarine that took them to Algiers.

That had been in just the last week. And in that time, Nola and Canidy had come to learn about the Nazis in Palermo having chemical and biological weapons.

And that the latter involved injecting yellow fever into the human hosts taken from the island prisons.

The men who had wheeled the pallet of fish into the warehouse were now coming out. The hand truck had another pallet on it, this one empty.

Canidy yawned again, then glanced at this watch.

*Now one hour thirty minutes past due.*

*Aw, to hell with it,* he thought, and was just about to head back up the hill to the OSS villa. He would try to arrange for some boat to take him out and look for the damn missing fishing boat, either tonight or at the crack of dawn tomorrow.

But then the longshoreman pulling the warehouse door closed pointed toward the dock.

"There," he said to Candidy, his rough voice emotionless. "The *Stefania*."

Candidy looked and, sure as hell, there he saw the silhouette of the fifty-footer sliding up to the top of the T-dock. There was a burst of diesel exhaust after the transmission had been bumped into reverse to slow the vessel, then the deck crew jumped down onto the pier, threw lines around the rusted iron mooring cleats, and secured the boat.

Candidy forced himself not to appear too anxious to reach the boat but still managed to nudge aside the longshoreman who had pointed out the boat's arrival to him.

On the pier, he maneuvered around the men unloading the first two boats and their gear and finally made it out to the *Stefania*.

Her diesel engine was now shut down. The door to the main cabin slid open and out stepped Francisco Nola. He was a tall, solidly built man, with an olive complexion, thick black hair and mustache, and a rather large nose.

"I thought that that was you," Nola said warmly.

"Frank," Candidy said with a wave from the pier, "I cannot tell you how good it is to see you."

Nola looked at him a bit oddly. "I appreciate the kind words, Dick. But . . . why?"

"I was worried that you —" Canidy paused and looked around cautiously.

Nola noticed that. "Come on board," he said.

One of the crew members pushed past Nola.

Nola called to him, "Go up there and tell Giuseppe that we have some kind of fuel-flow problem and that I want him to take a look at it now."

"Yes, sir," the crew member said and jumped down to the pier.

Canidy caught that. "So that's why you're late coming in? Fuel starvation? After we flew over you, I calculated how long it would take you to reach dock and you took twice the time."

Nola nodded.

"We lost power today more times than I want to count," Nola explained. "I found that if I kept the RPMs low, all was fine. But anything over nineteen hundred, she'd shut down. Just happened today, which makes me wonder if it's trash in the fuel from the bottom of the tank. We're very, very low on diesel."

Nola motioned toward the cabin.

Canidy stepped up onto the boat, and they went inside the cabin.

Nola left the door open, and, after a moment, Canidy understood why.

Stacked all along the walls of the cabin were cases labeled as containing canned almonds and pistachios. Two crew members came in and each picked up a case and carried it outside to a pallet that had been put on the pier.

*Nuts? Wonder if that's really what's in there?* Canidy thought. *But what else could it be?*

*And all this wasn't in here when they took us out to meet the submarine.*

Then another crew member came up from down below. In his arms were two cases of olive oil — each holding six one-liter bottles, according to the stencil on the side of the boxes — and he, too, went out the door and to the pallet.

Nola settled into the well-worn seat atop the rickety pedestal at the helm. There was a box at his feet labeled OLIVE OIL, its top flaps folded closed.

Canidy noticed that on the helm beyond the wooden spoked wheel was a large cutting board. On it was a knife that was long and thin, its blade sharpened so many times that it was almost picklike. Next to the knife was a slab of fish flesh, about a kilo in weight, and a beautiful, bright ruby red color that was not at all bloody. There were squeezed halves of lime and lemon, an open bottle of olive oil, the skins and an end of what had once been a whole onion, a few finger-shaped red peppers, and some sort of minced green-leaf spice.

He wondered more than idly what the hell that was — he hadn't eaten anything substantial since breakfast — but pressed on to more-important matters.

"We need to discuss Palermo," Canidy said. "Especially the cargo ship that I blew up."

Nola nodded. "What about it?"

"Have you had any word from Palermo?" Canidy asked.

Nola shook his head.

"Nothing since we left?" Canidy pursued.

"No. Why do you ask?"

"Is there any way to get in touch with someone there?"

*Assuming they're still alive,* he thought, *and not being dumped at sea, as the Nazis try to cover up the mass deaths from my Tabun cloud.*

Nola considered that a moment, then said, "Not without going there." He stared at Canidy. "What is this about?"

Canidy inhaled deeply, collected his thoughts, then exhaled.

"There was nerve gas on the ship —"

261

"Yes, I know," Nola interrupted. "Which was why you blew it up."

"But the professor we brought out — ?"

"Professor Rossi," Nola offered, his voice rising as it turned emotional. "Is he all right? Something happened to him on the submarine?"

"No, no," Canidy said, shaking his head. "Listen to me, Frank."

Nola stared at Canidy. He kept quiet, motioning for Canidy to continue.

"Rossi has explained to us that it is highly likely that the burning nerve gas from that ship created a cloud that caused mass deaths — anyone near the port, and possibly farther inland."

Nola's eyes grew wide and he quickly moved his hand from forehead to chest, making the sign of the cross over his body.

"Dear Holy Jesus," he whispered.

Canidy nodded solemnly.

"Rossi did say that there was some small chance that it was only the fuel that burned and that the Tabun went to the harbor bottom —"

Nola's eyebrows went up.

"But that's the long shot," Canidy finished.

Nola frowned.

After a moment, Canidy went on: "I have to find out exactly what has happened there.

And I need to know what happened with you after we got on the submarine."

Nola shook his head.

"I do not understand," he said softly and slowly, clearly still in shock over the realization of the atrocity that a nerve gas cloud could cause.

"Where did you go," Canidy said, "what did you see after the submarine left?"

Nola again shook his head.

Canidy sighed.

"Okay," he said. "Did you go back into the port at Palermo?"

Nola shook his head.

"Did you sit and wait for the villa to blow?"

Nola shook his head.

"Jesus Christ, Frank!" Canidy flared. "You've got to help me here!"

Nola looked hurt.

"Sorry, Frank."

After a moment, Nola finally spoke: "It didn't."

"What didn't?" Canidy said.

"It didn't," Nola repeated.

"You mean the villa did not explode?" Canidy said.

Nola shrugged.

"There was only one blast that night," he explained, then softly added, "the one from the boat with the gas."

*Jesus!* Canidy considered that for a moment.

*Well, there could be any number of reasons for that.*

*Maybe Rossi's men at the villa got cold feet after the cargo ship exploded.*

*Maybe they bungled the C-2 charges. Plastic explosive is mostly foolproof — but not completely.*

*Or maybe the charges were discovered by that Nazi sonofabitch, that SS Sturmbannführer Whatshisname.*

*Who the hell knows?*

"What would be the fastest method of getting news from Sicily?" Canidy asked.

"There should be another of our fishing boats arriving in the next day —"

"In the next day?"

"— or two. It's the one I met off of Marsala, when we took on these cases" — he motioned at the boxes stacked about the cabin — "before it continued fishing. And then there's another boat a day or two after that."

Canidy shook his head.

"Not good enough," he said. "That's if they got out of Palermo unharmed. And if they did, then if they didn't break down between here and there. And if not that, then if they didn't get waylaid by some goddamn

264

Kraut gunboat on patrol."

He sighed loudly.

"We don't have the time to wait on so many ifs. We need the intel now."

Nola shrugged.

Canidy looked him directly in the eyes.

"I'm going to ask you something, Frank," he said, "and I want you to think about it before replying. Okay?"

"Okay."

"I need someone to be my eyes and ears in Palermo, someone who is connected and can help me collect information on the Nazis — specifically, their use of the nerve gas and yellow fever. Would you —"

"Yes!"

"I said to think before replying. You don't even know what I want you to do. Because should you be caught, you will be killed."

Nola was silent a long moment, during which time he looked deeply into Canidy's eyes.

"Okay," he then said. "I have thought about it. And this is what I have thought: Sicily is my home and those people are my family. They are already dying. God willing, I will do what it is that you need, and what I cannot do I will find someone who can."

Canidy nodded slowly.

"Thank you, Frank."

Canidy glanced around the cabin, and his eyes settled on the cutting board with its fish and spices. At that moment, his stomach growled.

Nola could not help but notice.

"Would you care for some?" he said.

"What is it?" Canidy asked.

Nola reached farther back beyond the cutting board and from a spot out of Canidy's view produced a glass bowl. It appeared to have mixed in it a little bit of everything that had been on the board. Nola then reached back to the same spot and came up with a half loaf of a hard-crusted bread. He broke off a piece, ran it through the mixture in the bowl, then offered that to Canidy.

"Thank you," Canidy said, taking it.

He sniffed at the mound of food that was on top of the bread. It smelled sweet, mostly of citrus, with a strong spice he could not recognize and with the olive oil that he could. There were cubes of meat cut to the size of his pinkie fingernail and this he recognized as the fish, although it was more translucent, as opposed to the ruby red of the filet on the cutting board.

"Eat," Nola said, smiling. "Is very good."

Canidy nodded, then took a bite of just one corner of the bread and its mound.

The tart juices of the lemon and lime immediately made his cheeks involuntarily pucker. With the war, any citrus — any fruit, period — was extremely hard to come by. It had been longer than he could recall since he had enjoyed the tart taste . . . and the reaction it caused.

Then he tasted the delicate flavor of the fish.

*Tuna. Tender, full of flavor but not fishy.*

And that then was countered by a short-lived, searing-hot spice.

*The red pepper!*

He popped the rest of the bread into his mouth, hoping the starch would ease the fire. It did. And as the citrus caused his cheeks to pucker and then the hot spice flared again, they seemed more subtle this time, his mouth becoming more accustomed to the bold flavors.

He looked at Nola and smiled appreciatively.

"See?" Nola said, tearing another piece of bread from the loaf. He dredged it through the bowl and handed that to Canidy. "Is good, as I said."

Canidy took it, and said, "I could eat this all night! What is it?"

"*Sibesh,*" he said. "The Spanish, who claim they originated it, call it *ceviche*. But my family has been making *sibesh* since my ancestors first took to the sea to fish."

"Very nice," Canidy said, nodding.

"It is a natural marinade. It gently cooks the tuna as it flavors it."

Canidy nodded, wolfed down the second offering, then, with his mouth full, asked, "What is the leafy stuff?"

"Leaves of coriander," Nola said.

Canidy shook his head that he didn't immediately recognize it.

Nola added, "Is also called cilantro."

Canidy nodded.

"One more," Canidy said, "and then I'll stop, before I eat the whole damn bowl."

"You are welcome to the whole damn bowl."

"Thank you but no."

Nola tore off another piece of bread, then piled it so high with the *sibesh* that a third of it fell to the deck as he handed it to Canidy.

Nola shrugged. "I can make more. We have a boatful of fish."

Then Nola reached to the cardboard box that was at his feet and unfolded its flaps. He stuck his hand in and pulled out an opaque-glass one-liter bottle with a paper label that read OLIVE OIL. He then produced two slightly grimy jelly jars from the same box, and, using the cuff of his shirt-sleeve, wiped out the inside of the jars.

*Jesus, we're not going to wash down the fish with a shot of olive oil?* Canidy thought.

Nola took the bottle in one hand and, holding the jars side by side with his other hand — his fingers inside their rims — he began pouring.

Canidy laughed aloud when he saw red wine slosh out, some of the grape splashing on the deck but most making it into the jars.

Nola winked at Canidy. Then he handed one of the jelly jars to him and held up his own in a toast.

His smile quickly faded.

"To killing the Nazi bastards," Nola said.

Canidy looked him in the eyes and saw that he was sincere.

"To killing the Nazi bastards," Canidy repeated, touched his jelly jar to Nola's, and washed down the *sibesh.*

# [TWO]
## OSS WHITBEY HOUSE STATION
## KENT, ENGLAND
## 0655 3 APRIL 1943

"So how did you come about the body, Ewen?" First Lieutenant Robert Jamison, USAAF, said across the breakfast table.

269

Royal Navy Lieutenant Commander Ewen Montagu looked up from his plate that held a partially eaten, thick grilled ham steak, a mound of scrambled eggs, and slices of pan-fried potato. He motioned with his finger, asking for a moment to complete the chewing and swallowing of his mouthful of food.

The small breakfast room — fifteen by twenty feet, a quarter the size of the vast dining room nearby — was dim despite the fact that the dark brown, heavy woolen drapes had been pulled back. A gray light from the overcast morning filtered in through the handcrafted glass panes of the wrought-iron casement windows set in the sandstone wall. There was a single swinging door that led to the main kitchen.

Also seated at the table were Lieutenant Colonel Ed Stevens, First Lieutenant Charity Hoche, Commander Ian Fleming, Major David Niven, and Private Peter Ustinov. They, too, enjoyed their morning meals of ham and egg and potatoes.

A side table held two industrial-sized, restaurant-quality beverage dispensers — one containing coffee and the other hot water — a selection of English teas in square tins, three porcelain teapots, a bowl of sugar, a container of milk, and what was left of a pyramid of a dozen stacked porcelain cups and saucers. On a lone saucer, in a small puddle of cold tea, were four wire-mesh tea strainers and a collection of tea-stained spoons.

Before Montagu was able to reply, Niven, looking to be in some pain, sighed.

"We need a name," Niven said. "We simply can't continue referring to it as 'the body.' " He paused, then dramatically rolled his eyes. "And, my God! I cannot believe I'm discussing such matters over the breakfast table."

He put down his fork and knife, then reached into the front pocket of his pants and produced a small flat tin that contained a dozen or so white tablets. He waved it before the others.

"Would anyone care for an aspirin?" Niven said, politely.

Everyone declined.

"Didn't you already just take some of those?" Fleming said, conversationally.

Niven glared at him through droopy eyes.

"Must you really shout?" Niven said softly. "And for your information, Commander, I take these to thin the blood. They say a daily regimen of one tablet is good for the heart."

"I'd say all those martinis last night should have thinned the blood quite well," Ustinov said.

271

There were chuckles around the table.

Niven glared at Ustinov.

*"Et tu, Brute?"* he muttered, then popped two tablets in his mouth and washed them down with hot tea.

"You're right, of course, about the name," Ewen Montagu said, changing the subject. "We need one. And it must be the right name. But to answer your question directly, Bob, while the war sadly has created a steady supply of bodies — some from battle, some from bombings here, some from everyday natural causes such as old age and disease — none of these worked for our purposes. We needed a military-aged male who, if we were lucky, simply had drowned. But we were having no luck whatsoever."

Montagu sipped his tea, then went on:

"Then, if we did find what we needed, there was the matter of taking away the body from hospital or morgue. You cannot do it without questions arising. The paperwork involved alone is quite daunting, particularly when having to deal with the deceased's loved ones. You soon have too many people getting too close to the secret. So while we discreetly inquired about our needs to select administrators we had connections to at hospital and morgue, months passed, and we came up with nothing useful."

"So then what? You had to resort to getting one from the grave?" Jamison said.

"That was considered," Montagu said, "but for many reasons was dismissed, the primary one being we needed a fresh corpse for this ruse to be convincing. Then, last week, I was at my desk in the basement of the Admiralty when I got a call. A man who in December had lost all of his family — his wife had been staying with his parents — to a Luftwaffe bombing had become so despondent that he tried taking his own life by swallowing rat poison. He hadn't died directly from that. Rather, he'd collapsed in the shell of the bombed home, then exposure caused the pneumonia that ultimately did him in."

Niven dramatically put his fork and knife down on his plate with a *clank*.

"I really can't believe we're discussing this over our food," he said, then set about to sip at his tea.

Montagu glanced at Niven, then saw Fleming make a hand motion that said *Go on*.

Montagu looked back at Jamison and tried to wind up his story: "I put in a call straightaway to Sir Bernard Spilsbury, our distinguished chief pathologist who understands our needs, and explained the new circumstances. He said that it would take a pathologist of his advanced skills to discover the traces of the poison during an autopsy. There were maybe three such in all of Europe — he being one — and certainly none in Spain." Montagu paused and smiled. "Actually, when I inquired Sir Bernard had grunted, then replied, 'Absolutely, unequivocally none.'"

Montagu took another sip of tea and continued:

"He said that they would likely find only water in the dead man's lungs, caused by the pneumonia, which would make his death consistent with drowning and/or exposure at sea. Thus, with no family to make inquiries — all the easier for Sir Bernard to have the paperwork 'misplaced' — and the perfect cause of death, we had our man. He's in his early thirties. He's not in good shape, not physically fit at all, which was fine, as he only has to look like a staff officer."

Ustinov tapped Niven on the shoulder. When Niven turned, Ustinov pointed to the ham on Niven's plate.

"I take it you are not going to eat that?" Ustinov said.

Niven's eyes grew wide.

"Have you not even a semblance of decency?" he said. After a moment, he sighed, then pushed the plate toward Ustinov, motioning impatiently for him to take it. "Be my guest. I seem to have lost my appetite."

Ustinov shrugged, then quickly slid the ham steak onto his almost-empty plate and began cutting into it.

"Charity," Fleming said, spearing a nice-sized cut of grilled ham, "my compliments on the marvelous meals. Last night's beef roast and potatoes was a feast for kings. And now this fine breakfast. I have to admit that when I heard we were coming out here, I envisioned we'd be enjoying, as I heard that American radio commercial say over and over, 'two boxes of Kraft Dinner noodles for one ration point.'"

Charity's pleasant laughter filled the room.

"If you'd like some, Ian," she said in an accommodating tone, "we have a stockroom full of those blue boxes of macaroni and cheese. And Spam, too."

Fleming shook his head as he chewed.

Charity smiled and said, "But thank you for the compliment. Bob Jamison here is actually the one responsible for our finer staples at Whitbey House . . . in fact, is responsible for everything we get here at Whitbey House."

Fleming swallowed, then turned toward

Jamison and said, "My most hearty thanks, Robert."

"Not necessary," Jamison replied. "I'm only following the chief's standing orders. Dick Canidy said as long as we were here, and as long as we could procure what we needed, then that's what we would do. Dick always says that an Army marches on its stomach, and those who are well fed are more prone to follow orders for he who feeds them."

There were chuckles around the table.

"Well, then," Fleming said, raising his tea cup, "here's to Canidy."

The swinging door to the kitchen opened and a British woman in her midthirties appeared. She was attractive, pale-skinned and sandy-haired, about five-four and 125 pounds.

"Aha," she announced, looking at the side table. "There are the teapots!"

"Liz," Charity said, "good morning. Come in. Please join us."

Stevens noticed that Niven and Fleming were getting to their feet. He looked to the door, saw who it was, and also stood.

Stevens well knew the history of Elizabeth Alexandra Mary Stanfield, whose tunic bore the insignia of the Imperial General Staff and whose identity card read "Captain the Duchess Stanfield." Whitbey House was her ancestral home.

She had been assigned as liaison officer between the Imperial General Staff and OSS Whitbey House Station. Wild Bill Donovan had been the first to say that that meant she had been sent to spy on the OSS. When Dick Canidy arrived to run the station, he had immediately crossed swords with her — and ended their first meeting by telling Her Grace that she acted as if she had a corncob up her ass.

It had taken some time to get past that friction, but the Duchess had succeeded in convincing everyone that they were indeed fighting on the same side.

"Charity," the Duchess began, then glanced at the others. Her eyes grew wide when she saw the new faces. "Ian! How delightful to see you! And David and Peter! Now, isn't this a frightening surprise!"

"Please, Liz," Niven moaned. "Do you have to shout, too?"

The Duchess looked from Niven to Fleming to Charity, her eyes asking *What's that all about?*

"It's nothing personal, Liz," Charity said, grinning. "Someone last night had a few tea-many mar-toonies."

The Duchess smiled and looked at Niven. "I'm sure you'll be fine, David," she said warmly. "You always seem to land on your feet."

Fleming went around the table and lightly kissed the Duchess Stanfield on each cheek. Niven, exhibiting great effort, followed suit.

"I'm trying to recall the last time we all were together," the Duchess said. "Wasn't it in the bar at Claridge's right after Christmas?"

"It was," Ian Fleming said. "And while I cannot speak for David, I was more or less behaving myself." He waited for Niven to make the expected face, which Niven did, then went on: "And I'm afraid to ask, but I suppose still no word on the Duke?"

The Duchess shook her head and softly answered, "I'm afraid not. It's been quite some time now since his plane went down. It would appear hopeless. But one never knows for sure when someone is missing, do they? So, I keep my spirits up best I can."

Charity Hoche and Ed Stevens exchanged glances, and Charity was certain they were thinking the same thought: *The whereabouts of Ann Chambers. We have to move on that, too. How, we're not sure. But we must.*

Ed Stevens cleared his throat and said, "You're just in time, Liz." He turned to Montagu. "Lieutentant Commander Ewen Montagu, may I present Captain the

Duchess Stanfield?"

Montagu stepped forward and offered his hand. "I have heard much about you, Duchess. It is an honor. And your home in magnificent."

"Liz, please," she said. "And thank you. I'm grateful Whitbey House is being found to be useful."

Stevens said, "Have you eaten, Liz?"

"Yes, thank you."

"Well, then," Stevens went on, glancing at the table, "everyone would appear to be finished, and I think we can get into the plans of the operation."

Montagu nodded with enthusiasm.

"I should excuse myself?" the Duchess said, looking at Stevens, then at Fleming and Niven and Charity and, finally, Montagu.

Montagu looked ambivalent but was not about to speak before those who were superior.

"I believe that considering where we are," Fleming said, "this is one instance in which having more minds at work far outweighs any concern of too many people knowing about a certain secret operation."

"Agreed," Stevens put in.

"I know I'd like to have another female's perspective, particularly when we get into the writing of the love letters," Charity said.

The Duchess's face was questioning.

"Now there's no way I'm leaving," she said. "I'm intrigued!"

"Well, then, that settles it," Montagu said. "Welcome to Operation Mincemeat, Liz."

She raised an eyebrow at hearing that.

"Thank you," she said. "That is, I hope so."

There were chuckles as Charity pushed a button on the wall behind her. A moment later, two men came through the swinging door. They quickly cleared the table of everything but silverware and the side table of everything but the coffee and tea services.

## [THREE]

"Ewen," Lieutentant Ed Stevens began, "I think it would be a good idea if you gave everyone an overview of what has been going on, what has happened up to our coming here with" — he glanced at Major David Niven — "the, ah, about-to-be-named body."

"Very well," the lieutenant commander said and motioned to the Duchess that she was welcome to take his seat.

The Duchess smiled her thanks, poured herself a cup of tea at the side table, then settled into Montagu's chair as he began.

"Right now," Montagu said, "Hitler knows two things: one, that the Allies will not stop after taking Tunisia, and, two, that we could come in through any Nazi-occupied country or any neutral country. What he does not know is that, barring any major developments, the Allied strategy is to invade the island of Sicily, then go into Italy. This, of course, comes as no real surprise to anyone —"

Fleming interrupted: "Even Winston Churchill has said that 'anybody but a damn fool would know it is Sicily.' "

There were nods around the table.

"And it's our job," Montagu went on, "not to let that damn fool Hitler see that. Or at least believe it."

There were appreciative chuckles.

Montagu continued: "As we all well know, when something is indeed planned it is hard to keep a lid on it. 'Loose lips sink ships,' that sort of thing. Hitler has sympathetic ears in places high and low just waiting to intercept and pass along any news of Allied intentions."

*Like the Manhattan Project,* Charity thought, then glanced at Ed Stevens. When she saw him return the glance, she wondered if he had had the same thought.

"Which is why we came up with the idea for this deception," Montagu added.

"*Deceptions,* plural," Niven said.

"Yes," Montagu said. "David is of course correct. There are other minor *ruses de guerre* in play. One, for example, concerns Sir Henry Wilson. The field marshal's army, as you know, under General Montgomery and based in Egypt, is making motions so as to look as if it is preparing to invade Greece, with the continued threat of advancing up through the Balkans. That should get Hitler's attention."

"In support of that," Ed Stevens offered, "some of our agents at London Station for the last month have had their contacts not so quietly buy up all the Greek drachmas they can get their hands on. Collecting so much currency has gotten the attention of, as you put it, those with the sympathetic ears. It wouldn't surprise me if that information is already in Berlin."

Stevens looked at Charity and Jamison, and added, "Some of our agents here soon will be training to work with the Greek Resistance. We'll send them in to help increase operations to draw the Germans' attention from Operation Husky. That's so that when the Germans swallow Mincemeat and they begin shifting, say, armored divisions to

Greece, we'll blow railroads and highways, forcing them to move more slowly with the tanks under their own power."

Montagu nodded.

"All pieces of the larger puzzle," he said. "And our piece of deceit is the biggest, the one we devoutly hope will convince Hitler and his planners beyond any doubt, causing them not to reinforce the defense of Sicily."

"We're going to accomplish that with a frozen cadaver?" Bob Jamison said, incredulously.

The Duchess was sipping tea. She almost dropped her cup when she heard that. She turned quickly to look at Jamison, then at Montagu.

"I suppose it's too late for me to excuse myself?" she said lightly.

Montagu had not missed her reaction.

"We have preserved in a sealed steel case in the basement," he said to her, "the body of a man who we will outfit with certain papers that — again, we devoutly hope — will deceive the Germans."

"My home is now a morgue," she said wistfully before taking another sip of tea.

"I would not put it that way," Montagu said carefully. "What we will do with the body here is create the appropriate cover — papers, uniform, and other accoutrements

— then a week or so from now, take it to sea."

"Interesting," the Duchess said, nodding.

"But I'm getting quite ahead of myself." He reached down to the table for his cup of tea, took a sip, then returned the cup to its saucer and went on: "Our ultimate mission is to have, quote, most secret, unquote, information — disinformation — on the true plans for Operation Husky fall into the hands of those sympathetic to Hitler. It will then find its way to the German High Command, where it will be judged credible and acted upon."

He paused, then added, "And how do we do that?"

Montagu looked around the room while tapping his temple with his forefinger.

"By second-guessing the German mind," Montagu went on. "We have to consider not what we necessarily know to be true but, rather, what we believe is the German perception of what we know. If they think, for example, that we are inclined to take Greece — even though we know that we aren't — then it is easier to convince them that that is indeed what's going to happen."

"They already believe it," Charity said, nodding her understanding. "They're just looking for confirmation."

"Yes," Montagu said.

"Frankly," Fleming added wryly, "we're finding that second-guessing the German mind is not nearly as difficult as persuading our own superiors. And I'm not even including those in SOE!"

Ed Stevens made an exaggerated look of shock. "You mean to say you have trouble with your brass? And the exalted SOE!"

There were chuckles.

"I'm terribly afraid so," Montagu said. "And it often has been for the reasons opposite those concerning perception. To use the same example, our people knew we weren't invading Greece and then the Balkans, so this knowledge made it harder for them to believe our deception was solid."

"Also, when we first ran the idea up," Fleming explained, "everyone felt that they knew the German mind better than we did. It seemed that every part of our plan was questioned at one level or another. If it wasn't for the mastiff-like tenacity of Ewen here, Mincemeat would have died a long time ago."

Montagu looked at Fleming and appeared to take a quiet pride in the praise.

Montagu then turned to the others and went on: "We had made sure we had it pretty well worked out before we took it higher, to the head of British Naval Intelligence, then on up to Prime Minister Churchill, who ultimately approved it."

He went to the side table and refreshed his cup of tea.

Niven signaled for Ustinov to do the same for everyone at the table and the batman nodded, got up, retrieved a teapot, and began pouring.

Montagu went on:

"For example, our first idea — feeding information through a doubled agent using a wireless — we dismissed almost as quickly as we first thought it. Too obvious. If the disinformation we sent was not quickly dismissed at a low level — such being the nature of mistrust in a double agent — then it would be dismissed — or even lost outright — somewhere along the chain long before it reached the High Command. And we simply did not have the time to wait and see if that worked."

As Montagu took a sip of his tea, Fleming said:

"Likewise, another idea was to insert in occupied France an agent, similar to our man downstairs, but by parachute. He would carry a W/T, which we would expect the enemy to capture. They would then operate the radio as if the agent had in fact survived.

This in essence would have been the equivalent of their running a double agent. They would act as if they were the agent, and we would play along, sending both genuine factual information — harmless intelligence that they could authenticate — with disinformation supporting the deception."

"The first obstacle we found with that idea," Montagu said, "was making the dead body look as if it had died during the parachuting — not before. The obvious solution was to rig the parachute so that it opened only partially. Such an impact with the ground would of course kill any man. Unfortunately, it also would very likely cause the destruction of the W/T."

"And operation over," Fleming added.

"But even if the radio survived," Jamison said, "say, the chute snagged in a treetop, there would be another even bigger hole with that scenario. Agents don't carry their codes, and so whoever captured the W/T would find it about as useful as a rock."

"True," Fleming put in. "Agents are not *supposed* to carry their codes. We looked for a plausible reason around that, to have what might be a, quote, careless and absentminded, unquote, agent carrying only his code, or even thinking himself somewhat clever by burying the real code in a list of fictitious ones. But, not surprisingly, we failed in that miserably. It would be considered suspicious immediately. So we'd have a situation where we could send all the telegraphy messages we wanted and they could decode them as best they could using their usual means. But if they didn't have the unique code of the double agent, there would be no way for them to continue 'his' part of the conversation. So this idea also was dismissed with haste."

"After much back-and-forth over months with everyone between us and the prime minister," Montagu said, "we finally worked out a framework that was approved by all."

"What about AFHQ?" Charity said. "I assume General Eisenhower has signed off on it."

Montagu looked to Fleming, then to Stevens, for guidance.

Stevens and Fleming exchanged glances and seemed to have the same thought: *Innocence out of the mouths of babes. . . .*

"Did I say something wrong?" Charity said.

There was no way that either Fleming or Stevens could get into the real reasons why Operation Mincemeat had developed in the manner that it had. For that matter, damn near no one could — not unless they were privy to the personal communications between the President of the United States and the British Prime Minister.

Churchill was spending a great deal of time and effort trying to influence FDR — some said "manipulate the great manipulator" — trying to keep his focus on the war in Europe. There was more than a little reasonable fear in London that if the Americans accelerated the moving of assets to fight the growing war in the Pacific, the impact on Britain would be great — prolonging the war with Hitler perhaps to the point of losing it.

Thus, Churchill considered success in Sicily critical on a number of levels and was going to do whatever was necessary to see that Mincemeat was successful.

Including keeping Mincemeat hidden from that Yank commander at AFHQ.

What Stevens and Fleming did know was that Wild Bill Donovan had approved of this later-rather-than-sooner business of getting Ike's approval — going so far as to repeat what he'd personally told FDR: "It's hard to blow your nose anywhere near AFHQ without his explicit permission." The OSS director well understood that more often than not that was how things had to be done in their business — that secret services worked best in the shadows. And Donovan — who *was* privy to the fact that Churchill was working Roosevelt because Roosevelt had confided in him — believed in the soundness and necessity of the operation regardless of the political play at the top.

"Nothing wrong at all, Charity," Stevens said. "We are — how shall I put this? — in the due process of accomplishing that. Until we do, we want to keep it quiet. Which gets back to why we came out here in the first place."

Charity nodded her understanding.

"We are confident that we will get General Eisenhower's approval," Montagu said as he walked back over the side table, under which was a leather briefcase. He bent over, picked the case up, then put it on the table.

"Due to the complexity of what we have so far done," he went on, opening the case's clasps, "and what we are doing now, it will be easier to sell it not exactly as a *fait accompli* — but as close to one as possible. As Prime Minister Churchill says, time taken to cancel is quite shorter than time needed to plan."

"If Ike nixes the idea," Stevens said, "we can call off the op right up to the very last minute, when the agent is launched from the sub."

That triggered curious looks from Jamison, the Duchess, and Charity.

"Submarine?" Charity said.

Montagu was nodding as he pulled a folder from the case.

"The *Seraph,*" he said.

He opened the folder and produced a single sheet.

"This is an abstract of what I gave last week to Lieutenant Jewell, the sub commander," Montagu said. "I think it rather well sums up what we're trying to do."

He handed it to Charity, who immediately held it out to Stevens.

"Thank you," Stevens said, declining to take it by holding up his hand palm out, "but I've already read it."

"As have we," Fleming said, motioning to Niven and Ustinov.

Charity nodded, then let her eyes fall to the page:

— MOST SECRET —

DUPLICATION PROHIBITED

OPERATION MINCEMEAT

1. Object.

To cause a briefcase containing documents (both ones most secret and others of a personal nature) to drift ashore as near as possible to Huelva, Spain, in such circumstances that it will be thought to have been washed ashore from an aircraft which crashed en route from the U.K. to Allied Forces H.Q. in North Africa.

2. Method.

A dead body in the battle-dress uniform of a Major, Royal Marines, and wearing a "Mae West," will be taken out in a submarine, together with the briefcase, and a rubber dinghy.

The body will be packed in dry ice in a light-gauge metal container (6 feet 6 inches in length, 2 feet in diameter, and an approximate full weight of 400 pounds). As dry ice gives off carbon dioxide, container should be opened only on deck.

3. Position.

Body, briefcase, and raft should be put in water at same time as close to shore as Huelva as possible, northwest of river mouth.

4. Those in Know at Gibraltar.

Flag Officer in Charge and his Staff Officer, Intelligence are the only ones to be informed.

5. Signals.

If operation successful, signal "Mincemeat completed" from Gibraltar Staff Officer, Intelligence, to Director of Naval Intelligence.

6. Cancellation.

If necessary, signal "Cancel Mincemeat," then sink the case with body inside in deep water. Deliver briefcase to Gibraltar Staff Officer, with instructions to burn it unopened.

7. Abandonment.

If necessary, signal "Mincemeat abandoned." Follow Para. 6 above.

8. Cover.

Container label of "Optical Instruments" provides cover during operation. Afterward, cover is that we hope to trap an active German agent in order to get sufficient evidence to have Spaniards eject him.

It should be impressed on the crew that any leakage before or ever after the operation will compromise our power to get the Spaniards to act in such cases.

Also, if Spaniards ever suspect this as a plant, there would follow far-reaching consequences of great magnitude. Secrecy is paramount.

E.E.S Montagu

Lt-Cdr. R.N.V.R.

31.3.43

"Fascinating," Charity said as she passed the sheet to Jamison. "Okay, so now what?"

"Now," Montagu said, his tone solemn, "we create our man."

# [FOUR]
## OSS ALGIERS STATION
## ALGIERS, ALGERIA
## 0810 31 MARCH 1943

"My plan right now, Stan," Major Richard M. Canidy, USAAF, said to Captain Stanley S. Fine, USAAF, "subject of course to change at any damn moment, is to run a modified Special Operations team. Instead of an officer, a local liaison, and two radio operators, it's just going to be Nola and one commo man."

Canidy and Fine and Free French Forces Navy Commander Jean L'Herminier, captain of the submarine *Casabianca,* were seated in the main dining room of the villa. The morning breeze blew in through the open double doors that overlooked the harbor. The table had just been cleared of the breakfast plates. Canidy and Fine had china mugs of coffee. L'Herminier sipped tea from a heavy, clear-glass cup.

Over breakfast, Canidy had explained everything he had learned from Francisco

Nola — specifically, that they still had no clue about what had happened in Sicily after Canidy blew up the cargo ship, that the villa with the yellow-fever hosts might still be intact, and that Nola had agreed to be Canidy's eyes and ears in Palermo.

"What about the officer?" Fine said.

"Me," Canidy replied. "I'll stay as long as I have to stay." He paused. "Which may not be long, if what we expect to find is in fact there."

"Are you sure of this plan, Dick?" L'Herminier said.

Canidy shrugged.

"Hell if I know, Jean. We can always add more men later. Right now, though, we do not have that luxury. We just don't have time to wait for more. I need to know about the gas — and I'm really no further along in that regard than I was yesterday. After I get all that worked out — *if* I do — then we can get back to the discussion of setting up a resistance network on the island."

L'Herminier nodded.

"Well, I can certainly get you in," he said, trying to be encouraging. "The boat is being replenished as we speak."

"Thank you," Canidy said. He looked at Fine. "I need you to do something for me."

"Shoot," Fine said.

"The wireless operator for Nola."

"What about him?"

"There's a guy at Dellys, one of the ones Corvo brought with him from the States. I saw him working a SSTR-1 set — the suitcase radio?"

Fine nodded.

"Corvo won't want to lose him," Canidy went on. "And while I don't blame him, I do need him more than Corvo does right now."

"No one here in the villa's commo room would do?"

"Any of them Sicilian?" Canidy said.

Fine considered that a moment, then shook his head.

"I don't think so," Fine said. "We can go upstairs and ask. You do know that the practice message traffic from the Sandbox is with our radio operators here."

"I didn't," Canidy said, "but that doesn't surprise me. If Sandbox called Club des Pins, they'd probably only get static in reply. Literally."

L'Herminier's expression showed he did not follow that.

"We have agents training with the SOE there," Canidy explained, "and our British cousins aren't exactly being the model of cooperation with this fledgling organization we call OSS."

L'Herminier nodded his understanding.

"If it winds up being Corvo's man," Fine said, "do you have a name?"

"Shit," Canidy said, then thought a moment, then chuckled. "Jones," he added.

Fine started to write that down on the pad before him.

"No, no," Canidy said, chuckling again. "That's his training cover name — I think all of them are using it. I didn't get his real one."

He thought another moment, then said, "Just tell Corvo he looks Italian American, about age thirty, and probably comes from a sales background, very likely was the manager of some large territory."

Fine was writing it all down, nodding. "Okay. I'll get on the horn to Corvo."

"And have Darmstadter go fetch him from the Sandbox?"

Fine nodded as he noted that.

"Done."

"Am I missing anything?" Canidy said. "No doubt I've forgotten the most important element."

"It's not the most important one," Fine said. "But what about Professor Rossi?"

"Rossi! Good question," Canidy said. "Can you think of any reason to keep him here?"

Fine shook his head. "No, but you were the

one who wanted him on ice. I can think of plenty of reasons why he should be headed for the States. One big one in particular."

Canidy nodded at the reference to the Manhattan Project.

"I agree. Plus, with him gone, that'll be one fewer thing to worry about AFHQ sticking its nose in."

He took a healthy swig from his coffee mug, then looked at L'Herminier.

"Tell me what it was that that Owen at AFHQ wanted from you, Jean."

L'Herminier shrugged.

"I really don't know," he said. "When I finally got there — late, as I was pointedly told by his assistant, because something had happened with the driver he had sent for me —"

"I might know something about that," Canidy said, grinning.

"About what this aide to Eisenhower wants?"

"Well, maybe that. But I know what happened with the driver."

"They said his car was stolen," L'Herminier said. "Right there at the naval dock, where we tied up."

"Borrowed," Canidy said.

Fine chuckled.

When L'Herminier looked at him, Fine explained, "Canidy swiped your car."

"Borrowed," Canidy repeated. "I gave it back. So, not stolen, not swiped. *Borrowed*. If that ensign had damn well done what I suggested — run the professor and me up here, then gone back to get you; there was plenty of time for all that — then none of this would have happened."

L'Herminier nodded as he took it all in.

"Yes," he said, "but then I would have been timely with my appointment with Lieutenant Colonel Owen."

"Ha!" Canidy suddenly said. "Then it worked out perfectly after all!"

"Dick's probably right," Fine said. "Odds are that Owen needlessly would've caused you some grief. Or us some grief. It's what he does best."

L'Herminier shook his head, then said, "Owen's secretary said that I was to come again this afternoon. 'Fifteen hundred hours, sharp,' she ordered in that snippy Brit way."

"Damn shame," Canidy said, smiling.

"What is a damn shame?" L'Herminier said.

"That you're going to miss today's meeting, too. Fuck Owen. We have a boat to sail."

L'Herminier looked at him for a long moment.

"There is every chance," Fine put in, his

tone reasonable, "that if you were to duly report to Owen's desk at the appointed hour, you would be so informed by this snippy Brit lass that Lieutenant Colonel Warren J. Owen was in meetings and unavailable for an indefinite period of time, and, further, that the colonel had said, as aide to General Eisenhower and concerning matters of interest to the Allied Forces commander, that your orders are to await his return. Have a seat, and please don't disturb anyone."

Canidy was nodding his agreement.

L'Herminier remained silent for some time. Then he said, "Why is this?"

Canidy smirked.

"That's just the great kind of guy he is," he said, his voice thick with sarcasm.

"Remarkable," L'Herminier replied.

"Yeah, unfortunately," Canidy said. "Check the dictionary under REMF —"

L'Herminier looked confused.

"It stands for 'Rear Echelon Mother Fucker' —" Canidy explained.

L'Herminier's eyebrows went up at that.

"And next to the definition, you'll find that chair warmer's photo."

"You sound like you've had a bad run-in with this Owen," L'Herminier said.

"Not directly," Canidy said, glancing at Fine, then looking back at L'Herminier.

301

"But just about everyone else I know has — or knows someone who has — and it would seem to be just a matter of time till I have that distinct pleasure."

"The reason Owen and everyone else is out of sorts at AFHQ," Fine added in the even tone of a lawyer counseling a client, "is that Eisenhower has everyone running in circles with this divine declaration that there will be cooperation among the Allied Forces under his command. He means well. But we all know what happens when those who mean well —"

"They fuck it up for us few who are actually getting something done," Candidy interrupted, "that's what."

Fine nodded, then went on: "According to my sources there at AFHQ, it's causing more division than unity because Ike is bending over backward to accommodate the Brits —"

"And that," Candidy finished, his tone disgusted, "is making the Americans feel shorted — by their own commander! Our OSS agents being snubbed at Club des Pins is a prime example. Thank God we've got the Sandbox or I'd be out of luck finding a commo man ready to go." He grunted. "There's no end to the shit being swallowed thanks to Ike's steady drumbeat of 'in the interests of inter-Allied unity.' "

Fine laughed. "You sound just like Georgie Patton."

Canidy grinned. "That's who I was told said that. I stole it. Which doesn't mean I don't believe it, too."

"Beyond all that, there is some legitimate reason for the craziness at AFHQ," Fine said. "They're up to their asses in alligators with the fighting in Tunisia, where we'll soon have some three hundred thousand troops. At the same time, AFHQ is making early plans for the Husky op — and not doing well with that at all."

"Doesn't help that the Brits are in charge of the op," Canidy said, "making Eisenhower little more than a figurehead. Beating his own men up to 'Cooperate! Cooperate!' "

"I can't argue with that," Fine said. "Word is that Alexander's leadership right now is tenuous at best, and that has Tedder, Cunningham, and Montgomery squabbling among themselves."

Neither Canidy nor L'Herminier was surprised to hear that Air Chief Marshall Arthur Tedder, Admiral Andrew Cunningham, and General Bernard Montgomery held different opinions of how the invasion should proceed.

"Is nothing concrete getting done on Husky?" Canidy said.

"Oh, there are plans," Fine said. "Just too many. As you might expect, each man's thoughts follow the lines of his particular service. Cunningham wants to spread out the landings so that the Allied fleet has the most security. Tedder wants priority to be the taking of southeast Sicily's airfields so he can have them for his aircraft. And Montgomery, carrying Alexander's water, is pushing for an invasion of southeast Sicily with the ground forces attack as a single unit."

Canidy shook his head. "And what does General Patton have to say? Doesn't matter. He can't be heard over the *rat-a-tat-tat* of Ike — busier than a one-armed wallpaper hanger — beating the damn drum of inter-Allied unity." He paused, then dramatically added, *"C'est la guerre!"*

Fine and L'Herminier chuckled.

Canidy drained what was left of his coffee in one gulp and put the mug on the table with a *thud*.

"We need to get the hell out of here," he said, standing up. "And before we do that, Stanley, I have to raid your warehouse downstairs. But first, let's go talk to your commo guys."

# VI

## [ONE]
## OSS Whitbey House Station
## Kent, England
## 1155 3 April 1943

Private Peter Ustinov led a procession into the breakfast room that included First Lieutenant Robert Jamison and four men who wore British uniforms. All but one of the six were carrying typewriters; the last in line manhandled a very big, heavy cardboard box.

"The typewriters can go on the big table," Lieutenant Commander Ewen Montagu, of Royal Naval intelligence, said as he stood pouring tea at the side table, "and the box on the floor beneath it."

The Duchess Stanfield, Lieutenant Colonel Ed Stevens, Major David Niven, Commander Ian Fleming, and First Lieutenant Charity Hoche were seated at the big table. Stevens, Niven, and Fleming stood up and made room for the machines.

Charity studied the men helping Ustinov and Jamison. She had seen a couple of them when the caravan had arrived late yesterday with the ambulance bearing the body in the metal box. They wore, she saw, the uniform of the British Motor Transport Corps, but experience told her not to take that at face value.

Jamison and Ustinov each carried a nearly new British Oliver manual typewriter to the table. One was a Special Model 15 and the other a Special Model 16. They carefully placed both on the table.

The next two men followed with a pair of Hermes — the manufacturer plates stamped HERMES MODEL 5, PAILLARD S.A., YVER-DON, SWITZERLAND — and formed a line with these next to the Olivers.

The fifth man — who was brawny but still labored under his load — stood waiting with an Italian Olivetti Model M40 under one arm and a hefty Standard Model 16, made by the Remington Typewriter Co., New York, U.S.A., under the other. The men who had just put down the twin Hermes took these from him and put them on the table.

As they did so, the last man put down the heavy cardboard box on the floor beneath the Olivers. It made a loud *thud,* and the big man looked up at Montagu, his face apologetic.

"That's fine," Montagu said to him, then added to the others, "Thank you, gentlemen."

"That," Ustinov announced loudly as he shook his arms in a manner suggesting great relief, "was almost as exhausting as when we moved that canister down to the basement. Wasn't it, men?"

They looked at him, not knowing what to say.

"Of course it was," Ustinov answered for them. He looked at Niven. "Permission to retire for an hour's recuperation, sir?"

They now understood and smiled.

"Permission denied," Niven said. "You can take your bloody nap later."

Ustinov looked at the men in the uniform of the British Motor Transport Corps and shrugged.

"Sorry, I tried," he said.

"What makes me think you weren't doing that precisely for their benefit?" Niven said.

" 'He that sees his men well rested ensures a loyal soldier,' " Ustinov quoted. "Shakespeare said that."

Niven looked at him a moment in disbelief, then said, "Are you sure? And, regardless, what is it that you mean?"

Ustinov shrugged. "I'm fairly sure he did. If not, he should have." He paused and there

307

was a mischievous look in his eyes. "Just trying to keep my men satisfied, SAH! I hear
that's the mark of a good superior."

There were chuckles.

"If it's all right with everyone," Jamison
then said, "I really need to tend to some
tasks involving my regular duties. If I don't
get at least the requisition paperwork filled
out and signed, we may all very well find
ourselves starving."

Commander Fleming suddenly held out
his right arm stiffly and pointed to the door.

"Leave!" he said with great drama. "I for
one will not be responsible for you not being
able to fulfill your duties — or, more important, my stomach!"

Lieutenant Colonel Ed Stevens laughed
appreciatively.

"Do what you must, Bob," Stevens said.
"Join us when — *if* — you can. I have a feeling we're going to be at this for some time."

"Thank you, sir," Jamison said. "I'm sorry,
all."

"No apology necessary," First Lieutenant
Charity Hoche said, suddenly hoping her
tone did not make her sound as if she were
pulling rank on him as Deputy Director
(Acting) OSS Whitbey House Station.

"Thank you," Jamison said, not seeming to
have taken it in that manner. "Believe me, I

308

would rather be involved in this."

Jamison then turned to the men in the uniform of the British Motor Transport Corps.

"If you gentlemen have no other plans, I could use some help," he said.

The brawny one looked to Montagu and said, "Commander, would that be permissible with you? We've all about gone mad waiting for something to do." He looked at Ustinov and added, "With respect, bringing these machines up from the basement was a welcome diversion."

"That's it," Ustinov said. "Ruin it for me! Dig deeper mine grave!"

There were chuckles.

"Very well," Montagu said and looked at Jamison. "They're all yours."

"Don't wear them out, Bob," Ustinov put in. "I don't plan to move that massive metal box by myself!"

As Jamison and the men left, those remaining in the room sat back at the table.

"As you may have gathered," Montagu then said, "the typewriters are for the letters we're to compose. I collected a variety of brands in order to give each letter its distinct characteristic."

He pointed to the Olivers.

"These, for example," he went on. "You may know that the special models 15 and 16 were manufactured specifically for British government offices. Thus, we'll use them for those letters we write for the brass."

"I see," Charity said.

"And the box contains a great variety of stationery and business letterhead that we collected for our purposes," he added.

Charity nodded, now clearly in thought. She looked across the table, then motioned for the sheet that was before the Duchess.

"May I?" she said.

"Of course," the Duchess replied, and slid the Most Secret paper to her.

"Before we get into all that," Charity said.

"Yes?"

"You were speaking earlier about how everything came together to this point."

Montagu was nodding.

"I'm unclear on a couple of things."

"Ask away."

Charity picked up the paper and looked again at its first part.

1. Object.

To cause a briefcase containing documents (both ones most secret and others of a personal nature) to drift ashore as near as possible to Huelva, Spain, in such circumstances that it will be thought to have been washed ashore from an aircraft which crashed en route from the U.K. to Allied Forces H.Q. in North Africa.

2. Method.

A dead body in the battle-dress uniform of a Major, Royal Marines, and wearing a "Mae West," will be taken out in a submarine, together with the briefcase, and a rubber dinghy.

"Numbers one and two," she went on. "How was it decided that it would be a Royal Marine, a major, and that he would be put ashore at Huelva?"

Montagu raised his eyebrows and looked at Fleming and Niven.

"No offense intended," Charity added reasonably, glancing at them. "I do not mean to sound critical. It's just that I think it might be good to know as we get into all these letters."

"No offense taken," Montagu replied. "It's just that a great deal of effort went into it, so much so over many months, as we mentioned earlier, that frankly even if I could give you a complete chronology, we do not have the time for it."

Fleming looked at Montagu and said, "How about simply explaining how we arrived at numbers one and two?"

"That'd be fine," Charity said.

Montagu nodded. "Very well."

He took in a deep breath, composed his thoughts, then said, "As we have mentioned, we entertained many scenarios — some quite good, some absolutely worthless. We ultimately arrived at the idea of a courier of some importance carrying correspondence between higher-ups. These letters are to be so secret that they could not be sent by wireless or any other method. And to get our courier to the enemy — in one, credible piece — we decided to use a submarine, having discarded the use of a flying boat or an escort ship diverted from a convoy as being too risky."

He sipped his tea, then went on:

"Now, as to the Royal Marines, they are of course an elite force. And the rank of major is important, but" — he looked at Niven — "no offense to anyone present, not too important so as to draw undue attention."

"Quite all right," Niven said nobly, waving it off with a flick of his left wrist. "I'm accustomed to being unimportant."

"So a major in the Royal Marines met our criteria for 'a courier of *some* importance,'" Montagu finished.

"Okay," Charity said. "That's logical."

"We picked Spain," he went on, "because we know that Admiral Canaris of the Abwehr and Francisco Franco are quite friendly, quite close, actually. Accordingly, it's commonly overlooked that the quote neutral unquote country teems with German spies, including a very active one in Huelva. Which is why we selected Huelva specifically — nothing goes on there without this German agent's knowledge. We get our major and his briefcase to shore there, it's as good as being in Hitler's hands."

"We hope," Fleming added.

Montagu smiled. "Forgive me my exaggeration."

Charity smiled back.

"Once we had pinpointed Huelva," Montagu went on, "and began studying it, we found even more reason to use it. The hydrographer of the Navy at the Admiralty ran a number of scenarios for tides and weather. He determined that the conditions in April, particularly the prevailing southwesterly wind, were perfect for our purposes of, one, ensuring that the body would indeed make it ashore — not float farther out to sea — and, two, being logical that the body could have come from a plane that crashed at sea."

"A body wearing a Mae West?" Charity said.

"A life jacket. Sir Bernard Spilsbury — the pathologist? — explained to us that victims of plane crashes in water die from any number of events. It can be from the crash itself. It can be from drowning. Or, if they survive all that, then from exposure."

"Which is how our man died," Charity said.

"Pneumonia, triggered by exposure," Montagu corrected. "So all that came together. Most important, it was approved by the chiefs of staff and the Prime Minister, who then approved our use of a submarine en route to Malta. We then convinced Lieutenant Jewell to delay the departure of the HMS *Seraph* two weeks for us."

"And here we are," Fleming said finally.

"Okay," Charity said. "Thank you. Now I think I've got a good idea of where we're going with this."

"Incidentally," Stevens added, "you probably know you were lucky to get the *Seraph* and Lieutenant Jewell. They seem uniquely equipped for these sort of special operations."

"Indeed," Fleming said. "Then you've no

doubt heard what happened with Giraud?"

Stevens smiled. "Some of it."

"The French general who escaped from the German prison?" Charity said.

"He was at the Casablanca Conference with all the other leaders," the Duchess added.

Fleming nodded. "He almost cut off his skinny nose to spite his face. Had it not been for we Brits, he was this close" — he held up his index finger and thumb almost touching — "to spending the rest of the war back in a POW camp instead of there with Roosevelt and Churchill."

"How so?"

"In late October, prior to the Torch landing," Fleming explained, "Jewell carried a half dozen Allied officers, including General Mark Clark, to a lonely strip of beach forty kilometers west of Algiers. There, at the home of the head of the underground group Chantiers de la Jeunesse, they met in secret with Vichy French General Charles Mast. They tried to persuade Mast to bring his French forces in with the Allies, or, failing that, have the forces not fight the Allies during the invasion of North Africa. Mast said something could be possible — but only if General Henri-Honoré Giraud were there to lead them. Giraud was in Vichy France, having only months earlier escaped from a prisoner-of-war camp in Germany. He was more or less hiding from the Germans and their French friends, who wanted to lock him back up in Germany. Arrogantly, Giraud said he would consider being secreted to North Africa to command — but, ridiculously, he refused passage aboard any British vessel."

Stevens laughed.

"What's funny about that?" Charity asked.

"For one, it was a ridiculous demand from one with a bounty on his head," Stevens explained. "Then, General Clark desperately tried to locate a U.S. Navy boat — surface or submarine — close enough to accomplish the mission soon enough. He couldn't. So, cleverly, it was arranged with the British navy to allow the HMS *Seraph* to become the USS *Seraph* — flying a U.S. Navy ensign — and for it to be commanded by a Captain Jerauld Wright, U.S. Navy."

"What about the crew?"

"All Brits but for Captain Wright," Fleming said, grinning, "all putting on pitiful American accents. But the bastard Giraud got aboard."

"So you're lucky to have the *Seraph*," Stevens said. "Lieutenant Jewell is not afraid to be unorthodox."

"Lucky indeed," Montagu said. "Let us hope it continues."

# [TWO]
## PORT OF ALGIERS
## ALGIERS, ALGERIA
## 1745 31 MARCH 1943

A half dozen crewmen on the deck of the Free French Forces submarine *Casabianca* were systematically carrying the last of the provisions toward the loading hatch. A low wooden rack next to the hatch held two new, glistening torpedoes. The crew would secure the fish below, remove the rack to shore, then, with everything else onloaded, secure the hatch.

Near the gangplank, two of the four 6 x 6 GMC trucks, their cargo areas all now empty, were being fired up. The driver of the first truck engaged its granny gear with a torturous grinding of metal and began rolling away.

Free French Forces Navy Commander Jean L'Herminier was making an inspection of the boat, stem to stern. Major Richard M. Canidy walked with him, then saw a U.S. Army jeep pulling through the gates. Canidy recognized First Lieutenant Hank Darmstadter at the wheel.

"That would appear to be our man, Jean," Canidy said to L'Herminier. "With Frank Nola already belowdecks, we can go once this guy's aboard."

"Then you take care of that, Dick, and I'll finish up here."

At the OSS station that morning, Stan Fine had taken Dick Canidy upstairs to the commo room at the villa. There, they looked over the five operators on duty and spoke with them one by one. Two were women. When Canidy got to the last — a tall, intense fellow of maybe twenty-four, with somewhat-shaggy blond hair and unmistakable all-American facial features — he was about to blow his cork from frustration.

Canidy looked at the radio operator, then at Fine, and whispered, "I really do need someone who looks even remotely Italian or Sicilian."

Fine nodded agreeably.

The young man sensed someone was talking about him and glanced over his shoulder. When he saw that it was Captain Fine standing there with some stranger, he immediately removed his earphones and stood up from the radio.

"Sir," he said respectfully.

Fine nodded. "What's your name, son?"

"Jim Fuller," he said. "But call me Tubes, sir. Everyone does."

"Because of the radio?" Canidy put in, curious. "Those tubes?"

Tubes looked at Canidy and said, "It's become that in part. But I got the name from home."

"And home is?"

"California. I got the nickname surfing. When I was ten. Some like to ride on top of a wave, but I love to go under them" — he grinned broadly — "in the tube."

Canidy nodded. "Well . . . *Tubes* . . . inasmuch as I'd like to continue this, if you will excuse me. . . ."

"Yes, sir," Tubes said, sounding somewhat dejected. He started to sit back before his radio set.

"Out of curiosity . . ." Canidy said suddenly.

"Yes, sir?" Tubes said, standing upright again.

"There's one man at the Sandbox I'm interested in as a radio operator. I don't know the name he's using, but maybe you've worked with him on the air."

Tubes looked at Fine.

"Tell him whatever you know, son," Fine said.

Tubes nodded. "I'll try."

Canidy went on: "This is rough, but it's all I've got right now. It's my impression that he was in some sales job in the States."

"Sales?" Tubes said. "Well, there may be someone else out there who fits that. But Carmine — oh, man, that's *all* he talks about. And he has the worst skills of any radioman I've ever heard. It's like he's working the key with a booted foot."

Canidy was quiet a moment, absorbing that bit of new information.

*Shit! Now what?*

"Like I said, you could be talking about someone else," Tubes said. "Hard to say. But I can tell you that this Carmine isn't going to make it with a radio."

Canidy nodded. "Thank you, Tubes. I appreciate your expertise."

Tubes smiled. "You're welcome."

Canidy and Fine started for the door.

Then they heard Tubes call across the room.

"You want a good W/T guy," he said, his tone authoritative, "then the guy you want is Tony. He's a kid, with lots of energy, but he's got a great hand. Tony's who I'd pick."

Hank Darmstadter's jeep pulled up with a noisy screech of brakes. He shut off the engine.

Canidy got a good look at the kid in the passenger seat. "Tony" was indeed the excitable one he'd had in Max Corvo's classroom at the Sandbox. He had that unruly shock of wiry jet-black hair that stuck out at odd angles.

The kid was looking at Canidy, smiling, and making the connection, too.

Darmstadter got out. The kid did the same, then followed Darmstadter over to where Canidy stood.

"Major," Darmstadter said.

"Afternoon, sir!" the kid said, his manner excited. "Very nice to see you again. I had some follow-up questions about your lecture —"

"What's your name?" Canidy interrupted.

"Antonio Jones, sir. Tony."

"No, your real name."

The kid looked for guidance to Darmstadter, who motioned with his head *Go on, it's okay to tell him.*

"John Craig van der Ploeg, sir," he answered in a chipper tone.

Canidy studied him a moment.

"That's Dutch!" Canidy snapped. "How the hell are you Italian? And stop calling me sir."

Unnerved, John Craig van der Ploeg

grabbed a fistful of his hair.

"This look Dutch?" he said, smiling, then let go of the hair and motioned to his olive-skinned face. "This look fair?"

Canidy started at him impatiently. "So, what's your story?"

"I was adopted, sir. Lost my family to *La Grippe.*"

Canidy was about to snap at him again for saying "sir," but then thought, *Jesus! The 1918 Spanish flu? That wiped out tens of millions. . . .*

"I'm sorry," Canidy said, his tone genuine.

John Craig van der Ploeg shrugged, unbothered.

"I was two years old," he said conversationally. "It's ancient history to me. I have no memory of it — or them."

Canidy nodded.

"Do you know the name you were given at birth?" he said.

John Craig van der Ploeg shook his head.

"Well," Canidy said, "we'll have to come up with one that's more appropriate to the mission. Even if it's only a code name."

John Craig van der Ploeg nodded.

"You were told that this mission is one of extreme danger, one you may not survive, and one you cannot discuss with anyone?"

"It's why I volunteered," John Craig van

der Ploeg said.

Canidy glanced at the *Casabianca,* then looked at van der Ploeg.

"Okay, then," Canidy said. "Go grab your gear from the jeep and let's get aboard."

John Craig van der Ploeg looked past Canidy at the boat, then back at Canidy.

"Sir, we're not going by submarine, right?"

Canidy stared at him, not sure that he'd heard right.

"Say that again?"

"I asked if we were going by sub . . . because I can't."

*What the hell?*

"Do you want to tell me why?" Canidy said, trying to control his voice. "Or do I have to guess that, too?"

"I am claustrophobic, sir," John Craig van der Ploeg said. "Claustrophobia means —"

"I know what the hell it means!" Canidy flared. He stood there for a moment, staring at the kid, then said, "How did you expect to go behind the lines? The goddamn Germans would send a fucking Mercedes-Benz for you?" He shook his head. *"Claustrophobic!"*

"Surface ships I can do, sir," John Craig van der Ploeg said carefully. "Or drop me in by parachute. I don't really like airplanes, but if I'm near a window or an open door I can make do." He paused. "The last thing I'm trying to do is shirk my responsibilities, sir."

Canidy saw Darmstadter nod.

"Coming here," Darmstadter said, "he was more than a bit squeamish in the bird. At one point, I thought he was going to go out the jump door without a parachute. But I just wrote it off to nerves."

Canidy looked from Darmstadter to the kid.

"They didn't tell you about the sub at the Sandbox?" he asked.

John Craig van der Ploeg shook his head.

He said, "And I didn't ask. They teach us not to ask questions. Vincent Scamporino told me there was an important mission that needed a W/T operator and would I be interested in volunteering? I told him that as I'd already volunteered to be at the Sandbox, it followed —"

"Okay, okay," Canidy said impatiently. "I get it." He thought for a moment, and added, "What if I ordered you to go?"

"I could get aboard, sir, but when I lost it inside, well, it probably would not be pleasant for anyone."

Canidy looked furious.

"I'm sorry, sir."

"Stop calling me sir!"

John Craig van der Ploeg looked at his feet. "Sorry."

"Now what the hell do I do?" Canidy asked of no one in particular. "We don't have time to get someone else from the Sandbox, if there *is* even someone else usable there. . . ."

There was a long moment of silence.

Then John Craig van der Ploeg said, his tone upbeat, "If I may make a suggestion?"

Canidy glared at him.

"I think you may have caused me enough difficulty so far," Canidy said. "But if you're willing to stick your neck out again. . . ."

"I *am* willing to do what I can, sir," John Craig van der Ploeg said, somewhat indignantly. "It's why I agreed to follow Corvo and Scamporino here in the first place. If I could swim to where it is you're going, I would."

Canidy looked him in the eyes.

"Okay, you have my apology. For now. What's your bright idea?"

"Tubes," John Craig van der Ploeg offered brightly.

" 'Tubes' ?" Canidy repeated.

Then he thought, *He means that radio operator? The surfer . . .*

"The surfer?" Canidy said.

John Craig van der Ploeg nodded enthusiastically.

"Tubes is my commo partner. When we practiced our messages, we got tired of the

325

usual numbing stuff. You know?"

Canidy shook his head. "No. I don't know."

"You know, all the limbering-up exercises," he explained, and demonstrated by wiggling his fingers, then rotating his wrist. "And then there's the pronunciation practice . . . Alfa — di-DAH; Bravo — DAH-di-di-dit; Charley — DAH-di-DAH-dit . . ."

The look on Canidy's face was utter disbelief.

*This is getting more surreal by the moment,* he thought.

*I may be getting off the hook by* not *taking this kid.*

". . . and then the practice words, like ones with short sounds, TEE ATE EAT TEA MEAT . . . and the long ones, CUTE BAKER CHARLIE . . ."

"Okay! Okay!" Canidy said. "I get it."

Canidy glanced at Darmstadter, who had his hands firmly stuffed in his pant pockets and was finding intense interest in the toes of his shoes. He also was biting on his lower lip.

Canidy made a face of frustration, then looked back at John Craig van der Ploeg.

"There's a point to this tale?" Canidy said. "You realize you're holding up a complete submarine crew and its mission."

"Yes, sir — I mean, sorry. We just wanted to work our hand keys, because I had the Morse code down pretty good from my time in Boy Scouts. My touch typing on the type-writer, too —"

" 'In Boy Scouts,' " Canidy parroted drily.

He smiled and puffed out his chest. "Yessir. We were both in Scouts but not in the same troop. Or the same time. Not even in the same state. But, see? That's the point —"

"*What's* the point?" Canidy said and made a *Get on with it* motion with his hand.

Canidy, in his peripheral vision, thought he could see Darmstadter, his face flushed and eyes diverted, quivering.

"That's what we did," John Craig van der Ploeg explained. "When we got bored with all that other stuff, Tubes said we could move on, so we went about telling each other about ourselves."

"*And?*"

"And what I'm trying to say is that Tubes told me he had put in to train at the Sand-box and really wanted to go operational, not just sit in a dark commo room all hours of the day and night." He paused, then added, "He's one helluva radioman, sir."

Canidy stared at him, deep in thought.

*He's also the furthest from an Italian or Sicil-ian that I could possibly get.*

*He'd stick out in Sicily like a preacher in a whorehouse.*

*But if we find that the gas did the damage we think it did, then Tubes probably won't be staying, anyway.*

*Boy Scouts?*

*Jesus Christ.*

*But I should be grateful, I guess, because otherwise I right now would have zero other options. . . .*

Canidy looked at Darmstadter.

"Go get him, Hank. Take John Craig van der Ploeg here with you. Tell Stan that I want him to take Tubes's place at the radio there and that they're going to be each other's contact."

Darmstadter nodded.

Canidy looked at John Craig van der Ploeg.

"Anything unclear about that?" he said.

"Makes perfect sense," John Craig van der Ploeg said. "Thank you, sir."

Canidy glared at him.

"Hank," Canidy added. "And tell Tubes to get some clothes out of the wardrobe room. Especially a stocking cap — something, anything, to help disguise those California looks."

Canidy was standing in the conn tower with L'Herminier when Darmstadter returned in the jeep with Tubes two hours later.

Canidy was watching crewmen on the deck bringing some type of flattened contraptions to the conn tower. They were five feet long, had a wooden frame, and a fabric skin of canvas.

"What the hell are those, Jean?" Canidy said. "Some kind of boat?"

"Kayaks," L'Herminier said, an element of pride evident in his voice. "You said you didn't like the rubber boat you used last time to get ashore. I took it upon myself to procure these kayaks. They say they are very fast and maneuverable."

Canidy looked dubious. "Who's they? The Eskimos . . . ?"

The jeep stopped at the foot of the gangplank. Crewmen stood at ease on the dock, waiting to cast off the lines of the submarine and retract the plank.

Canidy saw Darmstadter point him out to Tubes, who then waved to Canidy. Canidy caught himself before he almost waved back.

Darmstader helped Tubes get a fat duffel bag's strap slung over his shoulder. Then Darmstadter reached back into the jeep and produced a cardboard box that was large enough to hold a couple of birthday cakes. He handed this to Tubes, then patted him on the back.

As Tubes started up the gangplank, Darmstadter went back to the jeep and brought out two green suitcases.

*There're the radios,* Canidy thought.

Darmstadter handed the suitcases over to one of the crewmen, who carried them aboard. Then Darmstadter waved good-bye at the conn tower.

This time, Canidy returned it.

The small tugs nudged the Free French Forces submarine *Casabianca* away from the docks and toward sea.

Tubes reached the foot of the ladder that led up the conn tower. He could not climb it with both the duffel strapped over his shoulder and the box in his hands, so he slipped the duffel to the deck. Then he went up the ladder with the box.

At the top, he saluted Canidy and said, "Sir."

Canidy looked at him and said, "Make that your last salute and use of 'sir.' Got it?"

Tubes looked confused.

"Where we're going, either of those could get both of us killed."

Tubes suddenly understood the gravity of that.

"They told me that this was a dangerous mission," he said.

"You can't begin to appreciate the understatement that that is," Canidy said.

Tubes nodded. He held out the box to him.

"What the hell is this?" Canidy said.

Tubes shrugged.

"Professor Rossi said you might need this," he said.

Canidy pulled back the lid of the box just enough to see inside.

"Christ," he said after a moment's thought. "Canaries."

L'Herminier leaned over to look, too.

"*Souris!*" L'Herminier said. "Not birds. Mice!"

"Yep," Canidy muttered. "But soon to be the same as canaries in a coal mine. . . ."

# [THREE]
## OSS WHITBEY HOUSE STATION
## KENT, ENGLAND
## 1155 3 APRIL 1943

"I say we move on to assigning the name," Niven announced. "And I say I'll just do it myself. . . . I say we call him" — he stared at the ceiling a long moment — "Martin. Major Martin."

"Why Major Martin?" Fleming said, making it a friendly challenge.

"Why not? Has a nice ring to it," Niven replied.

"That may well be true, but we can't bloody well just throw out a name and have it stick," Fleming said, trying to be sensible.

"Also happens to be the name of an unscrupulous chap in Hollywood I wouldn't mind finding bobbing breathless in the sea," Niven added.

There was silence around the table, then Montagu spoke up.

"Actually, Major Martin could work," he said.

Niven gave Fleming a smug smile. Fleming gave Niven the finger.

There were chuckles around the table.

Niven said to no one in particular, "Please, don't encourage him."

There were more chuckles.

Fleming looked at Montagu.

"How is that, Ewen?" he said.

"For the same reason that we selected the rank of major," Montagu explained. "There is no shortage of them. As I just recounted, we picked the Royal Marines because it is known as an elite service from which one could pull a courier for such a critical mission. Being elite makes it comparatively small, and it would not be unusual for many members to be familiar with others. I can name three Martins off the top of my head that I know personally —"

"You're right," Fleming interrupted. "I can think of two myself, though only one is in fact in the Royal Marines. A captain."

"There you have it," Montagu said. "I would expect there to be a long list of Martins in the Royal Marines, and certainly ones with the rank of major. Easy enough to confirm." He looked at Niven. "So there it is: Major Martin. Now, what about a first name, something equally common?"

"Bill," Niven immediately said.

*"William,"* Fleming put in, earning him a mock glare from Niven.

"Major William Martin of the Royal Marines," Montagu said, testing the sound of it. "By Jove, I think we do have it. Unless there are any objections?"

No one objected.

"Major William Martin of the Royal Marines it is, then," Montagu said.

"Bill, to his friends," Niven put in and grinned.

Surprising him, Fleming nodded.

"Yes," he said, "let's get into that — his

friends, his personal life."

Montagu said, "We know the main documents, the mission-critical ones, will concern the deceit, of course. But, getting to number one" — he motioned toward the Operation Mincemeat sheet — "we need companion papers for the purpose of padding, something that helps explain who Major Martin is."

"The love letters?" Charity said.

Montagu smiled. "It has been discussed that our man — our *Major Martin* — should be newly engaged."

"How charming," the Duchess said. "Love in bloom!"

"Discussed?" Niven put in. "I thought it had been decided, that we agreed on my idea."

"Right on both counts," Fleming said. "Decided and your idea. Now, let's discuss it. Ladies, any immediate thoughts?"

Charity found herself smiling.

*I have a thought or two on the subject, but I'm not about to bare my soul!*

"Charity?" Fleming said, looking at her. "Penny for your thoughts?"

"Um, nothing immediately."

"I'll raise that. A pound for your thoughts," Niven added, grinning.

She made a radiant smile.

"Sorry, no price can be put on them," she said playfully.

"If Major Martin is in his early thirties," the Duchess said, "then we can assume his fiancée is, oh, late twenties?"

"Why not?" Montagu said agreeably.

"And they're of comparable social background, say, middle class?"

Montagu nodded.

"That fits," he said.

"Is there any particular time frame for these letters?" the Duchess said.

Montagu looked to Niven and Fleming for their thoughts.

"They should be relatively fresh," Niven said. "They're newly engaged, and have rushed to it because of the war."

"That could be one theme in the letters," Fleming added, "where friends or relatives are cautious of a war wedding."

Niven nodded. "But as to timing, I would say no older than two months. The *Seraph* sets sail —"

"April nineteenth," Montagu provided. "Plan is to put Major Martin in the water on April thirtieth."

"So taking that into consideration," Niven said, "we must backdate our letters accordingly. Say, nothing before March first."

"Shouldn't these letters of hers be very

new?" the Duchess said. "Maybe written at her most anxious moments, right before he leaves?"

All the men smiled at once.

"That kind of lively thought, my dear," Niven said, "is why we came here."

The Duchess smiled softly.

Montagu reached down and opened the big box that was under the table. He pulled some blank sheets of typing paper and two pencils from the box and gave them to the Duchess and Charity.

"Would you please write your name on the sheet?"

They looked curious at the request but went along with it.

Montagu took the sheets, quickly reviewed them, then passed them to Fleming. They then made their way around the table.

"The letters from the girlfriend should be handwritten," Montagu explained. "And, no offense, Charity, but, as I expected, the Duchess has the natural British lettering necessary."

"That's understandable," Charity said, her tone agreeable.

Montagu then reached into the box and produced some off-white stationery with letterhead in black ink that read THE MANOR HOUSE, OGBOURNE ST. GEORGE, MARL-

BOROUGH, WILTSHIRE.

"This is from a nice little getaway where I once stayed," Montagu explained. "When I was there, I noticed a couple of mothers and daughters enjoying the weekend. In my mind's eye, I could see Major Martin's fiancée —"

"She doesn't have a name!" Niven interrupted. "Let's call her . . . oh, Pamela!"

"I could see Major Martin's *Pam*," Montagu went on, accepting the name without discussion, "there with her mother, discussing the pending marriage."

Charity nodded. "With her mother and sister."

"Even better," Montagu said, sliding the letterhead to the Duchess.

"The Duchess's lively thought just now about the letter needing to be anxious proves, I think, that it shouldn't be drafted," Montagu said. "It should be written at once, from the heart."

"I agree," Fleming said, nodding.

The Duchess's eyes went up. "Well, that certainly puts one on the spot!"

"That's not the intention," Fleming said, his tone apologetic. "It's just that it should result in a genuine feel. Charity can pitch in."

The Duchess looked at her. "And you will! Please?"

Charity smiled. "Of course."

The Duchess sat silently, in deep thought, then looked at Charity.

"I'm seeing her at this getaway with her mother and sister," she said, "her heart aching with the thought of having seen Major Martin off at the train station."

"And," Charity added, "though she longs for the time they spent together, at the same time she gets mad at herself for such a silly schoolgirl-like thought."

"Good," the Duchess said.

"All right, then," Montagu said. "Let's date it April eighteenth."

The Duchess began to write:

---

The Manor House

Ogbourne St. George Marlborough, Wiltshire

Telephone:
Ogbourne St. George 242

Sunday, 18th

I do think, dearest, that seeing people like you off at railway stations is one of the poorer forms of sport. A train going out

---

can leave a howling great gap in one's life
& one has to try madly — & quite in vain
— to fill it with all the things one used
to enjoy a whole five weeks ago.

That lovely golden day we spent together
— oh! I know it has been said before, but
if only time could sometimes stand still just
for a minute for us!

But that line of thought is too pointless.
Pull your socks up, Pam, & don't be a silly
little fool.

Charity read what the Duchess was writing,
then offered: "Maybe she mentions something
that he had written to her in a letter —"

"Something *about* her," the Duchess interrupted, looking at Charity. "Something vain
that she feels she must deny."

The Duchess looked at the ceiling a moment, then wrote on:

Your letter made me feel slightly better
— but I shall get horribly conceited if you
go on saying things like that about me —
they're utterly unlike _me_, as I'm afraid
you'll soon find out.

> Here I am for the weekend in this divine place with Mummy & Jane being too sweet & understanding the whole time, bored beyond words & panting for Monday so that I can get back to the old grindstone again. What an idiotic waste!

When the Duchess finished that, Charity said, "Very nice, Liz."

"Thank you. What about winding it up with some frantic words about their future?"

"Or possible loss of one," Charity heard herself say automatically.

As the Duchess began to write, Charity's throat constricted. She forced down some tea, as a mental image of Lieutenant Colonel Doug Douglass, completely out of uniform — as well as any other garment — came to mind.

*Loss of a future with Doug is exactly my fear.*

"There," the Duchess said, turning the page so Charity could better read it, "how's that?"

Charity looked at the paper.

> Bill darling, do let me know as soon as you get fixed & can make some more plans, &

please don't let them send you off into the blue the horrible way they do nowadays —

Now that we've found each other out of the whole world, I don't think I could bear it —

All my love,
PAM

*Oh, God. That's too close.*
*I'm think I'm going to cry.*

When she was sure of her voice, she said: "Perfect."

The letter was passed around the table. Everyone approved.

"Now we need another," Montagu said, "one written from her job."

He reached into the box and produced a short stack of blank typewriter stock he had taken from a typing pool at the Admiralty. He slid it to the Duchess.

"So she's now at the office," Montagu said. "Date it the twenty-first. She's bored out of her mind."

"I think it would be wise to pick up on what Charity so brilliantly suggested for the first letter," Fleming put in. "Have her make reference to a letter the major has written to her in which he talks of being sent on a hush-hush mission."

Niven added, "You could have her say something that violates a confidence. That is, she *won't* violate a confidence, the way women tend to do."

Charity and the Duchess immediately shot him daggers with their stares.

"I don't mean that in a vicious way, mind you," Niven said, trying to save face. "You know how women can be — proud of what their man is doing, trying to one-up their buddies in the course of conversation."

The Duchess looked away.

"Perhaps," she said. "But you just gave me an idea for an opening."

She studied the far wall a moment, then began writing:

Office.

Wednesday, 21st

The Bloodhound has left the kennel for half an hour so here I am scribbling nonsense to you again.

Your letter came this morning just as I was dashing out — madly late as usual! You do write such heavenly ones. But what are these horrible dark hints you're throwing out about being sent off somewhere — of course I won't say a word to anyone — I never do when you tell me things, but it's not abroad is it?

Because I won't have it, I won't. Tell them so from me.

Darling, why did we go and meet in the middle of the war, such a silly thing for anybody to do — if it weren't for the war, we might have been nearly married by now, going round together choosing curtains etc.

And I wouldn't be sitting in a dreary Government office typing idiotic minutes all day long — I know the futile sort of work I do doesn't make the war one minute shorter —

"Bloodhound!" Niven said, feigning indignation.

"Works for me," Fleming said, grinning.

"Okay, let's have her discuss how she spends her free time," Montagu said.

"Maybe going to the pub?" Charity said.

"No," the Duchess said, "that would not be proper for her to do, or, if she did, to share in a letter." She thought a moment. "To a dance! With friends!"

"A *dreary* dance with *ghastly* friends!" Charity added.

The Duchess smiled and nodded. She mentally composed it for a second, then started writing:

> I'm going to a rather dreary dance tonight with Jock & Hazel. I think they've got some other man coming. You know what their friends always turn out to be like

The Dutchess stopped, then looked to Charity for help.

Charity made a small frown, then looked across the table, and her face lit up. She giggled.

The Duchess looked to where Charity had looked — at Niven.

The Duchess grinned, then wrote:

> he'll be like that David we met — he'll have the sweetest little Adam's apple & the shiniest bald head!

The lead of the pencil snapped when the

Duchess added the exclamation point. She and Charity started to giggle again as they looked at Niven.

Niven got up and walked around the table to see what they had written about him.

"My head is not bald and shiny!" he announced.

Charity and the Duchess laughed aloud.

Then the Duchess added:

How beastly & ungrateful of me, but it isn't really that — you know — don't you?

"Perfect," Charity said.

Niven sighed.

"Not quite, but I suppose it'll do," he said.

"How about saying something about her engagement ring?" Fleming said.

"Good idea," Montagu added. "She'll be with friends and the ring would be a boasting point."

Then the Duchess added:

Dearest Bill, I'm so thrilled with my ring — scandalously extravagant — you know how I adore diamonds — I simply can't stop looking at it.

"Good," Charity said.

"Okay, let's wrap it up," Montagu said.

"Say the boss has come back a little early or something," Fleming suggested, "and that she has to finish quickly."

"She should try to make some plans to see him," Charity said, "even if they're futile."

*Like I do with Doug,* Charity thought.

*Now, that, gentlemen, was my personal thought — and you didn't even have to pay for it.*

"Easter is coming," Fleming offered.

The Duchess nodded and wrote:

Look, darling, I've got next Sunday & Monday off for Easter. I shall go home for it, of course, but <u>do</u> come too if you possibly can, or, even if you can't get away from London, I'll dash up and we'll have an evening of gaiety. (By the way, Aunt Maria said to bring you to dinner next time I was up, but I think that might wait?)

Oh! Here comes the Bloodhound — back sooner than he'd said —

Masses of kisses and love —

your

PAM

"Aunt Maria?" Charity said after reading the final passage.

The Duchess nodded.

"Everyone's got an aunt who never had a daughter and lives though the niece vicariously."

"That sounds rather clinical," Charity said, grinning. "Or should I say *cynical?*"

The Duchess laughed.

"I couldn't say. I just made it up."

"You two are finding much too much humor in this," Niven said with mock disgust.

"You'd like us to stop, David?" the Duchess said, smiling.

"No, no," Montagu put in. "This is going well."

"I would like for us to stop for lunch," Niven said reasonably. "Won't do Major Martin much good if we were to die of starvation in the course of our task here."

"I can always eat," Charity said.

"Indeed," Montagu said. "I think we could all use a bit of a break."

"Then we can move on to the more serious letters," Fleming said.

# [FOUR]
## 38 DEGREES 13 MINUTES 14 SECONDS NORTH LATITUDE 13 DEGREES 21 MINUTES 10 SECONDS EAST LONGITUDE GULF OF PALERMO, SICILY ABOARD THE *CASABIANCA* 2355 4 APRIL 1943

Dick Canidy, Frank Nola, and Jim "Tubes" Fuller were with Jean L'Herminier, all squeezed in the submarine captain's dimly lit drab-gray office. Each was seated in a metal-framed chair except Tubes, who stood.

"Dick, I'm sorry we could not get a better look at the harbor," L'Herminier said.

"Me, too," Canidy replied. "But we cannot risk going in any closer. One close call is enough."

"Agreed."

There were knowing glances among the men.

Only two days had passed since the *Casabianca* encountered the Kriegsmarine

348

patrol boat, and the memory felt like a fresh wound.

It had been just after midnight on their second night en route to Palermo.

The *Casabianca* was preparing to run on the surface, recharging her batteries for the electric motors while covering distance more quickly under the power of her diesel engines.

An hour earlier, L'Herminier had made the order for a slower speed and an adjustment in the planes so that the submarine would make an easy angle of ascent.

Now the boat had come to a stop, neutrally buoyant at periscope depth. For the last half hour, he had time and again raised the scope and carefully scanned the immediate area and seen nothing.

"Huh," L'Herminier now said.

"What is it?" his executive officer, a frail-looking, sad-eyed Frenchman a head shorter than the commander, said.

"There's a fishing boat that's dead in the water," L'Herminier said, still looking through the scope.

Nola said, "What could be the chance it's one of mine?"

He looked at Canidy and added hopefully, "We could ask them what they know about Palermo."

Candidy raised an eyebrow.

"Right," he said skeptically. "That'd be nice. But it's some long shot."

Two minutes later, L'Herminier added, "This is not good."

"What?" Nola said.

"A German patrol boat is coming alongside it," L'Herminier said.

The distinct profile of the Kriegsmarine fast-attack S-boat was unmistakable.

The advanced vessel was built in slightly different design variants, but all were essentially similar watercraft, all about a hundred feet long. It was their massive engines that earned them their name *Schnellboot* — the literal translation being "fast boat." One variant packed three Daimler-Benz twenty-cylinder, two-thousand-horsepower diesel engines that pushed the heavy wooden-hulled vessel almost forty-five knots.

The primary purpose of the S-boat was the rapid delivery of torpedoes on target. It would lie in wait in the dark, locate an enemy sub or ship — then hit and run. It carried 53.3cm torpedoes. Because of its methods, it rarely carried more "fish" than the ones in its tubes. The very nature of a fast attack — and a faster departure — did not allow time for the reloading of the tubes.

And the extra weight of the extra fish affected the agility of the craft.

S-boats carried other weapons on board — among them light machine guns, 4cm Bofors, highly efficient and effective four-barrel, 2cm Flaks — and these were for defending the boat.

L'Herminier recognized that this S-boat certainly was not operating in a fast-attack mode. He also saw that it did not appear to being using its deck guns defensively on this fishing boat.

The crew of the hulking patrol boat clearly had an aggressive stance.

"Looks to be a harassment stop," L'Herminier said.

He stepped back from the scope and looked at Nola.

"Can you tell if this fishing boat is one of yours?" he asked quietly.

Nola placed his face up to the periscope. It took him some moments to get his bearings, then to dial in the scope. When he finally did, he did not like what he saw.

It was a mostly moonless night but clear, and the sky full of brilliant stars cast a soft light on the water, putting the two boats on the surface in silhouette.

Nola had a reasonably unobstructed view of both vessels, their bows pointed more or less in the direction of the sub. He could see that the fishing boat, at about fifty feet in length, was not unlike the *Stefania*. The German patrol boat, sitting a couple meters off her port side, was about twice its length.

On the fishing boat, there were ten men standing on the port gunnel — most likely, the entire crew — looking up to face the sailors on the S-boat.

"I cannot tell," Nola said, his voice quavering. "But it very easily could be mine, or one of someone I know."

Suddenly, he saw the night erupt in flames. It was the muzzle flash from the S-boat's light machine guns laying a line of fire from bow to stern.

The fisherman were cut down where they stood, some falling into the boat, others into the sea. Dead.

"Great Holy Mother of God!" Frank Nola exclaimed, then turned away from the periscope.

L'Herminier grabbed the scope handles, stuck his eyes to the viewing glass — then immediately retracted the periscope.

"Dive! Dive!" the sub commander called. "Flood all tanks!"

"Dive!" the sad-eyed XO repeated to the helmsman. "All tanks flooded!"

"No!" Francisco Nola shouted to L'Herminier. "You must torpedo those bastards!"

L'Herminier turned to Canidy.

"Get him the hell out of here, Major!"

Canidy had never heard L'Herminier use that tone of voice.

But he recognized that L'Herminier was, in fact, right.

Canidy took Nola by the sleeve of his jacket and attempted to gently push him toward the compartment hatch.

"Let's go, Frank."

Nola tried to hold his ground.

"Now, goddammit!" Canidy said, and much more forcefully used his body to push Nola.

Nola stared shuffling toward the hatch.

"They just gunned them down in cold blood." He began crying. "We must do something."

They reached the hatch as the angle of the deck began to change.

"We can't, Frank," Canidy said, looking back over his shoulder at L'Herminier. "If we do, then our mission is compromised."

L'Herminier, still with a stern face, returned the look with a nod.

"Give me a depth of one hundred meters," L'Herminier then ordered his XO. "Then steer a course of zero-one-zero degrees. Full speed, if we can get it."

"Depth of one hundred meters," the executive officer repeated, "course of one-zero. Full speed."

The bow of the boat dropped dramatically. As the angle grew greater, mugs and papers and anything else not secured slid from tables.

Not ten minutes later, with the *Casabianca* passing through a depth of fifty meters, there came a thunderous boom from far above. It reverberated through the sub.

Canidy had Nola seated on his bunk. Canidy looked at him. His eyes — bright red and wet from crying — were now huge.

"That fishing boat just saved our lives, Frank. They diverted the attention of that patrol boat."

"This day, I vow, I never will forget," Nola had said.

In L'Herminier's office, Canidy said, "Our purpose here, then, is to clarify what happens next — in the next three days, and maybe in the next three months."

He looked at each man, then went on:

"One. Our main mission is to find out about the nerve gas. Was it on the boat? Did it do the damage we suspect? I think those questions will very quickly answer themselves.

"Two. Find out what happened with the villa and the yellow fever.

"Three. Assuming we get to three, then we set up Frank and Tubes to stay behind and send intel to OSS Algiers.

"And four. If we can progress to this point, we expand the team and begin building a resistance, the underground. Then sabotage teams from Dellys can come in."

He looked around the room.

"Okay? Any questions?"

"What if nerve gas was there?" Tubes said, his tone more serious than Canidy had ever heard it. "What do we do?"

"This mission was laid on to find out about the gas, period," Canidy said. "If it was used, we get evidence, then get the hell out. If it wasn't used, we try to find out, one, if it was there, and, two, what the plans were for its use, then get the hell out."

Tubes nodded.

"The answers are critical," Canidy continued, "because — and this is me talking, not anything told to me from above — if nerve gas was or will be used, then everything that anyone is doing right now — at AFHQ, in London, wherever — is, basically, wasted effort. Roosevelt said he was against chemical or biological warfare — but would not hesitate to use it in retaliation. And we all know

Churchill's take on it; he's for anything that ends the war yesterday."

There was silence for a long moment, then Canidy went on: "So we get in and get the hell out."

"And my part of that," L'Herminier said, "is that after we drop you, we will go out and lay on the bottom. Then between 2100 and 0400 hours we will rise to periscope level and stand by for your signal — either light from shore or via the W/T — at fifteen minutes after every odd hour. If there is not one, we will lay on the bottom a second day, then the next night rise to await your signal at fifteen minutes before every odd hour."

"And if you get nothing after that," Canidy said, "you get the hell out of here, Jean."

L'Herminier nodded solemnly.

"Reluctantly," he said. "But we still will maintain the radio watch each night on the same alternating schedule. And return, if necessary."

"Thank you, Jean."

The submarine was on the surface of the Gulf of Palermo, its decks still slightly awash. The night was clear and quiet, the air cool and still.

Inside the sub, L'Herminier was at the periscope, scanning the immediate area one last time.

At the foot of the conn tower, Dick Canidy stood squirming into dark brown overalls made of a thick cotton fabric that was coated with a stiff, impermeable rubberized material. The outfit had close-fitting, almost-constrictive cuffs at the wrists and ankles. The gloves were of the same construction as the overalls. As was the full hood, the big difference being that it had a heavy rubber mask vulcanized to the rubber-coated cotton fabric. The mask had two thick glass lenses, and a pair of round air filters that protruded down from either side of the chin like two massively swollen moles.

L'Herminier turned the scope over to his executive officer, who continued the scanning, and walked over to Canidy.

"How are you doing?" L'Herminier asked.

"How do you think?" Canidy said, picking up the hood to put it on. "It's hotter than hell in here."

L'Herminier nodded sympathetically.

"That's some spiffy suit — the real cat's meow!" Jim "Tubes" Fuller said.

Canidy looked blankly at Fuller, who was holding the box of mice.

"You like it so much," Canidy said, "it can just as easily be arranged that I hold the box while you go topside."

Tubes smiled.

"Aw, that's all right. You're already in it and all. I wouldn't want to stress out an old man."

Canidy stared at him, then grinned. They both knew they were only a year or so different in age. While Tubes's surfer mentality tended to annoy Canidy, he had found himself starting to like the guy. His laid-back personality certainly eased the gravity of the situation.

*Which really isn't all that grave.*

*This exercise borders on the academic. It's purely precautionary.*

*The risk of gas poisoning at this point is extremely low.*

*Yeah, that's right, Dick. Keep telling yourself that.*

*And keep discounting Rossi's scenario that those munitions are leaching gas from the harbor bottom.*

*See where that gets you. . . .*

Canidy glanced at Frank Nola. He looked extremely emotional, maybe even scared. He remained silent, lost in thought.

Canidy heard L'Herminier's encouraging voice.

"You should have no pressurization problem with the main hatch," the commander said. "The secondary hatch might be a bit stiff. We do not use it hardly at all. I personally tested it, then had one of the crewmen lubricate the moving parts as well as the seal."

*Was that for my benefit,* Canidy thought skeptically, *or yours, Cap'n?*

*Oh, hell, it is Jean's job to protect the boat and the lives of his crew.*

"Thank you, Commander."

Canidy, with some obvious effort in the heavy, stiff suit, clumsily made his way up the conn tower, his heavy leather boots clunking on the U-shaped metal bars welded to its side that served as steps.

When he got past the first round hatch, he sat on its lip and reached down with his right gloved hand.

"Okay, hand 'em to me," he called down. The hood made his voice sound distorted, and he figured what Tubes heard was probably garbled beyond understanding.

Tubes, though, reached into the box and nabbed two mice by the nape of the neck — a male and a female, in case one proved more sensitive to poisoning than the other — and put them in a soft cloth pouch that had a pull-string closure. He tugged the pouch closed.

He held up the pouch, which now wiggled,

to Canidy's gloved hand.

"Adolf and Eva coming up," Tubes said.

Behind the mask, Canidy grinned.

"Got 'em," Canidy said.

"Good luck!" Tubes said.

Canidy nodded and gave a thumbs-up.

Then he swung he legs up and inside the hatch opening. Carefully, he put the pouch of mice in a corner behind him, then turned to reach for the hatch door.

The heavy steel door, two feet in diameter and mounted on a hinge, almost closed under its own weight when Canidy started to rotate it downward.

*How much lube did that guy use?*

The door now covered the hatch, making the small space in the tower completely dark. Working only by feel, Canidy next found the V-shaped iron handle on back side of the door — there was another above his head, on the main hatch door — and he began turning the handle clockwise. This tightened the threaded "nut" that was at the bottom of the V, which cinched the door snug to the hatch.

*Watertight, airtight . . . and gastight.*

Canidy stood. He reached his right hand above him, carefully waving it back and forth in the dark in order to locate the main hatch handle. On the fourth pass, he rapped his knuckles on it. He turned his hand around, grasped the handle, and pulled, turning the handle counterclockwise.

The handle didn't budge.

*Shit!*

*I thought Jean said there'd be no pressurization problem.*

He reached up with his left hand, found the other end of the V-handle, then pushed it while pulling again on the right handle. Still no movement. Using the palm of his left hand, he started pounding on the left handle, trying to jar it, while his right hand pulled on the right handle. Suddenly, the left handle moved, causing his left hand to hit the thick metal of the submarine structure.

"Dammit!" he said, aloud, shaking his left hand to try to ease the pain.

He noticed that his voice, muffled by the mask and in the small space of the tower, sounded very strange.

After a moment, he reached up and spun the now-loose V-handle. There then came the sound of air hissing, and Canidy knew that that meant the air he was in was soon to be the air from outside.

*No turning back now.*

*Here goes nothing. . . .*

He pushed on the main hatch door and it swung upward on its hinge.

There was some light coming from the

stars, and he reached down and found the pouch of mice. He reached up through the opening and put the squirming pouch on the wet deck.

*Don't need to let them out. . . . They can breathe through the top of the pouch, if not through the fabric itself.*

*They'd probably go overboard if I did let them out.*

*And then this whole damn thing would really have been an exercise in futility . . .*

Canidy scanned the area as he waited for the mice to stop moving.

He saw nothing through the thick lenses of the mask.

The pouch continued to wiggle.

*That's good news.*

After some minutes, Canidy got tired of standing in the hatch. He climbed up and out, then sat with his legs crossed, staring down at the pouch.

It stopped moving.

*Whoooa! What the hell?*

He picked up the pouch and, with great effort due to the thick, stiff gloves, loosened the pull-string closure.

He held it up to one of the thick lenses of his mask and peered inside.

He saw a pair of fuzzy pink noses and a

small forest of whiskers looking back.

As best he could tell, the mice were not moving.

He loosened the string some more, tugging at the top of the pouch.

He peered back in — and suddenly Adolf and Eva lunged for their freedom.

*Shit!*

Canidy next saw them running in circles inside the conn tower.

He stared at them, watching and waiting for what seemed like half an hour.

Then he said, "Fuck it. Close enough."

And pulled off his hood and mask.

"I don't smell anything," Tubes said, standing on the wet deck.

"You wouldn't," Canidy said. "Tabun is odorless."

"No. I mean corpses. If there were dead bodies, there would be the stench of the dead. It's been — what? — eight, nine days."

"Depends on the wind direction," Canidy said. "But good point."

Two crewmen were pulling the folding kayaks onto the deck. Canidy watched as the wooden-framed, canvas-hulled craft were assembled quickly and put in the water, tethered to the sub by a short line.

Canidy lowered his rubberized black duffel

with the Johnson light machine gun, ammo, and other gear in his boat. He put one of the green suitcase radios in beside it. Then, after struggling to crawl in after them, he got to his knees and looked up at the sub.

"So this is your idea of bon voyage, eh?" Canidy said to L'Herminier.

L'Herminier shrugged.

"Jesus!" Canidy exclaimed. "This is akin to a high-wire act! I suddenly long for my little rubber boat . . . and I use the term *boat* loosely."

"If it makes you feel any better," L'Herminier said, "I understand that General Clark took a swim from one of these kayaks when the *Seraph* snuck him into North Africa before Operation Torch. At least you got aboard."

"That's supposed to make me feel better?" Canidy said. "I feel like I'm getting soaked just sitting in this thing."

"He had the same sort of problem, apparently. Story is, he'd taken off his trousers to keep them dry and keep safe the gold coins he carried in the trouser pockets. Or so he thought. The seas were rather rough — nothing like this here — and it all went in the drink. Clark clung to the boat while his trousers and gold found the sea bottom."

"Thanks, Jean. That really gives me a sense

of encouragement."

Once Canidy got settled in the kayak, L'Herminier called down, "You forgot something."

Canidy looked up and saw one of the crewmen holding the box of mice, in which Adolf and Eva had rejoined the others.

"Like hell I did," Canidy said. "Give 'em to Tubes. There's room for more than one big rodent on his raft."

"Hey!" Tubes protested.

Canidy looked at Nola and surprised himself by quoting, " 'But when it comes to slaughter / You will do your work on water.' "

Nola did not say anything at first, then asked, "What does that mean?"

"I'm not sure," Canidy said. "But in a very warped way, Gunga Din, I think it means we now go ashore."

"That's Kipling!" Tubes said, putting the box of mice in his kayak beside the suitcase radio.

"Yeah, that's Kipling," Canidy said. "Now paddle. And on the QT. We'll be in touch, Jean."

"Go with God," L'Herminier said.

# VII
## [ONE]
## OSS WHITBEY HOUSE STATION
## KENT, ENGLAND
## 1320 3 APRIL 1943

A large rectangular platter on the side table held the remnants of the luncheon. What had been a small mountain formed from a variety of sandwiches that had been cut into quarters — sliced ham and turkey, chicken and tuna salads — now was almost completely gone. The large glass bowl of mayonnaise potato salad next to it had been practically scraped clean.

The kitchen staff had prepared fresh pots of coffee and hot water for tea and brought in clean cups and silverware. They now efficiently cleared the plates from the table and the large platter and bowl from the side table.

"I do hope you will excuse my ill manners," Commander Ian Fleming said. "I shamelessly helped myself to too much food."

"You *should* be ashamed," Major David

Niven said to him between sips of tea. "And should you not be, I am prepared to be ashamed for you. Such an example of an officer and a gentleman you are setting for the young Private Ustinov here."

There were chuckles around the table from First Lieutenant Charity Hoche, Lieutenant Colonel Ed Stevens, and the Duchess Stanfield.

"I *am* quite impressionable," Peter Ustinov said as he stole the last quarter square of tuna salad sandwich from Niven's plate.

Niven looked at him in mock disgust.

"Well," Commander Ewen Montagu said, motioning toward the typewriters at the table, "shall we get on with it?"

"So we shall," Niven said and sat down in front of one of the Oliver typewriters, the Special Model 15.

"You're going to do this?" Fleming said.

"And why would I not?" Niven said. "We could have Ustinov here do it, but, then, it would take forever with the way he hunt-and-pecks out the characters with his index fingers."

"This first one is to be from the father to the son," Montagu said, reaching into the box and producing a small stack of letterhead from a hotel in Wales. "He's of course aware of the pending marriage, and, as a father would, is getting papers in order."

Niven looked at the Oliver, then at the Hermes Model 5 beside it.

"Then I'd better use that one," he said, getting up and sitting in front of the Hermes. "The Olivers should be used only for government correspondence."

"Right," Montagu said. He pulled out a second sheet of letterhead, then put it beside the Hermes. "Now, before you begin, you should know that the name of the solicitor firm is McKenna and Company." He pointed that out on the new letterhead. "My wife's brother F.A.S Gwatkin works there and agreed to provide this."

"I think I can make that work, with some minor changes," Niven said smugly.

"David," Montagu said, "we really should be rather faithful to —"

Niven held up his hand and said lightly, "Trust me."

"Last time I heard him say that," Fleming said, standing up and stepping behind Niven to read over his shoulder, "I was a wealthier man."

Niven turned to the Hermes. He picked up a sheet of hotel letterhead and fed it into the typewriter platen, rotating the sheet by expertly working the long, chromed carriage-return arm.

He placed his fingers on the keys of the typewriter in the practiced manner of a skilled typist. After again looking at the McKenna letterhead beside the typewriter, he stared at the ceiling in thought, then turned his attention to the blank sheet in the typewriter.

And began typing.

But, to everyone's astonishment, not just typing — his fingers flew in a frenzy, the machine noisily making a rapid series of *clack-clack-clack*s. As he went, this was then punctuated by the *ding!* of the bell at the end of each line and then the *rip-whir* as Niven worked the carriage return that advanced the sheet one line and reset the platen for the typing to begin again at the left margin. And then came another chorus of *clack-clack-clack*s. . . .

Black Lion Hotel
Mold, North Wales
Tele. No. 98

13th April, 1943

My Dear William,

I cannot say that this Hotel is any longer as comfortable as I remember it to have been in pre-war days. I am, however, staying here as the only alternative to imposing my self once more upon your aunt whose depleted staff & strict regard for fuel economy (which I agree to be necessary in wartime) has made the house almost uninhabitable to a guest, at least one my age. I propose to be in Town for the nights of the 20th & 21st of April, when no doubt we shall have an opportunity to meet. I enclose the copy of a letter which I have written to Gwatkin of McKenna's about your affairs. You will see that I have asked him to lunch with me at the Carlton Grill (which I understand still to be open) at a quarter to one on Wednesday the 21st.

I should be glad if you would make it possible to join us. We shall not however wait luncheon for you, so I trust that, if you are able to come, you will make a point of being punctual.

Your cousin Elizabeth Charity

"Elizabeth Charity?" Fleming said, reading over Niven's shoulder. "Who's that?"

Niven nodded at the Duchess and Charity, who clearly also were wondering about the mysterious but familiar-sounding relative.

"May I finish without having my every period and comma called into question?"

They all suddenly looked like schoolchildren reprimanded by the headmaster.

Niven's fingers flew on, the *clack-clack-clack*s filling the air:

> Your cousin Elizabeth Charity has asked to be remembered to you. She has grown into a sensible girl, though I cannot say that her work for the Land Army has done much to improve her looks. In that respect, I am afraid that she will take after her father's side of the family.

He pulled the sheet from the typewriter, picked up an ink pen, then handwrote the closing: *Your affectionate Father.*

The page was passed around the table for review. When Charity and the Duchess read the final paragraph, they both inhaled dramatically.

Niven stood his ground.

"If there can be a shiny balding David with a perky Adam's apple," he said, dramatically, "then, by God, there can be a homely Elizabeth Charity!"

Montagu didn't know what to say.

Fleming shook his head, smiling, but said, "Well, mentioning the cousin — injecting a family oddity in an otherwise-businesslike message — does add an element of authenticity."

"Very well," Montagu said. "Next, we need a letter from the father to the solicitor —"

"A *copy* of the letter that went to the solicitor," Ed Stevens put in.

"Right," Montagu said. "Good touch, Colonel."

Stevens shrugged. "I've been absolutely useless sitting here."

"Nonsense," Fleming replied. "Having a monitor is quite helpful. As you just proved."

"So, a copy of a letter that the father sent to his counsel," Niven said.

He looked at Montagu.

"I'll of course require a sheet of copying paper," Niven said.

Montagu produced a box of the papers and handed a single sheet to Niven.

Niven took it, put it between two fresh sheets of hotel letterhead, then, with some difficulty, fed all that into the Hermes. They went in slightly off center, and he pulled on the lever that allowed him to square the sheet to the platen. Then he made sure he had the McKenna letterhead handy in order to copy the address.

"Gwatkin?" Niven said to Montagu.

"F.A.S. Gwatkin," Montagu confirmed, then spelled the last name for him.

Niven nodded and began typing:

---

Black Lion Hotel
Mold, North Wales
Tele. No. 98

10th April, 1943

Dear Mr. Gwatkin,

I have considered your recent letter concerning the Settlement which I intend to make on the occasion of William's marriage. The provisions which you outline appear to me reasonable except in one particular. Since in this case the wife's family will not be contributing to the settlement, I do not think it proper that they should necessarily preserve, after William's death, a life interest in the funds which I am approving. I should agree to this course only were there children in the marriage. Will you therefore so re-draft the Settlement as to provide that if there are children the income is paid to the wife only until such time as she remarries or the children come of age. After that date the children alone should benefit.

---

I intend to be in London for the two nights of the 20th & 21st of April. I should be glad if you could make it convenient to take luncheon with me at the Carlton Grill at a quarter to one on Wednesday 21st. If you will bring the new draft with you, we shall have leisure to examine it afterwards. I have written to William & hope that he will be able to join us.

Yrs. Sincerely,

F.A.S. Gwatkin, Esq.
McKenna & Co.
14 Waterloo Place,
London, S.W.1.

He pulled the sheets from the typewriter, put them flat on the table, then handed Fleming a new pen from the box.

"Sign the top copy 'J.G. Martin,' so that it copies to the other page," Niven said.

When he had done that, Niven peeled off the top sheet from the copy sheet.

"Now write 'copy,' all caps, at the top of this one."

"Very well done," Fleming said after he had added the word. "That bit about the kids. Where did you get that?"

"From my uncle," Niven said, looking at Fleming as he handed the letter to Montagu. "He used very much the same language in his papers when my cousin — his son — prepared for marriage. Uncle Alex was frightfully worried that the woman was — as that delightful American phrase puts it — a gold digger. There was quite a large sum of money at risk, and his legal paper was far more complicated than this bit I just used."

"Interesting that you mention money," Montagu said. "We will need to address the personal spending habits of Major Martin. First, however, let's get finished with the legal part."

Montagu had folded in thirds the copy of the letter Niven had just given him and now was repeatedly unfolding and refolding it.

"With a reply from McKenna?" Niven said.

Montagu nodded.

"One to the father?" Fleming said dubiously.

"I agree, Ian. That would not be logical," Stevens said. "Martin would not have his father's letter in his possession."

"Then let's have it concern Major Martin's own legal papers," Montagu said. "He knows that he's off on a highly dangerous mission and, accordingly, wants his affairs in order for Pam should something happen."

"Like his aircraft crashes?" Charity said.

"And he drowns at sea?" the Duchess added.

"Precisely," Montagu said warily, not certain if they were mocking him or not.

"And maybe something concerning the payment of taxes," Niven went on.

"Ah, yes," Fleming said, "the only two things certain in this life, death and taxes."

Niven picked up the McKenna letterhead, then stood and went to the Olivetti Model M40. He spun the letterhead into the Italian typewriter and typed:

McKenna & Co. Solicitors.
14 Waterloo Place
London S.W.1.

19th April, 1943

Our ref.: McL/EG

RE: Your affairs.

Dear Sir,

We thank you for your letter of yesterday's date returning the draft of your will approved. We will insert the legacy of £50 to your batman and our Mr. Gwatkin will bring the fair copy with him when he meets you at lunch on the 21st so that you can sign it there.

The inspector of taxes has asked us for particulars of your service pay and allowances during 1941/2 before he will finally agree to the amount of reliefs due to you for that year. We cannot find that we have ever had these particulars and shall, therefore, be grateful if you will let us have them.

Yours faithfully,

McKENNA & CO.

Major W. Martin, R.M.
Naval & Military Club
94 Piccadilly
London, S.W.1.

Montagu took that, read it over, then passed it around the table.

"Very good," he said. "Now, as to his personality. Specifically, his personal spending habits."

"Thus far," Fleming said, "he has proven to be quite the responsible chap. There must be a chink in the armor. Everyone has one."

"Speak for yourself, sir," Niven said drolly. "My armor is impeccable. As is every other aspect of my personal being."

There were chuckles.

Niven then looked at Ustinov and said, "Didn't you recently get a letter concerning unpaid accounts?"

"It was in error," Ustinov shot back defensively. "And after my confrontation with the manager of the institution, was corrected to my satisfaction."

"Yes, of course," Niven said. "Sorry. I did not mean to suggest any armor problems on your part. What I was going after was, you are still familiar with the tone, the phrasing, et cetera, of that letter?"

"Oh, yes. It was short, sweet, and painfully to the point."

Niven gestured toward the Remington typewriter.

"Have at it," he said.

Montagu produced a new sheet of letterhead, this one from a familiar financial institution, and put it beside the big, heavy American typewriter.

Ustinov shrugged, then moved to the chair in front of the Remington.

He rolled the bank letterhead into the machine. Then he looked at Niven and held up both hands, making them into fists.

"There are ladies present," Niven cautioned, fearful of which digits were about to be displayed.

Ustinov looked to his fists. First the left index finger popped up, then the right index finger.

"I will now show you how this is properly done," Ustinov said formally, and slowly, *very* slowly, punched out the letter with a series of *tap . . . tap . . . tap*s:

---

Lloyds Bank Limited
Head Office
London, E.C.3.

14th April, 1943

Private

Major W. Martin, R.M.
Army & Navy Club
Pall Mall
London, S.W.1.

Dear Sir,

I am given to understand that in spite of repeated application your overdraft amounting to £79 19s 2d still outstands.

---

> In the circumstances, I am now writing to inform you that unless this amount, plus interest at 4% to date of payment, is received forthwith we shall have no alternative but to take the necessary steps to protect our interest.
>
> Yours faithfully,
>
> Joint General Manager

"Luckily for us, this was the short letter," Niven said.

Ustinov removed the sheet from the typewriter, signed it E. Whitley Jones above the title of Joint General Manager, and handed the page to Montagu.

"Any particular reason you used the Army and Navy Club address," Montagu asked, "as opposed to the Naval and Military Club we put on the McKenna letter?"

"He moved," Ustinov said simply.

Montagu made a face of appreciation. "I like that," he said. "Simple. Plausible. And another item for the Germans to confirm — or dissuade them."

He began folding and unfolding this letter, too.

"I'm not sure I like the next part of our exercise," Montagu said. "But we would appear not to have much choice with it. . . ."

## [TWO]
### GULF OF PALERMO, SICILY
### 0235 5 APRIL 1943

The three canvas-skinned kayaks were moving through the dark in a pyramid formation, Dick Canidy paddling on point, with Jim "Tubes" Fuller ten feet off his stern at five o'clock and Frank Nola a little farther back at seven o'clock.

There was a soft rhythmic sound coming from the paddles of Fuller and Nola as their blades dipped in the water. But not from Canidy's; his strokes were awkward, irregular, the blades occasionally making somewhat-noisy slaps as they broke the surface.

*I hate this goddamn excuse for a boat,* Canidy thought.

He had almost immediately decided that he did not care for the kayak over the tiny raft that he had used the first time he went ashore of Sicily. And he hadn't been a big fan of that damn rubber doughnut, either.

He granted that the kayak was faster. But

he was convinced that it could capsize at any second.

*And being faster probably also means faster to sink when the damn thing dumps over.*

Canidy also was more than a little apprehensive about transitioning from the rickety boat to shore. He mentally went over how he was going to accomplish it, then realized that that was pretty much an exercise in futility since he had never done it before.

*And, therefore, I have no fucking idea of what I'm doing and what's going to happen.*

*Except there's every possibility that I'll get soaking wet.*

*Which is okay as long as I don't dump the W/T.*

It did not necessarily help that both Nola and Fuller maneuvered like expert kayakers. They each worked their paddle, with the blades at opposite ends of the shaft, with the smooth, regular rotation of a windmill.

*Small surprise. Nola's whole life has been in boats.*

*Fuller probably learned at the beach or in Boy Scouts . . . or both.*

*Me, I was born to fly above all this damn nonsense.*

Out of the corner of Canidy's right eye, a motion in the darkness at about three o'-clock caught his attention. Carefully, so as not to upset the boat, he turned to look.

It was the bow of Fuller's boat. More precisely, it was the extra paddle Fuller had tied to the bow to project out in front of his boat.

And hanging from the tip of the blade was a veritable ship's figurehead — the squirming soft pouch dangling by its pull-string closure.

Canidy couldn't stop himself — he chuckled.

As Tubes paddled up alongside, he heard Canidy and smiled.

"Thought it'd be a good idea to use Adolf and Eva as our early-warning system," Tubes said, grinning.

Canidy just shook his head.

Wordlessly, Tubes paddled ahead and took point.

The sounds of small waves lapping on the pebble beach became louder and louder.

Canidy heard the sudden scraping of Fuller's boat running up on the shore, then some quick movement, then footsteps crunching on pebbles, then the sliding of the boat as it was pulled up onto dry land.

*Well, good for you, Tubes. You made it.*

*Too bad you can't show me how you did it.*

Canidy looked over his left shoulder. He saw the vague outline of Nola in his kayak.

He had already shipped his paddle, apparently in preparation for landing, and Canidy decided that he should follow suit.

Just as Canidy began to vaguely make out the outline of the shore, he heard footsteps crunching on the pebbles, then splashing in the water. They were coming toward him. He instinctively reached back to make sure he had quick access to the .45 in the small of his back. At the moment he touched the pistol, he saw the distinct shape of Tubes coming closer.

Tubes casually stepped sure-footedly through the shallow surf.

*With such ease, he looks as if he just as well would be headed out to go swimming.*

"I got it," Tubes whispered as he grabbed the bow of Canidy's boat.

He then towed the kayak to the shoreline, where he turned it parallel to the beach, and held it steady.

Canidy grabbed the gunnels of his boat, then awkwardly rose from his seated position and stepped ashore, his feet dry.

"Thanks," he whispered.

Just then, a few feet away, there came the sound of a boat scraping on pebbles. Canidy turned in time to see the bow of Nola's kayak coming out of the darkness, then the silhouette of Nola himself as he maneuvered the boat parallel to the shore and, with cat-like grace, leapt out and landed on his feet.

Nola then picked the bow of his boat up high and, with very little sound, moved the entire boat onto shore.

Canidy did likewise. Then he looked up and down the beach. There were no lights except from the stars, and he saw absolutely nothing inland but darkness beyond a distance of maybe ten feet.

He heard Nola's boots crunching toward him.

"I know precisely where we are," Nola whispered. "Is a popular bathing beach. And a ten-meter cliff is close by. Is where I told you there are small *grotta* — the caves — where we can hide the boats. Vergine Maria —"

"*Virgin* Maria?" Tubes whispered excitedly.

"Not *that* kind of a virgin," Canidy said drily. "It's the town's name."

Even in the dim of darkness, Canidy thought he could see disappointment on Fuller's face.

"Vergine Maria is where we are," Nola went on. "And, from here, is only two kilometers to my cousin's house in Palermo."

"Good," Canidy whispered. "Let's get our gear moved up there."

He then took a tentative sniff of the still air. It had a pleasant, salty smell mixed with

385

the light fragrance of some flowering foliage he did not recognize.

*Not a hint of stench of the dead.*

"How's Adolf and Eva?" Canidy whispered.

Tubes checked the pouch.

"Active movement," Tubes said, the hint of a smile in his voice. "I think they're procreating."

"You would."

Canidy saw that the folding boats were fairly easy to collapse — *Glad I didn't know that offshore,* he thought — then hide in two of the small caves in the cliff. Certainly not as easy as the rubber raft had been — that one he had deflated with a slice of his Fairbairn, then buried it in a small hole.

Farther down the cliff, they hid one of the green suitcase radios by itself in a cave. Moving with one of the cases without being seen was going to be hard enough. And stashing the other provided them with a backup in the event that the other was confiscated, broken, lost — whatever. They could retrieve the hidden case the next night, or even later.

And that took care of the evidence of their arrival. They had no worry about leaving tracks. The pebbles of the shore filled in naturally behind them as they went.

Canidy stood with his black duffel bag, the strap slung over his shoulder. Nola carried a small black leather bag in his left hand, the box of mice in his right. And Fuller, his duffel on his left shoulder, held the other suitcase radio in his right hand. He had tied the pull string of the mice pouch high on his duffel strap, the pouch itself touching his chest.

"Anyone have a cigarette?" Tubes suddenly whispered.

*What?* Canidy thought.

He hissed, "You can't light up! You could get us shot by coastwatchers!"

"It's not for me," Tubes whispered casually. "I don't smoke."

He held up the pouch and dangled it by the string in front of Canidy's face.

"Judging by their relaxed state, they would appear postcoital."

Canidy relaxed, then caught himself about to chuckle.

*No, not good . . . Need to focus.*

"Knock it off, Tubes!" Canidy whispered, trying to sound angry.

"Right," Tubes said in a mock-English tone.

"I mean it, dammit!" Canidy said.

There was silence, and Canidy guessed that he had hurt Fuller's feelings.

*Fuck it. Grow up. We've got a job to do.*

"Are we ready?" Canidy said evenly.

"Sure," Fuller whispered, with some ice in his tone.

"Ready," Nola whispered.

On the submarine, Canidy had debated with himself how they should go into town — armed to the teeth, or try to get there as quickly and unobtrusively as possible.

They were not at a loss for weapons.

Canidy had his Colt Model 1911 .45 ACP semiautomatic pistol, the Johnson .30-06 light machine gun, and the baby Fairbairn. Fuller carried a .45, too, and a Sten 9mm submachine gun. And Nola was armed with his own personal Walther P38 9mm semiautomatic pistol; he had declined the offer of an automatic weapon since he'd had no experience handling one.

In the end, Canidy had decided that each man should have his pistol close at hand. But the bigger guns could be held as backup, left in the duffels.

His reasoning, after all, was that there would be no firepower needed if they were to find a city full of dead citizens. Or if instead they were to encounter, say, a city overrun with German and Italian troops, they sure as hell were not going to engage in a firefight — not and get out alive.

*We're supposed to get in, get the intel, and get the hell out.*

*And that's exactly what I plan to do.*

"Lead the way, Frank," Canidy whispered. "Or tell me the direction and I'll take point."

"I can do it," Nola said and started walking.

After a dozen yards or so, Canidy felt that they were walking up a light grade. A few more yards beyond that, the grade became steeper. Then the path leveled off, and Canidy could see out over the water, the light from the stars reflecting on the surface. There was no visible horizon, and it appeared that the sky and sea had become one.

They began walking southwestward along a dirt path that paralleled the main, two-lane road. On either side of the uneven rocky trail grew hardy, dense shrubs, about chest-high to the men. The growth provided them with some cover. If necessary, they could duck down for total concealment.

There were absolutely no lights to be seen anywhere. Canidy could not determine if that was a good sign or a bad one. Where they walked was not at all populated — they had yet to pass any structure, residence or otherwise — but still he thought that there might be some man-made light somewhere in the distance.

*Of course, the absence of such man-made light could mean the absence of man himself.*

Off to their right, near the main road, Canidy noticed a low wall constructed of a white stone that showed up well in the dark. It followed alongside the lane, off into the distance as far as his eye could see. And it continued to do so, even after they had walked along for some five or so minutes.

"What's with the wall?" Canidy whispered to Nola.

"What do you mean?"

"The stone wall over by the road. What does it go to?"

"Oh. That is Cimitero dei Rotoli."

"That's what?" Fuller said.

"A monumental cemetery," Nola explained. "Is the size of what would be many, many city blocks, long and wide, and on up the mountainside."

*That's massive!* Canidy thought.

*Wonder how busy it's been lately?*

He was about to suggest that they make a detour and pass through it, looking for any evidence of mass graves. But then he decided that that wasn't necessary. He really wanted to get an eyeball on the harbor.

*It should tell me everything I need to know.*

Twenty minutes later, they reached the outskirts of a hamlet. The main road cut through its score of low, brightly painted buildings constructed of masonry.

"Palermo?" Fuller said.

Canidy realized that that was the first thing that Tubes had said since he had chastised him.

Then Canidy thought, *Not Palermo. Too small.*

"This is Arenella," Nola announced softly. "We are more than halfway there. Only about another kilometer."

"You okay with your gear, Tubes?" Canidy asked Fuller. "Need to trade, or take a break?"

"I'm fine," Fuller replied. "Thanks."

*So he's not pissed anymore,* Canidy thought. *Good.*

"And Adolf and Eva are still kicking," Fuller added. "I know you'd want to know."

"Thanks," Canidy said.

With Nola still in the lead and Fuller bringing up the rear, they passed Arenella, staying on the path between its outer edge and the seashore.

Canidy kept looking for lights. And kept finding nothing but black night.

*But it is — what? — maybe three, four in the morning.*

*Normal people are asleep at this hour.*

Suddenly, Nola made a noisy grunt — and stumbled forward.

*Find a nice rock there, Frank?*

Canidy whispered, "You okay?"

Then, just ahead of Canidy's feet, there came the painful moaning of a strange man's voice.

Canidy stopped in his tracks. He brought out his pistol as he crouched down beside some shrubs off the trail. He let his duffel slip to the ground.

Seconds later, Canidy heard Fuller coming up the path fast, and, with his left arm, Canidy motioned for Fuller to get behind him.

"Get your penlight," Canidy whispered to Fuller.

More moaning came from the man on the path.

"You okay, Frank?" Canidy called.

Far up the path, a tiny beam of light appeared. It was aimed at the ground; then it illuminated what looked like the box that held the mice.

Faintly, but clearly, Canidy heard Nola's worried tone: "*Dammit!*"

*He must have hauled ass after he fell.*

*Whatever it is, it scared the shit out of Frank . . . or still is.*

392

Then it occurred to him that Nola could get in the line of fire.

"Stay put!" Canidy called back. "And stay down!"

Canidy felt a solid tap on his shoulder.

"Here," Fuller said, holding out the pen-light.

"Shine it on him," Canidy said, "or whatever it is on the trail."

A moment later, a thin beam of yellow light appeared. It illuminated a tiny spot of shrubs across the path, then found the dirt path and meandered up it. The beam passed countless sun-bleached stones, then one large, dark rock — *Christ, that one alone could have tripped me,* Canidy thought — then finally found one of the man's legs, then the other. His pants were filthy.

Canidy thought, *Finally, we find someone . . . and he's damn near dead.*

The yellow beam danced its way up the leg, reached the buttocks, then continued up to the untucked shirttail. From what they had seen so far, the body was short and stout.

"Hit the face," Canidy whispered.

The yellow beam immediately went farther up — too far — first into the shrubs, then backtracked till it found the head.

The man's face was turned away from Canidy and Fuller, looking toward where

Nola was laying low. The man appeared to be older, maybe in his fifties, with wavy white hair.

*I can't see any signs of skin lesions,* Canidy thought, *no real evidence of gas poisoning.*

*Maybe he was farther away during the explosion, and what poison reached him is just now showing its signs.*

"Check his hands," Canidy said.

It took Fuller a moment to locate them individually. The man was splayed out, his arms awkwardly pointed in opposite directions, and Fuller had had to start with each shoulder and work the beam out from there, following each arm until he reached the hand.

*No lesions on the skin of his hands, either,* Canidy thought.

He said, "No weapons. Put the beam back on his head and hold it there."

Fuller did.

Canidy then stood up from his crouch and, with his pistol aimed squarely between the man's shoulder blades, carefully moved toward him. The man made no move whatsoever.

When Canidy reached him, he used the toe of his right shoe to nudge the man's hip.

The man groaned but otherwise didn't move.

Canidy stepped to the other side, trying to

get a look at the man's face.

"C'mere," Canidy called impatiently to Fuller.

Fuller came running with the penlight.

"Hit his face with that beam."

When Fuller did, Canidy said, disgustedly, "Oh, for christsake!"

"Is he dying?" Nola said, approaching slowly.

Canidy looked at Nola and said, "What happened up there?"

"The mice," Nola said, disappointment in his tone, "they got out of the box when it fell. The lid opened. I am sorry."

*You mean when* you *fell and* you *dropped the box?* Canidy thought.

*So we're down to two mice? No backups?*

*Oh, hell.*

*Nothing to do about it now.*

Canidy rolled the man over onto his back. When he did, Fuller moved the light, and it first found a wine bottle that had been between the man's chest and the path.

Then he shined the beam from the man's face down to his soiled shirt, then to his sodden pants. His fly was open, his penis barely out.

"The sonofabitch is stone-fucking-drunk," Canidy announced. "And it would appear that he passed out in the process of pissing his pants."

There was a moment's silence before Fuller spoke up:

"At least it's not gas poisoning. . . ."

They came to the edge of Palermo. As they skirted a piazza, then reached an intersection that Canidy thought that he recalled, an obese cat suddenly bolted out of an alley.

It saw the three men and raced straight for them.

Fuller instinctively reached up to his shoulder strap and, with his big hands covering the pouch tied there, protected the mice from attack.

Then, just as suddenly, the cat made a ninety-degree turn and disappeared down another alley near the piazza.

As Fuller exchanged glances with Nola, Tubes looking somewhat embarrassed, a wiry dog came flying out of the first alley. It was apparent that he was looking around for the cat. When he found the cat was gone, he shook his body from nose to tail, clearly pleased with himself and his little game.

The dog looked at the men, wagged his tail twice, then turned back for the alley.

*More signs of normal life,* Canidy thought. *Thank God.*

Nola began leading the way again, making

turns with the conviction of a citizen of Palermo that he was.

*It's interesting how attached they've become to the mice,* Canidy found himself thinking.

*Or maybe it's not the mice.*

*Maybe it's what the mice represent — a sure way to save their asses in a situation where, right now, nothing is for sure.*

*Because even now — especially now — the answers still are wildly unknown.*

From the time they had left the drunk to sleep off his bender in the path near Arenella, Canidy had been running scenarios based on that encounter.

*But what can you really make of one drunk?*

*No telling where that guy had been when the gas went up.*

*Or maybe it didn't, and the sonofabitch was just plain stinking drunk.*

*Who knows?*

*We should, very shortly.*

After another block, Canidy realized that they were headed back uphill.

"Where the hell are we going, Frank?" Canidy said.

"My cousin's," Nola said, "is ten blocks this way —"

"No," Canidy said.

Nola and Fuller stopped and looked with some frustration at Canidy. Clearly, everyone was tired — and more than a little apprehensive.

Canidy glanced at his watch. It was just shy of five o'clock. They would have to hurry to beat the sunrise.

He quickly looked around. When he glanced up, he saw a street sign bolted to the side of the building. It read VIA MONTABLO.

And he recognized that from when he'd first come to Palermo. He remember it intersected with Quinta Casa street. Which led to the port.

"This way first," he said, nodding downhill. "I have to see the harbor. It's only a few blocks. Then we go to your cousin's."

As they went, Canidy thought he heard the sounds of movement coming from one of the buildings they passed, then from another.

*I must be imagining things.*

*Willing there to be someone moving, getting up.*

But, he realized, it was the right time. It wouldn't be unusual for some people — one, two, a few — to be getting up.

*Even Sicily has to have its own early risers.*

At the next corner, where the sign on the building read VIA QUINTA CASA, they turned left.

Then across the street, in a window, Canidy saw something move.

It was a curtain being drawn back. Then, beyond that, a candle was being lit.

"Look!" he said, pointing.

Nola and Fuller followed to where he was pointing.

*Human life,* Canidy thought.

*Maybe it is okay here after all.*

*Or at least not a horrific human disaster. . . .*

He picked up the pace. They now were about two blocks from the fishermen's pier where the cargo ship had been moored.

And then they were within one block.

And then . . . they suddenly encountered a stench.

"What the hell is that?" Fuller said.

*Not fish decay,* Canidy thought. *It's a far more corrupted odor.*

He looked back at Nola and Fuller.

Fuller had the collar of his T-shirt pulled up over his nose, using it as a makeshift air filter.

Nola had buried his nose in the crook of his arm, breathing through the fabric of his shirtsleeve.

They finished walking the last of the final block and turned the corner.

Nola literally gasped at the sight.

*Shit!* Canidy thought, and instinctively stepped into the shadow of a doorway, out of sight.

Nola and Fuller followed him, their eyes

fixed on the heavy wooden beams that formed a fifteen-foot-tall framework over the foot of the pier.

There, from the uppermost beam, the bodies of two fishermen hung from wire nooses, their silhouettes backlit by the ruby horizon of the sun that was just about to rise. Dried blood caked their faces and upper torsos.

Canidy tore his eyes from the horror and scanned the port area.

He noticed that the T-shaped pier where the cargo ship with the Tabun had been tied up no longer was a *T*. It was a stub, only a third its original length. And then he saw that the pebble beach was stacked with the burned hulls of the smaller fishing boats.

"That explains why there was no fishing-boat traffic near shore," Canidy said softly. "No one is going in or out of this place."

Nola still stared at the sunbaked bodies.

"They look," he said, his voice beginning to quiver again, "as if they have been there for some time."

"About a week —" Canidy began.

He stopped when he heard behind him the wrenching sound of Jim Fuller violently throwing up on the sidewalk.

# [THREE]
## OSS WHITBEY HOUSE STATION
## KENT, ENGLAND
## 1550 3 APRIL 1943

"What exactly do you mean you're not sure you like this next part, Ewen?" Commander Ian Fleming said. "And that there's little we can do?"

Lieutenant Commander Ewen Montagu raised his eyebrows.

"It's not exactly a terrible thing," he explained. "Certainly, not what I feared it could be." He paused, gathered his thoughts, then went on: "It would appear that everyone likes to be a spy. No one more so than those so high that they could not possibly be one; they are stuck at their desks, making the big decisions."

"Who are we talking about?" Major David Niven said.

"As we were in the process of getting approvals for this mission," Montagu explained, "the Vice Chief became keenly interested in how this ruse would play out —"

"So Archie Nye wanted to play?"

Niven said.

Montagu nodded. "Very much so. Without any inquiries on my part, he offered up some scenarios. Then he approached Lord Mountbatten —"

"Oh, for christsake!" Niven interrupted. "Dickie got involved, too? Have they not enough to do?"

"Dickie?" Charity repeated.

"Mountbatten's nickname," Niven explained. "He got it, story goes, due to some nonsense concerning Czar Nicholas of Russia." He looked at Montagu. "Anyway, what exactly did Archie and Dickie have to offer?"

Montagu pulled two sheets of typewritten paper from his briefcase and handed them to Niven.

Niven quickly read the first page, making an occasional grunt as he went down the sheet. When he had finished, he slid it across the table to Fleming and began reading the second page.

Fleming picked up the first letter and began reading:

In Reply, Quote S.R. *1924/43*

COMBINED OPERATIONS
HEADQUARTERS

## 1A RICHMOND TERRACE
## WHITEHALL S.W.I

21st April, 1943

*Dear Admiral of the Fleet,*

I promised V.C.I.G.S. that the Major would arrange with you for the onward transmission of a letter he had with him for General Alexander. It is very urgent and very "hot" and, as there are some remarks in it that could not be seen by others in the War Office, it could not go by signal. I feel sure that you will see that it goes on safely and without delay.

I think you will find the Major the man you want. He is quiet and shy at first, but he really knows his stuff. He was more accurate than some of us about the probable run of events at Dieppe, and he had been well in on the experiments which took place up in Scotland.

Let me have him back, please, as soon as the assault is over. He might bring some sardines with him — they are on "points" here!

```
                          Yours Sincerely,

                          Louis Mountbatten

Admiral of the Fleet Sir A.B. Cunningham,
G.C.B., D.S.O.
Commander in Chief Mediterranean
Allied Force H.Q.,
Algiers
```

When Fleming had finished, he looked up and found Niven holding out the second sheet.

"I like the reference to Dieppe and the experiments," Fleming said. "Gives him a genuine air of being connected and in the know."

"And the sardines line is bloody brilliant," Niven said. "It screams *Sardinia* — yet subtly."

"And he doesn't want his major stolen," Fleming added. "Sets the mind not to think about something causing the letter not to be delivered. Clever."

Fleming passed the page that he held to Charity, then took the second page from Niven and read:

In Reply, Quote S.R. *1989/43*

COMBINED OPERATIONS
HEADQUARTERS
1A RICHMOND TERRACE
WHITEHALL S.W.I

22nd April, 1943

*Dear General,*

I am sending you herewith two copies of the pamphlet which has been prepared describing the activities of my Command; I have also enclosed copies of the photographs which are to be included in the pamphlet.

The book has been written by Hilary St. George Saunders, the English author of <u>Battle of Britain, Bomber Command,</u> and other pamphlets which have had a great success in this country and yours.

This edition which is to be published in the States has already enjoyed pre-publication sales of nearly a million and a half, and I understand the American authorities will distribute the book widely throughout the U.S. Army.

I understand from the British Information Service in Washington that they would like a "message" from you for use in the advertising for the pamphlet, and that they have asked you direct, through Washington, for such a message.

I am sending the proofs by hand of my Royal Marines Staff Officer. I need not say how honoured we shall all be if you will give such a message. I fully realise what a lot is being asked of you at a time when you are so fully occupied with infinitely more important matters. But I hope you may find a few minutes' time to provide the pamphlet with an expression of your invaluable approval so that it will be read widely and given every chance to bring its message of co-operation to our two peoples.

We are watching your splendid progress with admiration and pleasure and wish we could be with you.

You may speak freely to my Staff Officer in this as well as any other matters since he has my entire confidence.

Yours Sincerely,

"Well, I understand why it would be foolish for us not to use these," Fleming said. "That is to say, foolish to use a variation of them. The signatures are genuine." He looked at Montagu. "Right?"

"They are indeed by their own hands."

"I have proofs of the pamphlet, and photographs," Montagu said. "More filler for the briefcase. Which was the original idea — that there would be a logical reason why he'd have personal and business papers all mixed together, the mundane among the most secret."

He then produced a final letter.

"Which brings us to the big one," he said.

Niven took the two pages and began to read. When he had finished the first page, he passed it to Fleming, who then read it:

VICE CHIEF OF THE IMPERIAL
GENERAL STAFF
WAR OFFICE

# WHITEHALL, LONDON S.W.I

## <u>Personal and Most Secret</u>

23rd April, 1943

My Dear Alex,

I am taking advantage of sending you a personal letter by hand of one of Mountbatten's officers to give you the inside history of our recent exchange of cables about Mediterranean operations and their attendant cover plans. You may have felt our decisions were somewhat arbitrary, but I can assure you in fact that the Chiefs of Staff Committee gave the most careful consideration both to your recommendations and also to Jumbo's.

We have had recent information that the Boche have been reinforcing and strengthening their defences in Greece and Crete, and C.I.G.S. felt that our forces for the assault were insufficient. It was agreed by the Chiefs of Staff that the 5th Division should be reinforced by one Brigade Group for the assault on the beach south of Cape Araxos and that a similar reinforcement should be made for the 56th Division at Kalamata. We are earmarking the necessary forces and shipping.

Jumbo Wilson had proposed to select Sicily as cover target for Husky; but we have already chosen it as cover for Operation Brimstone. The C.O.S. committee went into the whole question exhaustively again and came to the conclusion that, in view of the preparations in Algeria, the amphibious training which will be taking place on the Tunisian coast, and the heavy air bombardment which will be put down to neutralise the Sicilian airfields, we should stick to our plan of making it cover for Brimstone — indeed, we stand a very good chance of making him think we will go for Sicily — it is an obvious objective and one about which he must be nervous. On the other hand, they felt there wasn't much hope of persuading the Boche that the extensive preparations in the eastern Mediterranean were also directed at Sicily. For this reason, they have told Wilson his cover plan should be something nearer the spot, e.g., the Dodecanese. Since our relations with Turkey are now so obviously closer, the Italians must be pretty apprehensive about these islands.

I imagine you will agree with these arguments. I know you will have your hands more than full at the moment and you haven't much chance of discussing future operations with Eisenhower. But if by chance you do want to support Wilson's proposal, I hope you will let us know soon, because we can't delay much longer.

I am very sorry we weren't able to meet your wishes about the new commander of the Guards Brigade. Your own nominee was down with a bad attack of 'flu and not likely to be really fit for another few weeks. No doubt, however, you know Forster personally; he has done extremely well in command of a brigade at home, and is, I think, the best fellow available.

You must be about as fed up as we are with the whole question of war medals and "Purple Hearts." We all agree with you that we don't want to offend our American friends, but there is a good deal more to it than that. If our troops who happen to be serving in one particular theatre are to get extra decorations merely because the Americans happen to be serving there, too, we will be faced with a good deal of discontent among those troops fighting elsewhere perhaps just as bitterly — or more so. My own feeling is that we should thank the Americans for their kind

offer but say firmly it would cause too many
anomalies and we are sorry we can't accept.
But it is on the agenda for the next Military
Members Meeting and I hope you will have a
decision very soon.

Laus Deo.
Yours ever,
Archie Nye

General the Honourable Sir Harold R.L.G.
Alexander,
G.C.B., C.S.I., D.S.O., M.C.
Headquarters
18th Army Group

"Jumbo Wilson is Field Marshal Wilson —"
Niven said.

"Right," Montagu interrupted.

"But what is Brimstone?" Niven went on.

"That's the fake code name for Sardinia.
Sir Archibald chose it. Clever, yes?"

Fleming nodded.

"And he used Husky for the eastern op,"
Fleming said.

"Reasoning behind that," Montagu said,
"is that it's not *if* but rather *when* the Germans will come across an operation with the
code name of Husky."

*"Laus Deo,"* Charity added. "Nice touch."

"Praise God," Montagu said solemnly. "Always appropriate."

"This letter covers a lot of ground," Fleming said. "As do the others. But this one, especially this big one, I don't think I would change anything in it if I could. It smells like the real thing because it is the real thing."

"Agreed," Niven said. "Just hope the Krauts think so."

Everyone else around the table nodded their assent.

Montagu then looked at the bulk of the work for the day and smiled.

"Well," he said, "thank you all. I do believe that we are finished with this aspect. That leaves us to collect only a few more minor miscellaneous items — his ID, the coins and such one would find in his pockets, et cetera. Tomorrow we can handle that, then Major Martin shall be dressed and the complete package prepared. Then we're off to the *Seraph*."

"Splendid piece of work," Fleming said.

"Thank you," Niven said.

"The compliment was meant for Ewen," Fleming said. "But, okay, you did brilliantly yourself."

"Thank you," Niven repeated. "And thank you, everyone." He paused, and, with raised eyebrows, added: "Formalities complete, then we are finished for the day?"

Montagu nodded. "I do believe so."

"Then I say it's to the pub for commencement of Attitude Adjustment Hour!" Niven said.

"I'm not certain there is any booze left after your bender last night," Private Ustinov said.

# [FOUR]
## PALERMO, SICILY
## 0650 5 APRIL 1943

Moving as quickly and as quietly as they could, Frank Nola led Dick Canidy and Jim "Tubes" Fuller back up the hill along Via Quinta Casa. They worked their way past the train station at Via Montepellegrino, and finally to a street off Via Altavilla that was lined with two-story apartment buildings.

The morning light was getting brighter by the minute.

And the sounds of people stirring was becoming greater.

*So, more and more signs that there weren't mass deaths,* Canidy thought.

It was not necessarily a well-kept neighborhood. There was some trash in the gutters of the street. The masonry exterior of the buildings had holes and large cracks that needed patching. Some appeared to have needed attention years earlier, as wild plants had taken seed in the cracks and were growing thickly there.

Nola stopped at a wooden door to one apartment house. It once had been painted a bright yellow color but now was faded and peeling. A small, weathered wooden cross was hung centered in a small niche above the door.

Next to the door was a large, single window with ornamental wrought iron protecting it. The rusted ironwork had a series of four iron baskets welded to it, and each of these held a clay flowerpot painted in elaborate colors. The plants in the pots looked unattended, their leaves drooping and dirt dry.

*Clearly, no one's tended to those recently,* Canidy thought.

The lace curtains behind the dirty panes of the window were drawn shut. There was no evidence of movement or light inside.

Nola knocked loudly on the door. There was no answer after a minute, and he banged even louder.

*That should awaken the neighborhood,* Canidy thought, *if not the dead.*

Nola looked impatient. He glanced over at

the window, then back at the door. Then his face registered something.

He went over the wrought ironwork and began lifting the far-right pot out of its holder. He looked inside the holder, under the pot, then immediately dropped the pot back in. He moved to the pot to its left and repeated the procedure. When he pulled out the third pot and looked inside, he shook his head. He then reached in under the pot, pulled out a big brass key, its finish mottled by minerals from the potting soil, and dropped the pot back in its holder.

"My cousin's wife," Nola said, rolling his eyes. "Nicole, she never puts anything back where she gets it. We are lucky there was a key in any of the pots."

He went to the door. He slipped the key into its lock, turned it, then worked the wobbly doorknob until it finally rotated. The door swung inward and they all quickly went inside.

The first room off the front door, which turned out to be the kitchen, was dark.

*"Ciao, Mariano!"* Nola called out as he walked to the window. *"Ciao, Nicole!"*

Nola put his leather satchel on the kitchen counter, then pulled the lace curtains open.

"That's not a good idea," Canidy said, "letting people see who's in here."

415

Nola looked at him a moment. He considered what Canidy had said, then looked around the room. He saw two large candles and a box of matches on the flimsy folding table in the middle of the kitchen. He pulled the curtains closed and then lit the candles.

"I will go check if anyone is here," Nola said, then motioned toward the two wooden chairs at the flimsy table. "Sit. This will be our home."

Canidy looked around the kitchen. It was filthy. A garbage can stood unemptied. The sink overflowed with foul-looking plates that were crusted with what was left of some rice and chopped meat, maybe pork or lamb. The tiled countertop had a collection of dirty glasses. One was half empty, a nasty growth of some type floating in it. A fat black cockroach scampered out of a chipped bowl, then disappeared into a gap in the grout where the counter met the wall.

*Our home?* Canidy thought. *Not in this dump, if we can avoid it.*

"Please, sit," Nola said, adding: "I be right back."

Nola started for the back of the apartment.

"Nicole!" he called as he went. "Mariano!"

In moments, they could hear him going up wooden steps, still calling out the names.

Canidy put his duffel on the floor beside one of the chairs, pulled the chair back from the table, moved it so that he would have a view of the window and door, and sat down.

He motioned to Fuller.

"Go ahead, Tubes. Take a load off your feet."

Fuller slid the suitcase under the table, then put his duffel on the floor, untying the pouch from its strap. He put the pouch on the table.

Canidy looked at it, and, when it showed movement inside, he grinned.

"Thank God for small comforts, huh?"

Fuller shrugged. "I guess."

"Keep an eye on them," Canidy said lightly. "Those two may not stand a chance in hell against the cockroaches in this place."

Fuller didn't respond. And Canidy now realized that he really had not regained all the color in his face. He still looked fairly pale.

"You'll be all right, Tubes," Canidy said. "We all will."

He looked at the pouch.

"So far so good, right, Adolf? Eva?"

Tubes made a small smile.

Canidy reached down to his duffel and began pulling out what Fuller recognized as pieces of a rifle.

As Canidy put the weapon's receiver on his

lap, he noticed Tubes was watching with interest.

"Johnny gun," Canidy said. "Officially, Johnson Model of 1941 Light Machine Gun."

"Never seen one."

"Not many have," Canidy said. "Marine Corps reserve officer Melvin Maynard Johnson, Jr. — a Boston attorney — wanted something to beat the Browning Automatic Rifle. So he built this. It's eight pounds lighter than the BAR, and a helluva lot more flexible."

He pulled its barrel out of his duffel, then quickly and effortlessly assembled it to the receiver.

"See?" Canidy said. "Unscrewing the BAR's barrel is such a bitch, it's next to impossible. Leave it to a jarhead to come up with a practical design for the easy swapping of barrels and for general field servicing. Plus, it packs compact."

He reached back into the duffel bag, brought out two curved box magazines and held one up.

"Twenty rounds of thirty-aught-six Springfield, same as the BAR," he said, then smacked the mag into the mount in the left side of the receiver.

"Presto. Ready to go."

He turned and stood the Johnny gun on its butt, leaning its muzzle against the cabinets where they formed a *V.*

"Helluva weapon," Canidy said. "Too bad the bureaucrats killed its chances of mass production."

Fuller nodded, then reached into his duffel, and brought out his British-made Sten 9mm submachine gun and a magazine.

Holding the Sten with its barrel pointed to the ceiling, he fed the magazine into the opening under the receiver, and checked to make sure the breech was clear. Then he slug its strap over his right shoulder, letting the weapon hang there, ready.

"Now what?" Fuller said.

Nola came back into the room. He had a look of worry.

"No one here —" Nola announced, then paused when he saw the long guns.

"That would mean that Tubes's question remains all the more valid," Canidy said.

Nola's face was questioning.

"To wit, now what?" Canidy said.

"I'm not sure," Nola said. "It doesn't appear that anyone has been here for some time."

"No shit," Canidy said and jerked his right thumb toward the sink. "Looks like they may have left in a hurry, too."

Nola glanced in that direction, then looked to be in deep thought.

"So far," Canidy went on, "the only thing we have confirmed is, one, that the cargo ship blew up and, two, that there weren't mass deaths from the nerve gas."

Fuller looked at Canidy.

"Those men who were hung," Fuller said.

Canidy raised an eyebrow.

"Yeah?" he said.

"What do you think they were trying to get? I mean, the people who hung them."

"Me," Canidy said.

*"You?"*

Canidy nodded.

"If they had hung them just to kill them," Canidy explained, "then that's what they would have done. They'd have strung them up, then disposed of them, probably just thrown their bodies to the sharks." He paused. "Hell, not even that. They'd have just made them get on their knees at the end of a pier and put a bullet in the head. *Then* fed them to the hammerheads and makos, kicking them into the sea if they hadn't fallen in when shot. They're evil *and* lazy."

*"They,"* Fuller said. "You keep saying *they.*"

"The SS," Nola offered. "Or the OVRA, the Italian secret police."

"It's the SS," Canidy said. "No question."

"Why are they after you?" Fuller said.

"They're looking for whoever blew up the cargo ship. "

"You," Fuller said.

Canidy shrugged.

"Yeah. That's what those SS sons of bitches do. That's how they smoke out anyone who's in or supports the Resistance. They'll literally crucify a whole village — slaughter men, women, children — to make them examples of what will happen to anyone else who works against the Nazis. Sometimes, it's not even for the message. Sometimes, it's just pure, unadulterated evil, often in the name of revenge."

Fuller tried to comprehend that. It was clear he had other questions.

And then, after a moment, he asked, "What happened to their eyes?"

"What do you mean?" Canidy said.

"The eyes of the men who were hung," Fuller said. "They were missing, nothing but bloody sockets."

"Birds, probably the seagulls, got them."

Fuller nodded. That he understood. He'd seen seagulls tearing into fish on the beach. They had, at once, disgusted and impressed him by how they got inside the fish — pecking in with their beak through the soft parts of the eyes and the anus.

"Very likely," Canidy added, "that happened after the SS gouged the eyes with a bayonet."

Fuller looked like he might be sick again.

"You going to be all right?" Canidy said.

Fuller nodded meekly.

Canidy went on: "It sends a message, too. 'You don't tell us what you see, what you know, then we will take your ability to see.' Same thing with the mouth."

Fuller narrowed his eyes. Then he shook his head to show that he didn't understand.

"Those shits in the SS," Canidy explained, "they take a special joy in smashing prisoners in the mouth with the butts of their Mausers. They do it till all the teeth are knocked out. Message being: 'You don't talk, then we'll see that you really can't talk.' " He paused. "Of course, the *real* message is for those who witness such atrocities: 'Cooperate or this will be you.' "

Fuller was familiar with the Mauser Karabiner 98k. He had fired one of the bolt-action carbines that the OSS had in Algiers — and painfully recalled the dense wooden stock with its butt plate made of steel. The mental image of that steel striking teeth made him uneasy.

Canidy looked at Fuller and felt obligated

to add, "I have to say that it certainly has gotten my attention."

Fuller nodded.

"But," Canidy said finally, "unfortunately for the SS, it's only served to piss me off."

Canidy noticed Fuller's unease and decided that he had said enough on the subject.

*Need to get his mind thinking about something else.*

"Can you give some thought to getting the radio set up?" Canidy now said to Fuller.

Fuller brightened slightly. He nodded. "Sure."

Canidy looked at Nola.

"Where's a good place, Frank?" He pointed to the ceiling. "Maybe the roof? Is there access?"

"Yes."

"Can anyone — a neighbor up the hill, say — look down on it?"

Nola thought about that, then said, "I don't think so."

"Okay," Canidy said. "But we'll let Tubes determine that."

He looked at the chronograph on his wrist.

"It's now oh-seven-thirty," Canidy said. "The *Casabianca* right now should be waiting on the bottom. Our first opportunity tonight to contact her is twenty-one fifteen. That's just under fourteen hours from now.

And the last chance is six hours after that, at oh-three-fifteen. That gives us a lot of time."

"To do what?" Nola said.

"To find out what happened to the Tabun that Professor Rossi said was on the boat. Did it go up in smoke? It does not appear that it did — at least, judging by the fact that the cloud did not cause mass death — so where is it? On the harbor bottom?"

Nola nodded his understanding.

"And then," Canidy said, "we need to find out about the villa with the yellow-fever lab. Or maybe we can do that first and it will lead us to the answer about the gas."

Fuller looked at Canidy and said, "If those fishermen were hung because the SS want to find out who blew up the boat, then wouldn't there be a price on your head?"

"As far as the SS is concerned, yes," Canidy said. "But I'm what's known as an asset. As are you."

"Me?" Fuller said.

Frank Nola cleared his throat.

He explained to Fuller, "My people will not stand for these atrocities — the hangings, the slaughter of that fishing-boat crew. We are a tough people. We can wait for the opportunity to beat these Nazi bastards and their puppets in the OVRA. And you are that opportunity."

Fuller nodded as he absorbed that.

"If we get this gas thing figured out," Canidy added, "we will arm the Resistance with weapons, radios, explosives —"

"Not *if,* my friend," Nola interrupted, "*when.* And until then, my people will take care of you two."

Canidy thought, *Better, I hope, than they took care of those guys hanging from those nooses.*

# VIII
## [ONE]
## OSS WHITBEY HOUSE STATION
## KENT, ENGLAND
## 0705 4 APRIL 1943

Charity Hoche rubbed her eyes, then yawned. As she sipped tea from the fine white porcelain china cup and found that it had turned tepid, her stomach growled. She looked at the clock.

*Okay,* she thought, *one more cup and then I'll head down the hall for something to eat.*

*I've been at this two hours — eight, counting last night — and I don't feel I'm any further along than when I started.*

Charity put the cup on its saucer, then reached across her desk and picked up the matching fine white porcelain teapot. With one hand on the teapot handle and the index finger of the other hand holding the teapot lid in place, she refilled the cup.

As the pleasant waft of fresh hot tea from the cup reached her nose, she thought about how acclimated to England she had become — at least, in one way. She almost never drank tea in the States. Yet here, despite the endless supply of coffee that was available — there always seemed to be a pot brewing — she not only had come to drink tea, she had come to drink only tea.

And she had become somewhat of a tea snob. She found that she preferred the Irish teas over the English ones, particularly the Irish Nambarrie for its remarkable full flavor and delightful aroma.

She found, too, that for some reason the caffeine in tea better suited her. It was easier on her mind and helped her to think more clearly and — if it were indeed possible — think more easily.

And she really needed that benefit now.

She had spent most of the previous night in her office — some six hours — having begged off the repeated offers to join everyone headed to the pub for the ministrations of Major David Niven's Attitude Adjustment Hour.

At the massive, ancient wooden desk — she envisioned a progression of English noblemen over the centuries also working at it — she had tried to list everything she knew about the missing Ann Chambers.

It had not been a very long list at all.

More helpful — though, in and of itself, that was not saying much — was the memo that Lieutenant Colonel Ed Stevens had brought from OSS London Station. It outlined the bare-bones basic information that was known to them: the date that Dick Canidy had last seen Ann, the date she had last been in her office at the Chambers News Service bureau, the date the bombs of the Luftwaffe had turned her Woburn Mansions flat to rubble, and what it was thought that she had been doing at the time of the bombing.

This last item proved to be essentially useless since it said nothing: "As her whereabouts immediately before, during, and after the bombing are an unknown, it can only be presumed that she was either at home relaxing or working, or away from home relaxing or working."

*Despite the fact,* Charity thought, *that no evidence of Ann or anyone else was found in the rubble.*

There also was a listing of twenty-plus people in London and the immediate area with whom Ann was known to have had more or less regular contact.

Each of the people listed had notations on the sheet of when they had been contacted about Ann's disappearance and what — if anything — they had known about it. Almost all had stated that they knew only that Ann had gone missing. The few people who had nothing noted beside their names had yet to be reached at all, and there was a penciled notation in the margin that read: "Ann w/any of these??"

Stevens had also brought to Whitbey House a very large and very heavy brown manila accordion folder that contained copies of Ann's last few months' work. The bureau chief — her editor — had put together the package at Stevens's request, and included a note stating that not all of Ann's stories carried her byline and so in the interest of thoroughness he had included everything he thought she had written and edited.

Stevens had passed the bulky folder on to Charity, saying that if nothing else she could at least get a feel from the stories as to what Ann had been up to just prior to her disappearance.

Ann had been busy.

Charity had begun the previous evening by separating out the articles with Ann's byline from the rest. The pile it made was almost equal to the pile that remained. Reviewing the features turned out to be difficult. The reading aspect was hard enough — some of Ann's subjects were very emotional — but trying to mine possible clues that could lead to someone — anyone — was mentally exhausting.

*Does this seamstress who donates her time stitching special garments for bombing victims who have lost a leg or arm know anything of Ann?*

*What about the nurse voluntarily making the regular rounds to the infirm in their homes, bringing food and medicine and a human's warm touch and kind words?*

*Possibly. Those and many others.*

*Yet the only way to find out is to actually find them all and ask.*

*And that is an immense task.*

Still, it had to be done, and she methodically took notes on all possible contacts.

By ten o'clock, when Charity's eyes began to water to the point they could no longer focus, she still had not finished reading all of Ann's byline pieces.

And so she had gotten out of bed just before five o'clock and returned to reading those that remained in the pile.

They were mostly in Ann's well-regarded Profiles of Courage series, human interest pieces that told of ordinary citizens rising in wartime to serve in extraordinary roles. More times than not, Charity found herself moved by the articles, and she wondered if that had been because of the power of Ann's prose — it was indeed powerful — or because of the realization that these, in fact, could very well be Ann's last words.

She sipped at her cup of tea, then picked up a news clip from the pile of Ann's bylined pieces. It was the last of the pile and turned out to be the last story Ann had filed before the bombs reduced her flat to rubble.

She began reading it:

---

**PROFILES OF COURAGE
ONE IN A SERIES**

*THE FACE OF GRACE UNDER
PRESSURE*

*A Brave Young Widow's Personal
Battle Against the Nazis*

By Ann Chambers
London Bureau
Chambers News Service

On the rolling hills in the quiet countryside of central England, a war widow opens her doors to those who have none.

At five foot four inches tall and one hundred five pounds, Grace Higham is not a

---

big woman in physical stature. But in the eyes of the men, the women, and the children she every day welcomes into her home, no one stands taller than the fair-skinned twenty-seven-year-old.

They are the injured and the orphaned, their lives horrifically altered by the attacks on London by the German Luftwaffe.

All come to Grace as strangers. And all become family.

Many stay after their recovery to work on the farm or in the kitchen, wherever they can, to help Grace help those who follow them to this haven on the hills.

One of those who helps here is Sara Spenser. Regular readers of this series will recall the profile of the young woman who, with the Light Rescue Section of London's Civil Defence, also tends to strangers struck down by Nazi bombs. Wearing a dented 1914 Tin Hat, scuffed men's Wellington rubber boots, and dirty, torn overalls, the intense and exuberant twenty-year-old works twenty-four-hour shifts, uncovering victims from the rubble of Luftwaffe bombs and transporting them by ambulance to hospital.

Sara on her off days brings the injured and the orphaned to Grace Higham and the handful of others who open their homes to the needy.

These outposts of compassion are necessitated by the fact that London hospital beds are far outnumbered by patients. While doctors and nurses perform nobly and efficiently in their jobs of saving and then stabilizing patients, there is no extra room in hospitals for the patients' extended care and recovery.

And so they are transported the hundred miles north of London by Civil Defence ambulance. Brought to Great Glen, a postcard hamlet so aptly named, where one woman's great work for hope and renewal began with a great personal loss.

William Higham, Grace's husband of three years, was killed in 1940 by German bombs as he fought in France with the British Expeditionary Force at the Battle of Dunkirk.

"Will was my whole life," Grace said. "And the heart and soul of this farm. Now there is new meaning for my life and for our farm."

Amid the patchwork of rich farmland, cut by a series of clear, cold streams, three of five farm buildings have been converted to an infirmary, an orphanage with classrooms, and a boardinghouse for the adults.

Grace said it gave her great joy to be able to share all that she and Will had. She added that, despite the circumstances that brought them here, being with the children was a particularly rewarding experience.

"Will taught me the true meaning of sacrifice. His life was centered on it. There was nothing he would not do for friends. And, of course, for me. He was always working harder so that he and I would have a better life, and a family." Her voice trailed off as she added, "But then he joined up and made the ultimate sacrifice."

Grace then quoted John 15:13: " 'Greater love hath no man than this, that a man lay down his life for his friends.' "

With so many people to take care of, so many tasks to meet in the course of a day, it was asked of Grace if there were any regrets.

She replied at first with a laugh. "Regrets? There is not time to wallow in such thought!"

And then she looked off, out across

the large yard where children played. She sniffled, and her eyes watered.

"Yet if I would have one, it would not be for me. It is for Will, and for others. A son, a flesh-and-bones embodiment of my dearly beloved husband, so that a part of a man so fine and so compassionate could carry on in this mad mad world of ours."

Grace Higham then turned away, softly sobbing, and excused herself. "Forgive me, but I must get back to my work."

Charity put down the page, and with her finger wiped absently at the tears rolling down her cheeks.

*Thanks, Ann.*

*That I really didn't need.*

She blew her nose.

*Time to take a break from this.*

*Eat, then go down and see if I can help with Major Martin.*

*Before Ann really gets me blubbering. . . .*

# [TWO]
## Palermo, Sicily
## 0750 5 April 1943

"Something is not right here," Francisco Nola said to Dick Canidy. "I would not be so concerned except that the house does not look right."

*How the hell can you tell?* Canidy thought, glancing around the filthy kitchen.

They were seated at the flimsy table, Nola having taken Jim Fuller's chair. Fuller stood near the window, keeping an eye on the street. The Sten 9mm submachine gun hung from its strap over his right shoulder.

"Nothing is put up," Nola went on, "as one would do if expecting to be gone long. And it is not just the kitchen." He pointed to the ceiling. "In the bedroom upstairs, on the table beside the bed, is a cup of mint tea. It has turned moldy."

*No surprise there,* Canidy thought. *They just didn't get it down here to add to the other dirty ones by the sink.*

*Doesn't necessarily mean anything more than that.*

"And," Nola said, "beside that cup is a book, left opened facedown on its pages. And in the closet, suitcases. They did not take a suitcase."

Canidy shrugged.

"I don't know what to say," Canidy said.

"Something is not right," Nola said again.

"There's a lot that's not right," Canidy said. "It's what we have to find out." He paused, then asked, "Those fishermen who were hung, did you know them?"

Nola shook his head. "Uh-uh."

Canidy considered that response, then said, "Probably a good thing."

"Why do you say that?"

"Because, then, they did not know you and could not link you to me. If they linked you to me, they would be looking for you."

"Others could, but they would not have talked," Nola said with conviction.

"Even as they watched their friends getting their eyes gouged out?" Canidy said slowly. "Their mouths smashed?"

Nola sighed.

"You underestimate my people," he said, his tone one of disappointment. "And *omertà*."

Canidy looked at him a long moment. The

437

Mafia's code of silence was legendary. And he instantly recalled one of its greatest examples, a tale of savagery that involved none other than Charlie "Lucky" Luciano.

After getting snatched off the streets of New York City, Luciano was taken to a warehouse — then strung up, beaten, his throat cut. He was left for dead. The tough sonofabitch, though, worked free of his ropes. He crawled to the street, only to be picked up by cops from NYPD's 123rd Precinct. No matter what they threatened him with, he refused to finger the goons who tried to whack him. The cops had to let him go. And Charlie Lucky settled the score with the wiseguy who had ordered the hit — successfully, and without breaking the code of silence.

"My apology," Canidy said.

Nola waved his hand, the gesture saying *That is unnecessary.*

"Who can we get to right away, Frank?" Canidy said after a moment. "What about Professor Rossi's sister, what was her name?"

"Diana."

"She lives near here, right? I remember it being in this area."

*And nothing like this dump. It was clean, well-kept.*

"Yes," Nola said. "We would have to be

very careful. When the SS discovered that the professor had disappeared, they would have gone looking for her, too."

"In which case, she may not even be alive," Fuller said, glancing at them from the window.

"Or she is in hiding," Nola said. "I know that the professor warned her before we left."

"Then the SS could have someone watching her place," Canidy said.

Canidy suddenly had a terrifying realization, and added: "And maybe this place, too."

Fuller automatically looked back out the window.

*But, then,* Canidy thought, *maybe not this place.*

*They don't know that Frank was involved with Rossi's disappearance — might very well not even suspect it.*

*And this is Frank's cousin's house.*

*Despite Frank's dramatics, the fact that the cousin and wife took off in a hurry could have a very simple — and innocent — explanation.*

*In which case, they're just plain lazy slobs who have no trouble living in filth.*

"I don't think there's real reason to worry about this place being watched," Canidy said. "However, we shouldn't discount it . . .

439

or anything else, at this point."

Nola and Fuller nodded their understanding.

They were quiet for some moments, each lost in their own thoughts.

"On the other hand," Canidy said out of the blue, looking at Nola, "you getting caught might not be a bad thing."

Nola and Fuller were shocked.

"You could become a pin on the map," Canidy said by way of explanation. "Especially when I start funneling men and matériel in here for the resistance."

*Not to mention,* he thought, *if I give you to pass out the ten thousand bucks in dollars and lire tucked in my money belt.*

Both men looked back with blank looks.

Canidy turned to Fuller.

"Weren't you at the Sandbox when . . . Oh, hell. No, that was John Craig Whatshisname —"

"Van der Ploeg," Fuller furnished.

"Right. Who, right now, better be filling the air with dummy messages to you."

"Building the traffic level?" Fuller said, but it was more a statement than a question.

Tubes had been schooled in the tactic of manipulating W/T message traffic in order to confuse the enemy. A sudden surge in traffic would suggest to the eavesdroppers that an operation was imminent — the larger the volume, the larger the op — and they could respond accordingly. Thus the key was to avoid peaks and valleys in the daily flow of traffic.

Conversely, one bit of subterfuge was to play to that — occasionally create an artificial peak of messages to make the enemy think something *was* about to happen. This would cause the Germans to apply more resources, diverting anything from the attention of a single radioman to a Panzer Division from other real ops.

"I'm sure John's got a credible volume going," Fuller said. "Enough to appear normal, but not enough to draw attention. I told you, he's really good."

Canidy snorted.

"And really afraid of the bogeyman," he added.

Fuller found himself grinning at that.

"He's just a kid," Fuller said loyally. "Maybe he'll grow out of that claustrophobia."

"Maybe," Canidy said, sounding unconvinced. "Now, getting back to the Pins on the Map Syndrome. I now assume that *Nebenstellen* — 'nests' — and *Aussenstellen* are also terms unfamiliar to both of you?"

They nodded.

Canidy sighed.

"Okay, then," he said, "I'm going to have to take this from the top."

He looked at the sink, then at Nola.

"What are the odds that there's actually something reasonably clean enough to drink out of," Canidy said, "and that the water coming out of that faucet isn't rancid?"

Fuller went to the cabinets and began opening the grimy doors. Behind the third one, he found glasses, no two alike. He stuck his fingers in three of them, then ran the tap. A discolored stream came out at first, and when that had purged and begun running clear he filled the glasses and distributed them.

As he did, Canidy began: "Pins on a map is another way of saying the tracking of assets. As I told you, Tubes, we are assets to the Allies. And Frank is an asset to the Allies — specifically, to the OSS. If the Abwehr could turn us, make us spy for them, we would become their assets. With me so far?"

Fuller nodded as he handed Canidy his glass.

"Thank you," Canidy said, and took a sip. "Surprise, surprise. Not bad for motor oil."

"Is rainwater from the cistern on roof," Nola said, and took his glass and drank it down.

"Great," Canidy said, putting his glass on the table. "Laced with Tabun ashes. I'll think I'll wait and watch what effect it has on you, Frank."

There was a *clunk* as Fuller put his glass on the counter. When Nola looked at him, Fuller shrugged sheepishly. "Sorry, Frank."

Nola shook his head, then said to Canidy: "Yes, I also follow you. So far. But I don't think I like where this is headed. Go on."

"Okay, I'll try to keep this simple," Canidy said. "The Abwehr collects agents like, well, like a boat hull collects barnacles. And with about as much discretion. The more the merrier. Why? The more assets, the more pins, the more power. And power corrupts . . ."

". . . and that brings us to the Abwehr's *Nebenstellen*," Canidy said, concluding what was basically the same thirty-minute briefing he had given to Max Corvo's men at the Sandbox. "These 'nests' have specialty teams called *Aussenstellen*, or 'outstations.' "

He looked at Nola, then added: "And if we can get you to talking to an outstation here in Palermo, Frank, we would have all kinds of answers."

Nola looked more than a little dubious.

"I don't know that I could get away with that, Dick," he said. "I am a fisherman. I have enough trouble paying the SS soldiers at Quattro Canti, the ones who report to Sturmbannführer Müller."

The SS had its local headquarters in the Quattro Canti, Palermo's "four corners" city center, which had been built by the Normans nine centuries earlier. Nola — reluctantly, after Canidy had cornered him — told Canidy that greasing the right hands there allowed him the freedom to move almost anything he wanted in and out of the port of Palermo.

Of course, these same crooked SS shits taking cash were also more than happy to "accept as a personal courtesy" the occasional skim of whatever it actually was that Nola's men were passing through the warehouses — from fresh fish to fruit and nuts to the always-appreciated cases of wines.

The irony that the SS used the squeeze technique on the Mafia — the very ones who arguably invented it, if not perfected it, in Sicily — was not lost on Canidy.

"Oh, *c'mon*, Frank," Canidy flared. "You've got connections. Don't go playing this *I'm but a simple fisherman* bullshit game with me again. I swallowed that once."

Nola looked back at him, intensely and wordlessly.

"If you're worried about money," Canidy

444

then said, "don't be."

"Money — that would help. But it's not that alone. I am thinking about the crew gunned down on the fishing boat and about those men hanging at the port. I cannot honor them if I, too, am killed. . . ."

"As long as the Nazis consider you are valuable to them — an asset — no harm would come to you," Canidy said.

Nola's eyebrows went up. "As you say, Dick. But I will think about it."

"If not you, what about someone else?" Canidy said. "What about the others who worked for Rossi? The ones I showed how to use the Composition C-2 on the villa?"

"Maybe."

"What were their names . . . Cordova?"

Nola nodded.

"Alfredo Cordova," he confirmed. "And Alessandro Paterno and Simone Cesareo. We, of course, would have to ask them."

"First," Canidy said, "we have to ask about the villa. If it went up, and, if not, why."

Canidy checked his wristwatch.

"We're coming up on eight-thirty," he said. "Tubes, when's the next set time for your buddy John Craig to throw the switch from SEND to RECEIVE?"

"Oh-nine-hundred," Fuller said. "That's when he'll stand by and listen for

445

our signals."

Canidy considered that, then said, "That works. That is, if you think you can get the radio rigged by then. Can you?"

Fuller nodded.

"I'll give it my best shot," he said. "If not, after that the next standby is twelve hundred hours, then fifteen and eighteen hundred."

"Let's try to get it done now, twelve-hundred at the latest," Canidy said. "I'll write the message while you do."

"Roger that," Fuller said.

Canidy looked at Nola.

"Frank, think you could in that time try to get an eyeball on Rossi's sister?"

*Oops,* Canidy suddenly thought, *poor choice of words, that. . . .*

Nola nodded.

"Is only minutes away," he said, then stood up.

*Well, he did not catch that or he's ignoring it.*

*Either way's fine by me. So long as we stay on track here.*

"When you come back," Canidy said, "make sure no one is following you. Walk in big circles, if you have to."

"Okay," Nola said, then went out the front door, locking it behind him.

As Canidy reached into his duffel for a small sheet of the thin flash paper — so named because when a match was put to it, it turned to ash in a flash of flame — Fuller slid the suitcase radio out from under the table. He then grabbed the pouch containing the mice and took it and the suitcase and the Sten upstairs.

Canidy put the flash paper on the table, noticed that the pouch of mice was gone, then looked up and saw Fuller walking away with it.

He shook his head and grinned.

And then he began composing the first message about their mission for Fuller to encrypt and send to OSS Algiers Station.

Fifteen minutes later, there came the sound of heavy footsteps from above, then the sound of boots coming down the wooden steps.

Jim Fuller appeared at the doorway of the kitchen.

"We're up and running," he announced excitedly.

"Good job, Tubes," Canidy said. "I'll be right up."

Fuller turned and went back up the steps with a thumping of his boots.

Canidy had just gotten up from the table to follow Fuller upstairs when he heard the key being worked in the lock of the exterior door.

He instinctively reached to the small of his back and pulled out his Colt .45 semiautomatic pistol. Just as he racked back its slide, the door opened.

Frank Nola stood there. He inhaled deeply — either at the sound of the slide having cycled forward, chambering a round, or at his view looking down the large muzzle. Or both.

Canidy brought down the pistol, decocked it, leaving the round in the throat.

When he looked back at Nola, he saw that someone was standing on the sidewalk behind him.

It was a young man, about five foot seven, with soft features and doelike eyes. His trousers, shirt, and coat looked to be two sizes too big, and of a style typically worn by a much older man. Even his woolen hat was oversize, its rim settling down almost over his eyes.

"C'mon in," Canidy said impatiently, now aware that the false alarm had triggered his adrenaline. "You caught me off guard for a moment there."

Nola exhaled loudly. He glanced at the gun, then back at Canidy, then made a sour face. He continued into the apartment. The young man followed, making cautious eye contact with Canidy.

As Nola pushed the door closed and locked it, Canidy studied the young man.

Canidy thought, *Why do I have the feeling something's not quite —*

Nola announced, "This is Andrea."

*I knew it! That's a young woman in a man's clothes.*

*And, for some reason, those clothes look familiar.*

*What the hell?*

"Are you just pulling people off the street now?" Canidy said to Nola.

Nola ignored that.

"Andrea," he said to her, motioning toward Canidy, then switched to Sicilian, "this is my friend. Forget how he answers the door."

Canidy looked at Andrea. This time, she made stronger eye contact. But she remained silent. He saw her eyes scanning the kitchen. When she came to the Johnny gun leaning against the cabinet, she seemed neither surprised nor bothered by it. The filthy dishes and glasses in the sink appeared to offend her more.

*If that's indeed the case, I like this girl.*

"Andrea's father is a fisherman," Nola said. "Luigi Buda is a fisherman on one our boats. It left out the same night that . . . that *I* left on the *Stefania*."

449

Canidy picked up on that. It was the same night he had Canidy and Rossi shuttled out to wait for the submarine.

And for the ninety-foot cargo ship to go up in flames.

"After the explosion in the port," he went on, "two SS soldiers came to her house, and she heard them asking her mother where her father was. Then they asked about her brothers. Andrea became frightened and slipped out of the house, and went to the Rossi house a block away. Rossi's sister taught Andrea to pray the rosary in church school. She wasn't there, but a box of his clothes was."

*That's why I recognized the clothes,* Canidy said, glancing at the girl.

*They are Professor Rossi's.*

Nola looked at Andrea and spoke again in Sicilian.

She shook her head and replied tersely.

"She speaks only Sicilian?" Canidy said.

"Yes," Nola replied. "She is in university and plans to learn English. I just asked if she had seen her mother since. She said no. She is afraid to go home, to dress in her own clothes. She's been at the Rossi house — dressed in the professor's clothes to better hide herself — all this time. She said the first days after the blast, there were SS all over, then not so much. When I knocked on

450

the Rossi door, she recognized me. . . . And here we are."

He said something to her in a fatherly tone.

She smiled softly and nodded.

"I said she should make herself comfortable, that this is home, too."

At that moment, she pulled off the woolen hat. Rich chestnut brown hair fell to her shoulders. She shook her head and air-fluffed the thick locks. Then she pulled off the jacket.

Now Canidy could see without question that she was indeed female. And beautiful. Maybe twenty years old, with dark, inviting almond eyes, and, defying Rossi's oversize shirt, magnificent breasts.

*This sure as hell ain't Rossi's sister.*

Then he felt badly.

*If by some coincidence that was her father's boat that that* Schnellboot *took out, she may be the only surviving member of her family.*

*Or, if not that patrol boat, then another.*

"So the brothers could've been lost with the father," Canidy said solemnly.

Nola looked at him. It took Nola a moment to comprehend what he was saying.

"Oh, no," Nola said. "The two brothers worked in the warehouses."

Nola said something in Sicilian to the girl.

Canidy recognized it as a question, and saw that, when she nodded and spoke her answer, her face brightened.

"She said they're alive. They were the ones who told her to stay at Rossi's sisters and keep using Rossi's clothes."

"Does she know where they are?"

Nola spoke to her. Canidy could tell from the tone that it was a question.

She answered.

"Near the warehouses," Nola said.

*Why do I have to pull the information out of Frank?*

*Is it conditioning from* omertà?

*Or is he just that damn dense?*

*Jesus!*

"Well, then, we have our first place to go," Canidy said in a somewhat-sarcastic tone.

He felt the flash paper in his pocket.

"After we take care of something," Canidy added. "You need to see this, Frank. Come with me upstairs."

Nola spoke to Andrea and she started to stand.

*I don't want her seeing the radio,* Canidy thought.

"She waits here, dammit!" he flared.

Andrea did not need that translated. She immediately sat back down.

Canidy noticed that her eyes were questioning, but it appeared that his outburst neither upset nor offended her.

*Tough girl . . . or a not very bright one?*

"*Grazie,*" Canidy said, hoping that his thanks sounded sincere despite his lack of a smile.

"Tell her we'll be right back," Canidy said and began walking out of the kitchen. He heard Nola translating, as he reached the foot of the stairs.

# [THREE]
## OSS WHITBEY HOUSE STATION
## KENT, ENGLAND
## 1145 4 APRIL 1943

Private Peter Ustinov was at the wheel of the dark green British Humber light ambulance as it rolled to a stop at a service entrance at the rear of Whitbey House. The ambulance's bold red cross on the large white square painted on its side panel and rear doors was bright against the gloom of the rainy day.

First Lieutenant Robert Jamison stood waiting beside the service entrance's pair of heavy wooden doors.

Ustinov ground the stubborn transmission into its reverse gear and let out on the

453

clutch. The truck zigzagged as it slowly moved backward, the front wheels cutting hard left, then hard right. Then Ustinov hit the brakes hard.

Jamison stepped over so get a better view of the cab. He found the befuddled face of Ustinov, having difficulty seeing anything behind him, staring into the rain mist on the glass of the rearview mirror.

"C'mon back!" Jamison coaxed.

He held up his hands and began making signals to guide him.

Ustinov revved the engine, and the truck again began to slowly roll toward the doors.

"A little right," Jamison called. "C'mon, that's it. . . . Now straight. . . . C'mon back straight two meters . . . one meter. . . . And *whoa!*"

The ambulance jerked to a stop and its engine died.

Ustinov had dumped the clutch.

Ustinov climbed out of the truck, slamming the door behind him.

"Nice work," Jamison said.

"Maybe for a blind man," Ustinov said, smiling. "My thanks for your aid."

He looked around.

"Have you seen the motor transport chaps?" Ustinov went on. "I said I wasn't going to lift that Major Martin in his casing by myself."

"I sent them inside," Jamison said, motioning with his right thumb toward the service-entrance doors, "to close the case."

"We have a pair of petrol jerry cans in here," Ustinov said, patting the palm of his hand twice on the shell of the ambulance. "At least one could stand being topped off."

"Okay, we can handle that in a bit," Jamison said. He nodded at the doors. "Let's get out of this rain, go see how close we are to getting your show on the road."

Lieutenant Colonel Ed Stevens, First Lieutenant Robert Jamison, First Lieutenant Charity Hoche, Major David Niven, Commander Ian Fleming, and Lieutenant Commander Ewen Montagu had spent most of the morning pulling together the last of the pieces of the puzzle that had become known as Major William Martin, Royal Marines.

The six-foot-six metal container containing the major's frozen body had been brought out of the cellar and up to the well-lit workshop near the rear service entrance. Still closed, the container rested on the stone floor, next to a wooden worktable.

On the table was a somewhat-scuffed, nearly new British-government-issue courier's briefcase. It had a metal handle, a special metal hoop for the secure attachment of a handcuff, and two heavy metal combination locks. The locks were open, the lid raised. Next to the briefcase was a six-foot length of stainless steel cable with small loops at either end. And, next to that, the pair of handcuffs.

Ewen Montagu, his back leaning against the wooden worktable, held various papers in his left hand. In his right there was a single sheet, which he was admiring.

Ed Stevens stood next to the opened briefcase, watching Montagu.

"This is very well done," Montagu said, moving the paper back and forth as he held it to the light. "Nice patina and well-worn creases. Excellent forgery."

"The guys who do our documents are the best," Jamison said.

Stevens put in, "Just don't ask where we get the talent."

"Where?" Montagu said.

"I told you not to ask," Stevens said, smiling.

"Prison," Niven said. "I heard they're felons serving time for the outrage against the government of having printed their own spending money and you pulled them out for your own, devious purposes."

"*Our* own, devious purposes," Stevens said evenly, still smiling.

"Personally, I find it a brilliant use of talent that otherwise would be wasted," Niven said and looked at Fleming. "Much like Ian's contributions with Major Martin here."

There were chuckles.

"I am ignoring you, Niven," Fleming said drily.

Montagu took another sheet and began examining it. This one was a jeweler's invoice — marked UNPAID — to Major Martin, for a single-diamond engagement ring.

"Well done," he said, then looked at another sheet, adding: "I think we were wise to go this route with Martin's ID."

Niven reached out, asking to see it.

Montagu passed it to him and said, "Ian and I made the executive decision that at this point it'd have been a genuine pain in the posterior to come up with a permanent Combined Operations HQ identification card. For starters, it would have been difficult making it look appropriately aged."

He produced his own ID, which was well worn, its plastic edges beginning to separate and its face cloudy with scratches.

"And so we chose to use a temporary replacement ID," he added.

"Besides," Fleming added, "being the forgetful type, it would be within reason that

457

our dear major could have lost the permanent ID."

"Looks quite official," Niven said, then suddenly added: "Dear God! They put the bloody date on this as March thirty-first!"

Montagu smiled. "Precisely."

"It means he didn't renew," Niven pressed.

"Give the major a break," Fleming said, grinning. "He's in love!"

"But the ID is expired!" Niven said, looking at them as if they had gone mad.

"Precisely," Montagu repeated. "Poor chap is absentminded."

After a long moment, there was a slow look of understanding on Niven's face. He sighed.

"Of course," he then said. "Well done."

Charity Hoche pointed to the table. Martin's dog tags — what the Brits called "identity discs on braces" — were next to some jewelry.

"The Saint Christopher and the silver crucifix there," she said. "They're nice touches. Any reason why both?"

Montagu nodded. "I believe both really quote makes unquote Martin a Roman Catholic. And with those Spaniards being the devout believers they are, the fact that Martin is anointed could very well be what keeps them from performing an autopsy.

Why abuse the sacred holy body of the deceased when it's clear the poor chap simply drowned?"

Charity nodded.

"And the snapshot of the lovely 'Pam,'" Jamison said. "Where did it come from?"

"The Duchess," Charity said. "It's some third cousin of Liz, twice or thrice removed. She offered it."

Montagu began putting the items in the briefcase.

There was a blank sheet of bond on the table next to the briefcase, and as every item was added to Major Martin, Montagu added it to an itemized inventory list.

When he finished, he had written:

---

— MOST SECRET —

<u>NOT FOR DUPLICATION</u>

PERSONAL EFFECTS OF:

MARTIN, WILLIAM, MAJOR, ROYAL MARINES

1. Identity discs (2) "Major W. MARTIN, R.M., R/C" attached to braces

---

2. Silver cross on silver chain around neck

3. Watch, wrist

4. Briefcase, containing:

   a. Photograph of fiance'e

   b. Letters from fiance'e (2)

   c. Letter top, torn

   d. Letter from Father

   e. Letter from Father to McKenna & Co.

   f. Letter from McKenna & Co.

   g. Letter from Lloyds Bank.

   h. Bill from Naval and Military Club, receipted

   i. Bill from engagement ring

   j. Book of stamps (2 used)

   k. St. Christopher plaque

l. Invitation to Cabaret Club

m. C.C.O. pass

n. Admiralty ID card

o. Key ring with keys (3) to flat

"And," Montagu said, looking up, "as he will have everything of value in the secure briefcase — which, of course, will be attached bodily to him by way of the cable and cuffs — it would be logical to include some cash."

There was an awkward silence, then Fleming said lightly, "You're the movie star, Niven. Out with it!"

Niven glared at him, then said, "Very well. But as I am an *unemployed* actor, I expect to be reimbursed."

He dug into his pant pocket and came out with some British currency: paper bills folded inside a monogrammed silver money clip and an assortment of coins.

"As he will be traveling on the government's shilling," Niven said reasonably, removing the clip from the notes, "he won't have need for a great deal of cash."

He peeled off three bills and handed them

to Montagu with the coins. Then he returned the clip on the folded bills that remained in his hand and put that back in his pant pocket.

Montagu took the money to the sheet, and wrote at the bottom:

| | |
|---|---|
| p. | 5 note (#227C45827) |
| q. | 1 notes (#X34D527008, #W21D029293, #X66D443119) |
| r. | 1 half-crown, 2 shillings, 2 six-pences |

"What else can we add?" Montagu then said. "Anything?"

Stevens felt compelled to look in his wallet, and removed it from the inside pocket of his coat.

"All I have are these four tickets to the Prince of Wales Theatre," he said, holding them fanned out.

"For which date?" Montagu asked.

"April fifteenth."

Montagu thought that over.

"That would work," he said. "Martin would still be in London and could very well have taken Pam."

As Stevens considered that possibility, it was clear by his expression that he was not too keen on contributing what were perfectly good, not to mention rather expensive, tickets.

"What the hell," Stevens said finally, and, as he handed the tickets to Montagu, added nobly: "Such are one's sacrifices for a higher cause."

Montagu looked closely at the tickets and saw that they were numbered seats: AA22, AA23, AA24, AA25.

He took the tickets for seats 23 and 24 and tore them in half. He put the stubs he tore off in the briefcase and returned the rest to Stevens.

Everyone had a curious look.

"I suspect if you were to take all that to the theater manager and, with your creative mind, convince him that the tickets were torn in error, the manager would honor the stubs."

Stevens nodded and smiled. "After all, no one else will be using the seats."

"Precisely," Montau said. "And our German friends, should they go so far as to somehow try and confirm the tickets were used, and are successful, will learn that indeed someone sat in those seats on that night." He paused. "But I really doubt they could be that thorough. The stubs themselves will say plenty."

Niven removed a pack of Cambridge cigarettes from his shirt pocket. As he took out a cigarette and lit it, he noticed he was being watched by Montagu and Fleming, who then exchanged knowing glances.

"What?" Niven said. "I put in the bloody money!"

Fleming made a *Let's have it* gesture with his hand.

"This I must say," Niven went on dramatically, "is a supreme sacrifice on my part." He began to hand over the pack, then said: "Wait!"

He took back the pack and shook out most of its cigarettes. Then he carefully crumpled the packaging over those that were left.

"Who's to say he had a nearly full pack?" Niven argued. "Probably burned through the new pack, what with being nervous about stepping off the abyss called marriage. A couple smokes is all he needs."

Fleming took the pack and said, "Matches, too, please."

Niven raised an eyebrow but handed them over also.

Fleming tossed both cigarettes and matches in the briefcase and Montagu added them to the inventory list.

"Let it not be said that I did not contribute to this worthy endeavor," Fleming said.

He dug into a pocket and pulled out a short pencil — a very short pencil — and tossed it in the briefcase.

"What in hell is that?" Niven said, indignant.

"Every man must have something to write with," Fleming said, "and so that is my contribution."

He smiled smugly.

"And *that,* Fair Lady and Gentlemen," Montagu said, grinning, "should suffice." He paused, and added: "Should *more* than suffice."

"There is one thing that's missing," Charity spoke up.

Everyone looked at her.

"And what might that be?" Montagu said.

"Something religious," she said softly. "A passage from scripture. Something. The man is about to be married — and maybe killed on a highly secret mission."

"Yes," Montagu said agreeably. "Very good."

"Do you have anything particular in mind?" Niven said. "Maybe the Twenty-third Psalm: '. . . Yea, though I walk through the valley of the shadow of death, I will fear no evil . . .' "

"Maybe," Charity said. "But not quite what I had in mind. What I'm thinking of is more along the lines of" — she paused — "I need to get a Bible and look."

Fleming said, "I have one in my room, a King James Version. I can go get it."

"Thank you," Charity said, "but I've got one in my room, too. I can use it."

Charity then saw First Lieutenant Bob Jamison reach into his pocket. He pulled out a three-by-five-inch book bound in blue leather that was well worn, its page edges gilded. He held it out to her.

"You're welcome to this," Jamison said, "if it's anything you're looking for."

Charity took the book and recognized it without having to read what was embossed in gold lettering on the binding: THE BOOK OF COMMON PRAYER, 1928. On the cover was a simple cross formed from two thin gold lines, and, under that, in block lettering across the bottom: ROBERT JAMISON.

Charity knew that when she opened it, she would find an inscription on one of the first few pages. It would congratulate Jamison on his having successfully completed his church's confirmation class and received the sacrament that officially made him a full member of the church. The page most likely would be signed by Jamison's mother and father — and, quite possibly, also by his god-parents and his grandparents.

Charity had a very similar copy, one with her name embossed in gold on the cover. It had been presented to MISS CHARITY HOCHE when she was fourteen and had completed her confirmation at St. Edmund's Episcopal Church near Philly. The bishop who had performed the Order of Confirmation had also signed her book.

As she began flipping pages, she found what she expected, and her throat muscles involuntarily constricted.

Charity Hoche looked Bob Jamison in the eyes and she fought back the urge to cry.

"Thank you, Bob," she said, softly, finding her voice. "This is exactly what I was looking for."

Fleming nodded knowingly. He, too, recognized the book. It was the standard worship for various Anglican and Episcopal churches around the world, as well as the Church of England. The language was virtually identical to that of the Catholic Church.

"I think it would be appropriate to include some reference to the marriage ceremony in his writings," Charity said. "Maybe even have him with a handwritten passage."

"That's credible," Fleming put in. "If I recall correctly, the section for the marriage ceremony runs only a few pages — half the length of the section for the burial of the dead." He paused, then added: "You can see which we Anglicans put the most faith in."

There was light laughter.

"Just a short piece," Charity said, scanning the pages. "Here. This: 'I, William, take thee, Pamela, to my wedded Wife, to have and to hold. . . .' "

She looked at Jamison. "It should be in a man's handwriting."

He nodded.

When Jamison was finished, and the page added to the briefcase and to the inventory list, Charity reached out for the Book of Common Prayer.

She flipped to a page.

"Before we close, would there be any objection to me reading a short passage?"

"Please do," Montagu said.

She looked to the pages, flipped quickly, then said, "This is from the Order for the Burial of the Dead." She read:

"I am the resurrection and the life, saith the Lord: he that believeth in me, though he were dead, yet shall he live: and whosoever liveth and believeth in me, shall never die.

"Amen," Charity then said, and all repeated it almost in unison.

Charity sniffed, then heard David Niven

struggle to clear his throat.

When she looked at him, and then at the others, she saw there wasn't a dry eye in the room.

Jamison returned to the workshop with Ustinov just as the two Motor Transport Corps men were about to lower the top shell of the case over the bottom shell that contained Major Martin.

Ustinov noticed that everyone in the room appeared somber. Charity's eyes were red, as though she had been crying or was on the verge of crying, and he wondered what might have triggered that.

He looked at the major in the case, resplendent in his Royal Marines uniform. The briefcase was in the case with him. The stainless steel cable had been looped around his waist, then handcuffed to the briefcase.

"And there you have it," Ustinov said, trying to lighten the mood. "The ultimate double agent."

"How do you figure that?" Niven said.

"He's going to be doubled by the Spaniards," Ustinov went on, undeterred.

"How the hell do you double a dead man?"

"You don't! That's what makes him the perfect one!"

"Oh, good God," Niven said in disgust.

The others chuckled, and Ustinov's eyes twinkled in delight.

More dry ice was added to the case. Then the Motor Transport Corps men secured the lid. A set of ten nuts and bolts was evenly distributed around the lip of the lid and then tightened using the two socket wrenches tethered to the lid by lengths of stainless steel cable.

Charity followed Jamison, Ustinov, and the Motor Transport Corps men as they carried the case containing Major Martin out to the ambulance. Jamison and Ustinov had begun talking about the logistics of the drive to the submarine and Charity looked at the ground.

*Leave it to men to move right to the discussion of automobiles,* she thought.

"So," Jamison was saying, "you're supposed to arrive at the dock at Greenock on April eighteenth?"

"That's right," Ustinov said.

"And that's up past Glasgow, right?"

Ustinov nodded.

"That's some trip."

"Indeed. Eight hundred–plus kilometers. I figure we can cover about three hundred kilometers on one tank of petrol. But we're being very conservative, allowing for any number of problems that might arise, and hoping to average at most two hundred a day. That gives us a five-, six-day margin of error."

"Better to be early than late?"

"Your Dr. Ben Franklin said, 'Never leave that till tomorrow which you can do today.' That doctorate was given to him by our Oxford University, by the way."

"I didn't know that."

*Try as I may, I cannot help but overhear this,* Charity thought.

She looked ahead and saw that the rear doors to the ambulance were closed.

Charity quickly worked her way around the men to get to the ambulance. She swung open its doors, and, with some effort, they slid the steel case into the ambulance.

"We get ferried by the HMS *Forth* the final five kilometers from Greenock to Holy Loch, where the *Seraph* is berthed, preparing to shove off. It had been in for repairs."

"Get there soon, maybe the sub can set sail earlier," Jamison said. "Who knows?"

"Just so long as we don't run the bloody hell into those Motor Transport bastards in Great Glen again," the brawny man in the Motor Transport Corps uniform said.

*What?* Charity thought.

"I thought you were those," she said to him. "MTC types, I mean."

The other MTC man laughed, looked at Ustinov, and said, "Don't want to lose the ambulance en route, do we?"

Charity said, "What did you just say?"

"Oh, nothing, miss. Just joshing. Pay no mind to us."

"No, I mean it. Did you just say Great Glen?"

"Yes, miss."

"What about it?"

The two MTC men looked at each other, then at Ustinov.

"It's rather complicated," Ustinov explained. "It took some doing — quite a bit, actually, as London had just been hit with a particularly nasty Luftwaffe attack — but we borrowed the ambulance. It's usually in service with the London Civil Defence. The Motor Transport Corps uses it to ferry the injured from hospital to a hospice and they said they desperately needed it. But they were not aware of *our* desperation. . . ."

Charity Hoche intercepted Lieutenant Colonel Edmund T. Stevens at the foot of the main stairway near the grand front door of Whitbey House. As she caught her breath, he looked at the clip of Ann Chambers's story.

He started shaking his head.

"I know it's a long shot, Ed," Charity said, "but, so far, it's the *only* shot."

"I don't know," he said. "But, then, I have no other suggestion. No one has come up with anything?"

He looked at Charity, studying her.

She was shaking her head. He could see genuine anxiousness in her eyes.

"You've got a good feeling about this, don't you?" he said.

"Yeah, I do."

"Okay. Take one of my staff cars. I'll bring Jamison up to speed."

"Thank you, Ed," she replied, then turned to go.

"And, Charity?" Stevens called.

"Yes?"

"Let me know what you find as soon as you can and if there's anything that I can do. I'll be at London Station."

"Will do."

And she went out the door.

# [FOUR]
## Palermo, Sicily
## 0855 5 April 1943

Canidy and Nola entered the upstairs bedroom. There were two small beds pushed together. Canidy noticed the bedside table that held the moldy tea and the book that had been left opened facedown.

Jim Fuller was at the far end of the room, near the window, which was pushed up. A chilly morning breeze blew in.

He had the suitcase opened, and the lid to the false compartment removed. The set of three instruments — the transmitter, the receiver, and the power supply — had been removed from the suitcase. They were now on a low wooden coffee table, connected by two thick black power cords with chromed plugs. A length of thin bare wire — the antenna — ran from the set, past a big bowl with a white, glazed finish, and on out the window to the plant shelf.

Fuller sat down on the floor, situating himself in front of the radio set, his legs crossed.

A pair of headphones hung around his neck.

As Canidy approached, he could see inside the big bowl. The mice were in it. Adolf — *Or is that one Eva?* Canidy thought — was nibbling on cut-up pieces of raw vegetable. The other was trying, in small bursts of energy, to run on the slick surface and getting nowhere.

Fuller saw him looking at the mice.

"I found some small sweet potatoes in a basket on the plant shelf," he said and looked toward the window. "When I strung the antenna out there on it."

Canidy nodded.

"I'm getting a little hungry myself," Canidy said.

Canidy reached into his pocket and pulled out the flash-paper message. He glanced at it one final time. It reminded him of Algiers, when the mission was laid on to find the chemical and biological weapons. Stan Fine and Canidy had had to come up quickly with its additional code names.

When Fine had suggested that they might use Roman mythology — "There's so much of that there," Fine had wondered aloud, "who's going to be able to separate it from the real thing?" — Canidy had embraced the idea.

And so now he had just written the message using the code names for the clandestine wireless radio station ("Mercury"), for the team ("Jupiter," "Optimus," "Maximus"), and for the submarine ("Neptune"). The code name for the nerve gas — "Antacid" — came from the earlier Sicily mission, when Canidy had pulled out Professor Rossi.

He held out the message to Fuller.

"Here's this," he said.

Fuller took the sheet and read it:

---

TOP SECRET

OPERATIONAL PRIORITY

05APR43 1200

FOR OSS WASHINGTON EYES ONLY GEN DONOVAN; OSS ALGIERS EYES ONLY CAPT FINE.

FROM MERCURY STATION

BEGIN QUOTE

JUPITER OPTIMUS MAXIMUS FIND NO SIGN OF ANTACID OR OTHER. SEARCH CONTINUES.

---

```
NEPTUNE STANDS BY.

END QUOTE

TOP SECRET
```

"Mercury?" Fuller said.

"That's your station name," Canidy said.

"Mercury?" Fuller repeated. "The planet? Oh, wait . . ."

He glanced down the message again.

"Jupiter Optimus Maximus!" Fuller suddenly said. "Hey, I remember. That's from mythology. Jupiter was the supreme god of Italy."

Nola had a blank look on his face.

"I have never heard of him," he said.

"Of Italy *and* Rome," Canidy said. "He was the great protector of the state and every part of life therein. Which, if you think about it, is what we are trying to accomplish."

"Wasn't he honored with the spoils of the generals and the sacrifices by the magistrates?" Fuller said.

"That's the one," Canidy said. "But one of my real favorites is that all places struck by lightning then belonged to Jupiter."

Tubes laughed aloud.

Nola could not quite understand why.

"Okay," Tubes said, "so I get it — you're Jupiter."

"Your supreme god finds it pleasing that you see such wisdom," Canidy said evenly.

"Then," Fuller went on, "who's Maximus?"

"Jupiter looked to the stars for guidance," Canidy said, waving with his arm toward the exposed beams of the roof, "and there Jupiter found that that name would go to the great radioman heretofore known as Tubes."

"Me Maximus? The greatest?" Fuller said with a huge grin. "I am duly honored."

Canidy nodded.

Tubes looked at Nola and said, "Then that makes you Optimus."

"Optimus?" Nola said tentatively. "Thank you."

"It means 'the best,'" Tubes explained.

Nola's eyebrows went up and he suddenly looked visibly moved.

"I am not worthy of such honor," he said softly.

*No shit,* Canidy thought.

"Well, you're probably right," Canidy heard himself saying. "But until I come up with something else — and it's really too late for that — we'll just have to leave you as Optimus."

Tubes grinned, then looked back at

the message.

"And since Neptune is god of sea," he said, "then that's the sub?"

"Good. And Mercury?" Canidy said. "Your station name?"

"Now I remember," he said. "Mercury was the messenger god."

"*Is* the messenger god," Canidy corrected, patting him on the shoulder. "Well done, Tubes. You surprise me."

Canidy looked toward the radio set.

"Okay, let's get this sent. Then you need to come downstairs. There's been — how do I put this? — an interesting development."

Fuller looked at him, then turned to the radio set.

After encrypting the message, he moved to the transmitter. He adjusted the box a little, enough to get his right hand to it comfortably.

The transmitter and the receiver were nearly twin black boxes, each about ten inches long and four inches wide and tall. They had black Bakelite faceplates that held an assortment of knobs, dials, toggle switches, and more. (Each weighed half the ten pounds of the similar-sized box that was the power supply.)

At the bottom right-hand corner of the transmitter faceplate was a button-shaped key. It looked somewhat like a black plastic drawer pull on a short shaft.

Tubes exercised his fingers and wrist, warming them up. Then he looked at the message he had encrypted, lightly put his right index and middle fingers on the key, and rhythmically began tapping out the Morse code.

Canidy and Nola and Andrea Buda were in the kitchen when Jim Fuller came thumping down the stairs and into the room.

He was holding out the flash-paper message to Canidy when he caught sight of Andrea.

He made no attempt to conceal his surprise.

*Praise the gods!* Fuller thought. *A real nymph!*

"Tubes," Canidy said, "this is Andrea Buda."

Fuller nodded and smiled, then stepped forward. He held out his right hand.

"Hello," he said. "It's my pleasure to meet you."

"She doesn't speak English . . ." Canidy began.

Andrea returned the smile, put her hand in his, and leaned forward, slightly turning her face to present her left cheek.

"But it would appear," Canidy went on, "that you're expected to perform the traditional greeting."

Fuller looked at Canidy, confused.

About that time, Andrea moved forward.

To Fuller's amazement, she touched her left cheek to his, made the sound of a kiss, then repeated it as her right cheek touched his.

Then she stepped back, smiled, and diverted her eyes.

"*That* is what I meant," Canidy said. "You can take the boy out of California, but you can't take the beach bum out of the boy."

Fuller smiled at Canidy and quietly said, "Can I change my name to Venus?"

*Venus?* Canidy thought.

Then it took every effort for him not to grin.

*Venus, goddess of love. . . .*

Canidy took a match from the box on the table and struck it.

"Tubes, touch her in any way that could be construed as anything but for the protection of her life," Canidy said lightly, "and . . ."

He touched the tip of the flame to the flash paper.

Andrea gasped.

# IX

## [ONE]
## GREAT GLEN, ENGLAND
## 1620 4 APRIL 1943

For the first eighty miles or so miles of Charity Hoche's drive north, the view from behind the wheel of Ed Stevens's olive drab 1941 Chevrolet staff car had been relatively unchanged.

It had been that of a big red cross painted on an even bigger square of white painted on a big dark green box.

Since leaving Whitbey House, Ann had followed the British Humber light ambulance that carried Major William Martin, Royal Navy Marines.

Then, just shy of Northampton, her view had changed somewhat. As the ambulance approached a fork in the road, she saw a right arm sticking out from what was the driver window and a left arm out from the passenger window. The arms did not belong to the same body, of course.

The passenger's arm — that of Private Peter Ustinov — waved an animated cheery good-bye. The other arm pointed dramatically forward, in the direction of the fork, a narrow macadam lane that split off to the right. The ambulance then followed the main road to the left, continuing north to Glasgow and then on to the docks at Greenock.

Charity came up on the smaller road, checked for oncoming traffic, and then took the turn, tapping the horn twice as she did to signal *Good-bye,* too.

The one who had pointed out the turn was the bigger of the two men who wore the uniform of the British Motor Pool Corps. Confirming Charity's suspicions, they were not actually assigned to the MPC; Ustinov had said it was their cover story for what he called "the unfortunate unauthorized reallocation of the Humber." The burly man had also given Charity written directions to follow from that point forward.

"Sorry we can't show you personally, miss," he had said. "Can't yet afford to lose the ambulance to the real MPC types, you know."

The instruments of the American Chevrolet staff car registered, of course, in miles. The speedometer indicated that Charity, now on the far side of Northampton, was making about twenty-five miles an hour over the rough surface of the uneven macadam. And the odometer showed that she had covered more than one hundred miles.

Generally, Charity had a little difficulty with the mathematical conversion of miles to kilometers — it wasn't that she couldn't do it; she just rather didn't care for the mental exercise — but this time it was easy.

*A round 100 makes it a snap.*

*The formula is to multiply the number of miles by 1.6 kilometers.*

*And that means I've just gone 160 kilometers.*

On the left roadside, she saw by the sculpted hedgerow a signpost that read GREAT GLEN 14 KM.

She glanced at the handwritten directions and confirmed that her destination was just shy of the town.

Charity could not recall the exact formula for converting kilometers to miles. But making a rough calculation was almost easier than multiplying by 100.

*A kilometer is roughly six-tenths of a mile.*

*That's slightly more than half a mile.*

*So that means I'm a little more than half of fourteen — or seven — miles from Great Glen.*

She noted the odometer reading: 42,215.

A little more than ten minutes later, as the odometer rolled to 42,220, she saw that the roadside hedgerow had ended. There now was a well-maintained, low wall constructed of fieldstone. And, as the odometer turned to 42,221, she came to a gap in the wall, an entrance, with a wooden sign that appeared somewhat new.

She braked as she read it: HIGHAM HILLS, A HOME TO ALL.

Charity felt her throat tighten as the car came to a stop.

She leaned forward in her seat, chin on the steering wheel, and peered down past the entrance.

There was a charming grassy drive with two tracks of bare soil rutted by automotive traffic. It was lined on either side by mature field maples, the canopies of the trees touching to form a tunnel. And outside of the tall trees, running along the edge of the farm fields, a simple wooden fence consisting of two parallel boards running between posts five feet high.

*This trip will turn out to be a complete waste of time and effort.*

*Not to mention most likely emotionally draining.*

*But I had to try. I owe Ann that much.*

*And when I'm done here, and with Major*

*Martin gone, I can double up my effort in find-*
*ing her.*

Charity sat back. She shifted the Chevy into first gear, turned the steering wheel as she let out on the clutch, and soon was slowly rolling past the entrance and into the tunnel of trees.

The lane wound along for almost a mile. Then the tree line and canopy ended, and the drive made a large circle in front of what appeared to be the main house of the farm.

Charity saw that the two-story residence was built of sturdy materials, with a façade of fieldstone and a roof of slate. And though nothing on the order of an estate such as Whitbey House, it was a rather large residence. It had a substantial covered porch on the front and two sides — where, perhaps, twenty or thirty people were sitting or milling about — and it looked to Charity as if each floor could have maybe ten to twelve large rooms.

She saw that there were three English automobiles and one somewhat-battered pickup truck parked together on the grass off of the circular drive, and Charity steered the Chevrolet beside the truck and shut it off.

She looked toward the porch and the people there and saw that her newly arrived vehicle was now the subject of some attention.

*Here goes nothing,* she thought and opened her car door.

As she made her way toward the shallow steps leading to the front porch, a man on crutches worked his way down the steps, then toward her.

He looked to be about sixty. His long face was clean-shaven and his thinning silver hair loosely combed over a shiny scalp. He was neatly dressed in a well-worn wrinkled brown suit with a white shirt, no tie. The right leg below the knee was missing, and the man had neatly pinned up the pant cuff so it would not drag on the ground. And though the man appeared gaunt, he moved on his crutches with a determined effort and an air of authority.

As the man approached Charity, he said with a cockney accent, "How can I help you, miss?"

Charity smiled, then noticed that the man had a clipboard tucked under his left arm, between the armpit and the cushion top of the crutch. She held out her right hand.

"I'm sorry to trouble you," Charity said with a dazzling smile. "My name is Lieutenant Hoche."

"It's my pleasure, Lieutenant," he said, shaking her hand. "Christopher Johnson. I'm the adjunct here."

"I was hoping to see Grace Higham," Charity said pleasantly.

"She's rather busy right now. If I could ask what this pertains to? Or perhaps I could assist?"

Charity considered that and nodded.

"Of course," she said and composed her thought. "There was a recent Luftwaffe bombing in London. A very dear friend has not been heard from since. I am trying to find her and coming here was one of my first leads."

"She's in recovery here?" Johnson said and pulled the clipboard from under his arm. "What's her name?"

"Ann Chambers," Charity said. "But I don't think that she's a patient."

Christopher Johnson flipped through a few sheets on the clipboard and scanned the names, running an index finger down the listing.

"If she were," Charity went on, "I believe we would have heard from her."

"No," Johnson said, still looking at the clipboard, "not a single Chambers listed here. Ann or otherwise." He looked up, and Charity saw genuine empathy in his blue-gray eyes. "I'm very sorry, Lieutenant."

Charity nodded. "Thank you. But, as I said, I did not exactly expect to find her here."

"I'm sorry," he said, "then I'm confused. What is it that you're looking for?"

"My friend, Ann Chambers, she has met with Mrs. Higham. Written about her, actually."

Charity reached into her pocket and brought out the clip of Ann's article.

"Oh, yes," Johnson said as he reviewed it. "I have seen this. We received quite a bit of favorable attention after it was published. Many boxes came, mostly from the States. Quite a few toys and stuffed animals for the children."

Charity smiled.

*Attagirl, Ann. You touched some hearts with that one.*

"That's delightful to hear," Charity said. "To answer your question, what I'm looking for is the woman who was driving an ambulance to bring patients out here. Sara Spenser, she's in the article. No one can seem to find her, either, and I was thinking that perhaps she had come out here. Maybe bringing in patients, maybe working for a period of time?"

Johnson was nodding his understanding.

"And if Sara was here," Charity went on, "perhaps I could speak to her and she might have some idea where Ann might be. She and Ann, as I understand it, became quite friendly after the profile Ann had written about Sara and then the one on Mrs. Higham."

Charity glanced at the steps to the covered porch of the house and saw an attractive, petite Englishwoman coming out of the main door of the house, then down the steps of the porch.

*That has to be the Higham woman.*

"Yes," Christopher Johnson said. "I mean, no."

Charity looked back to him.

"I'm sorry," she said, "I don't —"

"Sara is — " he began.

"Mr. Johnson," the petite Englishwoman interrupted as she approached, "is there something?"

Christopher Johnson turned at her voice.

"Mrs. Higham," he said courteously, then motioned with his left hand to Charity as he kept his balance while leaning on the crutch. "May I present Lieutenant . . ."

"Hoche," Charity furnished, holding out her hand.

"Lieutenant," Grace Higham said somewhat sharply, shaking her hand.

Grace Higham coldly eyed the well-endowed blonde who she thought was single-handedly giving credence to the British barb that the problem with Yanks was "they were overpaid, overfed, oversexed, *and* over here."

"What brings you to Great Glen?" Grace Higham went on.

"Sara Spenser," Christopher Johnson said. "She was hoping to speak to Sara."

Charity noticed that Grace Higham's face registered some shock or surprise . . . or maybe even some disappointment.

"Is there a problem?" Charity said.

"It was our understanding," Grace Higham said, "from Sara herself, that she did not have any family left. That they, too" — she glanced at the patients on the porch — "had been lost to bombs."

"The lieutenant has a friend who was friends with Sara," Christopher Johnson tried to explain.

"Ann Chambers," Charity said. "The writer?"

That registered immediately with Grace Higham. "Of course! How is Ann?"

"She's missing —"

"I'm terribly sorry," Grace Higham said.

"And I thought that Sara might have some idea where she is or maybe what happened to her. At the very least, just tell me the last time that she had seen Ann so I could try to retrace her steps."

Grace Higham was nodding. But there was clear distress in her expression.

She looked Charity in the eyes with a piercing gaze.

"I'm terribly afraid that that will be a bit difficult," Grace Higham said softly.

Christopher Johnson looked at Grace Higham and said, "If I may?"

Grace nodded.

"Sara," Johnson explained, "never made it here to Higham Hills. We are, as you can see" — he glanced over his shoulder at the people on the covered porch — "quite full. She was taken to Manor House."

"Which is . . . ?" Charity asked.

"Another residence that has taken on responsibilities similar to ours," he said. "It's near Yardley Hastings, just south of Northampton. I would think you passed it coming up here."

"We were informed," Grace Higham put in, "that Sara was taken to Manor House with another woman —"

Charity's eyebrows went up. "Really!"

"And that they had been injured not by a bomb directly but by loose bricks falling from a storefront. I was told that Sara's injuries were mostly superficial but that she was having difficulty speaking. Apparently, some severe type of shock."

"And the other woman?" Charity said.

Grace Higham was quiet, then looked at

Christopher Johnson.

Johnson began, "Her injuries were far worse —"

"There was significant trauma to the head," Grace Higham added. "The doctors were able to reduce the pressure on the brain, we were told, and believed that she was ready for recovery. And so she was picked up by the runners at Manor House and taken there."

"Runners?"

"People who help out doing odd jobs. We have a few. They have many more. The Motor Transport Corps has been stretched rather thin, their vehicles in short supply, so Manor House does not bother relying on them."

*Well,* Charity thought, *they should soon have another ambulance at their disposal.*

*Soon as it is "re-allocated."*

Charity said, "You say believed that she was ready for recovery. That suggests —"

"She didn't make it, I'm afraid. There was an aneurysm . . ." Grace Higham said, her voice trailing off.

Charity suddenly had trouble hearing anything clearly for a moment. She found herself hyperventilating. Tears flowed down her cheeks.

"I'm very sorry to have to tell you that,"

Grace Higham was saying somewhat stiffly. "But you do realize that this may not be your friend. There sadly are too many such stories. . . ."

Charity struggled to hold back her deepest emotions.

"Can you tell me how to find this Manor place?" she said after a moment, her voice shaking. "I pray you're right, that it's not Ann. But, if it is, I need to know. And, if it isn't, maybe I can get Sara to tell me something."

Grace Higham thought about that, then said, "I have been meaning to get over there to visit but simply have not had a moment to spare. I do think that I could go with you now."

"Thank you," Charity said. "Can you drive? We can take my car. But I don't think I'm right now in any condition to do so."

"Of course," Grace Higham said, surprised by the lieutenant's vulnerability and how she was unafraid to show it.

She studied Lieutenant Hoche a moment, then decided that maybe she had been indeed a bit quick to judge this book by its cover.

The forty-five-kilometer drive south — with a ten-minute stop for Charity, who thought

she might be getting sick to her stomach —
had taken them just shy of an hour.

Charity Hoche and Grace Higham stood
with a squat woman who wore a white
nurse's outfit. They were in the doorway of
what not very long ago — no more than a
month — had been a working barn at Manor
House.

The four horses that had been there had
been moved to another barn nearby. The dirt
floor had been improved, concrete poured,
and the stalls modified so that they now re-
sembled small rooms. Additional rooms had
been built, fashioned from boarding. And
wooden bunks had been built to hold straw
mattresses.

Charity Hoche had been shocked by all
that she had seen as they had walked
through the main building of Manor House,
past the patients there, then out to the barn.

There were indeed patients, all progressing
well in their recovery, as Ann Chambers had
written in her article. And there were the
children. But also there were patients who
looked like ghosts, some with grave injuries
that had left them looking horrid.

Charity could not help but notice that
these extreme cases even had a smell of
death about them.

*Ann hadn't written about them because*

*what she had written about was bleak enough.*

*Ann knew her audience. They wanted to read about the good that Grace Higham was doing.*

*Dwelling on the darkness would have lost a lot of readers — ones who would not have finished the piece, and then not have sent the packages of toys and animals for the children.*

Then Charity had another thought and it was a struggle for her to contain the wave of emotion that came with it.

*Was that how Ann looked — and smelled — before that artery burst in her head?*

"Now, I must caution you," the squat nurse was saying, "that what you're about to see may be disturbing."

"We'll be fine," Grace Higham said, then looked at Charity and added: "Both of us."

*This little lady has a backbone of steel,* Charity thought.

"Very well," the nurse said in an officious tone.

They came to one of the stalls converted into a room. There was the shape of a female on her back under the white sheet. The sheet was slowly rising and falling with her breathing.

The nurse motioned that they could go in.

As they stepped forward together, Grace Higham suddenly exclaimed, "Oh, God!"

Charity inhaled deeply, then whispered, "Ann!"

"Say that again," Charity Hoche told the squat nurse as Charity, her eyes red, gently stroked Ann Chambers's dark hair.

"She has amnesia."

"She can't remember who she is?" Charity said.

"Or where she came from," the nurse said.

Charity turned and looked Ann Chambers in the eyes.

"You're Ann," she said softly. "Ann Chambers, remember?"

Ann blinked her eyes, and when she opened them again, Charity was convinced she saw some sign of recognition, some acknowledgment.

*And even if there wasn't, there will be eventually.*

"She kept muttering, 'Sara, Sara,' " the nurse explained. "And she would write it down. We thought that that meant she was trying to tell us her name."

Charity's and Grace's eyes met.

"Then what happened to the other woman?" Grace said. "The one who died of the aneurysm?"

"We have our own cemetery, and a full, appropriate burial service was performed," the nurse said. "Was that a mistake also? We were told there were no relatives."

"In this case," Grace Higham said, "that was true about Sara."

"It wouldn't be with Ann," Charity added softly, looking down at her. "She has plenty of family . . . including me."

Charity turned to the nurse. "She's well enough to travel?" she said, more a statement than a question.

"Oh, no. The doctor said that she needs quiet time to recover."

"No," Charity said evenly. "You misunderstood me. What I said was: She *is* well enough to travel. I'm taking her home. Right after I pay my respects to Sara. Can you show me her resting place?"

Grace Higham felt a lump form in her throat.

*Oh, how I like this Yank!*

*Not only is she taking charge of her friend, she's taking the time for Sara, too — not at her "grave" but at her "resting place."*

*Ann Chambers, you are indeed one fortunate soul to have such a friend.*

# [TWO]
## WHITBEY HOUSE
## KENT, ENGLAND
## 2150 4 APRIL 1943

Charity Hoche surprised herself at how fast she made the return trip to Whitbey House. She realized that that was in part thanks to Grace Higham's having arranged for a runner to shuttle her back to Great Glen, saving Charity a two-hour round-trip, and putting her — with Ann Chambers in the backseat — that much closer to Kent.

When they had arrived, Charity had not exercised a great deal of self-control. She had been impatient; she found it difficult not to bark at anybody who she felt got in her way or who did not immediately do what she asked of them in a manner she considered satisfactory.

Bob Jamison had had to delicately take her aside and say that he would handle the details, including getting Ann down to the dispensary.

"You just went through a hellish emotional

roller-coaster ride," Jamison had said. "Catch your breath and let me worry about the little things."

When Charity had looked him in the eyes, Jamison saw a fury mixed with fear.

Then, slowly, her eyes softened, her body grew less tense, and she nodded.

"Thank you, Bob."

"She has a mild amnesia," Major Richard B. Silver, M.D., said to Charity Hoche and Bob Jamison. He held the medical file that the staff at Manor House had put together on Ann Chambers and given to Charity. "It's a dissociative amnesia."

They were in the left wing of the mansion, in the dispensary, what had once been the ballroom of Whitbey House. Ann Chambers lay sleeping peacefully in one of the sixteen field-hospital beds. Under Dr. Silver's supervision, the medical staff had given her a complete checkup, then a bath, and then she had been made comfortable.

Silver was a tall man, easily six-four, with a deep, commanding voice that he modulated with the skill of a radio broadcaster. His tone could be strong, but at the same time the sound of his voice would carry no farther than those in the immediate conversation — all the while conveying an utter confidence and authority that was not to be questioned.

He was good at what he did. He knew it. And those he dealt with knew it.

"Dissociative?" Charity repeated.

Major Silver nodded.

"Amnesia is too commonly misunderstood," he went on, "and, accordingly, very often misinterpreted. Broadly, amnesia is defined as profound memory loss. Ann has dissociative amnesia. A person blocks out critical information, usually something that is stressful or traumatic. Thus, she would be dissociative to that event."

Charity looked at Ann, then back to Silver.

"I believe that we can rule out transient global amnesia," he said.

It was obvious from Charity's expression that that meant nothing to her.

"Transient global amnesia is the loss of all memory," he explained, "but only temporarily. It has elements of severe anterograde amnesia, which is caused by brain trauma and involves the ability to form new memories, and retrograde amnesia, the ability to recall memories only hours old. The reason we can discount it is because it's most commonly associated with vascular disease."

"Vascular disease?" Jamison repeated. "Isn't that an older person's disease?"

Dr. Silver nodded. "Right. Which brings us

to the dissociative amnesia called fugue amnesia."

Jamison shook his head.

"Also known as fugue state," Silver explained. "As in, a disoriented state of mind. Some even call it 'hysterical amnesia.'"

Jamison noticed that Charity seemed to respond to the term *hysterical*.

"What causes it?" Charity said.

"A traumatic event," Dr. Silver went on, "something that the mind simply is not able to handle. Such as witnessing a murder, a particularly bad automobile collision, a —"

"A bombing?" Charity interrupted. "From an air raid?"

"Yes," he replied, nodding softly. "I am thinking that she must have seen her friend struck down by the bricks, as you described. That could cause it."

Charity considered that.

"Is there any treatment?" she said.

"Time," Major Silver said. "Time and love. Sedation sometimes is necessary. Pyschotherapy, talking with a psychiatrist, can be helpful. In extreme cases, there's hypnosis and sodium amobarbital, which helps recall lost memories. Left alone, however, the memory can slowly return. Or it can suddenly return. And the patient may or may not recall what caused the trauma."

Charity smiled. "That's the best news I've heard in a long time. Thank you, Major."

Bob Jamison found Charity Hoche in the pub. She was at the bar, nursing what appeared to be a martini cocktail made with Prime Minister Churchill's personal recipe.

She heard his footsteps approaching and turned toward him as he took the seat beside her.

"Just got off the secure line with Ed Stevens in London. He said to tell you congratulations, and thank you, and that he will speak with you personally tomorrow about quote saving the OSS unquote from the wrath of Ann's father —"

"Brandon Chambers," Charity furnished.

"— whom he is right now trying to contact via the transcontinental telephone line. He said he'll then have our doctors here talk with whatever doctors Chambers wants and then they can decide where Ann goes next."

"What about Dick?"

"I have had the news that Ann is here sent to Stan Fine at OSS Algiers. But nothing more, not any details."

She nodded.

*Dick deserves to know,* she thought. *But not to worry about her condition.*

*There's nothing that he can do for Ann from*

*there — or wherever he is.*

They were quiet a moment, then Charity looked at Jamison.

"Bob," she said, "I've been debating myself about this."

"About what?"

Charity took a sip of her martini, then went on: "I cannot personally issue the order, for what would be very obvious reasons. Nor can I order you to issue such an order. . . . Oh, what the hell. I can deny I ever said it."

"And I'll deny I ever heard it," he said, agreeably.

She nodded, then said, "I don't care what lie or lies you have to tell, Bob, but please figure out a way to get Doug Douglass here."

Jamison looked at his watch.

"He should already be here," Jamison said simply.

Charity's face brightened.

"I was afraid you would return from your trip upset," Jamison explained. "And, as Colonel Stevens had me assume command of Whitbey House in the absence of the Deputy Director, Acting" — he nodded at Charity — "and with the authority provided me as Major Richard Canidy's adjunct, a message under the major's signature went out that required the personal attention of Lieutenant Colonel Douglass at OSS Whitbey House Station for a period not to exceed thirty-six hours concerning a mission to be laid on —"

Jamison suddenly heard what he just said, and added, "Charity, I'm so sorry. I didn't —"

Charity Hoche let out a deep belly laugh.

"I believe," she said, "having just heard enough hocus-pocus shrink talk, that the good Dr. Freud would have something to say about your little slip."

Jamison smiled, relieved that she was taking no offense.

Charity looked at Jamison a long moment, then leaned forward and kissed him on the cheek.

"Thank you, Bob. I'm grateful."

She turned back to her martini.

*My God,* he thought, *she's in her cups.*

He saw her ample chest rise, then fall, with a sigh.

*Make that in her double-D cups.*

*What a beautiful woman — physically and emotionally.*

Charity drained her drink, put the glass on the bar, then said, "I must visit the ladies' facilities. Have them make me another, please. And when my flyboy lands . . ."

Jamison was smiling and nodding.

"My seat is his seat," he said.

# [THREE]
## PALERMO, SICILY
## 0930 5 APRIL 1943

Dick Canidy was having difficulty concentrating on the mission and he knew that made for a dangerous situation.

He and Jim "Tubes" Fuller were backtracking, following in reverse the path through Palermo that they had taken with Frank Nola to reach the apartment home of Nola's cousin.

They were headed for an area near the warehouses on the northern end of the port.

*This isn't the time to think about Ann.*

*But I just can't help it.*

After Fuller had come into the kitchen and damn near drooled all over Andrea Buda, Canidy had said that it was time to go see the Buda brothers. He decided that it was better that Nola should go first, separately, and that Canidy and Fuller would follow.

After some discussion between Andrea and Nola in Sicilian, it was agreed that she would lay low there in the apartment. Then Nola left.

Canidy and Fuller went back upstairs to stash the long guns and secure the W/T radio station.

Nola had shown them the makeshift door that had been cut in the floor of the upstairs bedroom. It was under the thick, woven-hemp mat that lay between the beds. When the mat was pulled away and the door removed, there was access to the dead space between the joists. These long joists supported both the floor of the second level and the ceiling of the first floor. They found that with a light forcing, the suitcase would fit snugly between them.

There had been room in the dead space also for the Johnny gun and the Sten, but when Nola suggested putting them in there Canidy had said no. He wanted to get to them more readily and planned to simply camouflage them by wrapping each in clothing, then putting the Sten in the closet upstairs and the Johnny in a corner of the downstairs hall closet that was under the foot of the stairway.

Tubes was sitting on the floor at the table holding the W/T set.

He put one of the headphone ear cups to his left ear and quickly tapped out code to Algiers Station that Mercury Station was going off the air in five minutes. He then threw the toggle switch on the Bakelite face-plate to RECEIVE. With the one can still held to his ear, he awaited confirmation while watching Canidy pull a sweater and an overcoat from the closet.

Suddenly, Fuller said, "What in the world?"

He sat erect and quickly pulled the cups over both of his ears.

Canidy turned to see what was going on.

Fuller was quickly handwriting the incoming message.

After a moment, he turned away from the radio and held up the paper.

"This was sent out in the open," Fuller said, pulling off the cans.

"What the hell is it, Tubes?" Canidy said.

"For you. No encryption, but it's in some code."

Canidy walked over and took the sheet of paper.

URGENT

UNRESTRICTED

05APR43

```
FOR JUPITER

BEGIN QUOTE

EXCELLENT NEWS, EXCELLENCY.

YOUR GODDESS HAS RETURNED TO YOUR
CASTLE.

END QUOTE

CAESAR
```

"Who's Caesar?" Fuller said.

He looked at Canidy, who had turned his back to him and was looking out the bedroom window.

Fuller wasn't certain but he thought he saw Canidy's body shake. And then he heard Canidy clear his throat as Canidy looked at the message again.

"I'll explain later," Canidy said after a moment in an odd, strained tone. "Acknowledge receipt, then take it down."

Fuller nodded, and put the cans back on his ears.

*At least now I can think about Ann without choking up,* Canidy thought as he and Fuller came to the railway station they had passed earlier.

He found himself smiling.

*And smile about her.*

*But I need to pay attention to what's here and now.*

*I'm anxious, I know.*

*And with so many things that can go wrong, I have to keep my nerves controlled and my attention focused.*

Canidy and Fuller then walked north a few blocks and found Quinta Casa street, then took it downhill toward the port.

There were more people out on the streets and in every piazza. But their mood was somber; despite the clear sunny sky, it seemed a dark cloud hung heavily over them.

*Small wonder,* Canidy thought.

*A couple ripe bodies swinging by the neck in the bright sun can cause that kind of oppressive effect.*

Canidy and Fuller tried to blend in. They wore the civilian clothing from the OSS villa in Algiers. Fuller had on a woolen stocking cap; Canidy had insisted he cover the bright blond hair that would stand out among the darker tones of the Sicilians. They kept their gaze downward, avoiding eye contact. And they stayed silent.

As they passed an alleyway, Canidy tapped

Fuller on the shoulder and motioned toward it.

They wound their way back into the alley, and when Canidy saw that they were far enough out of sight and earshot of the street they stopped.

"What is it?" Fuller said.

"I meant to mention this earlier but either forgot or, when I remembered, we weren't alone."

Fuller raised a questioning eyebrow.

"Look, Tubes, I've got to be brutally honest with you. I don't know how safe this situation is." He paused. "More to the point, I should say, I don't know how off-the-deep-end dangerous this situation is."

Fuller reached into an outer pocket of his coat. He pulled out the pouch with the squirming mice in it.

"So far, Adolf and Eva say we're good."

"No, Tubes. Not about the gas, though that's still unanswered. Only thing we know about that is that there weren't mass casualties. There're no signs of deaths by gas. And the people we see don't exhibit any signs of being sick from it."

"Then what?" Fuller said, carefully returning the pouch to his pocket.

"For all I know, Tubes, we could be walking into an ambush, a setup, something that could fuck us up no end. While our luck with these Guinea sons of bitches has held so far, I do not trust them any farther than I can throw them."

Fuller nodded as he absorbed that.

"And you're thinking now — ?"

"I don't know," Canidy interrupted. "That's what I'm telling you. My gut says Nola is more or less on the level with us — as long as it meets his needs. But these new guys . . . We're about to add two new unknowns. For all we know, they could be trying to fuck over Frank and he doesn't even know it."

Fuller nodded.

"And, if not them, then others," Canidy said.

"So what do we do?"

"Well, we have to move forward. Otherwise, coming here was a waste of time."

"Not a complete waste . . ." Fuller grinned.

"Try to think with your big head, Tubes," Canidy said. "If these goons even suspect you're having carnal thoughts about their baby sister, that makeshift gallows could get awfully crowded."

Fuller made a face. "Okay, okay, I get your point. So what now, then?"

"We need a code word for my contingency plan."

"What's the contingency?"

"Take this next meeting as an example. We're talking with the Buda brothers and Nola. And we determine that, despite their profound oaths of being our loyal agents, the bastards are working for the Krauts . . . Pins on the Map, right? . . ."

Fuller nodded.

". . . and about to burn us. So, one or both of us says the code word, calmly in conversation, then we both silently count to ten — and *then* we blow away every last one of the two-timing sons of bitches."

Fuller's eyes were wide.

"Severe case of lead poisoning?" he said. "That certainly is a definitive contingency plan."

"Beats hell out of the alternative," Canidy said.

"Which is?"

"Not having one and getting the shit shot out of us," Canidy said pointedly. "Or strung up for the seagulls' entertainment. You wanted to go operational, Tubes. This is what you get. I don't know about you, but I damn sure plan on going home alive."

*And the sooner, the better, now that I know my goddess is in my castle.*

Fuller nodded slowly, then said: "Fins."

"What?"

"That's our contingency plan's code

513

word. Fins."

"I'm guessing, as in a surfboard's?" Canidy said drily.

"No. Like a shark's."

They came to where Quinta Casa made a *T* with the intersection of Christoforo Colombo, the street that ran parallel to the northern section of the port. The horrid smell was not there, and Canidy noticed that the wind had shifted, a fresh breeze was coming in off the sea.

As Canidy started to lead Fuller to the right, he automatically glanced to the left, checking for traffic.

He did a double take and stopped.

Fuller almost ran into the back of him.

"What?" Fuller whispered, then looked to where Canidy stared as if he'd seen a ghost.

Four blocks up, moored to the dock next to some warehouses, was a ninety-foot cargo vessel. It was under the armed guard of four sailors from the *Regina Marina.*

The rusty, utilitarian vessel looked very much like the one that Canidy had blown up — a small main cabin at the bow, and the rest of the topside a long, flat deck with large hatches and a pair of tall booms.

And, to the best of his memory, it had not been docked in the port of Palermo earlier that morning.

*I damn sure would've seen it sitting there,* he thought, *even as I was distracted by those poor bastards swinging on the gallows.*

"Does it mean anything?" Fuller said.

"Hell if I know."

Two blocks down Christoforo Colombo, the single-story brick building that bore the address that Frank Nola had given Canidy looked barely habitable. Canidy wondered if it was the right place.

*Did Frank fuck this up?*

*And now Tubes and I have to go back to the apartment and wait for however long it'll take him to show up so we can start the whole process all over again?*

*Jesus. . . .*

Canidy stood to the side of the heavy wooden door, using the masonry wall for protection, and leaned over to knock. After a couple of minutes, and a second series of louder knocks, there came from the other side of the door the metallic sound of latches being undone.

The door cracked open, and, when Canidy looked, he saw Nola's pronounced nose.

Frank Nola waved Canidy and Fuller inside, opening the door enough for them to just pass through. Then he swung it shut with a *slam* and secured the latches.

Apparently, Canidy realized as he looked around the dimly lit main room, the place was somewhat habitable.

*It's set up about half and half . . . half office, half landfill.*

A pair of desks piled high with paper were pushed together back-to-back in the middle of the room, a wooden office chair at each. There was a row of five battered, wooden filing cabinets against the near wall. And the rest of the room was random clutter — half-eaten German ration boxes, empty wine bottles, upturned wooden cases, overflowing cans of trash.

Canidy looked at Nola, who motioned toward a door on the far side of the room and said: "This way. And hurry. We do not have much time. The brothers have to get back to work at the warehouse."

At the doorway, Nola stopped and nodded toward the next room.

"In here, Dick," he said.

Canidy looked at him.

"Why don't you go ahead, Frank? You know the fucking way."

Nola frowned.

"Just being polite," Nola said, sounding hurt.

"After you, Frank," Canidy said.

When Nola had started through the doorway, Canidy glanced at Fuller, who shrugged.

The next room was another office, a smaller one, with a single desk, a wooden chair behind it, and a wooden bench against the wall.

The brothers Buda were seated on the bench. Each had been reading a different section of a newspaper and now looked up at the strangers, Canidy and Fuller, who followed Nola inside.

The Budas were about thirty years old, maybe five foot five and two hundred pounds. The dirty overalls they wore fit tightly, the cotton fabric stretched and defining the rolls of fat of their midsection. They had an olive skin, but their face and neck and hands were coarse from long exposure to wind and sea and sun.

Their mop haircuts looked to have been done by placing a small bowl on the head and then trimming any hair that stuck out with dull scissors.

*Or maybe hacked with a single-edged knife,* Canidy thought.

*Jesus, they look like they couldn't possibly be smart enough to read a newspaper.*

*And no way in hell could they share the same mother as Andrea.*

Nola said something to them in Sicilian as he motioned to Canidy.

*Great. They don't speak English, either.*

All Canidy could recognize from Nola's rapid-fire introduction was "Antonio," "Giacomo," and what he thought was the word for "friend" — *amico.*

From under fat, heavy eyelids, the brother Budas's deep-set eyes stared without emotion or recognition at Canidy.

*Calm down, guys.*

*Your enthusiasm is over the top.*

"Frank," Canidy said evenly, "by any chance did you explain to Tweedle-Fucking-Dee and -Dum here what we're trying to accomplish?"

Canidy heard Fuller chuckle behind him. He also noticed some response in the brothers' expressions to that crack.

*Well, maybe you bastards do understand English.*

"Yes," Nola said. "And they are willing to help. You must understand that they're upset about what happened at the port."

*And they're pissed at me?*

*I hope you didn't tell them I blew up the boat, Frank.*

*Otherwise, ol' Tubes is behind me with an itchy trigger finger on his .45 and about to yell, "Fins! Motherfucking fins!"*

518

"Yeah, let's talk about that," Canidy said.

He looked at the brothers and added: "Who did that hanging?"

Nola began to translate. Canidy held up his hand for him to stop.

"Let them answer the damn question," Canidy said.

The brothers remained silent. Then the one on the left spoke in Sicilian.

Nola translated: "Antonio says they understand some English but cannot speak it well."

*Bullshit*, Canidy thought. *But no need to call them on it right now.*

"What about who strung up the fishermen?" he said.

"The SS," Nola said. "I asked them that earlier, before you came. Sturmbannführer Müller's men, on his orders. Müller himself was at the pier when they were" — he searched for the appropriate words — "put there."

Nola looked at the Budas, then went on: "Antonio said three SS officers from Messina arrived the next day. One was an *obersturmbannführer*. He stayed for only a few hours, had angry words with Müller, then left."

Canidy nodded but was not sure what to make of that.

"Did you ask about the nerve gas, Frank?" Canidy went on, still looking at the brothers.

"Yes."

*"And?"* Canidy said, turning to Nola. "Jesus, don't make me pull this out of you like a bad tooth."

"And," Nola went on, "they said that they know nothing about any poison gas."

"Did they say if they knew anything about what was aboard the cargo ship that blew up?" Canidy said.

Nola turned to the brothers and asked the question in Sicilian.

There was some discussion, first with Nola, then between the brothers, then again with Nola.

"They say," Nola finally explained, "Sturmbannführer Müller ordered the ship unloaded of all contents. They got everything off except the last of the canisters of fuel. They were to get that remaining gas off the next day, but then . . ."

*What? Canidy thought. Just gas was on it?*

He said to Nola, "There was only fuel in the cargo hold when the ship went up?"

Canidy saw that Tweedledee — *Or is Antonio Tweedledum?* — nodded.

"Only fuel, nothing else?" Canidy said, looking directly at Antonio.

*"Sí,"* Antonio replied.

Nola said, "He said yes."

Canidy glared at Nola.

"No shit, Frank . . . I know what *sí* means."

Fuller chuckled again.

Canidy looked back to Antonio.

"What did you take off of the ship? And where did it go?"

Nola answered, "It went in the warehouse."

"But what was it, is my question," Canidy said.

Nola looked to Antonio and repeated the question for him in Sicilian.

There then came a long involved reply, with input this time from Brother Giacomo, and much gesturing of hands and waving of arms by both brothers. Canidy recognized the name Müller.

"There was a little of everything," Nola said, now making the same gestures as he spoke to Canidy. "There was mostly cases of food, what I believe is called 'field rations' for the soldiers? There was the fuel cans. And there was some crates of ammunitions, 'bullets'? Müller wanted those off first."

Canidy considered this, and nodded.

"And," Canidy said, "all this went into one of your warehouses?"

"Yes," Nola said. "The one that the Germans have begun to take over."

"How do you mean?"

"We have two working warehouses," Nola said. "One is still all ours. The other, the Germans are slowly taking over. As part of our agreement, they *allow* us to unload their matériel and store it, alongside whatever we have in there. But they have posted armed guards, and we do not have same freedom in that warehouse as we do in the other."

Canidy thought that over, then looked at Antonio.

"Bullets?"

Antonio nodded.

"Many bullets," he said. His thick tongue made it sound like *buh-lets*.

"Is there any way that I could get inside the warehouse?" Canidy said to Antonio, then looked at Nola. "Any way to get past the guards?"

Antonio said something in Sicilian.

Nola shrugged. "Not impossible. The military items, they are very careful about. Not so much everything else of ours. They do not check it closely. Particularly if they are expecting to get a piece of it."

Canidy thought about that.

"I might need to get in and take a look," he said.

"Okay," Nola said.

There was a long moment's silence. Then Canidy said, "What about the villa?"

"I didn't ask," Nola said. "There wasn't time."

"Have at it," Canidy said, waving his arm toward the Budas.

Nola went on for some time in Sicilian. When he was done, the brothers didn't say a word. They just simply shook their heads.

Nola said something else and their reply was terse.

"As far as they know," Nola said to Canidy, "there was only one explosion. The ship. No explosion from the villa. And they have not heard of anyone else speaking about any villa exploding."

*So,* Canidy thought, *the damn thing still is in one piece?*

*And still full of yellow fever. . . .*

"Do they know Whatshisname Cordova?" Canidy said.

Nola spoke to the brothers, and Canidy recognized the names when he said, "Alfredo Cordova," "Alessandro Paterno," and "Simone Cesareo."

The brothers shook their heads.

*Shit,* Canidy thought. *But no real surprise.*

*Those are Rossi's people from the university. Not fishermen from the docks.*

"When can I get in the warehouse?" Canidy said to Antonio.

Antonio shrugged and replied in Sicilian.

Nola translated: "Anytime after today."

Canidy glanced at Fuller, who tried to maintain a stoic face, but Canidy could see uncertainty in his eyes.

Then, out of the blue, Fuller yawned massively, which almost caused Canidy to do the same.

He checked his wristwatch.

*We've been going almost twenty-four hours — damn near nonstop since we got off the submarine.*

*We've got to be careful not to get so tired that we get sloppy.*

Fuller made an apologetic face.

Canidy turned back to Nola and thought about what had just been said.

"Anytime after today?" he repeated.

Antonio stood up. Giacomo did the same.

"Why not today?" Canidy said.

*"Buh-lets,"* Antonio said by way of explanation, then rattled off something to Nola in Sicilian.

Nola translated: "They've got to go to work. They've been told to put the crates of bullets from the warehouse aboard a ship that has docked here from Messina."

"And if I can go into the warehouse tomorrow," Canidy said after a moment, "then that means they'll be done with that by tonight."

Nola nodded.

# [FOUR]
## PALERMO, SICILY
## 1301 5 APRIL 1943

The two warehouses that Francisco Nola ran his import-export business out of were six blocks up Christoforo Colombo from the office building. When they got to the warehouse that the Germans were not using, Nola went upstairs to its small box of an office that overlooked the floor, brought a pair of binoculars down to Canidy, then went back inside the office.

The warehouses had skylights and each was reasonably well lit by sunlight.

Canidy stood with the binocs to his eyes. He was just inside the great double doors. Fuller was behind him, also out of sight of anyone on the docks, watching the activity at the other warehouse over Canidy's shoulder.

Under the gaze of the armed guard, Giacomo and Antonio Buda supervised the work of maybe ten longshoremen. The workers hand-carried or wheeled on low manual lifts the crates and other containers. Their steady line went from inside the great double doors out to a staging area on the dock beside the ship. There the cranes on the ship's deck lifted the matériel up and into the cargo holds.

Canidy looked intently through the glasses at some pallets. They were topped with the Germans' version of jerry cans, these particular ones painted a sand color.

*I could've made them with my naked eyes.*

*They're damn near identical in looks — and, I'd bet, function — to our jerry cans.*

*Probably meant for North Africa and never got there in time.*

The metal sides were stamped with lettering and Canidy focused in on that:

---

WEHRMACHTKANISTEREN.
KRAFTSTOFF 20L
FEUERGEFÄHRLICH

---

*Leave it to those tight-ass Krauts to label the obvious.*

*I sure as hell hope they're flammable.*

Beside the pallets were wooden boxes the size of footlockers. These were labeled: 8MM MAUSER.

*Well, those are the rifle rounds.*

And then he saw larger wooden crates. These were huge. Two or more of the Mauser boxes of ammo would fit in a single one.

Canidy adjusted the eyepieces of the binocs to get a clearer view. Then he read the stenciled marking: SONDERKART.6LE.F.H.18 T83 10.5CM.

*Sonofabitch!*

*Those certainly are some* buh-lets.

*Those are fucking 105mm field howitzer rounds!*

He took out a pencil and paper and started writing down the stenciled markings. This took some effort, and he had to go back and forth between holding the binocs and writing with the pencil. Then he read back over what he had written and peered again through the glasses to confirm he'd gotten it right.

He looked at Fuller.

"Think you can find your way back to the apartment?"

Fuller pointed to his nose.

"By scent," he said, grinning.

Canidy looked over at the other warehouse. Antonio Buda was helping wheel a manual lift that carried a crate out through the big doors. Canidy nodded in Buda's direction and said, "Should I share that with our new friends?"

"We'll just keep it our little secret," Fuller said, smiling.

"And you'll just keep your hands to yourself when you get there."

"Okay, okay."

Canidy handed Fuller the paper and Fuller read it:

```
TOP SECRET

OPERATIONAL IMMEDIATE

5APR43 1500

FOR OSS WASHINGTON EYES ONLY GEN
DONOVAN; OSS ALGIERS EYES ONLY CAPT
FINE.

BEGIN QUOTE

NO ANTACID REPEAT NO ANTACID BURNED
OR SUNK IN PORT.

NO KNOWN REPEAT NO KNOWN ANTACID
ASHORE.

AMMO FOR SMALL ARMS AND FOR HOW-
ITZERS FOUND. CRATES LABELED 8MM
MAUSER AND SONDERKART.6LE.F.H.18 T83
```

```
10.5CM.

AMMO AND FUEL CANS BEING ONLOADED
SHIP. DESTINATION UNKNOWN.

MORE TO FOLLOW.

JUPITER

END QUOTE

TOP SECRET
```

"When you're done, after you get the confirmation," Canidy said, "burn the message."

"Right."

"Then get some rest, and I'll see you there
as soon as I can," Canidy added. "No telling
what's coming next."

# X

## [ONE]
## VILLA DEL ARCHIMEDES
## PARTANNA, SICILY
## 1720 5 APRIL 1943

Dick Canidy, sound asleep on his back, was startled awake by a loud, high-pitched cry.

As he sat upright, struggling to get his bearings, there was a raucous flapping of wings as a score of seagulls took flight.

Canidy was up about a hundred yards on a ridge of the hillside that overlooked the Villa del Archimedes. The villa was another five hundred yards, give or take, to the northwest.

A cobblestone roadway had been constructed on the ridge, along with a stone wall two feet tall at the lip.

*For whatever reason,* he'd thought earlier, *the goddamn Krauts or Wops took it out of play by taking a chunk of it, probably with more of those 105mm rounds from a field howitzer.*

What remained of the wall provided for nice concealment, not to mention a place to fall asleep. And it served as a solid platform for the bipod of Canidy's Johnson light machine gun.

Now Canidy thought: *Dammit! I fell asleep!*

*Not surprised. I was exhausted.*

He watched the birds disappear into the distance.

*I probably disappointed those flying rats.*

*They were hoping for another tasty snack of eyeballs.*

He shook his head, trying to shake the numbness he felt.

*Jesus! That was a close call!*

*If I'd slept through till it turned dark . . .*

Canidy had an almost-due-west exposure, which was exactly what he wanted — bright light to help mask the brightness of muzzle flash — but the brilliance of the sunset was forcing him to squint.

*If I'd slept past dusk, the damn muzzle flash would've looked like a Fourth of July fireworks show. . . .*

He looked over the wall and down.

The ridge afforded Canidy one helluva view. In the distance was Cape Gallo, the northernmost point. To the northeast was Mondello, and he could make out the crescent beach where they had landed with the folding kayaks.

And here, below his feet, was Partanna . . . and the Villa del Archimedes.

Canidy had been looking down with the binoculars, waiting and watching — *and snoozing* — since he had come back alone from the apartment, where he'd left Frank Nola with Jim Fuller and retrieved the Johnny gun.

Having left the warehouse where the cargo ship was still being loaded, Nola had walked with Canidy the five kilometers to Partanna. There he'd pointed out the hillside to Canidy, somewhat needlessly as the looming rock was as hard to find as an angry zit on the forehead of a teenager.

They had followed the roadway up to where the hole had been blown into it and then sat watching the coarse-stone villa for more than an hour.

Canidy had had the binoculars to his eyes and was studying the big electrical power generator on steel skids that had been put beside the villa. It had a diesel engine with a manufacturer plaque that read MANN. And there was a wooden pallet covered with jerry cans, a few lying on their side, empty.

*Ah, the well-labeled* Wehrmachtkanisteren kraftstoff, *the "armed forces cans" of "fuel."*

*And my favorite part:* Feuergefahrlich . . .

*"flammable."*

Nola tapped Canidy on the shoulder, then pointed out the dust cloud being kicked up on the dirt road by a car approaching the villa.

When the car, a 1940 Alfa-Romeo sedan, had gone through the gate in the stone wall surrounding the villa and pulled to a stop, Canidy trained the glasses on the driver's door. It opened.

"Well, look at who we have here," Canidy said.

He handed the binoculars to Nola.

"Is that your sturmbannführer?"

Canidy got his answer when Nola grunted derisively.

"That is Müller," Nola added needlessly.

"I've seen enough," Canidy said. "Let's go. I need my Johnny gun."

The Alfa-Romeo was still at the villa when Canidy had returned alone, but now it was parked for whatever reason near the generator.

*Maybe they refueled it while I was gone,* Canidy thought.

He looked at the sun and figured he had maybe a half hour till sunset, and that this was the last of the brilliant light before it started turning softer.

He peered through the sights of the Johnny gun and thought, *"If you want something done right . . ."*

When fired, the muzzle of the automatic tended to walk upward from left to right. So he put the bead of the tall front sight just to the left and a little below the dozen *Wehrmachtkanisteren kraftstoff* that were on the pallet beside the generator.

He took in a deep breath, then let out half of it as he squeezed his trigger finger.

The Johnny gun began to bark, the first of the ten-round burst kicking up dirt as it stitched a line of lead toward the generator.

Canidy paused a moment, holding his position and aim, and wondered if he had hit anything other than ground.

*Dammit!*

He squeezed the trigger again and the Johnny gun responded with another series of *bam-bam-bam*s until the twenty-round clip was empty.

There were men — Müller's — running out of the villa now.

*Damn diesel is slow to blow.*

He pulled the empty magazine from the left side of the weapon.

He put in a fresh one — and one of the Kraut jerry cans exploded.

The men ran back inside the villa.

*Not sure that's a wise decision . . .*

And then another jerry can erupted.

And then four or more went up at once, like a string of firecrackers.

*Very loud firecrackers.*

The fire from the multiple explosion hit the main fuel tank of the Mann engine. It caught, and that fireball blew off the boards that covered the windows of the villa.

And then the first of the Composition C-2 inside cooked off.

The concussion that followed was so severe that Canidy instinctively ducked behind the low wall, covering his head and ears.

*God, I love this job!*

# [TWO]
## PALERMO, SICILY
## 2020 5 APRIL 1943

Canidy had hid in a cave until just after dark before making his way back to the apartment. When he got there, he found only Frank Nola and Jim Fuller.

"Where's the girl?" he said.

Fuller shrugged.

"She left when Frank and I went upstairs," Tubes said.

*She's not off telling anyone about us, is she?*

"Do we need to worry?" Canidy said. "Is she dependable, Frank?"

"Yes, as good as me."

*Jury's still out on that one, Frank.*

*But so far, so good.*

He looked at Fuller.

"Messages go out okay, Tubes?"

He nodded.

"But I think you need to see this," Fuller said.

He held out a handwritten decrypted message.

Canidy read it quickly.

"Great," he said. "I guess."

"What?" Nola asked. "Is good news?"

"Fine says that Rossi's notes state that the Tabun shells are clearly marked. The cases are stenciled with 'T83' — just as we saw — and the shells themselves are marked 'GA,' with a ring of green around the tip."

"But most of those crates did not have the T83," Fuller said.

Canidy nodded. "Yeah, there were a bunch of regular howitzer rounds in there. So how the hell are we supposed to get a look in the crates with the T83 designation and confirm the GA and the green ring?"

Then he smiled.

*We don't have to confirm it.*

"What is it?" Fuller said.

"Need to shoot a message to *Le Casa*," Canidy said.

He looked at his watch and began thinking out loud: "Not going to make 2115. And, even if I ran, I'd probably miss 2315 —"

Fuller figured out what he was doing. "You're leaving?"

Canidy nodded. "But 0115 would work. Time to get to Mondello, then paddle out. And if I miss that, 0315 is my backup. Meanwhile, there should be plenty of excitement out at what's left of the villa. Enough for diversion."

He saw that Fuller and Nola were regarding his ramblings oddly.

"Sorry about that," Canidy said, then asked Nola: "How are they coming with the loading of that ship?"

"One of the booms broke," Nola said. "Is taking longer than they wanted."

"How long?"

"Should be done by dark."

"It *is* dark, Frank," Canidy said.

Nola nodded. "Should be done."

Canidy shook his head.

*I'm not going to miss these intellectual exchanges one bit.*

He then took a sheet of flash paper and wrote:

```
TOP SECRET

OPERATIONAL IMMEDIATE

05APR43 2115

FOR NEPTUNE

FROM MERCURY STATION

BEGIN QUOTE

JUPITER HEADED HOME ALONE
06APR 1ST SURFACE.

END QUOTE

TOP SECRET
```

He handed the paper to Fuller and said, "Get on the air to Mars —"

"You mean Neptune?"

"L'Herminier is Mars, god of war."

"Got it," Fuller said softly.

He was quiet a moment, then added: "Why?"

"Why Mars?"

Fuller shook his head.

"Why am I leaving?" Canidy said.

Fuller nodded.

"We did it, Tubes. We found what we were supposed to. It's all I need for now and you're going to radio me the rest. You and the follow-up teams. You're still up to it, right?"

Fuller pursed his lips. He tried to keep a straight face, but his expression showed he had his reservations.

Canidy put a hand on each of his shoulders and looked him in the eyes.

"Look, Tubes, it's never easy," he said. "You're always looking over your shoulder, always on edge. But then when you get out, you discover you miss that rush. You find nothing compares to being in. *Ever.*"

Fuller stared back and said, "Really?"

Canidy then suddenly grinned from ear to ear.

"Why the hell do you think I keep coming back in?" he said. "This time tomorrow, I'll be itching to get back in."

Canidy then checked his watch again.

"It's 2050. Go get this on the air. And sometime soon — not tonight — get that backup suitcase radio set and find a secure place for it that only you know."

Fuller nodded, and Canidy detected that he was feeling a little more confident.

"You can count on me, Dick."

"I know I can, Tubes," Canidy said solemnly. "You're going to be all right." He paused, then added with a grin: "As long as you let the big head do all the thinking."

Canidy, floating and waiting in the kayak a little after midnight, heard the diesel engine of the cargo ship before he saw its vague outline on the horizon.

*With my luck, the damn thing will plow over me right before the submarine gets here.*

The boat slowly rumbled past.

*It's going around to the south of the island.*

*That's the long way to Messina.*

*Or are they going to stage the nerve gas at a southern port?*

*And that boat is in no hurry.*

*What does that mean?*

Twenty minutes later, Canidy was startled by the sudden rocking of the kayak.

He grabbed the gunnels and quickly lay down in the wet bottom, trying to keep his center of gravity low.

*Damn ship wake.*

*Now's not the time to sink, Dick ol' boy.*

The rocking subsided after what seemed an eternity.

Over the next half hour, Canidy worked at getting his breathing back to normal. He'd just about accomplished that when there was an enormous *whoosh* of large volumes of water being displaced.

Canidy about came out of his skin.

Then he looked and sighed when he saw the silhouette of the submarine conn tower.

"But what if this gas burns?" Commander Jean L'Herminier, chief officer of the Free French Forces submarine *Casabianca,* asked Dick Canidy.

They were in the captain's office and drinking coffee.

"How much water are we in?" Canidy said.

"Maybe a thousand meters."

"Then it really doesn't matter if it burns," Canidy said. "We're far enough out, and at a point where no one is around. If there's a cloud, it will dissipate. No concentration, no harm. And what doesn't burn goes to the bottom."

L'Herminier nodded.

"Most important," Canidy said, "the Germans don't get the gas."

The speaker of the inner-ship radio built into the wall of the office crackled alive.

"Commander, we've got her," the nasally voice of the executive officer said.

When Canidy and L'Herminier came into the control room, the executive officer was at the periscope. The XO heard them enter and stepped back.

"She's at eleven o'clock, Captain," he said, gesturing toward the scope.

"Thank you," L'Herminier said.

He put his face to the periscope.

After a moment, L'Herminier said, "Ninety-, ninety-five footer. A nice-sized target."

He began turning the tube, making the start of a slow three-sixty scan of the surface. He did it in forty-five-degree segments, stopping to study each segment before moving to the next. When he had come back to the cargo vessel, he said, "Well, well. Looks as though she does have company. Maybe an escort?"

L'Herminier stepped back from the scope and motioned for Canidy to see.

Canidy looked but could not make out anything. He adjusted the optics.

"The cargo vessel is at eleven o'clock, just to the port of our bow," L'Herminier said.

After a moment, Canidy said, "Got it."

"Now, look to about two o'clock. Same size as the cargo ship but armed to the teeth."

"Oh, shit! Another S-boat."

Canidy stepped back from the periscope. When he looked at L'Herminier, he saw that the commander had his eyes closed and his head down.

*What the hell is he doing?*

Then L'Herminier brought up his head, and, as he opened his eyes, he crossed himself.

When he saw Canidy's questioning look, he said softly, "I understand what it is we do and why. But still I say a prayer for the souls of the lives I must take."

Canidy nodded. Then he quickly closed his eyes and lowered his head.

*Merciful Lord,*

*Bless the souls of these men whose lives we are about to take.*

*Bless the fish we're about to fire so that our sword is swift and sure.*

*And . . . and bless this boat and crew so it's only the enemy's ass and not mine.*

*Amen.*

Canidy opened his eyes. L'Herminier was at the scope, looking in the direction of the S-boat.

*Well, that might not be the prayer my father would have chosen.*

*But it'll have to do.*

"On my mark," the sub commander said to the XO. "She's settled in ahead of the cargo vessel and matched her speed. Steer one-zero-six degrees."

"One-zero-six degrees!" the executive officer called to the helm.

After a minute, the captain calmly said, "Distance seven-five-zero meters."

The XO repeated that.

"Fire torpedo two," L'Herminier ordered.

Canidy felt the *Casabianca* shudder as the fish shot forward. There was silence for what seemed like an eternity, then L'Herminier crossed himself again — and a muffled roar reverberated through the ship.

Then all was quiet.

L'Herminier calmly turned the scope in search of the cargo vessel.

"Ah, she's starting to run," he said.

L'Herminier looked at Canidy.

"I like it when the target runs," he added. "Not as easy as the S-boat just now. You have to lead them."


# [THREE]
## OSS ALGIERS STATION
## ALGIERS, ALGERIA
## 1245 10 APRIL 1943


As Major Richard M. Canidy, United States Army Air Forces, looked out at the *Casabianca* among the ships in the harbor and barrage balloons above them, Captain Stanley S. Fine, United States Army Air Forces, came out onto the balcony, a fat manila folder in his hand.

Faintly, Canidy heard a familiar sound, and his eyes caught movement in the sky. He immediately pinpointed the USAAF P-38Fs — a small V formation of five Lockheed Lightnings — and grinned knowingly. The sound of the 1,475-horsepower Allison V-12 engines was like recognizing the voice of an old friend.

*All things being equal,* he thought, admiring the twin-engine fighters, *I'd rather be in that lead aircraft, going wherever the hell it's going — even if that's air combat . . .* especially *air combat — because* that *is where I feel the most comfortable.*

It had been only months earlier that Canidy — flying with Doug Douglass, protecting a stream of B-17 bombers over Germany — had been blasting Messerschmitt Me 109s out of the sky with his Lightning's battery of eight .50 caliber Brownings.

"Those birds make a pretty sight," Fine said. "I miss flying, too."

Canidy nodded.

Fine was widely admired not just for his creative ability — as Canidy put it, "at silencing the rear-echelon bureaucratic bastards in Washington and their endless paper-work" — but also because, despite his some-what-frail appearance, he was absolutely fearless. And one helluva pilot.

"Here's the stack of everything we've re-ceived from Mercury Station," Fine added. "No more reports on either the Tabun or the yellow-fever program."

"Thanks, Caesar," Canidy said with a smile. "That's good news."

"There's also an update in there from Whitbey House. Says Ann is doing well."

"Any reason she wouldn't be?" Canidy said. "No word where she was, what happened?"

Fine shook his head. "No — to all the above."

Canidy said, "I'm planning to get back to London —"

"And so you shall," Fine said. "Soon as we knock this out."

Canidy was more than halfway through the manila folder of messages — chuckling at one of the lines that Tubes had stuck in: "Adolf and Eva send regards" — when John Craig van der Ploeg appeared on the bal-cony. He was holding a single typewritten message. He had a look of uncertainty.

"What's this?" Canidy said, looking at the message. "You miss one?"

"It's the latest from Mercury," van der Ploeg said.

Canidy took it from his hand and read it.

"Tubes says Nola wants more money for bribes and to start stockpiling weapons?" Canidy said. "So we send 'em."

"There's a Sandbox team getting ready to go in," Fine offered. "Soon as *Le Casa* can get herself provisioned."

"That's not the problem," van der Ploeg said.

"What is?" Canidy asked.

The radioman nodded at the message that Canidy held.

"That's not his hand."

"What do you mean?" Canidy said.

"The way he sends Morse code on the wireless key," the radioman said, "I can tell that Tubes isn't doing the —"

"I know what it means," Canidy interrupted.

"But it's his radio frequency," John Craig van der Ploeg finished.

Canidy considered that.

"It *was* his hand for those" — van der Ploeg went on, nodding at the messages Canidy had been reading — "but at noon it suddenly wasn't his hand. I even made him resend the messages."

"You're sure?" Canidy said. "Absolutely

one hundred and ten percent certain?"

John Craig looked as if he took offense at the question.

"As certain as anyone can tell the difference between who's blowing the blues horn, Miles Davis or Jack Benny. Or maybe the tone of airplane engines?"

"Your ear is that good?" Fine said.

"More like Tubes's hand is that good. He has a natural rhythm. He makes his keying seem effortless. It's almost art —"

"Shit!" Canidy flared.

"And whoever's operating Tubes's W/T has all the finesse of a ham-fisted gorilla."

"Did he send the code for a compromised station?" Canidy said.

John Craig van der Ploeg shook his head. "Negative, sir."

Canidy glared at him. "Don't start with that sir shit again."

"So you think he's been turned?" said John Craig van der Ploeg. "He's a double agent?"

*The station is compromised,* Canidy thought.

*Jesus Christ, I led that poor sonofabitch there like a lamb to the slaughter.*

*Tubes, I pray you're all right . . . as I promised you would be.*

"Ask him," Canidy said evenly to John Craig van der Ploeg. "Ask him, quote, is there another barnacle on the hull?, un-quote."

Canidy looked at John Craig van der Ploeg, then took the typewritten message he had just handed him and wrote on it: *Is there another barnacle on the hull?*

He handed it to him.

"What — ?" John Craig van der Ploeg said after he read it.

"Just fucking send the message!" Canidy snapped.

When John Craig van der Ploeg had left the balcony, Canidy looked out in the direction of the Lightnings, their twin tails now tiny points on the horizon.

Stan Fine saw that, too.

"Don't think about it, Dick. You're *not* going back in, by air or sub. You did your job."

Canidy stared at him.

"That's really not your call, Stan."

Resignedly, Fine nodded, then went on, "Corvo's team from the Sandbox will be en route any day, maybe even tomorrow. They'll find Tubes."

Canidy didn't say anything.

*"As long as the Nazis consider you are valuable to them — an asset — no harm will come to you."*

*Hope I'm at least right about that.*

"Okay, meantime, we keep working him," Canidy said coldly. "Double agents are useful. We can feed him info. Maybe that will buy time to keep him alive."

Canidy looked out over the Mediterranean Sea, in the direction of Sicily, and sighed loudly.

"You can call me FDR," he said. "I'm also going to accept only the unconditional surrender of the goddamn enemy."

# [FOUR]
## OSS LONDON STATION
## BERKELEY SQUARE
## LONDON, ENGLAND
## 1701 14 MAY 1943

Lieutenant Colonel Edmund T. Stevens reached toward the tray on David Bruce's desk that held two bottles of Famous Grouse scotch, one full and one about empty, and three glasses. He picked up the open bottle, then looked at David Bruce and Major Richard M. Canidy.

They both had glasses dark with scotch.

"I was about to wave the bottle at you," Stevens said, "and offer you more, but it would appear that I'm drinking a bit faster than everyone else."

"I'd suggest it's an evaporation factor," Canidy said, smiling. "Air is terribly dry this time of year."

Stevens finished filling his glass, then touched it to Canidy's in a toast. "I'm just damn glad you're here, Dick."

"Thank you. Me, too."

David Bruce said, "You were saying about our agent who's been doubled?"

Canidy nodded. "We're feeding him disinformation with some really low-level real stuff. There's a team that's trying to get to him, see if he's really turned or just controlled. We don't know. It's my opinion that he's under duress. Tubes is a good guy with no ax to grind, no reason to aid the enemy."

"Tubes?" Bruce said.

"Maximus, if you prefer."

Bruce smiled. "Oh, yes. Thank you, *Jupiter.*"

David Bruce sipped his scotch, then said: "Will the Germans see Maximus as a sign we're going to invade Sicily? And what about the S-boat and the ship you took out?"

Canidy drank from his glass as he considered his answer.

After a moment, he said, "As to the boats, I don't see why they would not simply be seen as targets of opportunity. And we have agents in Sardinia, too, so why would we *not* in Sicily? And before you ask about blowing the villa, that could have been done by anyone, including the Mafia, pissed at the hanging in the port."

David Bruce's expression suggested that he did not exactly agree with that assessment.

"What about Ike?" Bruce then said.

"What about him?" Canidy said defensively.

"Has he been told?" Bruce went on.

"Told what?" Canidy said, his tone incredulous. "That we fucking took out a ship carrying nerve gas that his people said did not even exist? Jesus!"

Canidy drained his glass, then looked at Stevens.

"Give me that bottle, Ed. I can use another now."

David Bruce made a face.

"Dick does make a good point," Ed Stevens said evenly after he passed the bottle to Canidy. "Why muddy the waters?"

After a moment, David Bruce nodded.

"Sorry, Dick," he said. "I'm just trying to keep all the pieces in perspective. Now's not the time for us to slow down. We're making real progress. Thanks to our OSS agents in Sardinia you mentioned, eighty-four B-24 Liberators bombed La Maddalena on April tenth. They even sank the Italian heavy cruiser *Trieste.* And, of course, we took Bizerta and Tunis on May seventh."

"More than a quarter million German and Italian prisoners," Stevens said.

"And now," Bruce added, "thanks to Ed Stevens and his new pals, it would appear the path to taking Sicily and Italy is clearing."

Canidy looked at Stevens. "New pals?"

Stevens gave Canidy a copy of Lieutenant Commander Ewen Montagu's OPERATION MINCEMEAT outline. When he'd read it, Stevens then gave Canidy an overview of the OSS's contribution.

"We put together Major Martin at Whitbey House," Ed Stevens said.

As he explained OSS Whitbey House Station's participation, Canidy found himself laughing aloud at various points.

"I am really sorry I missed being a part of that," Canidy said.

"I wish I had been of more help," Stevens said, "but the others handled it marvelously."

He then produced another typewritten page.

"That's the report from 'Jimmy' Jewell — formally, Lieutenant N.L.A. Jewell — captain of HMS *Seraph.* Confirmation and details of the transport of the body and its launching off Spain on April thirtieth — two weeks ago. Pretty straightforward. Borderline boring, actually, as it all went according to plan."

Canidy glanced at the page and nodded.

"Immediately after we got that signal," Stevens said, "Montagu had the message traffic at the Admiralty reach a fevered pitch, all cranked up about the missing of Major Martin."

Stevens took a moment to refreshen his scotch.

He went on: "On May second, the naval attaché in Madrid signaled that the body of Major Martin had been picked up off the coast. So the Admiralty responded to the naval attaché about the briefcase and its, quote, most secret, unquote, documents. The attaché then got hammered with urgent messages to get back every damn document — but don't be too obvious. Don't want the Spaniards getting suspicious, wink, wink. And return those documents to DNI immediately!"

Canidy chuckled.

"May fourth, they gave Major Martin a full military burial in Huleva."

"And the briefcase?"

"Returned," Stevens said. "Very, very carefully put back together."

"Meaning, they read the contents? The writings finely crafted at Whitbey House?"

Stevens reached for a stack of papers and said, "Commander Fleming brought these over. These are far more interesting to read."

"And they are . . . ?"

"Intercepts of German wireless traffic courtesy of the fine folks connected to the Golf, Cheese, and Chess Society."

Canidy grinned. He knew a little about the Brits' code-breaking operations at Bletchley Park, some forty miles northwest of London. Golf, Cheese, and Chess Society — GCCS for short — came from its Government Code and Cypher School there.

Canidy flipped through the documents.

"I'll give you the executive summary," Stevens said, clearly enjoying himself.

"I'd say a bit of Niven or Fleming or Ustinov rubbed off on you, Ed."

"They're great guys, Dick," Stevens replied. "Anyway, in the first week of May the German agents telegraphed the contents of the letters to German intel in Berlin. They stated that, due to time — the Admiralty was hammering the naval attaché to get them back, right? — they're unable to examine documents for authenticity."

Canidy nodded.

Stevens went on: "The first message sent to Berlin that was intercepted was boldly detailed and gave us a marvelous step-by-step. It said that the body of the Royal Marine had been found on the beach at Huelva by a fisherman who then had brought it to the attention of personnel at the nearby naval station. There a naval judicial officer took charge of all documents and personal effects. And the body was sent to the morgue, where a doctor certified that Martin had fallen into the sea alive but died of asphyxiations from five to eight days 'exposure to sea.'"

"Ah, those brilliant Spanish physicians," Canidy said, sipping his scotch.

"They even had a Captain Ron Bowlin, USAAF, who'd crashed into the sea there on April twenty-seventh, brought in to identify the body. He couldn't, of course, but now we know where ole Ron is."

Canidy chuckled.

"Meanwhile, German intel, working from photos of the contents of Major Martin's briefcase, had determined that the documents were indeed genuine. That information then got forwarded to Admiral Doenitz."

"Commander in Chief, Naval Staff," Canidy said. *"Ding, ding.* We have a winner."

"Even better, the cover letter read: 'The genuineness of the captured documents is above suspicion.'"

Canidy shook his head in amazement.

"Then just yesterday came the sweetest piece," Stevens went on. "His Heil Hitler himself now believes that the Sicily invasion is a diversion. He's demanding that, quote, measures regarding Sardinia and the Peloponnese take precedence over everything else, unquote."

Stevens stopped to take a sip.

"And now we hear that General Keitel —"

"Corporal Schickelgruber's commander in chief," Canidy said, impressed. "Very nice."

"— has passed word down that they expect Sardinia, Corsica, and Sicily to be attacked all at once, or perhaps one at a time, when we take Greece."

"I heard you were sucking up all those drachmas. Guess they did, too."

Stevens nodded. "It was more than drachmas, but they helped."

David Bruce finally spoke up.

"We couldn't have asked for more out of an operation," Bruce said. "They clearly believe that the Allies have enough troops for both assaults. And that can only cause them to defend — or not defend — territory accordingly."

"So the radio traffic confirms that Mince-meat was swallowed?" Canidy said, but it was more a statement than a question.

"Whole," a familiar voice said from the doorway.

"Jesus Christ!" Canidy said, seeing who it was, and struggling to quickly get to his feet.

"Not quite," Wild Bill Donovan said, laughing. "Only a common general. But I thank you for the promotion."

Canidy was smiling. He put out his hand.

"Very good to see you, General. And congratulations."

"That was nice work, gentlemen," Donovan said. "Even Ike and the boys at AFHQ are impressed."

Donovan looked at Canidy. "You've been busy, too, Dick. Why don't you fill me in."

"Of course. I —"

Donovan, looking at Canidy's drink, interrupted: "Why don't you first pour me a little of whatever evil spirit that might be. I suspect, with your history, I'm going to need a taste."


". . . And that was the story that the Mafia guys were getting out of the SS office in Palermo," Canidy said. "That Müller was scared and going to use the Tabun without authorization. The Germans had sent it to

Palermo, without his knowledge, to be staged as insurance. Not as an offensive weapon. Of course, that can be all wrong. . . ."

Donovan was quiet a moment, sipping his scotch.

"Thankfully," he then said, "it would appear that you are right. We had corroborating evidence."

"Confirmed?" Canidy said. "By who?"

"Hans Bernd Gisevius," he said. "But ultimately Canaris."

"Admiral Canaris in the Abwehr?"

He nodded. "We doubled Gisevius. He's a leader of the German underground who Allen Dulles uses as his pipeline to Canaris. And Canaris also is tight with Fritz Thyssen."

Canidy knew Dulles was the OSS station chief in Switzerland. The Thyssen name was unfamiliar to Canidy and his face showed he didn't recognize the name.

"The Ruhr Valley industrialist. Who in the early days funneled a helluva lot of money into Hitler's pockets. Then he finally saw the writing on the wall, packed up the kids and grandkids, and fled for Switzerland in 1939. He's still a player in the Ruhr Valley, and tightly connected with Wolfgang Kappler."

"Why is that name familiar?" Canidy wondered.

"Kappler Industrie GmbH," Stevens furnished, "chief provider of coke, steel, and other materials to Mann and Daimler-Benz."

"Engines," Canidy said.

"Engines," Stevens confirmed.

"And there is an SS *Obersturmbannführer* in the Messina office named Oskar Kappler," Donovan went on. "And Thyssen has both been seen in the company of Wolffy Kappler and sniffing around industrial sites and the docks in Buenos Aires."

It took Canidy a moment to put those pieces together in his mind.

"So the real reason they don't want to use the gas," Canidy ventured, "the reason they don't want the war to become any worse than it has, is because they are making plans to get the hell out of Dodge."

"There are some who would agree with you, Dick," Wild Bill Donovan said. "I happen to be one of them."

"Then the war is — ?"

"Unfortunately, long from over," Donovan said. "And we have a lot of work yet to do until it is."

# [FIVE]
## WESTMINSTER TOWER
## PARK LANE AT ALDFORD STREET
## LONDON, ENGLAND
## 2020 14 MAY 1943

"No more jokes about my memory — the doctors said that's mostly over and done," Ann Chambers said playfully, one hand under the bedsheets, searching. "I've got a clean bill of health . . . and I'm beginning to remember why you drive me crazy."

Her hand found what it was looking for, wrapped around the prize . . . and gently but pointedly squeezed.

"Okay, okay," Canidy said. "No more jokes. And be easy with those. They only come in pairs — very, very delicate pairs."

Ann moved in closer to Canidy. She pressed her nose into his neck, kissed it, and practically purred.

After a long quiet moment, she glanced around the room and suddenly sat up.

"This place is absolutely amazing," she said.

She looked out the large picture windows of the twelfth-floor luxury apartment. The view overlooked Hyde Park.

Although it was now dark, she had spent the last few hours waiting for Canidy by sitting in the plush armchair at the window. She now clearly recalled the last rays of the sunset casting long shadows of the trees across the Serpentine, the park's long, curved picturesque pond.

"Thank Uncle Max," Canidy said.

"Who?"

"Stanley S. Fine, Esquire, on leave as vice president of legal affairs for Continental Motion Picture Studios, is the nephew of Mr. Max Liebermann, chairman of the board of Continental Motion Picture Studios."

"I think I knew that. I can't —"

"The studio," Canidy went on, "maintains this apartment for stars and executives — and very, very select friends of the family — who might be visiting London."

"I see," she said, rubbing his chest hairs.

When Stanley Fine had first arrived on duty in London, he had been temporarily housed in a shabby flat. The flat also had been a very long Underground ride away from the office. After a good deal of mental debate, he had put aside whatever pride had told him that he should take what he was given in the interest of the war. And he had made the luxurious Westminster Tower apartment his quarters.

His argument, at least to himself, was that he could walk the ten or so blocks to and from the office. This allowed him to spend more time on the job, in the interest of the war.

Now, of course, he was holed up in the OSS villa at Algiers.

"I'll remember to thank him," Ann said, sounding like the proper Southerner that she was.

"You realize, don't you, that the Dorchester Hotel is only two blocks from here? We could go down, sit in Stan's famous spot, where he held court. I believe it even has a brass plaque engraved with his name; if not, it should for all the money he and I have left there. Anyway, there was a pretty nice-sized crowd at the bar when I went by just a little while ago."

"I got a nice letter from Charity," Ann said, ignoring the suggestion and his ramblings.

Canidy could hear excitement in her tone.

"Really?" he said.

"She's preggers."

*Whoa . . . oh, shit!*

"Really!" he repeated, trying to make it

563

sound excited. "Well, congrats to her. Does Doug know?"

*What I really want to ask is: Does Douglass know what he's doing?*

*Well, hell, he is a big boy. . . .*

"He's already given her the engagement ring."

Canidy was silent. And he realized it was making for an awkward moment.

"What's on your mind, Dick?"

Her hand was making faster circles on his chest.

He looked her in the eyes and thought, *I think I know what's on yours, baby.*

He said, "What's on yours, baby?"

Ann was quiet, looking out the window at the park, clearly searching for the right words.

She said, her voice chipper, "I think we should, too."

"I thought we had an understanding," Canidy heard himself automatically saying, "that it's the guy who's supposed to —"

His voice trailed off when he caught sight of the tear on her cheek.

He kissed it.

"Sorry I said that, Annie. You know I love you. Yes?" He paused, then went on: "No one has ever reached me the way that you do."

Her hand stopped making the circles.

"There's a 'but' coming," she said somewhat icily.

"Baby, if I were to ask for a hand in marriage, my heart tells me that there is absolutely no question it would be yours —"

"But . . ." she repeated.

"But my brain tells me that I'm just not ready. This is not the time. For us, for *anyone.*"

Canidy saw more tears on Ann's cheeks.

He wiped them away as he went on: "It just would not be fair to you, Annie. Not with this war, not with my job."

Ann sniffled. She was quiet a long moment, then nodded gently.

"Maybe this damn war will end soon," he continued, "and then everything changes."

She cleared her throat.

"Then," she said, trying to sound strong, "I'll just have to settle for right here and right now."

He leaned over, wrapped his arms and legs around her, and gave her a long, soft kiss.

Then he whispered, "Why are we in this bed?"

"I . . . why, I forget," she said with a straight face.

And after a long moment, she giggled.

And then her hand was under the sheets again, searching . . . and finding what it was looking for.

# AFTERWORD

This book is a work of fiction based on actual events.

We may never know the exact depth of aid that Mafia boss Charles "Lucky" Luciano and his syndicate of ruthless wiseguys provided to fight the Axis in America and abroad.

What *is* known is that on V-E day — the very day that victory was declared in Europe — Thomas Dewey, the former prosecutor who was then governor of the great state of New York signed for the release of Luciano from Great Meadow Prison.

It was May 8, 1945, and Luciano had served just shy of ten years of his thirty-to-fifty-year sentence. He would not have been eligible for parole until 1956.

Charlie Lucky was deported — aboard a cargo ship — from the United States of America. He died in Italy in 1962.

What also is known is that the Nazis did

have chemical and biological weapons programs. And that President Roosevelt had nerve gas munitions manufactured with which to retaliate should the Germans use theirs.

Understanding such history allows us today — in the noise that is the daily media — to better understand the difficult decisions of who we fight, why we fight, and how we fight. It is never simple.

Every day around the world, the United States of America has warriors putting their lives at risk so that our freedoms are protected. We owe them our everlasting respect, gratitude, and, most of all, support.